Flood

Richard Doyle left school at fifteen. After graduating in law from Oxford University he worked briefly on the London Stock Exchange before turning to writing as a career. Following the successes of his early books, Richard led a peripatetic life in America and the West Indies. He is now based on a farm in Devonshire with his wife and twelve-year-old son.

Also by Richard Doyle

Executive Action

Pacific Clipper
Havana Special
Imperial 109
Deluge

FLOOD

Richard Doyle

Published by Arrow in 2003

3 5 7 9 10 8 6 4 2

First published in the United Kingdom in 2002 by Century
The Random House Group Limited
20 Vauxhall Bridge Road, London SW1V 2SA

Random House Australia (Pty) Limited
20 Alfred Street, Milsons Point, Sydney,
New South Wales 2061, Australia

Random House New Zealand Limited
18 Poland Road, Glenfield, Auckland 10, New Zealand

Random House (Pty) Limited
Endulini, 5a Jubilee Road, Parktown 2193, South Africa

The Random House Group Limited Reg. No. 954009

www.randomhouse.co.uk

A CIP catalogue record for this book is available from
the British Library

Papers used by Random House are natural, recyclable products
made from wood grown in sustainable forests.
The manufacturing processes conform to the environmental
regulations of the country of origin

ISBN 0 0994 2969 1

Typeset by SX Composing DTP, Rayleigh, Essex
Printed and bound in Great Britain
by Cox & Wyman Ltd, Reading, Berkshire

For Desmond
with affection

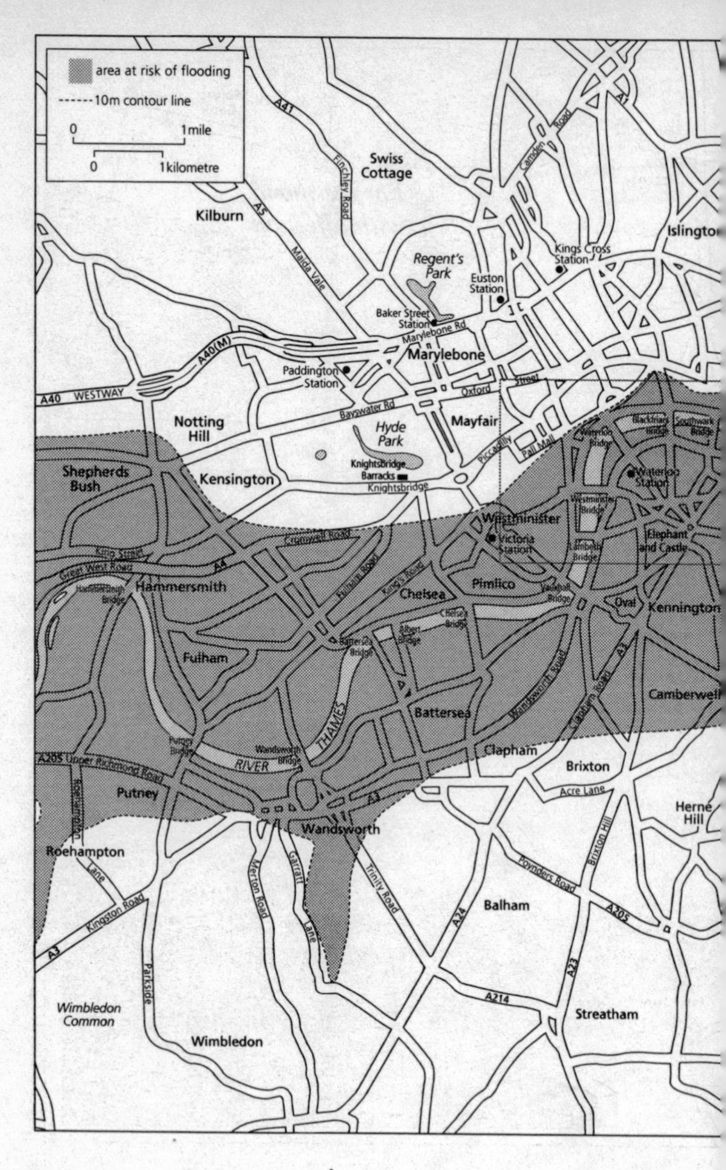
area at risk of flooding
10m contour line
0
1 mile
0
1 kilometre
Swiss Cottage
Kilburn
Islington
Regent's Park
Euston Station
Kings Cross Station
Baker Street Station
Marylebone Rd
Marylebone
Paddington Station
A40 WESTWAY
A40(M)
Notting Hill
Hyde Park
Mayfair
Bayswater Rd
Oxford Street
Piccadilly
Pall Mall
Shepherds Bush
Kensington
Knightsbridge Barracks
Knightsbridge
Westminster
Victoria Station
Waterloo Station
Elephant and Castle
Cromwell Road
Hammersmith
Great West Road
King Street
A4
Chelsea
Pimlico
Oval
Kennington
Fulham Road
Kings Road
Fulham
Battersea
Camberwell
Clapham
Brixton
Wandsworth Road
Clapham Road
Putney
Upper Richmond Road
A205
RIVER THAMES
Wandsworth
Roehampton
Acre Lane
Herne Hill
Balham
Trinity Road
Merton Road
Garratt Lane
Kingston Road
Poynders Road
Brixton Hill
A214
A24
A23
A3
Streatham
Wimbledon Common
Wimbledon
Parkside
Finchley Road
Maida Vale
Camden Road
A41
A5
A1

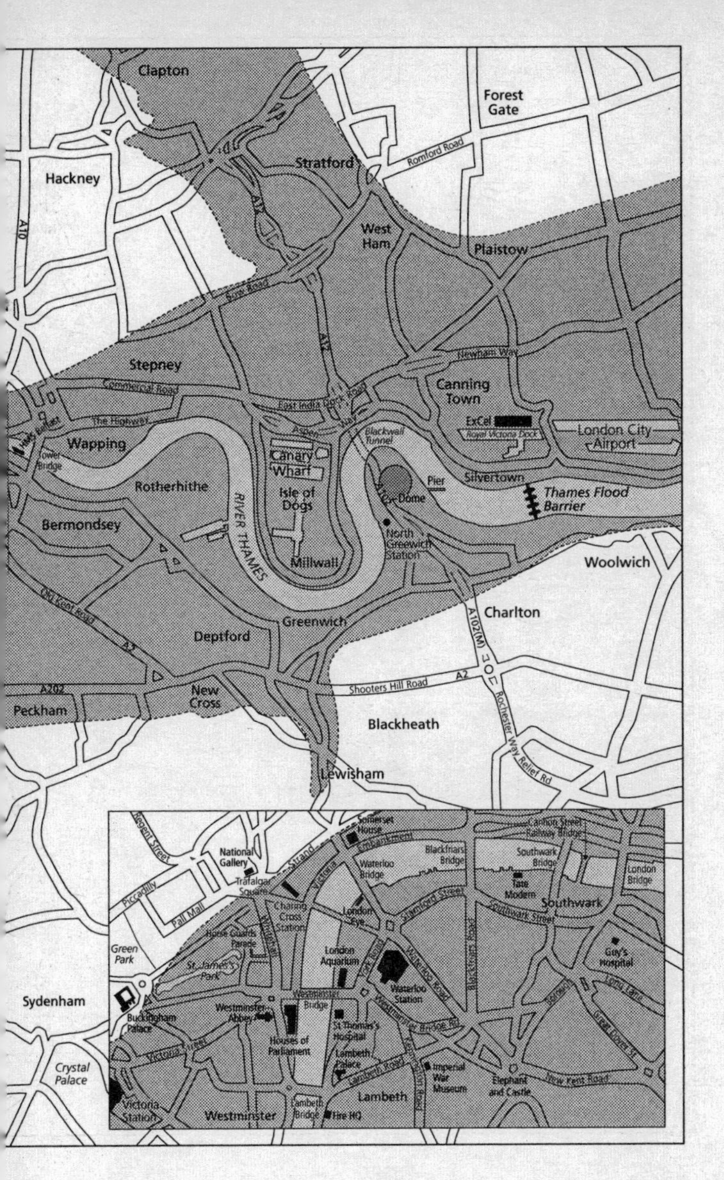
Clapton
Forest Gate
Romford Road
Stratford
Hackney
A10
A12
West Ham
Plaistow
Bow Road
Stepney
Newham Way
Commercial Road
Canning Town
East India Dock Road
The Highway
Aspen Way
Blackwall Tunnel
ExCel
Royal Victoria Dock
London City Airport
Wapping
Tower Bridge
Canary Wharf
Rotherhithe
Isle of Dogs
Dome
Pier
Silvertown
Thames Flood Barrier
RIVER THAMES
Bermondsey
North Greenwich Station
Millwall
Woolwich
Old Kent Road
Charlton
A102(M)
Greenwich
Deptford
A2
A202
Shooters Hill Road
New Cross
Peckham
Rochester Way Relief Rd
Blackheath
Lewisham
Regent Street
Somerset House
Embankment
Cannon Street Railway Bridge
National Gallery
Strand
Blackfriars Bridge
Southwark Bridge
London Bridge
Waterloo Bridge
Trafalgar Square
Tate Modern
Piccadilly
Stamford Street
Southwark
Charing Cross Station
London Eye
Pall Mall
Southwark Street
Horse Guards Parade
Whitehall
Blackfriars Road
Green Park
London Aquarium
Guy's Hospital
St. James's Park
Waterloo Road
Waterloo Station
Long Lane
Sydenham
Westminster Bridge
Westminster Abbey
St Thomas's Hospital
Westminster Bridge Rd
Buckingham Palace
Great Dover St
Houses of Parliament
Victoria Street
Lambeth Palace
Imperial War Museum
Lambeth Road
Kennington Road
Crystal Palace
Elephant and Castle
New Kent Road
Victoria Station
Lambeth
Westminster
Lambeth Bridge
Fire HQ

24 December

After the tides recede, one of the boat parties searching the estuary chances across a taped plastic box. When they open it up they find a newborn baby inside. This is at Gravesend. The storm has finally blown itself out after thirty-six hours and the immensity of the disaster is still sinking home. The channel is choked with wreckage brought down on the ebb: timber, plastic sheeting, steel drums, sections of roofing, half-submerged hulks of lighters and burned barges, mobile homes washed out from Canvey Island, anything that can float. Fuel oil, pumped out from scores of storage tanks up and down the estuary, coats the banks and fills the air with a diesel stench. Victims of the flood are also coming downstream and the boat parties' task is to recover the bodies.

All day, crews have been hauling the dead from the water till they grow numb with the horror of it. Till they are sickened of bloated abdomens and waxen faces; of young and old, men and women and children heaving slackly on the swell. However many they take out, still always more come in a ceaseless flow of misery, as if all the cemeteries of London are giving up their dead at once.

The box bumps alongside one of the boats in mid-stream. It is wrapped in a plastic bin bag for protection and tied with wire, and a man grabs it from the current thinking it might contain valuables. Besides, anything is better than another corpse.

The child inside is only days old. By any standard, its survival is a miracle. Even in normal conditions the box should have gone under within moments of being set adrift, and last night wind strength over the southeast exceeded eighty knots. Seven-metre breakers hammered the Thames bridges. Somehow the box stayed afloat and the plastic covering kept out the oil and other pollutants. The child is dehydrated, weak from hunger and cold, but it is alive.

They get it aboard and into the warmth. Someone finds a blanket and they call up the emergency frequency because no one knows how to treat a kid this young. Tied to one wrist is a wedding ring. Nothing else, no name or message. The man who had made the rescue sits on the deck, his hands trembling. Why, he wonders, has fate chosen him to save a life?

What thoughts ran through the mother's mind as she consigned her child to the waters? Was the father there as she pulled off her wedding ring, the only gift she had left to bestow? Death must have been close then. They must have known there was no escape for them. The child was all they had left. A son who would never remember their tears or the name they cried as they cast him adrift. Parents who could never guess that their prayers would be answered, at least in part. That of all those who died that night, this one should be spared.

1

The storm had its origins ten days before over the Great Lakes of North America. A fluctuation of the upper-atmosphere jet stream sent a surge of freezing air spilling down off the Canadian Shield. Where its leading edge encountered a warm front of sub-tropical air, eddies formed. One such eddy of warm air became detached from the rest of the front and began to rotate. More air was sucked in towards the centre, increasing the rate of spin. A trough of low pressure developed and a storm was born.

Propelled eastwards by the earth's rotation, the depression moved across into Maine and New Brunswick. Already it was generating wind speeds of fifty knots, enough to send boats off the Banks running for cover. Out in the open ocean the rate of spin increased to a point that air was spewing out the top of the vortex faster than it could be replaced at sea-level. Pressure within the system was down to 980 and dropping by a millibar an hour.

With the unpredictability of its kind, the storm changed course, swinging south to vent its spite on Portland and Cape Ann. North of Boston it dumped forty-four inches of snow on Highway 113, marooning a thousand vehicles for three days. It stripped the beaches of Marblehead and killed six people before veering back out to sea.

Now it is travelling east across the Atlantic towards the British Isles at a steady forty knots, tracked by the radars of six nations.

Thursday December 18. Seven-fifteen pm at Stranraer on Scotland's bleak west coast. Snow flurries sweep across the blackness of Loch Ryan like white smoke, rattling against the steel sides of a Royal Navy transport landing ship, the 6000-tonne RFA *Sir Gareth*. A line of paratroopers files slowly up the gangway, heads ducked against the weather. On the dock, trucks and Land Rovers prepare to board through the vessel's gaping stern door.

Inside the cavernous hold, vehicles are backing and filling, manoeuvring into position. Men's shouts echo with the crash of iron blocks and rattle of chains as vehicles are secured into position. The soldiers dismount and pick their way among bolt heads and fixing rings, skirting pools of water to the stairwells. There is a noise of machinery and the massive hull doors slowly wind shut, closing with a clang that resounds through the hold.

Four decks up, on the bridge, Captain Ferguson is talking over the phone to the Harbour Master. He is concerned about the weather for the 36-mile crossing. Conditions in the Irish Sea are currently given by the Meteorological Office as very rough, winds Gale Force 8, with a forecast increase to Force 9 before midnight, indicating winds of forty to fifty knots and twenty-foot seas. The Barra Island lifeboat is out searching for a trawler adrift without power off Eriskay. Ferguson is not impressed. According to the latest Navtex report, the storm track is northeast, bearing away from the ship route. Journey time is only just over two hours, a good part of that in sheltered waters. He has made the trip before many times and is accustomed to crossing in all weathers. He is confident of being able to handle anything short of a full hurricane. He will sail. The Harbour Master does not try to dissuade him. The decision is Ferguson's. He is the captain; the ship, its crew and passengers, his responsibility.

The warps are cast off and the *Sir Gareth* edges out from the quay at 8 pm, half an hour behind schedule. From Stranraer to the open sea is a distance of ten miles. For the first thirty minutes of the trip, the wind's strength is not fully apparent. Halfway down the loch though, the swell becomes severe. The seas are heaped up with white foam blowing in streaks. Captain Ferguson orders equipment to be secured and warns everyone to expect a rough crossing.

On the troop deck the paras are unworried. Rough seas are the norm in winter. Many have taken travel sickness capsules and the medication is making them drowsy. As the lights of the port disappear astern, an officer checks his watch, less than two hours till they reach Belfast.

Shortly before the *Sir Gareth* rounds the mouth of the loch out into the open sea, the Meteorological Office upgrades its forecast for the Irish Channel to Severe Gale Force 9. On the Beaufort Scale this indicates wind speeds of 41 to 47 knots, gusting as high as 60 knots. Sea state is described as 'very high', with waves reaching above 7 metres. 'Dense streaks of foam along the direction of the wind. Crests of waves beginning to topple, tumble and roll over.'

Wind operates on the sea by friction. Rough spots on the surface give the moving air purchase on the water. The first ripples appear at two knots, at five knots wavelets form and at nine knots the crests start to break. The first white horses are seen. At Force 4, a moderate breeze with airspeed of thirteen knots, wave heights reach a metre. But double wind speed to twenty-six knots, Force 6, and wave sizes triple to three metres. Double the wind speed again to fifty knots and waves are touching twelve metres. Wave height rises exponentially with wind speed. The suddenness with which seas can become very much more violent with a comparatively small increase in wind strength can mean the difference between life and death.

Emerging from the loch into open water, the *Sir Gareth* receives the full force of the wind on her starboard quarter. Driving spray all but blinds the searchlights. The ship shudders under the impact of massive seas driving out of the darkness. She rolls the port rail under, digging deep, and the crests hammer bursts of spray against the bridge wing.

Oceanographers measure wave size using a figure called 'significant wave height', the mean of the largest third of waves. At this moment an ERS-1 remote sensing weather satellite is passing south of the Mull of Kintyre. From eight hundred kilometres up, its sophisticated radar altimeter measures ocean levels to within three centimetres of accuracy over a kilometre-wide footprint. The raw data is downloaded to an earth station in Holland and piped direct to the Met Office. Significant wave height in the region of the Irish Sea is now ten metres.

This is what the *Sir Gareth* is facing.

All at once a huge trough seems to open in the sea right at the foot of the bows. The ship plunges downward, burying the foredeck up to the helipad. While she is still struggling to lift her bows clear, she is struck by three enormous waves in succession, the so-called 'three sisters' phenomenon dreaded by sailors. A breaking wave can exert a pressure exceeding ten tonnes per square metre. The first of these actually breaks over the bridge, sweeping away radar and communications masts on the bridge housing, destroying the stack and spewing a torrent of water through the forced draft blower intakes down into the engine room. The next in succession is even bigger. It wrenches the sixty-tonne main crane jib off its mountings and stoves in the main bow loading doors.

For the engine room crew there is no warning at all. One moment they are snuggled away down in their warm and waterproof world, the next they are fighting for their lives in total darkness through chest-deep icy water to reach the hatches before they close on them.

Unlike civilian vessels, the *Sir Gareth* is not fitted with TV monitoring equipment and bilge alarms to warn of internal flooding. Between the bow doors and the landing ramp is an unlit compartment reaching the full height of the vessel. Into this space now flood hundreds of tons of seawater. Some escapes down into the bilges, as it is designed to, but the pumps are unable to cope with the volume. As the level rises rapidly it begins to force its way through ducts and cable runs into other sections of the ship. The extra weight pulls the bows down deeper, increasing the pressure of sea coming in. Soon water is pouring down stairwells onto the lower decks.

The bridge is washed clean out, every man knocked off his feet. Half a dozen injuries but Ferguson has no time for them. His engines are out, navigation systems wrecked, the ship wallowing without power. An urgent distress call has already been made. He calls for emergency pumps to clear the engine compartments and orders watertight doors sealed to limit flooding. The ship is hard hit but she is afloat. All they have to do is hang on till the rescue helicopters find them.

An urgent message is faxed from the Meteorological Office to all government ministries in London. Central Forecasting has issued a severe weather advisory for the next twenty-four hours for Scotland, eastern England and the North Sea.

Simultaneous with this message comes a second, routed from Clyde Coastguard Maritime Rescue Centre, relaying from the sub-centre at Portpatrick to the Cabinet Office at 40 Whitehall. The RFA *Sir Gareth* is adrift off Corsewall Point in a storm. Heavy seas have damaged the vehicle-loading door, flooding the engine room. The master radios that the vessel has an 8-degree list and is not under command. Trapped aboard are a civilian crew and 160 soldiers of the Parachute Regiment.

The duty clerk notes that the Air-Rescue Co-ordination Centre at RAF Kinloss in Scotland has already been alerted. Helicopters from Prestwick and Valley are on route to the stricken vessel and the Portpatrick lifeboat has been launched.

Aberdeen rings off and the clerk dials the home number of the Secretary of the Cabinet Office, Commander Roland Raikes. The Commander answers on the second ring. Twenty years of naval service have accustomed him to being called out at all hours. A graduate of the rigorous 'Perisher' selection course that has made British nuclear submarine commanders feared by every other navy, Raikes has been on secondment to the Cabinet Office for the past eighteen months.

Raikes's first action, after speaking to the clerk, is to dial the Defence Ministry switchboard and identify himself to the officer on duty. He establishes that Coastguard are declaring a Class A major incident emergency, requesting all possible assistance from the military. A Class A emergency denotes an immediate threat to life. It means officers on the spot can sanction the need for equipment and expenditure without having to seek higher approval. This will cut out delay and speed decision taking.

Raikes tells the clerk he is coming in. Normally he would walk to work along the embankment from his flat in Pimlico, but tonight he takes the car. It is raining again. It has been raining all month with more to come. If the temperature drops, London could yet have a white Christmas.

With little traffic around he is at the 40 Whitehall entrance inside ten minutes. His pinstriped suit is freshly pressed. Always look smart even at night, he has learned. You never know how long a crisis will last. You could be facing TV cameras or be summoned to the Prime Minister in whatever you are wearing. The same experience has taught him to keep a clean shirt and shaving kit in his office overlooking Horse Guards' Parade.

One floor up, the Emergency suite is an open-plan room with dedicated phone and fax lines to military, police and other emergency service switchboards. There are direct links, too, to the principal ministries most of which have their own operations rooms. Other equipment includes workstations for handling hazard-modelling-system images and closed-circuit feeds, fax machines and telex facilities. The walls are papered with maps and lists of call-out numbers for utility companies, local authorities, hospitals. The night clerk here has just come off the phone to the Coastguard. He gives Raikes the latest breakdown.

The situation is far worse than at first appeared. In fact it is appalling.

At 9.53 pm comes yet another message from the *Sir Gareth*. The ship is taking in water through the bow with flooding to the troop deck and engine room. This message ends, '*hove to and not under command*'.

Minutes later, at 10.05 pm, Portpatrick coastguard takes a call on the telephone emergency switchboard. The caller identifies himself as speaking on a cellular phone from the *Sir Gareth* and requests immediate lifeboat assistance. '*Ship down by bows. Listing 10 degrees.*' Estimated position is given as ten miles off the Irish coast.

The nearest Coastguard Search and Rescue helicopters are based up the coast at Prestwick.

Both Prestwick's aircraft are already in the air on route to other calls, so Prestwick passes the request to the RAF which operates an SAR squadron based at Valley, 120 miles south on the island of Anglesey.

The declared aim of the SAR helicopters is to be airborne within ten minutes of a call-out by day, forty-five minutes by night. Because of the number of lives at stake, Valley orders both machines into the air. It will take them the best part of an hour to reach the search area.

Down in London, Raikes asks for a weather update. The office has been monitoring the storm's progress since yesterday. There are warnings of Force 8 gales in the southern North Sea, with offshore waves of five metres plus. Tide levels are predicted to hit danger levels along the east coast from Immingham in Humberside to Dover.

The latest area forecast reads like a litany of things sailors don't want to hear. *Sea areas South-East Iceland, Faeroes, Fair Isle, Viking, North Utsire. Severe storm moving East 40 to 50 knots. Pressure 965mb and falling. Forecast winds 60 to 65 knots, gusting 90 knots, becoming cyclonic. Seas 11 to 15 metres.* Put simply, this means the hurricane is tracking eastwards across the tip of Scotland into the North Sea. Technically it is not a hurricane since hurricanes as such only occur in warm latitudes, but to any vessel caught up in its path the difference will be purely semantic.

What's the position on tugs? Raikes wants to know. The night clerk checks. There is an ETV, an emergency towing vessel, at Stornoway on stand-by for the offshore oil industry. She has steam up heading for the scene but at her top speed of twenty-five knots it will be eight hours before she can get a tow alongside.

The Navy has a minehunter, HMS *Vixen*, at Faslane on the Gareloch. The distance is less than a hundred miles but the sea state in the Firth is very violent, with fifteen-metre waves. Raikes shakes his head. He doesn't believe a lightly built vessel like a minehunter will be capable of much assistance in those conditions either. It is looking like a helicopter evacuation.

The clerk is back on the phone. The helicopters haven't located the ship yet, he says. They're still searching. She's not showing up on the radar. It's high ground up there. Mountains down to the coast. There could be interference.

Raikes disagrees. He knows those waters well. They hold submarine exercises up there and he is familiar with the capability of the helicopters' radar. It is very effective and wouldn't be thrown off by the mountains. If it can't detect the ship on the surface, then the probability is that she has sunk. Get on to Portpatrick, he tells the clerk. Ask them, have they picked up a signal from the *Sir Gareth*'s EPIRB?

All military vessels, the *Sir Gareth* included, carry an EPIRB float-free radio buoy. If a ship goes down, this will bob to the surface and begin automatically transmitting a distress message to a C-S satellite, one of four in near polar orbit. C-S location accuracy is normally between five and twenty kilometres. Maximum wait time between activation and detection should not exceed ninety minutes.

It takes only a minute for the answer to come

back. A signal from an EPIRB was detected by satellite ten minutes ago. The signal was localised and passed to the United Kingdom control centre in Plymouth where it has been confirmed as originating from the *Sir Gareth*. The fix places it on the fringe of the coastguard's search box and corresponds with their estimate of the ship's last known position.

A flash of fire bursts over the *Sir Gareth*, triggering a surge of hope aboard. Surely the helicopters have arrived at last, their flares staining the clouds as the crews scan the raging seas for sight of the transport? A crash of thunder dashes spirits again and even as the lightning dies away, Captain Ferguson braces himself for the storm's next onslaught.

He can't understand why air-sea rescue is taking so long. The ship can't survive much longer. They've managed to restart one engine, restoring a measure of power, and the helmsmen are struggling to keep her head onto the seas, making 2 or 3 knots, no more. It is anyone's guess how much longer the engines will keep going. Repeated hammering by gigantic seas has strained the propeller shafts, causing the bearings to overheat. The bridge, wheelhouse and radio deck were all wiped out by the impact of the three gigantic waves that shattered the ship. Radar, communications and navigating systems down. Ferguson is conning the vessel from a jury-rigged station on the main deck. The ship is lying deep in the water, weighed down by the flooded vehicle deck. Huge seas are breaking over the sides, sweeping the main deck, hammering at hatches and scuttles. Each time the bows dip into a trough, Ferguson thinks she will never come up again.

The troop deck is awash and the senior army officer, a major, has gathered his men together in the stern accommodation. Life vests have been issued and the crew are going through the drill for abandoning ship. God help them all, Ferguson thinks listlessly, if they have to take to the lifeboats. His own officers are exhausted; they stagger about their duties dazed by the relentless battering of the storm.

2

With the storm comes the surge. Atmospheric pressure affects the level of the ocean; high pressure depresses the surface and low pressure raises it. A storm is a low-pressure system, a depression. Put simply, there is less weight of air on the ocean under a storm so the greater weight around the edges squeezes water in the central area up into a hump. Over open ocean the effect can sometimes be as much as a metre. The hump moves with the depression and is called a surge.

Right now the surge is increasing as it moves from the Atlantic into the shallower waters of the continental shelf. Along the western isles of Scotland, tide readings are hitting decade levels. North Rona has touched four metres and Stornoway, on the Isle of Lewis, is equalling its own record of 4.45 metres.

Now the storm swings eastwards across the northern tip of Scotland. The mass of water travelling with the depression enters the narrow confines of the North Sea. There is high pressure to the east and strong winds blow on the flank of the depression, rolling the surge southwards at the same time that the earth's rotation throws it against the east coast. The North Sea shallows towards the south and the converging coastlines of Britain and the Continent act like a funnel, squeezing the water higher. By the time it arrives off southeast England, a surge that began at seventy-five centimetres can reach as much as three metres, occasionally more. If the gales persist in strength, an enormous volume of water will be forced up the Thames estuary into London. The funnel effect of the river will increase the height by half as much again. The surge that arrives at the Thames Barrier will be 4.5 metres, not three metres.

Surge heights have risen by 10 per cent in twenty years, matching the increased violence of winter storms. Scientists are divided on the cause; some see it as a component of generalised global warming, others as part of a more localised variation in weather patterns. Either way, the consequences are ominous.

Nineteen miles from the northernmost tip of the Scottish mainland, the Wick lifeboat is putting to sea and volunteer coastguard Callum Mackay is helping on the jetty. Sheets of rain sweep the quayside as the storm hammers the slate roofs of the town. A crewman in an orange survival suit passes him the stern warp and retreats inside the deck-house. Callum and the rest of the shore party watch the Trent class boat motor into the outer harbour and line up for the harbour mouth. Callum can't think how she's going to make it.

The storm is pounding the outer piers relentlessly. As each roller comes driving in, the sea heaves up and avalanches over, burying wall and pier. The lighthouse at the entrance to the outer harbour is completely hidden in leaping bursts of spray. Streaks of yellow spume coat the surface of the harbour and waves are surging over onto the quaysides.

Another savage gust batters the town. There is a sustained howl to the wind, a continuous keening note that only the big storms generate. In winter months Wick endures gales one day in three, but tonight is turning rough even by Wick's standards. The streetlights flicker and cut out for a moment, then come back on. Rain falls in blinding torrents that drive horizontally off the sea. All the men are wearing oilskins; all are soaked. The boat reaches the gap between the piers. It looks as if she must be smashed against the walls, but somehow she slips through. This is the worst moment. Beyond South Pier she is broadside on to the seas, exposed to the full violence of the weather. The coxswain has to judge his timing, seizing a break between the big waves.

The boat is corkscrewing in the swell, burying her sides as she rolls. Her searchlights stab out into the tossing crests. The bows rear up and plunge steeply down into a trough. Another roller cascades over the piers. The lights cut off abruptly. The lifeboat vanishes from sight, just disappears as if it has been blotted out. There is no way of telling what has happened. The watchers stare into blackness. Seconds crawl past. No one speaks. Spray lashes their faces. Has the boat capsized or is she lost to sight behind mountainous seas? At last a shout goes up. Someone has spotted lights out in the bay. She is away.

The group on the quay disperses. They have done their part; the rest is up to the lifeboat. Callum Mackay returns to the Coastguard Land Rover and checks his pager. There is one message: the tide gauge has malfunctioned.

It is Callum's responsibility to maintain the gauge at Wick and he checks it without fail every day of the year. High tide at London Bridge occurs approximately thirteen hours behind Wick. Wick is one of five stations with a direct landline to the Met Office so that its gauges can be observed in real time. Wick is a tripwire for the entire system.

The tide gauge hut overhangs the foot of the North pier in the inner harbour next to the boatyard slipway. Alongside it is the tide pole, a white painted length of wood fixed to the pier with the height marked off in tenths of a metre. The heaving of the inner harbour makes the level difficult to read tonight but it looks to Callum like all of five metres, maybe more. Higher than he can ever remember seeing it.

Callum lets himself into the hut with a key. Rain and spray beat against the sides and roof. The floor is several inches deep in water. At that moment a great jet of spray bursts up from behind the equipment bench, drenching the interior of the hut. There are two gauges here. The main one is a modern 'bubbler' type. Nitrogen gas is passed down a tube at a controlled rate while a transducer measures the pressure resistance proportional to the head of water. More pressure equals deeper water, hence a higher tide. The system is simple and very accurate. A microprocessor samples the gas flow several times a second, averages the readings and transmits the result down a dedicated phone link south to the Met Office.

Alongside this is an old Admiralty pattern gauge in a wooden case with a clock-driven brass drum and a pen worked off a float. The float is mounted inside a pipe extending down into the water, called a stilling well because it is designed to damp down the motion of the waves. The sea has risen so high it has smashed the float right up against the top of the pipe and burst the seal. Callum experiences a jolt of alarm. The equipment in this hut is sited to catch any surge as it moves round from the Atlantic into the North Sea. For it to explode the gauge like this means there must be a tide of truly awesome dimensions forming out there.

Callum hurriedly locks off the valve to the well to stop any more water coming in. His priority is to get the bubbler gauge restarted. The Admiralty model is only kept as a stand-by. He makes sure the compressor is working properly and checks for gas pressure and water head. He opens the purge valves on the twin bubbler units. Silt or algae can get sucked into the air lines and block the flow. A blast of gas does the trick if so. But the gauge seems to be working normally. It looks like the problem has to be with the telemetry system electronics.

There is a phone in the hut and he uses it to call the Met Office and speak to a technician. Callum did twenty years as an engineer with British Telecom, so the two can talk on equal terms. He tells London he suspects that water may have got into the power supply and blown a circuit. They discuss suggestions for testing connections. Callum wedges the phone into his shoulder as he tries different switch settings and calls over the results.

The noise of spray hammering at the hut is frightening and makes it hard to think. Finally they succeed in isolating the fault. A new circuit board is required. Callum hunts around in his box of spares. To his relief he finds one that seems dry. When he fits it the modem lights up and starts transmitting data. The process has taken just over twenty minutes.

Callum dismantles the older gauge to save it from further damage and emerges out into the howling night, ducking against the spray as he locks the door behind him again. The tide is surging against the quayside of the inner harbour. The outer pool is completely hidden by huge rollers smashing over the breakwater. The whole bay feels swollen, charged with mountainous seas. London had better watch out.

As yet, none of this is in anyone's mind at Whitehall. Surge tides are not a concern of the Cabinet Office. The Department of the Environment, Food and Rural Affairs is responsible for precautions against flooding. Storm surges are a regular feature of winter months; most fade out as the winds die away. Rarely do gales persist long enough for a tide to threaten London. And if one did, the Thames Barrier would protect the capital.

Raikes is on the phone to the Met Office calling for an update on the projected course of the storm. This will have a general bearing on operations. The immediate concern is to locate the *Sir Gareth*. In an emergency, Coastguard can call on any available assets in the country, military or commercial. By international convention, even foreign ships and aircraft can be tasked to a rescue if one of them happens to be closest to the scene. All nations co-operate when it is a question of saving life.

There are twenty-four dedicated SAR helicopters in the country. The two based at Valley on Anglesey are already at the scene. They will be joined by three more Sea Kings, two from RAF Leuchars in Fife and another from Prestwick, in addition to a Coastguard Sikorsky from Stornoway.

Valley's Sea Kings are searching off Corsewall Point. They can home in on the radio beacon from thirty miles out. Conditions are atrocious, with snow and sleet rendering searchlights useless and hampering radar. In spite of this they manage to locate the beacon but can find no trace of the ship or survivors. They commence a box sweep, flying below the cloud cover and firing flares. After another fifty minutes with no result they divert to Prestwick to refuel. One of Prestwick's own Sea Kings, which has returned from an earlier rescue, takes up the hunt, and the search box is extended southwards following the calculated rate of drift.

What is needed is a tanker aircraft to enable the helicopters to stay on station. Raikes calls Defence and establishes that the RAF is aware of the problem. The nearest tanker aircraft is currently inbound from the North Sea, empty after refuelling a Nimrod on anti-submarine patrol. It will have to land and top up at Leuchars before flying on to Portpatrick. There is a second tanker at Leuchars but it is grounded for lack of spares. There are no other aircraft that could reach the area in time.

Matters are looking critical till an appeal to NATO Command produces an offer of American help. A USAF tanker aircraft, currently deployed on exercise with Strategic Command over the Atlantic, can be diverted. Her tanks are full and from her present position the aircraft can reach Portpatrick in fifty minutes. Raikes promptly calls the US Embassy in Grosvenor Square. Speaking to the duty officer, he expresses his gratitude on behalf of the British Government. He has learnt from past experience that politeness pays. And in this case perhaps it does, for within minutes there is an offer of further American assistance in the shape of an E-3 Sentry AWACS on the same exercise that has been instructed to extend its patrol to provide on-the-spot command and control over the missing vessel.

While Raikes is speaking another phone rings. A newly joined clerk picks it up. 'For you, Commander,' she says.

Raikes takes the receiver and recognises the deceptively soft tones of the Number Ten press secretary. 'If you have a moment, Commander, the Deputy Prime Minister would like a briefing before she has to go out.'

It is a command not a suggestion, Raikes knows. He leaves the office and takes the stairs down two steps at a time. He walks briskly along the passage to the green baize door at the far end, inserts his pass into the swipe lock, and goes through into Number Ten.

The house feels silent and still. It is late and the Prime Minister is out of the country at the economic summit in Melbourne. In his absence

Venetia Maitland, Home Secretary and Deputy Prime Minister, is conducting affairs of state from the Cabinet Room next door. 'She's expecting you,' an aide tells him without looking up from a stack of papers. 'Walk right in.'

The lights in the long room are dimmed and the curtains drawn. Venetia Maitland sits at the famous table with her narrow back to the door, two red leather ministerial dispatch boxes, filled with files, open in front of her. A single lamp reflects off a spill of bright hair and trademark jaunty scarf. Her legs are crossed to one side, half in shadow. Dancer's legs, Raikes remembers.

At his knock she turns quickly, as if pleased to see him.

So tell me about this naval ship? she says. Is it as bad as it sounds?

When Raikes first came to the job he was cautious when talking to ministers, nowadays he finds it easy. And Venetia is a good listener. 'So how do we lose a ship with all the modern aids?' she asks. Mostly by looking in the wrong place, he tells her. 'It's easily done, particularly with the weather they're having up there tonight.'

'Is there anything I can do?'

No, he says. There is nothing any of us here can do. It is a straight matter of finding the ship if it hasn't sunk or the survivors if it has.

'According to the Met Office, the storm will spread to the rest of Scotland tonight and reach northern England and the East Coast by morning.' Raikes is letting her know there could be more bad news on the way. 'Oil and gas platforms are being evacuated and the Thames Barrier may have to close.'

'Yes, I'm aware.' Little escapes Venetia Maitland's attention. 'I'm on my way down to the Barrier in a few minutes to see HMS *Belfast* come through. If there is news of the *Sir Gareth*, I want to be told.'

3

Coastguard radio stations in Scotland and Ireland have been monitoring the *Sir Gareth*'s cellphone transmissions. Using the GPS navigation satellites it is theoretically possible to plot the origin of the signals with an accuracy of three metres. Unfortunately the readings are distorted by mountainous country, giving a position fix thirty or forty miles west of the search area somewhere off the Irish coast.

Four helicopters are now combing the sea for her, aided by the USAF Sentry, an RAF Nimrod aircraft and several ships. Then, just before 2 am, another telephone transmission is picked up. In a last appeal to Portpatrick, the caller reports that he can make out the lights of the Irish coast. The situation aboard the *Sir Gareth* is desperate. The list has increased to 30 degrees. The ship is on her beam-ends and her engines have stopped.

This is the first intimation to the searchers of the dreadful mistake that they have made. At no time has the *Sir Gareth* mentioned that she is still under engine power and headed for the Irish coast. The searchers have estimated her position according to drift by sea and wind, backed up by the bearings emitted by her EPIRB buoy, which, unknown to them, had been washed overboard. Throughout the search they have rejected Ferguson's estimate of the ship's position in favour of their own.

By '*hove to, not under command*', the coastguard have understood Ferguson to mean that the ship was wallowing helplessly at the mercy of wind and current. The position he gave had to be an estimate because his radar, GPS and Loran navigation systems were all inoperative. Their own calculations for the ship's drift placed her to the southwest of her given position, and they vectored the helicopters accordingly.

Radar operators initially misidentified the ship, wrongly tagging it as an Irish vessel that had turned back from Larne. From then on the *Sir Gareth* effectively vanished from their screens. It is a compounding of errors that Raikes has seen before. An initial wrong assumption is made and everything builds on that, leading to the inevitably tragic result.

A frantic signal is dispatched to all aircraft and vessels in the vicinity to make for the fresh coordinates with utmost speed. Even while it is being transmitted, however, a final message comes from the sinking transport. '*Preparing to abandon ship.*'

Only later is it possible to reconstruct the vessel's final moments.

With the vehicle deck flooded, the ship's rolling is becoming more and more prolonged, choking the engine air intakes. She has turned broadside on to the waves, exposing herself to the full fury of the elements. Hatches are blowing in, bulkheads failing. Ferguson can feel her movements slowing, becoming sluggish and knows she is readying herself for the plunge.

The first officer has warned the troops aboard that the end is near. There is no panic. A human chain is formed to help the injured out from below onto the deck. Floats and rafts are dropped into the sea, but the launching of lifeboats has been delayed because of the expectation of rescue. The searchlights are wrecked or dead. In the blackness of the night the only visibility comes from the violently frothing waves. The first boat away is smashed and overturned by mountainous seas. A few men reach the rafts but most are swept away into boiling surf. Raging seas swing up, plucking off groups of men as they cluster aft by the floats, sucking them back out to their death.

The final throes take less than a minute. The bows dip and snort under and at the same time the stern lifts clear of the sea, exposing the screws. There is no way for those still left aboard to get clear and anyway they have no time. The ship corkscrews into the water as if she is driving herself down into her grave. Two more boats that have succeeded in getting away are swept under the keel and capsized. The suction of the sinking ship drags the survivors under as she heads for the 50-fathom line.

The first rescue craft on the scene is a helicopter from an American naval vessel. The crew report the water filled with struggling men. They rescue twenty-eight with their winch and remain on station to vector in other aircraft. By the time these arrive many have drowned, unable to cling on to the rafts any longer. Sea Kings pull another sixty-three from the water. The Donaghadee lifeboat, which is already at sea, reaches the area an hour after the *Sir Gareth* goes down and takes in tow a raft with two bodies aboard.

In all, one hundred and eleven lives are lost, including nine from the civilian crew, Captain Ferguson among them. It is the biggest British naval disaster since the Second World War.

At 11 pm, the tragedy off Ireland is still in its final stages when Venetia Maitland and a press secretary climb into the ministerial Jaguar outside the front door of 10, Downing Street. A police driver is at the wheel, with an armed bodyguard alongside, and an escort car with more heavily armed officers travels behind. As Home Secretary, Venetia is a prime terrorist target and rates protection second only to the Royal Family and the Prime Minister. The car is armour-plated, with windows of two-inch thick polycarbonate. Like being in a fish bowl, Venetia thinks. And all for a three-minute journey.

A guard in the gatehouse retracts the hydraulic security barrier into the surface of the road and the convoy glides through the heavy steel gates erected in Margaret Thatcher's day. An officer on foot holds back the traffic in Whitehall. The Jaguar shoots straight across the street and dives into Richmond Terrace, another restricted road that leads past the massive white façade of the Ministry of Defence. At the far end the traffic is held up again for the ministerial car to turn right on to the Victoria Embankment. After only a few hundred metres it pulls up alongside Westminster Pier.

Venetia is forty-four, divorced, with a daughter at university. She lives in Notting Hill, owns a cottage in her New Forest constituency and has the use of a country house in the Cotswolds for official entertaining. As a senior minister she draws a salary of £160,000, a figure she could multiply by five by moving to the private sector. Occasionally she is tempted, but no amount of money can replace the buzz of being at the centre of events.

Tonight HMS *Belfast*, the former WW2 heavy cruiser, preserved as a floating museum opposite the Tower of London, is returning to the Thames from a six-month refit at Portsmouth. Her passage up-river has had to be brought forward in view of the projected Barrier closure. Venetia has agreed to attend and the Environment Agency, which controls the Barrier, has sent its launch.

Officials from the Agency are on hand to greet her. No minister of Venetia's standing can move without an entourage. The stone steps of the dock on the Thames are slippery from rain. The boat alongside rides restlessly at its moorings. Venetia takes the hand of one of the crewmen and steps confidently aboard. The press secretary and bodyguard climb after, ducking their heads to enter the cabin.

Radios crackle in the night air. An escort boat from the River Police looms up and the launch's engine throbs as it moves out into mid-stream. From here, London is suddenly beautiful. The gothic stonework of Westminster and Big Ben takes on a romantic glow under the floodlights. Bridges are picked out with lights, chains of lamps spangle the embankments. Shining windows strike bright shafts into the darkness and the iridescent blackness of the river, running swiftly between the banks, throws back a thousand coloured reflections. Three hours to go to low water. This is the time of maximum flow.

A white wake curls under the stern as the launch passes by the London Eye, the spectacular observation wheel on the south bank. A diameter of 135 metres, its thirty-two glass viewing capsules glow against the sky. Beyond Blackfriars, the great dome of St Paul's Cathedral rises against the northern skyline on Ludgate Hill. There is a new pedestrian footbridge here, spanning the river from the old Bankside power station in a slender arch of steel.

A mile further down, the Tower of London stands behind its floodlit walls, a fantastic sight, half hidden by skeletal trees, romantic and magnificent. Beneath Tower Bridge the pilot turns on the orange light and opens up the throttles. On the far side a moored pleasure boat throbs with revellers.

They pass Wapping and Rotherhithe. Once shabby streets and warehouses, converted to million dollar apartments. Docklands comes into sight; the 243-metre tower at Canary Wharf dominating the Isle of Dogs, centrepiece of the massive developments that have rejuvenated this sector of the river, the green lamp on the pinnacle flashing at forty beats to the minute. On the opposite bank, the façade of Greenwich Palace glimmers palely in the dark, the loveliest sight on the river.

Downstream, the river does a double loop around the Greenwich Peninsula, an 800-metre-wide spit of flat ground projecting a mile out from the southern bank. Formerly occupied by a gasworks, it is now the site of the Millennium Dome.

As they round the peninsula the pilot is on the radio, talking to Barrier Control. The approaches to the Barrier are strictly policed. The authorities have always been concerned it might be a target for terrorists. Each year the military hold a tabletop exercise to simulate the recapture of the facility.

Dead ahead on the water, clusters of red and green lights indicate the piers. Green for open gates, red for closed. As the launch slows and draws close, the huge scale of the project becomes fully apparent. The four central gate openings each span more than sixty metres, equivalent to the opening of Tower Bridge, and there are six side gates half as wide. The most striking feature of the Barrier, the stainless-steel hoods that surmount the 20,000-tonne concrete piers, house operating machinery and control equipment.

The gates are hollow and over twenty metres in height, made of plated steel. Each can withstand an overall load in excess of nine thousand tonnes. If a dangerous surge threatens, the gates swing up through 90 degrees from their riverbed positions to stem the advancing tide.

Tonight all ten gates are open.

The street address for Canary Wharf Tower is One Canada Square. In the offices of the *Daily Telegraph* on the twelfth floor, journalist Lauren Khan is watching the Internet news traffic generated by the unfolding tragedy off the Scottish coast. Half an hour earlier she was warned to fly out to cover the story, only to be stood down at the last minute when it was decided to use a team from Northern Ireland instead. Now one fact catches her attention: a source notes that the storm could pose a surge tide threat to London.

This is a reference to a fax sent out by the Meteorological Office at 10 am on Thursday, almost thirty-six hours before the tide is due at London Bridge. It linked the approaching storm with disturbances in sea-level, and gave predictions for danger points along the east coast, together with tide heights and timings. At this stage the levels for Division 5, which affects London, were forecast to reach just below danger point.

Lauren runs a check through the *Telegraph* archive. Back in 1953 a two-metre surge struck the east coast in one of the worst storms of the century. The brunt of the sea's attack fell on the East Anglian shore, particularly in Essex where the defences failed along wide stretches of the coastline. On Canvey Island alone, fifty-eight people drowned. The tide brimmed the walls in the capital but the embankments held.

It might have been very much worse. Tide levels that day were moderate and the surge came up-river at low water. Had it coincided with high water on a spring tide, more than forty-five square miles of London would have been flooded.

The narrow escape focused attention. A government committee recommended that a barrier be built to protect the capital against surge levels of the kind to be expected once in a thousand years. The so-called 'thousand year flood'. But costs were daunting, politicians prevaricated and it took twenty years to decide on a site at Woolwich, three miles below London Bridge, and fix on a design.

Construction of the Thames Barrier started in

1972 and was completed in 1982. Reinforced concrete piers, twelve storeys high and founded on solid chalk, support steel gates weighing 3300 tonnes apiece, half as much as the Eiffel Tower. In the normal position the gates are lowered into sills in the riverbed to allow the passage of shipping; when a surge threatens they can be raised hydraulically to form a solid wall spanning a third of a mile from bank to bank.

The project was bedevilled by cost overruns and strikes. Seventy miles of riverbanks downstream had to be raised and strengthened. Five subsidiary barriers were required on creeks and tributaries. The final bill came to half a billion pounds, 70 per cent over budget. In February 1983 the gates were raised in anger for the first time, more than thirty years after the Essex flood. At last Londoners could feel safe.

Global warming is the joker in the pack. Melting of the polar ice caps is raising sea-levels appreciably. Waves are getting larger and extreme weather patterns more frequent. Also, warmer sea water expands and this increases levels. Taking the worst-case scenario, by the year 2030 the odds against a high water level reaching the top of the Barrier gates shorten to once in three hundred years, and some studies put the safety factor at nearer one in a hundred years, a tenth of the intended degree of protection.

Lauren figures there might be a story here. She starts to make some calls.

The Met Office press officer is on his guard. He tries to fob her off with generalisations about forecasting. 'It is a man-machine mix, part high-power computing, part intuition and experience. Standard practice is to run several models or possible scenarios. These are then compared with incoming data and adjusted until the emerging pattern can be predicted with confidence . . .'

Lauren wants something more specific. 'Is tonight's surge a threat to the capital?' she repeats.

A moment's hesitation. 'It's a spring tide period, but the model has the surge peak well behind high water at London Bridge.'

Lauren scribbles a query over the words 'well behind' and moves on. She wants some figures about surges, she says. How a surge builds as it comes south.

'Currently the model shows tide heights peaking at Division Four, that's East Anglia and Essex. The surge will have reached approximately two metres by then, but of course it will be running behind high water so levels are forecast to be only half a metre above danger.'

'Does your model ever get it wrong?' Lauren asks.

Again, the hesitation. 'The model is only as good as the forcing data that goes in to it,' the press officer admits. 'Our surge model uses wind and pressure data from the Limited Area Model of the regional forecast for the British Isles. Any inaccuracies in these data, particularly wind speed and direction, will be reflected in the output from the surge model.'

'Garbage in, garbage out,' Lauren summarises succinctly. 'One final question. What is the highest these surges reach?'

*

Lauren Khan's story is beginning to shape up. She is acute enough to have detected the note of caution. Whatever the Met Office are saying, they are less than one hundred per cent confident right now. Surge residuals of up to three and a half metres have been recorded in the Thames estuary.

The next step is to contact the Thames Barrier and here she has a break. A couple of photographers are hanging around the newsroom, waiting for transport across the river to the Thames Barrier to cover the passage of HMS *Belfast*.

Lauren grabs her coat.

It is pitchy black in the Arctic night as the Boeing C-135 of the Royal Dutch Airforce Weather Reconnaissance Squadron, sixty minutes out from Den Haag in Holland, heads across the North Sea for the Long Forties and the Devil's Hole.

The plane is forty years old, a veteran of the Cold War, originally employed for intelligence duties, flying snooping missions against the Russian navy. Now she carries a full suite of meteorological gear, so many computers and processors that air scoops have had to be mounted either side of the fuselage to cool the electronics. There are cloud probes, air sample pipes and a temperature gauge mounted on a nine-metre red and white painted probe that projects from the nose.

The airframe may be elderly but the crew holds the KC, known to them as Snoopy, in affection. In service the plane has proved reliable and safe. Tonight she needs to be, her mission is to fly into the eye of the storm.

Behind the cockpit is the main cabin with the computers and technical stations. The C-135 usually carries up to five scientific officers. One of these is British, an oceanographer, on secondment to the European Centre for Medium-Range Weather Forecasting from the Met Office's Hadley Research Centre. The technicians sit harnessed to padded seats at their consoles, each with its own VDU displaying wind speeds, wave heights and other data being monitored by the onboard systems.

In the tail is the rest room, actually a chemical toilet, little more than a bucket with a curtain for a screen. The curtain is a concession to the only woman on board, Heidi Winkler, another oceanographer. Heidi has charge of the rack of meteorological buoys that can be deployed via a chute appropriately located alongside the toilet.

Immediately opposite is a recess holding the ditching gear, including the life raft in a big yellow pack that can double as a tent in the event of the plane being forced down in the sea. The red rubberised dry suits of the technicians hang from the rail above. They have all done the survival course run at the base. This includes being dumped overboard from a launch into the freezing sea and has taught them that there isn't a cat in hell's chance of surviving a ditching in the kind of conditions they mostly fly in.

Tonight's mission calls for a flight due south to rendezvous with the storm and transect the eye of the depression, estimated to be not less than fifty miles in diameter. ECMWF wants a forecast on the storm's future strength and for that they need to know how the internal pressure is holding up. They are searching for so-called sensitive spots, regions where conditions change rapidly. Research has shown these spots are most often to be found at altitudes of 4000 metres, just below the jet stream. The crew will be seeking out regions of sudden extreme turbulence that indicate rapidly deteriorating conditions.

They are literally looking for trouble.

4

The boat is pulling into the Barrier dock on the south bank. There is heavy security here and again at the ten-storey control building. Barrier Control used to recruit from the services, chiefly from the Royal Navy Engineering branch, and the Operations Room still retains the air of a ship's bridge. There is the same sense of order and attention to detail, the same quiet professionalism among the staff, though nowadays they come mainly from industry. Running the Barrier has many features in common with managing a big power plant. The routine is geared towards maintenance, a ceaseless checking that things are normal.

Seventy staff work here around the clock. Of these, only about six are required on duty in the operations room on any one shift. Once a month the entire Barrier is test-raised to the closure position, a procedure that takes around two hours. In an emergency the gates can be raised in just thirty minutes.

The operations room has windows on three sides looking right across the full length of the Barrier and up-river to the Dome. On the opposite bank lies the former Royal Victoria Dock, now the site of the London City Airport. The lights of an aircraft lift silently off the runway, climbing away eastwards to vanish in the overcast. Somewhere up there a full moon is waiting if only the weather would clear.

The Barrier piers are floodlit, their stainless-steel hoods gleaming against the stark blackness of the water. And here at last is HMS *Belfast*. She is further off than Venetia was expecting, about five hundred metres. The six-inch turrets of her main armament are trained fore and aft; she looks magnificent and not a little sinister in her chill battle grey, evoking images of winter seas and Arctic convoys. There are two tugs ahead towing and another couple astern. A Port Authority launch rides hard alongside.

Angus Walsh, the Barrier chief, is on hand to greet the ministerial party, his short red beard bristling under his safety helmet. His previous experience was at Bradwell, the pressurised water reactor on the Essex coast. Venetia has had a briefing on Angus. She knows that he is a first-class engineer, top of his class at Imperial College. That he is a solitary man who prefers his own company. For relaxation he likes to fly gliders, alone. He is forthright, argumentative and truthful, and everyone who has worked with him respects him. The Barrier is his life.

Tonight Angus leads off with a lecture to the company on the Barrier and its operation. He reels off statistics: the enormous strength of the gates, the simplicity of the mechanisms, the monthly program of test closures. Every control system, every power feed, every hydraulic link is duplicated.

Over on the north bank is a back-up control room, also manned twenty-four hours a day. In the unlikely event of both rooms being put out of action, gates can still be operated from individual piers by independent hydraulic mechanisms.

Angus is the gatekeeper. It is his job to decide when the Barrier closes. For him surges are just one component of the picture. He has to consider fresh water flow down river from Teddington Lock and predicted tide levels, as well as the height and timing of surges. Any combination that will generate a tide height at London Bridge of 4.85 metres or above triggers a Barrier closure.

The magic figure is 4.85 metres. If a tide at London Bridge is forecast to exceed that level, the Barrier closes. End of story.

Venetia Maitland and the accompanying journalists have moved over to a bank of screens.

'So this is the surge crest moving down the east coast?' Venetia points with her finger. The screen trace shows a hump rising above the base-line. It starts small, then grows higher and wider, taking on a lumpy appearance. By the bottom of the screen it has become large and menacing. 'And this is it at Southend? That's what, thirty miles by river from here?'

'Thirty-five miles,' Angus corrects her. His mistrust of politicians is instinctive. The Barrier would have been in place years earlier if the government of the day hadn't spent the money allocated for it on building a motorway instead. As it is, politicians only need engineers to pin the blame on when things go wrong.

It takes an hour for the tide crest to travel from there up-river to the Barrier, he explains, adding witheringly, 'And the reason the surge looks threatening on the chart is because you are seeing it in isolation.'

'So will you shut anyway?' one of Venetia's aides interjects.

Yes, of course the Barrier will still close, Angus snaps. 'We take no chances. It is quite a big surge, and if for any reason the model wasn't performing properly or the surge began overtaking, then there might be a risk of the danger limit being exceeded.'

The journalists are clamouring for Angus's attention. Reluctantly he turns to them. Lauren Khan catches his eye, 'You said overtake? You mean speed up? Does that happen?'

Angus is disconcerted. 'It is possible,' he admits, 'but unlikely.' Surges tend to fall off as they progress south. Only occasionally does a surge come up the estuary and never on the high tide. He searches for a way to put the answer simply, without a lot of technical details. 'Mainly it's due to interaction with the rising tide coming up the estuary. The two moving bodies of water cancel each other out. It's one of those patterns you learn to recognise. You watch these threatening situations building up and you can almost guarantee they'll fall off as they approach the estuary.'

Only very occasionally does a surge override the strength of the tide, he adds. Obviously, it happened in 1953. But it's rare. The Barrier closes in anger two or three times a year on average and in more than two decades there has not been a threat event yet.

Further discussion is interrupted by a flurry of excitement. While they have been talking the *Belfast* has moved much closer. A warning buzzer sounds in the control room. The journalists crowd the windows. The lead tugs are only some 500 metres from the gates, drawn close together to pass through. The cruiser looks huge close up, even against the massive piers of the Barrier. The muzzles of the four-inch secondary gun batteries are pointing straight up at the tower. There are men stationed in the bows and waist and, less distinct, figures on the bridge.

The Environment Agency media team intervene to urge people down onto the piers. Hard hats are produced and everyone files out to the lift. Venetia and Angus get in together with Venetia's bodyguard and her press officer. Angus presses the button. It is a long way down. There are two basement levels and he takes the lower. The lift stops. Venetia steps out into a stairwell with walls of bare concrete.

Angus leads the way through a steel door into a broad, brightly lit passage, as spacious as a tube tunnel. Along the sides are water conduits and racks of cable runs. Fire mains to the left, power and communications and alarm cables to the right, he explains as they go. All duplicated. Fire suppression systems include water sprinkler and deluge, carbon dioxide, foam and halon. Drains run beneath gratings in the floor. The central gangway is wide enough for two people to walk abreast.

After about seventy-five metres the passage ends. They exit through a metal door into a stairwell and descend two flights of concrete steps. Another door brings them back into a second tunnel, identical to the first but at a deeper level. They are now passing beneath the central portion of the river, Angus tells them.

Twelve metres below the river, this is one of the hidden marvels of London. The twin tunnels, there is a second lying parallel with this one, run inside the concrete sills sunk into the riverbed in which the Barrier gates rest. They extend from bank to bank, a private crossing reserved solely for Barrier staff, a permanent and safe means for engineers to reach the gate piers, regardless of weather, and to bring equipment in and out.

Angus hurries along and the others follow. Signs over the fire doors indicate pier heads. 'Which gate?' the press officer calls breathlessly.

'Echo,' Angus responds curtly, not pausing. They pass through three doors, then take a turn off left marked Pier 6. A door opens onto a stairwell. 'We have some climbing to do now,' Angus apologises gruffly. This proves to be an understatement. Twelve steps, then a turn, twelve more to a landing. Level 6. After five floors of this there is another door off. A new stairwell, concrete steps this time. Two more flights, signs reading Oil Storage and MV Switch Room. Angus opens a door into a vault-like chamber containing a pair of enormous yellow hydraulic rams. This is the upper machinery room and these are the pistons for rotating the gates. They are idle at the moment. The gates are lowered, lying flat in their sills on the bed of the river.

Angus leads the way through double doors, out onto the platform of the pier. They have arrived only just in time. The tugs are already entering the gate. They seem tiny, but from this distance the 10,000-tonne cruiser appears truly gigantic, a moving mountain of masts and funnels and guns bearing down on them. It is hard to believe a vessel on this scale can possibly squeeze between the piers.

'Great shot if she gets stuck!' a photographer cracks.

Angus scowls. She won't, he says crossly. The gate is sixty metres wide and the ship's beam only twenty. The Barrier has seen many larger vessels through safely. The biggest was the aircraft carrier, *Ark Royal.*

Venetia is not so easily convinced. The Barrier is not infallible. In October 1997, a sand dredger scuffed one of the piers in thick fog and was holed. The 3000-tonne *Sand Kite* was taking a mixed cargo of sand and gravel for construction use to a wharf up-river. The dredger regularly made the passage three or four times a week. This time, however, something went wrong.

Just before 7 am the master of the vessel radioed Barrier Control, following normal procedure, to announce his approach. Visibility was 400 metres but he could see the Barrier without difficulty. He was instructed to make for Echo gate. Minutes later the *Sand Kite* collided first with Pier 5 then swung over to strike Pier 4. The impact caused a 12-metre split down the ship's starboard bow and dumped 4000 tonnes of ballast onto Foxtrot gate.

The vessel settled onto a cushion of sand with its hull lying across the gate. To the relief of Barrier Control, divers reported no signs of structural damage to the submerged gate. The salvage operation took six days. The ship was temporarily patched, water was pumped from the hold and it was refloated. The two adjacent gates were closed so that the incoming tide would flush as much as possible of the dumped gravel up-river off the gate. During all this time Echo gate was jammed in the open position. Finally, on November 1st, the dredger was towed clear.

Venetia's thoughts are interrupted by the camera crews. They want shots of her in the foreground of the ship. She obliges. This, after all, is why she has come. Stately and majestic, the warship enters the gate. The men in the bow wave down and call a greeting. Venetia leans against the rail, her profile towards the cameras, trying not to shiver from the cold. There are fog crystals in her hair and a film of mist clinging to her clothes. The cruiser slides by with a waft mingled of oil and steel and salt water, the unmistakable, romantic smell of a big ship.

Slowly, the *Belfast* processes through the gate and out the other side into the pool of London. The group on the pier watch her lights recede into the distance till they are swallowed up in the glitter of Docklands.

As they return to the tower, one of Venetia's aides fields a call for her. It is Raikes with the news that the *Sir Gareth* has finally gone down with heavy loss of life.

5

London is the most closely watched capital city in the world; on average an individual will be captured on camera more than three hundred times in a day. This surveillance is a response to terrorist outrages as well as to rising crime figures. Public areas such as the Underground system, Westminster and other high-risk zones are monitored around the clock.

Ever since a failed IRA bomb attack on Hammersmith Bridge, all the main crossings of the Thames have been under surveillance. At New Scotland Yard, an officer observing a bank of closed circuit television monitors peers at one of his screens. A camera trained on the bridge at Waterloo has detected a figure moving into view.

At this time of night any pedestrian on this spot is sufficient to warrant closer attention. Pressing a switch to bring the camera under remote control, the officer pans across to centre the figure in its field of vision. The person, it is not possible to say if it is male or female, appears to be attempting to climb onto the parapet. A touch of a dial calls up a zoom lens powerful enough to read a newspaper headline at a hundred metres.

The officer makes immediate contact with the Central Command Complex. 'Monitor Room here. Waterloo Bridge up-river side, young white male on the parapet and preparing to jump.'

On the second of July 1798, two London magistrates, John Hariott and Patrick Colquhoun, persuaded the West India Merchants' Committee to finance the world's first police unit to combat piracy and theft on the river. The new force was an immediate success. Equipped with cutlasses and blunderbusses, and patrolling in rowing galleys, in the first six months of operations it recovered over £100,000 in stolen cargo.

The docks have been replaced by office development, the warehouses turned into luxury flats. Today the hundred officers of the Thames Division are more likely to be found rescuing swimmers or boarding pleasure cruisers in search of drugs than chasing river pirates.

The Thames Division is the world's oldest police unit. It still operates from the original site in Wapping High Street, overlooking the river, patrolling fifty-four miles of banks from Staines to Dartford Creek, as well as having responsibility for all other canals, lakes and reservoirs in the Greater London area.

Every couple of days, a launch pulls somebody out of the river. Most are alive, but about one a week is a corpse. Some of the swimmers are drunks who just want to cool off. 'People think: it's not so far, I can swim to the other bank easy,' says Sergeant Arthur Bell. 'But they don't reckon with the currents. It takes all their strength just to stay afloat. The river walls are too sheer to climb out or they get stuck in the mud at low tide.' Officers used to receive a corpse allowance of £25 a body or £17 if there was more than one. Such payments are no longer seen as appropriate.

Arthur has spent nineteen years on the river force. He is one of the longest serving officers. For a while he was with the élite anti-terrorist unit on watch off Westminster. In 1989 he took part in rescue operations after the pleasure cruiser *Marchioness* was rammed on the river at night by the dredger *Bow Belle*. Fifty-one people drowned and another eighty were saved, fifty of them by Arthur and his men.

The launch creams down river from Westminster, blue lights flashing. There is an RNLI boat at Tower Pier and another at Chiswick, but Arthur's boat is the nearest. It is a race to reach Waterloo Bridge before the young man jumps. If one of Arthur's crew can grab him quickly, they can save him. If he goes down deep, the chances are they will lose him. The currents will seize the body and tow it under. Bodies disappear for days, weeks even.

They reach the bridge and Arthur cuts the blue light array. He doesn't want to frighten the jumper. They can make him out just by the crest of the bridge on the up-river side. He is facing out towards the water, leaning forward with his arms gripping the rail at his back. The classic suicide's pose. Behind him on the road are police and ambulance men. They have closed the bridge to traffic and for a moment the situation is static.

Radio messages crackle to and fro. Everyone is waiting to see what will happen. Arthur switches on

Up close he looks younger still, hardly more than a teenager. With practised skill Arthur flips him over on his front, checking to see that the tongue is free, and starts pressing on the back and ribcage to bring up water. The boy coughs and gags. At least he is breathing. Arthur rolls him over onto his back again. The dark hair is plastered down, framing the thin face. 'All right, son,' he says gently, tucking a blanket around him. 'You're safe now. We'll take care of you.' This one was lucky, he thinks to himself. Over the radio he contacts ambulance control and arranges to dock at Festival Pier on the south bank.

A minute later he watches the boy carried up the steps and placed in a waiting ambulance. The victim is now a patient. Arthur wishes him well.

St Thomas's Hospital occupies a triangle of land between Westminster Bridge Road and the Thames with a frontage on Lambeth Palace Road. It is administered as a joint trust with Guy's, two miles down river, and the hospitals share a formidable international reputation. They are a major centre for cardiac and cancer services, and have important renal, respiratory and dentistry units as well as housing the National Poisons Centre. They also operate the largest accident and emergency service in the UK. About 90,000 patients are treated annually in Guy's and St Thomas's and the Trust employs 6,000 staff.

Melanie Sykes started here as a junior doctor last summer. Competition was tough and she knows she was lucky to get the job. The training at Guy's and St Thomas's is second to none.

Melanie is twenty-six years old. She is a little under average height and when not working hard has to watch her weight. Her eyes are dark like her hair which she wears long and tied up in a knot that tends to slip down when she is busy. She has a quick smile and a direct manner that manages not to be blunt.

Melanie's parents want her to be a GP but she is aiming higher. A consultant, she hopes, but she hasn't settled on a speciality. At present she is attached to the Lane Fox Respiratory Unit at St Thomas's, a centre for patients needing artificial ventilation. The unit has sixteen beds and state-of-the-art equipment. Some patients are in for rehabilitation, others, like the post-polio cases, are longer term. Working here can be harrowing, but it is all experience.

This morning Melanie has been part of the team re-admitting a former patient who has had a relapse after a bout of pneumonia. The man was fetched from Intensive Care in Birmingham by the unit's customised ambulance and it has taken the best part of two hours to get him settled. Lane Fox is on the ground floor, which makes transfers, with all the ventilators and kit, easier.

The north side of the unit faces towards the Thames. When she first arrived, Melanie used to go down into the garden here and walk along the river front. The path runs alongside a hip-high wall of white stone shaded by plane trees; behind is a metre and a half drop down to the embankment walk and then the river wall itself. The upper area is private to the hospital and a pleasant place on a sunny day, with benches looking out over the river and the

Houses of Parliament opposite. At this time of year, though, the garden is bleak and the river brown and unattractive.

Friday December 19. It is after midnight. The tube network is shut down for the night. Between now and five is when essential maintenance is done. The power to the rails is off and the lights on. Night becomes day. This is a period of furious activity underground when the passengers are gone and stations and platforms are taken over by engineers and maintenance gangs, signal testers, ballast crews, billboard men and cleaners.

London's is the oldest system of the world's great cities and the most extensive. Over a billion passengers a year travel the 800-mile network, approximately four million each working day.

Paul Suter leads a twelve-strong team equipped with jackhammers and portable power packs. Front-line troops in the constant battle to keep the system running. Their task tonight is to replace a set of points on the Bakerloo Line beyond Piccadilly Circus. The worn sleepers are first dug out by hand and then a track dolly is wheeled up to hoist the rails clear. It is a frustrating job. They have only a few hours to work each night and tonight the last train was delayed, leaving them even less time than usual. By the time they have managed to isolate the station and get their plant and equipment down onto the platform, the knock-on effect means it is too risky to attempt all the planned work. If a job is left unfinished, the morning rush hour will be thrown into chaos. Patch and mend is the best that can ever be hoped for. It is a vicious circle: the system breaks down for lack of maintenance but there isn't time to do maintenance because the system keeps breaking down.

Paul logs off items on his clipboard. Yesterday a missing spare part costing all of £25 brought the entire Central Line to a halt. Paul's colleagues talk with anger about under-investment, crumbling brickwork and fifty-year-old signalling equipment. Everyone agrees it is only a matter of time before something really big goes, a bridge or a tunnel roof collapse.

A battery-powered works unit takes the team and their equipment into the tunnel. They are travelling through one of the deepest spots of the line, midway between Waterloo and Charing Cross, right under the Thames. The tunnel is constructed of triple layers of brick. Sides and roof stream with water that gurgles as it trickles away. Just being down here makes Paul nervous. He knows of engineers who refuse to work this section. The bed of the river is officially put at eight metres above their heads. Actually, in places it is much less. The depth of the river is not uniform. Tides and currents scour the bed, constantly carving out trenches and deep holes. There are people who claim that if you lean over Waterloo Bridge at low tide and peer down into the water, you can make out the hump of the tunnel roof in the mud of the river bottom.

If a river tunnel were to collapse, within three minutes water would be gushing through into the stations at each end with catastrophic consequences for the rest of the system. There would be no time to warn the public, thousands would perish. Floodgates were installed at the tunnel entrances during the Second World War as a protection against air raids, but these have long since been locked off and are no longer operational.

Paul looks away along the rails to where the lights disappear up the tunnel, wondering how long it would take to cover the five hundred or so metres to the first platform, uphill and in bulky overalls and boots. Longer than three minutes certainly. He tries not to picture the roof cracking open, the roar of water rushing in.

The engine begins to climb again under the northern bank. They pass through stations at Embankment and Charing Cross, reach Piccadilly Circus and slow to a crawl, halting a short distance beyond the platform. As Paul climbs down he feels a draught of air in his face. They have stopped opposite the entrance to a cross-over where trains can switch tunnels. This adds flexibility to the system, allowing trains to overtake or a breakdown to be withdrawn. The cross-over is controlled by signals and two sets of points. It is one of these they are here to replace.

Something is moving on the rails. An unmistakable humped shape that saunters boldly across the track. The black rat of the old plague days is re-establishing itself in the Underground. It was never totally eradicated from the docks and the new development there suits it. More food around, new drains laid. Rats like people. Now they are spreading westwards. They no longer carry plague-bearing fleas, according to health experts, but Paul is not so easily convinced. Cases of the disease have been reported in Paris.

By 4.30 am the work is done and tested. While

his team packs the shovels and picks onto the battery unit, Paul takes a last check around. There is still the debris to clear away but that can wait until the next shift. Assuming nothing else goes wrong tomorrow.

Away in the West Country, Claire Panton wakes and reaches out in the darkness for her bedside clock. As she does so there is a faint click, followed by a shrill electronic beep. Claire feels for the button and quickly switches the noise off. Her husband rolls over with a sigh. 'What time is it?'

'Four. That was the alarm. Phil will be here in twenty minutes.'

Claire rolls out of bed and pulls on her dressing-gown. By the time she is dressed and ready, her husband has made tea. There is a soft tap at the door. Claire checks her shoulder bag. Money, credit cards, map, telephone, everything is there. She puts on her raincoat and kisses her husband. 'We should be back around ten tonight. If there's any delay I'll call you.'

Claire and Phil are teachers at St David's secondary school. Today the entire school, all 460 pupils, are travelling up to London by train to see this year's Christmas show at the reopened Dome. It is only a five-minute run to the school at this time of night. The lights are on and their colleagues are already gathered by the main entrance. Colin Gynn, the head teacher, is in charge. As Claire and Phil hurry over, the first buses are turning into the forecourt.

The entire outing has been meticulously planned. There is a ratio of one adult escort for every nine pupils, plus two qualified first-aiders. Pupils are marshalled in the assembly hall as if for the start of a normal day. They have been told to bring one small bag only. Personal stereos permitted at the owner's risk. When the last bus has disembarked a roll call is held. The head then reminds everyone of the arrangements.

'On arrival at Paddington, groups must stay close to their leader. We will go down onto the Underground and take a Circle Line tube train to Westminster. At Westminster we change onto the Jubilee Line for North Greenwich, which is the station for the Dome.'

When everything is ready, boarding begins. Claire checks off names by the door of her bus. Some pupils have been to the Dome before but for others this is a first visit to London. The older girls are in their tightest skirts while the boys are deliberately sloppy, shirt tails dangling, ties askew. 'Remember,' she tells them, 'so long as you stay with your group you can't get lost.'

'Yeah, Miss,' they chorus.

At the station a handful of parents are on hand to wave goodbye. Several pupils are smoking which the teachers pretend not to see. No one wants to start the day with a fight. Claire takes a seat by the aisle and unfolds a newspaper. The weather in London is forecast to be damp and windy but in the West Country they are used to rain. She is looking forward to the trip. It will be a day to remember.

6

Twenty-five miles east of Hull, the seaside hamlet of Kilnsea lies at the base of Spurn Head, a hook-shaped five-mile spit of sand and shingle that juts out from the Holderness peninsula into the Humber estuary where the river meets the sea. A mosaic of dunes and wetlands as little as fifty metres wide in places, Spurn Head is internationally important as a wildlife sanctuary, one of the great refuges for wading birds and wildfowl that migrate through the estuary or overwinter.

The coastline has suffered the worst erosion in Europe. During the last Ice Age the Yorkshire coast was a line of chalk cliffs standing thirty kilometres east of here. Even since Roman times the shore has retreated by four hundred metres and thirty villages have disappeared completely, swallowed up by the sea. Fifty years ago the low cliff and sea wall were breached south of Easington at a point known today as the Lagoons. Waves poured across the neck of land from the seaward to spill out again into the Humber between Skeffling and Kilnsea. Inland, the flood lapped the cobblestones in Easington village square over a mile from the coast.

Outside the village, on the North Sea coast, a couple of caravan and holiday parks cater for summer visitors. It is a precarious existence. There are no sea defences here, just soft cliffs of boulder clay. On days when the North Sea has a big swell on, the waves break right over and the backwash drags material down the beach. Each time this happens a bit more of the cliff is eroded away. The level of the defences is dropping all the time and the sea is eating into the lower land at a rate of two metres a year.

Adam Thorne is the Environment Agency officer for the Spurn Head Heritage Coast. He is twenty-six, tall and instantly likeable, with a thatch of fair hair, a man who enjoys his work, loves the coast. Tonight, because of the flood Red Alert, he has turned out to chase up residents of beachfront properties who haven't responded to telephone warnings. Three households have taken his advice and are moving to higher ground; he has one more left on his list. Turning south out of Easington towards the peninsula, the full force of the wind hits the Land Rover and the headlight beams are full of spray mingled with flying sand and sleet. It is nearing high water and he can hear the deep roar of the sea pounding the shingle banks.

The lane leading to the caravan park has a lot of water running down it. Adam hopes it is rain and not flooding from the sea. Until a few years ago an old WW2 anti-aircraft tower stood at the corner of the site, twenty metres inland from the beach. First the beach was swallowed by the sea, then the tower. The owner has done what he can, compacting his site, drawing his chalets and vans back inland. He has brought in a bulldozer to carve out a berm along the shore, but the waves carry the spoil away faster than he can throw it up.

Adam brakes for a moment at the gate. The headlights are pointing out in the direction of the sea. Adam can't make out much, just occasional spouts of whiteness which can only be breakers bursting over the sands. They seem horribly close and it strikes him forcibly that he is right out on the limit here. If the car breaks down and the sea comes over, this is a place where one could die tonight.

There is a light on at the lodge and the owner's pick-up is parked outside. Somewhere out in the field to the left, being battered by the wind, are the chalets and mobile homes. He can hear crashings and screeching of metal and he wonders how many of them will survive the night. Hard to believe, right now, that this is an attractive spot in summer. There is water running several inches deep across the forecourt. Adam leaves his engine running, squelches through the wet and pounds on the front door.

'I'm not going,' the man repeats stubbornly.

'Mr Lindsay, you have to go. If you stay here you could drown.'

The owner stares at him, eyes red-rimmed with strain and tiredness. 'I might as well,' he mutters. He might as well die as leave, he means. He has sunk his pension money into this park, everything he possessed. Day by day he sits here watching his livelihood disappear. What is there left for him? 'They should build a wall,' he says. It is an old wish. The Agency builds floodwalls to protect other people's homes, why not his? 'If they won't build me a wall, they should at least offer me compensation.'

His words are barely audible above the noise of the storm. The sound of the waves seems to be growing by the minute and spray is beating so hard against the shuttered windows that Adam expects them to break under the impact. Water is seeping through into the living room from some rear part and soaking into the carpet. Every time there is a big gust the entire house shakes. If they stay here much longer they will both drown, he thinks.

Adam doesn't know what to do. It is his duty to get this man to safety but he can't compel him to leave. Even the police have no power to order evacuations. He feels desperately sorry for him. The man is in his sixties. He has worked hard all his life. If he leaves, where can he go? He is too old to start again. He has nothing except what is here. The government denies him compensation, yet a mile or two up the coast they are spending £10,000 a metre to build a rock revetment in front of a gas terminal. Eventually the council will condemn this house and order its demolition at his expense. Last year a family up in Hornsea were billed £3,500 for having their house knocked down against their will.

Another thunderous gust shakes the building. When waves strike the land with great force, the pressure of water compresses air into cracks in the rock. Then, when the air escapes under pressure, it shatters the rock like an explosive charge. The sea is literally blasting the cliffs apart.

'If you refuse to come now and have to be rescued later you'll be putting other lives at risk as well as your own. A helicopter sent to help you might be needed somewhere else.'

The man shakes his head stubbornly. He doesn't want to be rescued. He is staying put.

Adam decides he can't wait any longer, he must go. 'I'm leaving now,' he tells the owner. 'If you want to stay, then that's your decision.'

Outside again, Adam uses his mobile phone to contact Rivers House. The owner's refusal to accept evacuation is officially logged. The man has made his decision and will have to take the consequences. Adam swings the Land Rover around and heads back up the drive. He does twenty metres, then stops short. One of the caravans has broken loose and been rolled across the track by the wind, completely blocking it. He gets out to take a look but he can see at a glance there is no way that he is going to be able to get past. The caravan is on its side, jammed up between the hedge and the bank. It will have to be dragged clear, probably by a tractor. Adam hasn't got a winch or any chains and he doubts if the Land Rover would have the power to shift the blockage anyway. He will have to go back to the house and get help from the owner. Perhaps he will be staying here too, after all.

Then he remembers there is a way out across the fields to the south of the site if only he can find it. He backs the vehicle around. Yes, there is the gateway over to the right. He steers through and starts to follow a rutted track. This should lead through to join up with the road to Kilnsea. Within yards though the track gives out or else he loses it. Visibility is so bad he can't tell which. Sleet and spray are lashing at the windscreen and the wipers are useless. The ground is uneven and the Land Rover lurches from side to side, crawling through mud and water. He fetches up against a bank and follows it along, thinking he must come to a gate eventually. A fence post looms up in the headlights, he twists the wheel over to avoid it and only just in time realises he is on the edge of the cliff.

He backs up again, retracing his course across the fields. The bank must have bent round towards the sea without him noticing. He tries to keep going as straight as he can away from the beach, but within minutes all sense of direction is gone again. He is beginning to think he might have been better off taking his chances at the lodge when the going gets suddenly easier and with relief he sees that he has come out on to the road at last.

The relief is short-lived. He keeps looking out for lights but there is no sign of the village anywhere. Visibility is worse than ever and he can't make out any landmarks in the dark. It is all he can do to keep on the road. It is about a mile up to Kilnsea and he must have done twice that by now. The road seems to be headed downhill and that's confusing. At first he thinks it is just a dip he never noticed before, then an awful thought hits him. This is the only road on the peninsula. It was built by the military in 1940 and leads all the way down through the nature reserve to the lifeboat station at Spurn Head. Suppose he has become so disorientated in the darkness that he is driving away from the village?

Adam struggles on for another half-mile looking for a place to turn. The dark and the flying spray breaking over the spit of land makes it impossible to see more than two or three feet in front of him and he daren't risk straying off the road and ending up in a ditch with a damaged vehicle. Water is washing over the roadway and he is thinking the sensible course may be to keep going till he reaches the lifeboat station. By his calculations it shouldn't be more than another mile.

The road takes another dip and all at once the water is axle deep and flowing fast all around. He peers through the windshield, trying to make out if the road rises again, but he can't see anything. He drops down into low ratio and keeps the throttle steady. A Land Rover will keep on running so long as the air intake is above water. In practice that means a depth of up to a metre. The trick is to keep the speed down otherwise you create a bow wave that washes over the engine.

Above the shrieking of the wind, he can detect the heavy thudding of waves beating on the clay cliffs. Bursts of spray slam against the side and roof of the Land Rover. Adam fights to keep the wheel steady as they lurch through potholes. This is one of the narrowest parts of the spit. The land here is barely fifty metres wide, studded with marram and buckthorn. Sections of road get washed out all the time in bad weather when the sea comes over.

There is so much water that it is hard to make out where he is going. Waves are foaming around the doorsills. It is like driving through the sea itself. He has completely lost sight of where the road is and he is beginning to feel really frightened. He fumbles inside his coat for his phone. The time has come to stop trying to be a hero and call for assistance. The wheel bucks in another pothole. He grabs on with both hands, gunning the engine to climb out again. Then without warning the vehicle tips sickeningly sideways as a great slab of ground supporting the roadway collapses into the sea. Adam has a fleeting glimpse of surf boiling in the headlights before water engulfs the cab.

7

It is 6.02 am when the call comes in to Humber Coastguard Maritime Rescue Sub-Centre at Bridlington. The owner of a caravan site on Spurn Head, south of Easington, is trapped in his house and the sea is breaking in. The road out has been cut; he has no means of escape. Help is needed urgently.

There is a Coastguard volunteer section based on Easington that covers this section of the coast. It is equipped with a rigid inflatable towed by Land Rover. They have turned out and are near the scene, but the team leader radios in that the sea has broken through the peninsula south of the village in the area known locally as the Lagoons. Heavy waves are smashing across the salt marsh; a boat rescue is impossible. These are experienced men and no one questions their decision or their courage. It will have to be a helicopter extraction.

Bridlington puts in a request to Air Rescue Co-ordination at RAF Kinloss in Scotland for a military helicopter. The nearest Sea King base is at Leconfield north of Hull. Its machines have had a busy night assisting in the evacuation of a drilling platform and searching for a trawler fisherman washed overboard on Dogger Bank. He was subsequently picked up by Bridlington lifeboat. One of the base's two Sea Kings, Rescue 39, has now returned and can be in the air again as soon as it has refuelled. Estimated time of arrival at the scene of the emergency is forty-five minutes.

The Sea King HAR-3 is the primary SAR aircraft for UK waters. A big rugged machine with a range of three hundred miles, it carries a crew of four and up to nineteen passengers. It is fitted with advanced all-weather search and navigation electronics and a computer-aided automatic hover control system that effectively enables the winch operator to fly the aircraft during a rescue. Standard equipment includes enhanced thermal imaging cameras for picking out survivors in the water and powerful night scanner lighting.

Locating the caravan site is straightforward using the Sea King's GPS system. There are no hills or high structures to worry about, but there is a lot of turbulence close to the shore and the helicopter bounces around as though they are riding over potholes. Visibility is poor due to the amount of rain and spray. As they close in on the target zone the crew switch on the searchlights. It is immediately apparent that the sea has cut right through the neck of the peninsula. Breakers are streaming unchecked through a channel a quarter of a mile wide. The clay cliff east of the site has collapsed taking the house with it. Much of the rest of the site has been overrun by water. Then the winch operator calls out he can see coloured smoke coming from a patch of higher ground that is still dry. Someone there has lit a flare. It is the owner waiting to be rescued.

With no trees or other obstructions nearby, the pilot elects to go for a ground recovery. The use of the flare is helpful because it provides a visual clue of wind direction. He brings the helicopter down carefully till it is hovering just feet off the ground. The park owner is crouched over, shielding himself against the wash. Rhys Jones, the winchman, jumps out and hauls him on board and the rescue is over. It has taken all of six minutes.

In fact it is only just beginning. As they are lifting off again a message comes over the radio: an engineer from the Environment Agency is missing in the area. He was last reported leaving the caravan park at Easington. This is Adam Thorne and the park owner confirms the account.

The pilot's name is Terry Spencer, a lieutenant with four years experience in helicopters and married with two children. He is a small man with a solid physique, strong in the arms and shoulders. He needs to be to hold the aircraft steady in these conditions. He takes the Sea King up to five hundred feet while he works out a search plan with his co-pilot, Doug Neering. The most likely probability is that Thorne was trying to make it over the Lagoons when the sea broke through. They will start their search there.

Spencer brings them back to the area of the breach and flies a close search pattern back and forth across the peninsula, while Doug Neering scans the surface below on the FLIR display. FLIR stands for Forward Looking Infra Red, basically a heat-seeking camera mounted under the nose of the aircraft. The system is so sensitive that it can detect whether a body floating in the water is alive or dead.

Tonight though it picks up nothing. Either Adam has been washed right out to sea or, more likely, he found the way blocked and turned back.

Spencer banks round onto a new heading and starts to fly southwards, parallel with the coast down the centre of the spit. They know Adam is using a Land Rover so they are hoping he has stayed with the vehicle. A mile south of the caravan park the seas are much worse. The helicopter has now been over Spurn Head for approximately half an hour and during that brief time weather conditions have deteriorated sharply. Even with military night vision goggles it is hard to make out features below. The FLIR display is a little better but moisture in the atmosphere tends to degrade infra-red and there is a huge amount of airborne water around tonight.

They fly down as far as the Point, circle and return. It is hard to distinguish any land at all now. There is just a broad white strip of tumbling seas with waves powering across and breakers exploding into sheets of spray. Twenty minutes into their second run Doug picks up something on his display. He guides Spencer down for a visual check and there it is, a vehicle on its side, buried among breakers. According to the GPS read-out they are directly over the beach on the east shore but the fix is a notional concept. None of the crew can remember seeing seas like this on the coast before. It is not simply that they are coming in fast. There is a massive quality about them that is awesome. A relentless succession of mountainous crests riding unstoppably out of the darkness.

They put the light on the vehicle and, sure enough, there is a figure in the surf clinging to the roof-rack. There is only one way to play this – a straight lift. While Spencer holds the aircraft in position for the rescue, Doug sets the Sea King's hover computer with the datum. The system then takes over control and automatically brings the helicopter round to hold an into-wind hover position at fifty-five feet. The wind speed is sixty knots plus and the engines are labouring to keep position. It is like flying into soup. Rhys, the winchman, clips his harness to the cable and slides open the starboard side main hatch. Instantly the cabin fills with air so full of spray and rain that it is an effort to breathe. Like Spencer, Rhys is twenty-three. He joined the RAF on leaving school at seventeen and trained as a rescue swimmer. He has also qualified for Britain's Olympic team. He is in a long-term relationship with a girl named Sue who works on the base, and there is a child due in the New Year. Inshore rescues like this are 'a lot more exciting' – his words. Out in the ocean you can ride out a big roller, but a wave breaking against a shelving beach is dumping all its energy as it hits. It can crush you against rocks or bury you so deep under a backwash of sand that you never come up again.

He crouches in the hatch concentrating on the scene he is going down into. The spray flying in the rotor wash makes it hard to see, even with the beam of the searchlight. It should be a straightforward lift, no boat rigging to worry about. The vehicle looks to be grounded on the sand; it is a matter of getting the sling onto the survivor and riding back up with him. With no hitches the recovery should be over in five minutes.

He gives the thumbs up signal to Jacob, the winch operator, and pushes himself off from the hatch sill. He is wearing full survival clothing, quarter inch neoprene thermal body suit, dry suit and boots, gloves, safety helmet and life vest. The winch lets him down at about six feet a second. With winds gusting to seventy knots the idea is to complete the drop as fast as possible before the winchman drifts off target. For the final fifteen feet Jacob slows the descent to give a controlled impact. The transition from the safety of the helicopter cabin to the boiling sea takes less than ten seconds.

Rhys drops down into the surf, not quite within arms' reach of Adam. His immediate impression is that the sea state is even wilder than it seemed from above. The water is chest deep and there is a savage undertow dragging at his legs. It is all he can do to stay upright and stop himself being smashed against the side of the car by waves breaking over. He can also see that Adam's strength is failing fast. He has obviously been out here in the water for a considerable while and the cold and exhaustion have almost done for him. He has no life jacket; if he loses his grip on the vehicle he will be swept out to sea. Death will come not from hypothermia but from the cold starving his limbs of oxygen and blood. Unable to stay afloat, he will quickly drown.

Doug, the co-pilot, is monitoring the rescue. Visibility in his words is 'bloody diabolical – next worst to a white out'. Each time a wave rolls in, the Land Rover disappears completely. Behind in the main cabin, Jacob is leaning out from the hatch. He wears a safety line and he is following the rescue with one hand on the winch controls. It is his job to see Rhys has enough slack on the cable to move freely but not so much that it can get snagged.

Timing his movements between incoming waves, Rhys starts moving round the vehicle towards where Thorne is clinging onto the roof. The brilliance of the searchlight beam freezes the scene; every wave crest, every particle of spume picked out with a knife-edged clarity. The Land Rover is dangerously unstable; it is heaving and rocking in the swells, at any moment it may go over. Out of nowhere another wave hits. It is so huge Rhys can't see its crest. He has an impression of a great black wall hanging over him and the next instant he is fighting for breath under an avalanche of water. He struggles to keep a hold on part of the vehicle but he can feel it sliding away. The suction of the backwash is pulling the Land Rover bodily out to sea, carrying both men with it. Rhys is being tumbled over in the surf. He senses something huge rolling down upon him and realises that it's the Land Rover. He flails desperately to escape, thrashing with his limbs. He can move but he can't reach the surface. He is upside down under water and unable to see. His safety harness is holding him under. The cable must be snagged on part of the vehicle. He has to free himself or drown.

Fifty feet overhead, as Rhys is hit by the wave, the helicopter is experiencing sudden fierce turbulence. A violent downdraught is immediately succeeded by an equally savage updraught. The Sea King shudders and drops thirty feet like a stone, only to soar back upward again as a high-pressure air pocket bursts beneath its keel. The winch is designed to maintain only a light tension on the cable otherwise the winch man risks being jerked off his feet during a rescue. When Rhys slips and falls under the wave, the cable becomes trapped beneath the Land Rover as it topples over. A second later, the air pocket punches the Sea King skywards, the tensioning system which has just gone into reel-in mode scrambles to reverse, but can't react fast enough. The clutch freezes, snatching the cable tight. The cable is designed to lift 275 kilograms and now it is trying to lift a Land Rover filled with sand and salt water and weighing more than a tonne by the rear suspension. There is a sheer pin in the winch assembly that is supposed to fail if the 275-kilogram limit is exceeded, dropping cable and reel into the sea. For some reason this doesn't operate. Probably the wire severed on some sharp projection of the vehicle. With a violent twang, the cable parts and the loose end, thirty metres long, flies up and wraps itself around the tail rotor.

Rhys is fumbling for the release latch on the harness when he feels a terrific jerk and a thrumming vibration that shakes the Land Rover. Then suddenly he is free again and fighting his way back to the surface. And he thinks, Oh shit, that was the cable parting.

The purpose of a tail rotor is to provide horizontal stability. Without it the fuselage of the helicopter would spin round under the influence of the main rotor. Damage to the tail assembly is the commonest cause of catastrophic crashes among single-main-rotor helicopters. The Sea King's tail rotor blades are made of an aluminium honeycomb protected by a carbon-fibre outer layer. The winch cable tightens around the rotor head and blade pitch-change mechanism, locking it solid instantly. The violent deceleration causes the blades to sheer off from the rotor head. It also sheers the pin inside the winch assembly, ripping the reel mechanism off the fuselage and jerking it into the arc of the main rotor. The blades of this rotor are heavier and more strongly built than the tail assembly; also, the blade tips are weighted to keep them in balance and they stand up better to the impact. When the winch reel comes in contact with the blades it is hurled away backwards and out of the spinning arc. One blade tip disintegrates and another blade edge is damaged, but the rotor continues to function.

Spencer's reactions are instinctive. The helicopter is uncontrollable and spinning chaotically. He knows this can only be a tail rotor failure, most probably resulting from a collision with a solid object. Why is not important. All that matters now is to get the aircraft down before it dives into the sea. He is low over the water and that only gives him seconds literally in which to act. There is no time for checklists or even to shout a warning to the two other crew on board. They are as aware as he is they are about to crash. Doug has hit the radio button and is screaming out a Mayday message. They may be his final words. Jacob, who has almost been jerked out of the hatch, at least knows what has happened but he can't do anything except hang on and try to remember his ditching drill.

Spencer hits the engine cut-out switches. There is a moment of strange silence in the cabin as the engines die. The spinning steadies, the mass of the heavy fuselage is acting like a break on the rotors.

The helicopter is now somewhere between a stall and a glide and going down fast.

The Sea King is sixty-five feet, twenty metres, above the sea at the moment of the disaster. Aircraft are designed to withstand a ground impact with a vertical velocity of three metres per second. Effectively this means that a plane will break up if it drops onto a solid surface from a height of just half a metre. A falling object accelerates at ten metres per second per second. If the Sea King tumbles straight into the sea, it will be travelling at over seventy kilometres an hour when it strikes the surface. At that speed it will be equivalent to flying into a mountainside.

Helicopters do not float. This is one fact drummed into flight crews. Actually, it is an understatement. A Sea King fully loaded weighs eight tonnes. That weight is concentrated at the highest point in the fuselage where the engines are located. When a helicopter ditches in the sea it immediately becomes unstable. It turns turtle and starts to sink with deadly speed. Attempts have been made to add flotation collars and air bags but these can't overcome the fundamental characteristics of the aircraft.

All the crew have done escape training. They have been through the simulators where they are strapped into a fuselage section on a hydraulic arm, which is then dunked into a tank of freezing water. Even though everyone is anticipating what will happen, nothing prepares one for the disorientation and terror of being upside down in the dark under water. Emergency lights help and so do HEEDS bottles – cut-down scuba sets with enough air for three minutes – and so does the training, but a sea ditching remains the hazard a crew dreads.

Spencer's one thought is to keep from dropping back onto the Land Rover. Not only will that kill Rhys and Adam but it will almost certainly do for the rest of them as well. Their best chance is to try to ditch far enough off the shore so that they will not strike the bottom and break up on impact. He has only the barest control on the joystick. He can't see anything through the windshield. All he can do is pray.

It is a tribute to Spencer's skill that the Sea King actually stays aloft for all of six seconds. The difference between that and the two seconds it would have taken to hit the sea in a straight dive is enough to reduce the impact speed from a lethal seventy kilometres per hour to a just survivable twenty-three. The helicopter plunges into the water a dozen metres further out from the Land Rover and another fifty metres south. In one sense the crew are fortunate there is a storm raging, because in normal conditions the aircraft would have fallen into a bare half a metre's depth of water whereas now there is a good five metres to cushion their impact. The helicopter hits in a nose down attitude and cants over onto the port side.

Rhys has watched the crash in disbelief. All his instincts tell him to forget what he is doing and go to help his buddies. Then his training reasserts itself. There is a man here to be rescued first. Without the helicopter lights, the darkness is near total. He fumbles his way around the Land Rover till more by luck than anything he locates the engineer, gets a grip on the man's clothing and lugs him, staggering through the waves, back up the shelving shore. He drags him beyond the worst of the breakers and dumps him down. Thorne collapses, too weak to move further. Rhys unzips his own survival suit and tells him to put it on. Then he sets off down the coast to try and find his friends.

In a ditching it is Jacob's duty to inflate the life rafts ready for deployment as soon as the helicopter hits the sea. In the few seconds they have, there is no time to do anything more than brace himself against the bulkhead. The caravan park owner is strapped in his seat looking terrified. He has only just been plucked from the sea and now he is going through it all again. The impact of ditching throws Jacob across the cabin. It is lucky for him that they roll over to port otherwise he might have been thrown through the hatch. He picks himself up and can see the hatch now over his head with water pouring through. They don't seem to be sinking and the auxiliary lamps are still on. They are battery powered and designed to function under water. The park owner is nowhere to be seen. His seat is under the water and he is still strapped into it. Before Jacob can go to his help the man splashes to the surface gasping; he has managed to unstrap himself. Jacob finds a life vest and thrusts it at him. Then he pulls out one of the rafts and inflates it ready for use. He wonders about putting on his survival suit but can't see it anywhere.

Doug's head appears in the cockpit hatch. The skipper has injured his leg and he needs help getting him out. The cockpit windows have been stoved in and the cockpit itself is chest deep in water.

Together the two drag Spencer through into the rear cabin and force the cockpit hatch shut. Waves are pounding against the hull outside and they can feel the fuselage grinding and shifting on the sea bed beneath them. The water is now waist deep inside and the noise is terrifying. No one knows how long the aircraft can take this kind of punishment. The question is, do they stay where they are or try to make for the shore? The Sea King's emergency homing beacon has been triggered so rescuers can locate the wreckage easily. Going outside means fighting through the surf and breakers against waves as high as houses. Spencer's leg feels broken and he has doubts whether he can make it. He is not certain about the others either. Against that it will take the best part of an hour for help to reach them here, quite possibly longer. If the helicopter doesn't break up in that time it will almost certainly roll over, trapping them inside.

They have to go for it now, while they still can, Spencer tells the others. It is clearly the only choice. Doug though is worried about the skipper's leg. He asks what about taking the raft? Spencer shakes his head. 'I can swim,' he says as if that will make any difference. All four men have inflated their life vests. Spencer starts to pull himself up onto the lip of the hatch but Doug pushes him aside. Let me go first, he says, and launches himself through. He hangs onto the starboard landing gear with the water surging around him while Spencer grits his teeth and his two buddies help him out. As soon as he is clear, the park owner follows, with Jacob bringing up the rear.

*

On the land, Rhys can just make out the gleam of the helicopter's cabin lights among the spray and plunges towards them through the waves. There is a cluster of yellow dots glowing in the water close to the wreck that can only be survival beacons on crew life vests. He struggles out to them and finds Spencer and the other three clinging on to the fuselage. The skipper is injured and incapable of pulling himself through the surf and the others are refusing to leave him. All four are losing strength fast in the cold. Rhys and Jacob each take one arm and together swim Spencer towards the shore. They have almost made it when a thirty-foot comber breaks over them, flinging them apart. Rhys rolls over in the surf, fighting the undertow trying to drag him out to sea again. He manages to regain his feet and finds he is on land. The wave has thrown him up the beach like a piece of flotsam. He looks around and sees the skipper lying face down nearby. Rhys starts dragging him up out of reach of the waves. From out of the dark Jacob staggers up to help. They get Spencer safe in among the dunes and leave him there to go back for the others. Two lights are bobbing on the edge of the surf. It is Doug and the park owner. Somehow they have all made it. When Rhys looks out to sea he realises something has changed. The Sea King's cabin lights have vanished. The hull has been broken up or turned over. Either way, anyone who had remained aboard would now be dead.

An hour and a half later they see lights in the sky and at first they think they must be hallucinating. Adam Thorne is so numbed with cold he can't move his limbs when Rescue 38's winchman comes down. He and Spencer have to be stretchered up into the helicopter. What had seemed like an easy rescue has seen a helicopter lost and has almost cost six lives.

8

In London it is two hours before Low Water. At Barrier Control, wake-up calls are going out to those members of the closure team who have not spent the night in the accommodation block, reminding them that they must be on site by 8 am for a 10 am raising. Angus Walsh is already awake. He has managed six hours' sleep, which isn't bad considering all the razzmatazz over the *Belfast*. He listens to the weather forecast and the news while he dresses, then walks across to the control tower to check on the tide predictions. It is still dark outside and very wet. The river is full. No cause for concern, just not as low as experience tells him it should be considering the state of the tide. Most likely the rain over the past twenty-four hours has something to do with it.

At the tower reception area the status board shows 'RISK OF CLOSURE – HIGH'. Up in the control room, the duty controller confirms Angus's observation on the water level in the river. The outgoing tide is definitely lagging behind prediction. It is the same all down the estuary. Southend is up around ten centimetres. He puts it down to a combination of exceptionally heavy rain and wind conditions.

He and Angus discuss the situation on the east coast. The Met Office has issued new predictions for East Anglia showing an increase in levels for the south part of the coast, which are already over danger limits. The figures for Southend remain unchanged for the present, but the Met Office is warning these will shortly be revised upward substantially. It is beginning to look as if a record tide may be generated in the estuary. The control room is also monitoring levels at Plymouth on the south coast. There are indications that a small surge may be moving towards the Straits of Dover. Surges from this direction, what is known as 'the back door route', can add to London's problems in critical periods.

Angus surveys the charts and grunts. High Water is still eight hours away, a lot can happen in that time. Closing procedures are in place and the gates will be raised at ten o'clock. Any surge coming up-river will find the passage barred.

Angus takes a mug of coffee down in the lift and through the tunnels to inspect the gates. He likes to go round at this hour when there is hardly anyone on duty and he can poke about without interruption. On Pier 6 he steps outside onto the deck overlooking Echo gate. He stretches his shoulders and takes a couple of deep breaths. The wind is from the northeast. About him he can hear the rising hum of traffic entering the city.

He looks east down the river towards Southend. Somewhere there out in the sea is the surge, approaching steadily and inexorably down the coast, smashing and drowning as it comes. In another eight hours it will reach the Barrier and it will be up to him, Angus Walsh, to ensure that it does not pass. London is in his hands.

River Blackwater, Essex. It is a bitter morning out on the marshes. Dawn is still half an hour away. The wind is cold enough to freeze the bone and rising towards gale strength. It moans through the cables of the steel-frame pylons that stride out from the coast westwards to London. As the speed picks up, the wires begin to swing. Momentum builds till two lines clash. The result is a flashover and spectacular burst of flaming sparks. The heat released severs strands of wire on the cables that begin unwrapping back along the line.

This process, the technical name is conductor galloping, hits the 400kV Rayleigh to Romford circuit. A network control station in Rayleigh detects the fault. Managers close off the section before more damage results and try to re-route supplies around the breakage. It is not easy. This is a major feed into the M25 corridor. Many installations are powering up, drawing maximum current. People are switching on kettles, heaters, cookers, TV sets. Already demand in the southeast is breaking records. A dead sector in this place at this time will black out a substantial portion of the area network.

During the night freezing temperatures have deposited a coating of ice on the pylon towers leaving them too dangerous for engineers to climb. Instead the live-line helicopter will have to be scrambled to attempt repairs.

Out at Ilford on the outskirts of London, Diane Herring is leaving home for work. Diane is a network control manager with London Electricity. It is her job to oversee the smooth running of the transmission system within the capital. Her control centre is in Brixton. Most days she takes a train into the city and changes onto the underground Northern Line.

The power goes off as she is walking to the station. It is pitch black. All the streetlights are out too, which means it has to be a main feed somewhere. Supplies in this part of the country come from the Magnox nuclear plant out at Bradwell. She stands there in the dark, trying to get her bearings, all her senses heightened. She is aware of the wind bending the trees alarmingly. And there is a strange smell on the air. It is salt. She can smell the sea. Suddenly she feels afraid. 'I was frightened because I had never smelt the sea in Ilford before. All I could smell was salt.'

North Kent, near the Dartford Crossing. It is dark still as the shuttle bus, with Kerry Rosin and other workers aboard, comes up the rise from Greenhithe. The woods beside the road open out and all at once there is Bluewater.

A mile from the Thames, a former chalk quarry has been excavated down to a depth of forty-five metres to create a 240-acre man-made amphitheatre walled on three sides by sheer cliffs. Within it, architects have built a futuristic city of white stone that might have been carved out of the surrounding chalk. Thirty million people a year come here to the largest shopping complex in Europe.

Bluewater's statistics are formidable: seven thousand employees, a quarter of a million square metres of retail space containing three department stores and 320 shops, spaces for 13,000 cars, a park with seven lakes and a million trees. When research showed that 15 per cent of moviegoers go shopping before or after, the designers added a twelve-screen state-of-the-art multiplex. They also added a subtropical Winter Garden with eighteen-metre-high eucalyptus trees, a leisure village with cafés and restaurants, a water circus with an ice rink and revolving performance floor. To prevent partners getting bored they provided fishing, boating and biking in the parkland, and clusters of sports-goods shops and bars with sports TV for men to hang out in while waiting.

The quarry is a blaze of light. Down the access road from the A2 rolls an unending line of delivery vehicles. The goods depot here is open round the clock. Because this is Christmas, Bluewater's normal opening time has been brought forward an hour to nine o'clock and tonight the centre will stay open till 11 pm. In spite of the fact that they have a long day ahead, workers on the bus are in high spirits. Two hundred thousand visitors are expected today. Yesterday's average spend was £200 a head. That translates into £40 million of takings. And this is only one day. People are speaking already of the Billion Pound Christmas. Kerry is looking for a good bonus to make this year special for her eight-year-old son.

The ToyStack manager has already opened up when Kerry arrives. He says yesterday's sales were a best ever for the store. As a result, though, there is a huge amount of stock to be replaced. The stockroom is completely bare. The first delivery is out the back and for the next hour sales staff work without a break, refilling racks and shelves as fast as the boys bring the cartons through. Decorators appear with a new Christmas tree, which looks wonderful, but takes up so much space the Lego display has to be moved. By 8.40 they are done. The juniors vacuum the floor. Empty cartons are flat-packed and pushed out back for collection. The manager sends people off in twos for a quick coffee break.

When Kerry's turn comes she heads down the South Mall, known as Thames Walk, for a cappuccino at Prêt-à-Manger. Bluewater is designed as a triangle, with the three anchor department stores at the apexes, linked by two-storey malls. In the minutes before opening, the halls and galleries are busy with cleaners, window stylists, decorators and maintenance men. As she passes Dixons, Kerry pops her head round the door hoping to see a friend. Sasha waves but she is busy unpacking a pile of stereo equipment. The store looks to be in even more turmoil than ToyStack.

Fresh displays have gone up since yesterday; best of all, an enormous red and gold sledge with flying reindeer circling overhead beneath the Wintergarden roof. Her boy will adore that. The street entertainers are about too. Bluewater employs clowns and jugglers, mime artists and stilt walkers to amuse the shoppers. There is even a robot Santa Claus.

At the entrance to Thames Walk is the Moon Court welcome hall, with stairs climbing to the upper galleries. In the centre, a tall black slate column with steel markings rises between the stairs to the dome in the roof. This is the Thamesometer.

A sliding gauge on the column points to the height of the tide down on the river at Greenhithe. Right now at 8.50, it is showing half a metre. Low water or thereabouts.

Docklands. At the start of the 1980s, a twelve-mile swathe of derelict land blighted both banks of the Thames down river of the Tower of London. Behind high walls in Wapping, Rotherhithe, the Isle of Dogs and Silvertown, the docks stood abandoned, their cranes stilled, their quays deserted, given over to scrap-metal dealers and rubbish tips. There were no buyers for the Victorian warehouses; the cost of clearing the sites exceeded their auction value. On the Isle of Dogs there were only a few hundred jobs among a population of thirteen thousand; 90 per cent of housing was publicly owned.

Then in the Christmas of 1984, a civil engineer, Philip Beck, submitted proposals for a new airport to be constructed five miles from the City on the south side of Royal Albert Dock. His choice was influenced by the fact that the Docklands region was free from radio interference and therefore safe for aircraft navigation systems. This chance discovery had other benefits. Telecommunications companies were encouraged to set up satellite earth stations on the Isle of Dogs and North Woolwich linked by a fibre-optic main ring.

Other projects were in the pipeline. An American group seeking office space came to Docklands. Coincidentally, a restaurant chain invited a Swiss banker onto a barge moored at Canary Wharf. He discovered that the infrastructure for state-of-the-art business communications was already in place.

The synergy sparked by these events led directly to the consortium submitting plans for a £4-billion commercial development.

Today Canary Wharf is the jewel in the docklands crown, a self-contained mini-city covering seventy acres. Ninety thousand people work here in thirty separate buildings, including hotels and apartment blocks, 150 shops, bars and restaurants, five underground car parks, and stations for the Jubilee Line and the Docklands Light Railway. Dominating the development is One Canada Square, otherwise known as Canary Wharf Tower, and, at 243 metres, one of Britain's tallest buildings.

Sophie de Salis, an American banker, slots her black BMW coupé into its reserved space in the basement car park underneath the tower. As she climbs out and shuts the driver's door a shadow blocks the light behind her. Sophie glances up. Two muscular youths have appeared from round a pillar, noiseless in their Nike trainers, and are staring at her.

'Hi, guys' she says.

'Hiya, Mrs S. You want the car done?'

She surely does, Sophie tells them. 'I'll need it by . . .' she pauses. Better be safe, she thinks, 'Four this afternoon, no later.'

'No problem, Mrs S. Full valet?'

'Please, inside and out.' She hands over the keys. 'Four o'clock. And see you make her shine, hey?'

The boys flash smiles. 'Sure thing, Mrs S, Christmas special,' they promise.

Sophie leaves them to it. They are nice boys. The bank picks up the tab and she always adds a generous tip. She hates to drive a dirty car. She takes the lift up to the promenade level; the shopping mall is busy as usual. The Forex dealers have been in since five. Half the world's major financial institutions have office space here. By the stairs a Porsche agency has a 911 Cabriolet on display, with a leggy girl in a Father Christmas outfit helping a guy into the driving seat who doesn't look any older than the kids from the car park. Sophie buys a paper and stops by Miami Coffee for her morning caffeine fix.

AmBank's offices are on the forty-second floor of the tower. The lift takes forty seconds. On Sophie's desk are photographs of her husband and daughter. Randal is a banker, also London based, and currently seeing clients in Boston. He flies back in tomorrow. Chrissie is twelve and attends an English school in Hammersmith. Outside the windows day is just breaking; Docklands can be seen emerging through the morning mist. Just below is the gleaming new 213-metre HSBC building. To the south stand five more recently completed tower blocks: 400,000 square metres pre-let to blue-chip tenants at a rental income of £180 million.

Opposite, the river loops around the Greenwich Peninsula with the Dome on its tip. Away to the east stretch the three Royal Docks, Victoria, Albert and King George V. Together they cover 250 acres; the largest artificially contained water system in the world. Everywhere she looks, spindly tower cranes peck at fresh emerging offices, hotels, apartment blocks and expressways. The pace of construction is frantic: £10 billion invested in infrastructure alone. Twenty years ago none of this existed. Now half a million people work here and land costs five million an acre. The world changes so fast, she thinks. What will it be like for my daughter when she grows up?

A mile to the east, the Tricolour flutters jauntily from the mast of a French patrol boat moored alongside the sprawling ExCeL exhibition centre fronting Royal Victoria Dock. ExCeL is huge, a linear city encased in a glass-fronted hangar, supported by an exoskeleton of roof trusses. The Dome across the river is only half the size. Together with Canary Wharf, it has shifted London's centre of gravity permanently down river towards the east.

The exhibition hall stretches for half a mile. Its main floor of lightweight reinforced concrete is designed to allow access to articulated trucks. It is strong enough to take a seventy-tonne main battle tank. With eighty-five acres of water in the adjacent dock, ExCeL can host the London International Boat Show; display a submarine or a frigate.

The first of eight hundred delivery vehicles are arriving on site. Marshals direct them up a ramp to the three-lane roadway round the building, with entry points to the halls every fifty metres. It is a slick operation. Trucks enter the bays, discharge their loads and move off again in a constant flow. Exhibitors' parking is on the lower ground floor, beneath the main exhibition halls. Sub-floor ducts carry power and cabling to stand sites, ducting for heat, ventilation, water, drainage and sprinkler systems; £100 million has been spent on telecommunications and computer networks.

The current show is titled World Defence International. Twenty-two months in the planning, it is into its fifth day and a runaway success, with a thousand exhibitors and record level sales. Today it is open to the general public. Fifty thousand visitors will climb the steps to the glass entrance pyramid. ExCeL has seven thousand parking spaces. A dual carriageway links the centre to the M25, with a journey time of fifteen minutes outside the rush hour. Canary Wharf is ten minutes away by road. Three DLR stations serve the centre and a two-minute shuttle-bus ride takes visitors to Canning Town station on the Jubilee Line. London City Airport is right next door.

Six hotels and 150 serviced apartments have opened on the waterfront, along with shops, bars, restaurants and a conference centre for three thousand delegates. Everything possible is arranged to speed visitors to the site and ensure their comfort and convenience. Nothing is left to chance. Nothing can possibly go wrong.

9

At the Barrier, preparations are rolling down for closure at 10 am. The Closure Warning message has been sent to the Agency regions, to electricity companies and power stations, London Fire Brigade, Metropolitan Police, Thames Water and London Underground.

Before the Barrier itself can close, thirty-seven subsidiary gates and barriers downstream of Woolwich have to be confirmed shut. Some of these, like the barrier on Barking Creek and the King George V dock gates, are massive structures in their own right. The thirty-metre barrier across the River Darent at Dartford is the responsibility of the Agency's Southern Region, while on the opposite side of the estuary Anglia Region takes care of the Tilbury barrier. Then there are the private owners of riparian properties, such as Tate & Lyle and the Woolwich Ferry, which have their own floodgates.

Closure of these gates and barriers is remotely monitored from the Control Room. Most gates have telemetry equipment feeding back to screens at Woolwich. Since dawn the Agency launch has been patrolling the upper estuary, conducting a physical check as well. It is a slow and painstaking job but it has to be done. Just one missed gate could mean disaster.

Jack Lamar, Chief Executive of the Dome Sports Stadium is talking on the phone. He is also trying to steer his Jaguar XKR in heavy traffic and juggle figures in his head. Jack is responsible for the day-to-day running of the Dome. Has been ever since the big tent reopened as a sports and entertainment complex. It is a high profile, stressful job. Most days he is at his desk by 8 am, leaving when the last event finishes, usually not before eleven at night. He lives, works and dreams about the Dome.

This year the theme is winter sports. Dry ski slopes, bob sleigh simulators, snow boarding ramps, and an ice rink in the central arena as big and advanced as any in the world. It is proving a runaway success. Hockey and curling matches have drawn capacity crowds and in the New Year the Dome is to host the European Figure Skating Championships.

For Christmas, though, Lamar has opted for pure entertainment. An ice dance extravaganza with performers from twenty different countries, three rock bands and a laser show to end all laser shows. It has been running a week to rave reviews and heavy bookings. Which is just as well; the staging costs are frightening.

Right now Lamar is on to Marketing. It is always his first call of the day. They will give him the projections for today's visitor figures. Their computer program summarises advance bookings, special events, phone enquiries, school holidays, competing attractions, even the weather, and comes up with a forecast of how many feet will cross the threshold on a given day. The program is supposed to be accurate to within plus or minus 3 per cent. Personally Jack thinks he can do better. Today he estimates 45,000 will pass through the turnstiles.

The traffic starts to move at last. Lamar takes the Blackwall Tunnel approach and turns off on the slip road to the site. Parking is one problem he has yet to solve. There is room for only a few hundred cars and the local council refuses to release more land. Lamar is working on them but for the present a car exclusion zone remains in force for two miles around the Dome. Visitors arrive by public transport, the unreliable London Underground's Jubilee Line, by coach or by boat from one of the up-river piers. Security on the gates recognise the Jaguar and wave him through.

A billion pounds has been spent here, reclaiming a former gas works. A giant gas-holder still dominates the southern approach road. Two centuries ago this was marshland, underwater at spring tides. Eight thousand piles had to be sunk to stabilise the site. The ground was so contaminated with toxic residues that it had to be sealed with half a metre of crushed stone before building could start. Another three and a half billion has gone on extending the Jubilee Line eastwards from Westminster. Supporters claim the result is the regeneration of southeast London. Social engineering on a grand scale. To detractors it symbolises greed and profligacy.

This morning Lamar reaches the main concourse to find the coach park awash. Two of his juniors are outside with engineers from the council. There has been heavy rain during the night. A storm drain has become blocked and the water is backing up. The council's chief engineer arrives. He looks tired; he has been out since four am. It is the same story across the borough.

They discuss ways of dealing with this one. Lamar grows impatient; the first visitors of the day will begin arriving in thirty minutes. Maintenance has sent for duckboards to make a walkway. Lamar demands to know why something can't be done to sort out the flood. He suggests pumping into the Thames. The trouble is there are no pumps available, none powerful enough anyway.

'You're in a dip here. The pumps have to lift the water over the flood banks in order to discharge into the river,' the engineer explains. He makes a sweep of his arm to take in the defences that ring the head of the peninsula.

Lamar suggests if they can't pump the water out, then they could cut a channel through the bank and let it run out. 'We have a JCB on site,' he adds pointedly.

The engineer eyes him narrowly. 'I can't do that,' he says, 'and I'd have to stop you if you tried. That's a flood defence. Protected by statute. You need a legal permit in order to touch it.'

'I thought we had the Barrier for flood defence?' Lamar objects.

The engineer shakes his head. These people, he thinks. Patiently he explains the Barrier is for defence against surges, exceptional flooding brought about by storms in the North Sea. Protection against ordinary high tides comes from defence works along the river. 'Most of Greenwich is below sea-level.

You cut a hole in that wall and your visitors could be getting more than just their feet wet.'

Lamar scowls and leaves them to it. He has more important things to do than listen to a lecture on the river. As he pushes through the doors of the administration block he is phoning his secretary, telling her to get on to Greenwich Council and see they get the necessary pumps up here fast. Otherwise the press is going to see just what kind of a reception the borough puts on for its visitors.

Across the river in the *Telegraph* offices at Canary Wharf, journalist Lauren Khan's day starts with a trawl through the Internet news channels. One item makes her sit up. It is a claim that London-based Environment Agency staff are being advised to leave their cars at home today for fear of flooding in the capital.

Calls to the Agency for confirmation result in angry denials. Lauren dials Angus Walsh's number at the Barrier but he is too busy to speak to her.

Out over the North Sea, the C-135 of the Royal Dutch Air Force Weather Reconnaissance flight rocks in a patch of turbulence at 13,000 feet. For the past two hours the team has tacked back and forth through the roughest weather Europe has seen all year, searching for so-called 'sensitive spots', critical nodes signalling imminent switches in the weather pattern, and comparing measurements from these with data from other sectors of the storm.

Full analysis of the results from tonight's mission will take several days. Already though, features about the storm pattern are apparent. Most importantly, the pressure in a newly formed subsidiary low is falling steeply, giving the system potential for a fresh lease of life. This information is being transmitted to the Dutch authorities at Den Haag in the Netherlands, who in turn will pass it on to the British Meteorological Office. Dutch experts too are finding the situation hard to read. One thing is becoming clear, though. There is now a strong possibility that fifty-knot winds will extend right across the southern North Sea by midday.

In the rear fuselage, Heidi takes a parachute buoy from the rack and makes a careful note of its identification number. Flight test observers move around the aircraft as their experiments demand. She unlatches the chute fixed in the aeroplane's floor. A shrill whistling sound fills the fuselage along with a blast of cold air. Heidi lifts the metre-long buoy and slides one end into the breech of the chute. 'Preparing to drop buoy,' she calls over her intercom. Up in the cockpit, the navigator notes the position on his log and gives the okay.

Heidi braces her legs and shoves hard on the end of the cylinder. It slides down the chute and drops smoothly away. A thousand feet clear of the plane its parachute will deploy and the instrument package will begin radioing back readings as it descends to the sea. She closes the chute, then goes back into the boxed off section known as the Van to follow its progress.

The Van is unheated. A digital thermometer attached to an outside air analyser reads –5 Celsius, which is only to be expected at this altitude. Touch the inlet pipe and you get instant frost-bite. Other instruments measure ozone, CO^2 and atmospheric pollutants from the nose-mounted cloud probe, which shoots a laser between two prongs to analyse water droplets. Heidi, who is wearing a parka and mittens, blows on her fingers to warm them before using the keyboard of her workstation.

A shrill beep blasts from the radio set on the desk. Snoopy's receiver has picked up a signal from the buoy and is preparing to download data. The instrument probe has extended and is sampling the atmosphere as it swings from its parachute. Heidi turns down the sound and watches the figures rolling down the screen. '. . . 968 . . . 967 . . . 965 . . . 960 . . .' These are among the lowest pressure readings Heidi has ever experienced. She watches awestruck as the figures continue to unravel. '. . . 959 . . . 958 . . .' She presses the record button and fires the data into the modem for transmission to base.

There can be no doubt now that a fully developed secondary depression is following close behind the storm's main eye. The isobar pattern shows the pressure gradient growing ever steeper, sucking in gale-force winds behind and fuelling the system with energy. On the weather radar, cloud formations twenty and thirty miles out tell a similar story.

If this continues, the storm will take on a whole new momentum.

10

From Docklands the A13 road to Southend passes through Beckton and its sewage farms, across Barking Creek with its own barrier rising above the factory roofs and past the Ford engine works at Dagenham, before cutting inland to the M25 interchange at Dartford. Traffic is heavy here at the only river crossing between London and the sea, with freight from the ports of Tilbury and Grays coming up to join the motorway and shopping centres on either bank. This is an unlovely stretch of coastline, former marshland now given over to industrial use and docks. Clustered along the north-east of the estuary, at Holehaven and Coryton, are oil refineries and storage terminals where there is deep water close inshore for the tankers to berth. At Basildon, the A130 forks off to the right towards the Thames, running for a mile through scrubby ground till it dips between bluffs down to a newly built bridge over a creek. This is Canvey Road leading to Canvey Island.

As late as the seventeenth century Canvey appears on maps as an indistinct area of mud flats and saltings, much of it under water at high tide, the higher parts providing useful pasture for sheep in summer. When land reclamation became fashionable, Dutch engineers were employed to build dykes and wall in four thousand acres from the sea. With the coming of the railway, Canvey was marketed as a residential seaside resort for Londoners. By 1953 the population had risen to 11,500, all living on ground below sea-level, with a single bridge connecting them to the mainland.

Though there had been repeated floods over the walls during the previous half-century, the warnings were ignored. In fact, Canvey was nothing short of a basin of death. In 1953 the surge came over the walls shortly before midnight with deadly speed. Within thirty minutes the bridge was impassable. There was almost no warning for the island's inhabitants. People were woken by the crash of water breaking down doors and windows, splitting timbers and shattering glass. Most houses were flimsy single-storey constructions. Terrified and bewildered, they struggled to reach the safety of lofts. Some smashed holes in the ceilings to climb outside onto the tiles in their nightclothes. Others clambered onto furniture or stepladders. Parents clung to the tops of doors, desperately holding their children above the icy water, while wave after numbing wave swept through, sapping the strength from their arms.

Fifty-eight people died on Canvey that night.

The walls are stronger now and a second bridge has been constructed. Against this, the population has more than tripled to 36,000. The houses may have been rebuilt but most are still single-storey dwellings and nothing can be done to raise the level of the land. Canvey remains a dangerous place.

From the bridge, Canvey Road runs eastwards on an embankment across the marsh, then bends south between fields, with horses grazing into the town. West of the road is still mainly agricultural and south of it, between Long Road and Hole Haven, the predominately industrial area.

Holehaven Road leads down to the southwestern tip of the island, bounded by the narrow Holehaven Creek and a foreshore studied with jetties and terminals. Long stone groynes protect the anchorage and the air is heady with the stench of petrochemicals. To the east are the tanks of an oil-storage depot, row upon row of giant drums, some silver or black coloured, others a dull red. Beyond them is the Calor Gas terminal with pressurised tanks holding 35,000 tonnes of highly inflammable liquid petroleum gas, one tonne for every man, woman and child on the island.

An overhead oil pipeline spans the creek. The shore opposite is one long, solid mass of steel tanks, pipework and industrial plant, that stretches away unbroken for more than three miles in the direction of London. A fifth of Britain's refinery capacity is located here at Coryton, operated by Mobil-BP. Twenty million tonnes of crude oil pass through Shellhaven and Coryton annually. Both companies are required by law to keep three months' stocks in the UK and some of the largest tanks hold 100,000 tonnes of oil apiece.

In recent years studies on the probability of very large non-nuclear accidents have focused on the Canvey installations. The potential for disaster here is recognised. Safety standards are high and rigorously enforced. It has been estimated that the chances of a major accident, defined as resulting in fifteen hundred deaths or more, are in the order of one in five thousand. These statistics do not take into account the possibility of a major flood.

Town place names tell the history of the island's battle with the sea: Sunken Marsh, Small Gains Creek, Newlands. Others recall the long association with the Dutch: Delft Road, Zuyder Road, Kamerdyk Avenue. The combination of heavy industry and high-density population would strike many people as astonishingly irresponsible, given how low lying Canvey is. The entire island is below the level of a spring tide.

The Thames is an old river. Before the ice melted and the North Sea was formed, it ran east to become a tributary of the Rhine and the two then flowed southwards out through the Straits of Dover. When the seas rose, the submerged delta off the river's mouth became a wide area of shallows and sandbanks stretching for fifty miles from Felixstowe to North Foreland on the Kent coast. A consequence of this is that all very large vessels entering the Port of London have to be piloted in along buoyed channels from the north.

Ten miles out to sea off Harwich, white foam crests are beginning to blow in streaks over heaping waves. The *Pearl Princess*, a Very Large Crude Carrier, inward bound for Coryton Refinery with 154,000 tonnes of Arabian crude, has spent the hours of darkness anchored in Sunk Deep Water Anchorage. Sunk Deep is the holding point for large vessels waiting for the tide to take them up the estuary. On the bridge with the master is an Inner

List Sea Pilot, tasked with navigating the super-tanker through the thirty miles of shoals to the river mouth where the tugs will meet them.

The pilot is studying the latest shipping forecast. The big storm moving down from the north is still hammering King's Lynn. Within the next three hours the winds are predicted to moderate to twenty-five knots, inside the limits for an approach. Even so, he hesitates. The Deep Water Route at the Sunk is exposed and if the ship starts to roll, her underwater clearance will be affected. This is a serious matter because at points on the approach the vessel's under keel clearance will be between four and five feet. And if conditions deteriorate once they are underway, there can be no turning back.

It is a difficult decision, not made easier by the clear impatience of the *Princess*'s master, a Latvian who speaks little English. The length of the estuary requires that a VLCC depart the anchorage as soon as possible after low water so she can be swung on the flood tide off Canvey before high water. Ebb tide berthing at Coryton is prohibited for vessels of this size because, should a problem develop, there will be insufficient time to get out again down the Sea Reach Channel to deep water.

As a final gesture the pilot uses the ship's radio to contact the Port of London Authority and speaks to the Harbour Master at Gravesend. The answer comes back promptly: the weather is forecast to moderate; the vessel is cleared to approach.

The pilot goes to the corner of the bridge to look out at the sky. It is still his decision. He is the one who will face a charge of criminal negligence if disaster results. Yet any delay on his part will cause furious complaints from the owners. The tanker must sail now or else, at the very least, forfeit half a day before the next tide. A full day or more if the weather worsens. On top of this, the tide for 13.20 is predicted to run very high, giving extra clearance under the keel. It is this factor that decides him. He nods to the captain. The ship will sail.

Thirty minutes later the tanker is underway from the anchorage, setting to the southwest towards the shoals. This is a critical area where a pilot has to pick up the Deep Water Route 232 degrees through the shallows east of Trinity Buoy. If the charted approach is jeopardised he will have to abort and start again, losing precious time. The light is still poor, visibility is further obscured by intermittent rain. The wind is astern though and the ship does not appear to be rolling. The single screw, right-hand turning propeller cants the vessel's head to starboard with headway on due to transverse thrust. Otherwise the computer-managed engine system seems to provide a quick powerful response.

In common with all modern generation VLCCs, *Pearl Princess* is double hulled to prevent pollution in the event of collision or grounding. Such protection comes at a price. That price is five metres extra freeboard, virtually doubling the windage to more than seven thousand square metres. Windage is the area of a vessel giving air resistance. In gusty conditions a ship's side can act like a sail, causing alarming handling problems. While the new hulls reduce the risk of oil spillage, they increase the chances of grounding or collision.

On the positive side, the bridge is well laid out for

one-man operation, with good radar and GPS navigation aides. The only omission is a Doppler-type ground track log. In poor visibility it can be hard to gauge the lateral movement of a large ship travelling at slow speed.

They pick up the route without incident and the supertanker slides on past Sunk Head light tower into Black Deep. Three miles further on there is another tense period when the channel narrows and the pilot has to position the ship carefully for the entrance to Knock John Channel. Shivering Sands light tower marks the start of Oaze Deep, after which the ship is brought round 30 degrees to starboard before swinging again to port to pick up the centre-line buoys of the Yantlet Channel at Number 1 Sea Reach.

The VLCC is now in a ten-mile long channel with a width of only 156 metres, and fully committed. Aborting, that is putting the vessel about, is impossible until she reaches the refinery. From this point on there is no turning back.

11

Whitehall, Department of the Environment, Food and Rural Affairs. The decision phase of the flood scenario has never been exercised. Met Office scientists think in terms of probabilities – '*50 per cent chance of precipitation over the South-East*' or '*70 per cent chance of gales*'. This approach will not do for ministers, who demand yes or no answers: do we go for it or don't we? Sitting at the cross-over point is Lester Gordon of DEFRA. It is Gordon's job to translate between two distinct communities: the scientific and the executive, each with its own mind-set and special language.

Gordon has to decide whether to throw the switches that will bring all the apparatus of central government into action. It means claiming the attention of very busy and important officials. Millions of citizens will have their lives disrupted; tens of thousands will be driven from their houses. The entire Underground system could be emptied. Schools will be closed; hospital operations cancelled, patients sent home, fire brigade and ambulance services withdrawn. It is highly possible, probable even, that injuries and deaths will result.

These big surges have come down the coast before, only to die away. He is determined not to be bounced into sounding the alarm just because someone at the Met Office has lost their nerve.

Gordon decides to contact Home Office Emergency Planning Department and speak to them informally. By sharing his knowledge he will be covering himself in the event of a crisis developing, while at the same time, if the surge fades away as is likely, he cannot be accused of spreading unnecessary alarm. This is the classic civil servant compromise.

He talks to the deputy-director. Through its contacts with local authority emergency planners, EPD is already well briefed on the position on the east coast. The department is also aware of the surge threat to the Thames. Like DEFRA, EPD finds it hard to conceive of the Barrier being unable to cope. 'If I read you rightly, you are suggesting that we wait until the next computer run from the Met Office, at which point we shall have firmer grounds on which to base a decision?' the Deputy-Director says at length.

'Broadly speaking, yes. I don't see that we have enough to go on at present. Of course, these events can look alarming and the Met Office is right to bring them to our attention.'

'And High Water in London is still six hours away?'

'Six hours and twenty minutes, according to the Barrier.'

'So we do have a little time then. But by waiting, we risk more people moving into the danger zone.

Whereas if we declare an emergency now we could stop the schools from opening, cancel commuter trains, turn back traffic. Shut London down, in effect, before the day gets started.'

'Nice fools we'll look if it turns out to be a false alarm.'

'Quite. At the moment then, you feel the situation does not warrant drastic measures?'

Gordon winces. The Deputy-Director has neatly thrown the ball back at him. 'The information I have at the moment does not support calling a general emergency,' he says carefully. 'Even the worst possible case suggests that water levels will only just reach to the top of the Thames Barrier. These calculations have a safety margin built into them and the probability is that actual levels will fall short of prediction. By the time of the nine o'clock run, the position should be much clearer.'

'Which will still leave us five and a half hours,' the EPD man reflects. 'We will abide by your advice and wait for the revised forecast at 9 am.'

'In the meantime, you might care to brief your people on the general situation, informally of course. As a precautionary measure.'

'Don't worry,' is the bleak response. 'We are doing that already.'

Hammersmith, West London. Jo Binney is twelve. Her school, Godolphin and Latymer, is three streets away. Jo bikes there, calling by at the home of her best friend, Chrissie de Salis. Chrissie's parents both work so she and Jo spend a lot of time together in Jo's house. Jo's mother holds the door for her daughter to wheel the bike out. Harriet

Binney is in her early forties, dark haired, pale, pretty and hesitant. She and her husband have been separated for five years.

Harriet goes back inside and shuts the door against the cold. Her elder daughter, Miranda, who is studying modern languages, arrives back from Brussels today. Harriet has to meet her off the Eurostar at eleven. It will take her half an hour at least to get to Waterloo. Tonight the girls' father, Henry, is coming round for a family supper. He will be expecting something festive for Christmas so she must get food in.

Outside the Home Office in Queen Anne's Gate, a wintry sky hangs low over the city. Along Petty France pedestrians hurry to work, muffled against the wind. The day has a smoky, yellowish cast as if at any moment it might sputter out altogether, leaving London in twilight.

The Home Office is one of the great departments of state and the Home Secretary is the keeper of the Queen's Peace. Responsibility for law and order makes it the most exposed position in the Cabinet. Before Venetia took the post, she was warned it was the graveyard of politicians. So far she has proved the doom mongers wrong.

Venetia's workload is immense. Besides overseeing the police and prison service, over the years the Home Secretary's remit has swollen to cover such widely disparate areas as the exercise of the Royal Pardon, the Security Service MI5, nudist beaches, betting and gaming, burials, fire brigades, ice cream vans and the regulation of au pairs. High among these comes Emergency Planning.

The part of the building where Venetia works is known as the Private Office. The corridor outside is lined with black and white portrait photographs of her predecessors. Half a dozen of Venetia's senior staff are crammed into the outer office which is a scene of organised chaos. This is where the red boxes are handled; document trays overflow and papers are heaped on any surface and stacked on the blue carpet. One desk, piled with buff-coloured files marked Secret, handles nothing but phone tapping and deportation warrants.

Twenty years ago the Home Office was housed in the Victorian grandeur of Whitehall. The new building by St James's Park, erected at the height of the terrorist campaigns, resembles a concrete fortress of unrelieved brutality. Some walls are two and a half metres thick. Venetia has the use of a corner room with a low ceiling and a great many windows. Furnishings are characterless, seventies-style modern. Venetia's desk faces the door with two hard chairs in front and a second desk to one side for her computer terminal. In the corner behind, placed so she can swivel her chair to watch it, is a large screen TV. Beyond the desks is a seating area with a sofa and armchairs covered in an ugly floral pattern that Venetia is longing to have changed. A conference table of blond wood over by the far wall can seat twelve.

Here Venetia has summoned her top advisers for an emergency meeting on the storm. They enter in order of precedence, led by the Permanent Secretary. Under the constitution, the role of ministers is to set policy. Day-to-day administration is in the hands of the career civil servants. In a very real sense it is the PS's who run the country through their departments.

The PS is followed by Venetia's principal private secretary, another senior civil servant but working for her rather than for the depart-ment. After him comes the Director of Emergency Planning and his deputy to whom Gordon of DEFRA spoke earlier. It is that telephone call that has prompted Venetia to summon the meeting. The rear is brought up by officials from the Fire Inspectorate and the Police Support Unit and policy advisers from Venetia's staff bearing files and notepads.

Venetia is already seated at the centre of the conference table with her back to the windows. The others take their places without formalities. Venetia can't be bothered with them. At a nod from her, the EPD Director leads off with a summary of the past twelve hours on the east coast. It is pretty much what everyone has been hearing on the news.

Is this unprecedented? Venetia wants to know. The EPD contingent exchange glances. They have been discussing this among themselves. The consensus is no. Conditions are bad, but they have been worse. Sea defences have been breached in Norfolk, at least two lives lost, a helicopter brought down. There is flooding at King's Lynn. More or less what would be expected from a severe winter storm of the kind that appears once a decade.

The EPD Director continues: 'I've spoken to county authorities and the sea-levels are as high as any of their people can recall. The defences are coping reasonably well, given the conditions. The worry seems to be that the surge is overtaking the high tide as it comes south. In which case we can anticipate even higher levels along the Essex coast. The big question is, will the levels continue as far as the mouth of the Thames and up into the estuary?'

'What does the Met Office think?' the PS asks.

'At the start of the storm, they forecast that winds would start to ease by morning, resulting in diminished surge heights. This is the usual pattern. But in the past few hours they have revised their opinion. They now say severe gales will persist beyond midday, bringing high surge levels as far as Southend.'

'And thereafter?' Venetia's attention is focused on him. On her right an aide is taking shorthand notes.

'It has always been EPD's understanding that high surge levels in the estuary itself are extremely rare.'

'But not impossible or presumably the Barrier wouldn't have been built,' Venetia observes tartly. 'I'm not interested in what our understanding has been. What's the position now?'

The Director looks unhappy. Opinion is divided, he explains. According to DEFRA, the Barrier will meet any challenge. The Met Office seems less confident.

'And whom do we believe?'

The Director shakes his head. From the scientific standpoint he would normally say the Met Office. 'But they admit that the Barrier does have special experience where the Thames estuary is concerned.'

Venetia's lips tighten. There are no simple solutions here. 'What's the time frame on this?' she asks.

'High Water is predicted at 2.25 pm at the Barrier.'

Venetia makes a note of that and glances round

the table. 'Likely scenarios please?'

A redheaded young man with the EPD takes over. He unfolds a map of the estuary on to the table. Surges get higher as they proceed up-river, he explains. This is called the squeeze effect. Overtopping, if it does occur, is most likely at pinch points where bends in the river constrict the flow. 'One area Barrier Control is uneasy about,' he indicates with a pencil, 'is here, on the south bank down river of the Barrier at Thamesmead.'

There is a moment's silence while everyone stares at the map and at the long blue channel that winds and curls up to the heart of the city. Till now none of them has ever thought about the river much except as an obstacle to be crossed by bridge or tunnel.

'Thamesmead used to be called Plumstead Marsh before the redevelopment. A mix of housing and light industry, all very low lying.'

'Housing, light industry and a high security prison,' another civil servant adds. 'HMP Belmarsh is sited there, right on the river.'

A discussion of the area follows. Greenwich and Docklands are mentioned.

'But they are safe behind the Barrier, surely?' someone says.

'Enough,' Venetia breaks in abruptly. 'Before we go further we must know if this is going to happen or at least get some idea of the probability. What is DEFRA telling us?'

She is addressing the EPD Director. He shakes his head. 'They say they won't know anything for sure until the latest forecast comes off the Met Office computer. That should be soon after nine.'

Venetia makes an exasperated sound. Her contempt for DEFRA's ponderous workings is well known. 'Well, I am not going to sit on my hands till they make up their minds. We need to bring experts from all departments together to work on a strategy. I intend to convene the Triple-C Committee without delay.'

The Prime Minister is on the other side of the world. Venetia phones through to Number Ten. She speaks to the head of the Prime Minister's secretariat. 'At once please. I'll keep my line clear.'

Of course it is important or I wouldn't be interrupting him, she feels like saying, but checks herself. Nothing will be gained by antagonising those close to the Prime Minister.

Australia comes on the line. The Prime Minister is in the middle of an official dinner. They are calling him out now.

Minutes pass. Venetia waits. At last the phone rings again. The Prime Minister is irritable. At first he does not appreciate the seriousness of the situation. Venetia tries to be realistic and at the same time not give a sense of panic. The PM agonises about not being on the scene. He wants to fly back. No, his staff are telling him. It will take twelve hours; by the time you reach Heathrow the crisis will be over anyway. Besides, if the surge fades out in the meantime, you will be left looking a fool.

The Permanent Secretary passes over a note suggesting a conference call with Ministers. Venetia returns him a withering look. The more people involved, the more talking, the longer to reach a decision. Instinct tells her it will be disastrous to permit the PM to micro-manage the crisis from a distance. She can't push too hard though for fear it might look as if she wants to take over.

She says she is convening Triple-C. What for? the PM asks suspiciously. Venetia explains it is her duty as Home Secretary to take responsibility. The PM concedes the point with a grunt. Venetia can hear the bitterness in his voice. The man can sense power slipping from his grasp. The capital faces its gravest crisis since the war and he is powerless to intervene.

'As quickly as possible please, Roland. Time is short.'

Responsibility for ensuring that a lead government department is nominated in good time to respond to an emergency rests with the Cabinet Office. Specifically, this responsibility is exercised by the Secretary to the Civil Contingencies Committee. Triple-C is a group of ministers and officials which meets as and where necessary under the chairmanship of the Home Secretary. If an emergency arises where it is unclear which government department should have the lead, it is the duty of the Committee Secretary to make an appropriate nomination quickly. The Secretary of Triple-C is Commander Roland Raikes.

Raikes has been anticipating Venetia's order. She uses his first name which underlines the urgency. Section 7.11 of the Government Emergency Planning Guidance states that 'In the event of an exceptionally serious or widespread disaster which could lead to massive devastation and casualties, the Home Secretary will provide the focus for central government from the Cabinet Office.'

Venetia Maitland's intervention can only mean that she is expecting the worst.

12

At the Met Office the Limited Area Model has finally come off the computer, fifteen minutes late. The surge appears as an ominous lump that swells in height and mass as it advances down the Essex coast. The peak will now be reached at Felixstowe and Clacton. Two and a half metres, not so high as in 1953 but still alarming. The town defences will probably be able to cope, but a lot of farmland and marsh will be under water.

More worrying is the way tide levels are remaining high all down the coast. Hull has seen virtually no change for the past three hours. Cromer is still rising and will continue to do so for half an hour to come. There does appear to be some slight fall off at the approach to the Thames estuary. The predicted level for Southend is 1.99, a fraction under two metres. Sufficient to give the Barrier a scare but not enough to drown London.

One nagging doubt persists. Surges this big are rare events so data on them is patchy. There is a suspicion that in the past the model has tended to under-forecast levels. On one notable occasion the negative error was more than three-quarters of a metre at Southend.

*

One of the telephone calls Raikes has to make is to the London Fire Brigade headquarters by Lambeth Bridge on the Albert Embankment. The headquarters complex is an austere pre-war building surrounding a courtyard at the rear. The topmost floor houses the Command Support Centre, set up to handle major incidents and manned by specialist officers. The centre has access to databases on chemical sites and building use as well as communications facilities to control major disasters requiring multiple appliances.

The senior officer on duty reacts with dismay to the Cabinet Office call. The Brigade has only two boats and tidal flooding is not part of its remit. 'If you're talking about serious water over the walls our first priority would be to withdraw all vehicles from the danger zone.'

Raikes reassures him. This is an information call, he emphasises, not yet an advance warning, it may not come to anything. 'Just be aware of the weather situation as it exists.'

The officer in charge puts the phone down with a shrug. He is fifty-three, coming up for retirement, which is why he is up here in CSC. The call, he thinks, is typical of civil servants, spreading rumours, then telling people not to panic. If London does flood all he can do is order his chaps to man their appliances and drive like hell for high ground. The pre-Barrier flood plan gave the emergency services a clear hour's warning ahead of the public to get their vehicles away before the roads became jammed with traffic. He hopes the current administration has the sense to adopt the same policy.

'Going for a smoke,' he tells his second in command. The Support Centre is perched on the flat roof of the headquarters building. From up here there is a view over the river in both directions. To the east is St Thomas's Hospital, on the far bank the Palace of Westminster and, almost opposite him, the offices of MI5. Looking west, he can make out Tate Britain and, swinging back over Vauxhall Bridge to the south bank again, the vast futuristic headquarters of MI6, the Secret Intelligence Service. Closer at hand still, at Citadel Street, is NCIS, the National Criminal Intelligence Service. All those buildings have big computers in their basements. If water comes over the walls there will be hell to pay.

And it is not only computers that will suffer. On this bank, between the two bridges and Kennington Road, he can list six schools, a day hospital, a health centre, two community centres used by the elderly, and a covered reservoir belonging to Thames Water.

He moves to the west edge of the roof and leans over the parapet. He is looking straight down into what appears to be a narrow rectangular reservoir walled off from the street. This is an old draw dock, an inlet from the river on this side of the embankment, with a steep ramp up to road level, formerly used to put boats into the river. No longer in use, it sits between Black Prince Road and Albert Embankment, an historical relict. The entrance is closed off by strong gates, but if the river were to rise the water would spill out into the surrounding streets.

Two doors down from the London Fire Brigade HQ, Nikki Fuller works in the Environment Agency's Planning Office. Her job is to ensure that building standards are observed on the river's banks and floodwalls, and critical height levels adhered to.

The double gates at the end of the draw dock towards Black Prince Road are floodgates and so are part of her responsibility. Aside from their sheer bulk they also employ rubber seals across the sides and bottom. These have to be checked and maintained in good condition because otherwise over a period the rubber becomes brittle.

The draw dock is right outside Nikki's office window so she takes a particular interest in it. It is also on her route to the bus stop going to and from work. This morning it occurs to her that she hasn't been down to check on the gates for a while. It will only take a moment. Instead of turning in at the door of No. 10, she carries straight on down the ramp. It is quite steep in heels and she has to walk carefully. At the bottom there is the usual rubbish collected in the trough but also quite a lot of water. She is standing below the river level down here. Nikki frowns. She can definitely see a trickle coming through the gate and it is not even high water. She makes a mental note to contact the local authority and have it sorted out.

She turns about and walks briskly back up the ramp. One or two passers-by eye her curiously. The time is now 9.15 am.

The computer run from the Met Office takes ten minutes to download at the Barrier control room. It takes another ten to crunch the calculations in the computer before the Barrier's North Sea model spits out. Finally they run the Thames model. This takes the data off the first model for Southend and produces a forecast of levels at all points along the river over the next thirty-six hours. Reliability is estimated to be within a tenth of a metre, based on the original data.

Angus and Martin Simpson, the Tidal Defence Manager, study the chart together. The tide level shows in profile as a blue lined hump moving left to right across the screen, growing in height as it travels up-river. A flat red line climbing in a series of shallow steps represents the danger level along the banks. The two lines twine together like snakes till just past the Barrier, where the blue line climbs ominously clear of the other.

'This is with a residual peak of 2010 millimetres at Southend at High Water plus twenty minutes,' Martin interprets. In plain language, the model assumes a surge crest a little over two metres in height will start up the estuary half an hour behind the tide. 'This is without the Barrier raised.' He taps a key. 'This is with closure four hours before High Water.'

Angus leans over his shoulder, one hand on the desk. The blue line of the water level stops short at the Barrier and continues up-river well below the red danger mark. 'Let's see the level at the gates according to this.'

Martin selects the sector and zooms in. The display switches to a scale diagram of the Barrier. Angus reads off the figures, 'Seven metres ten.' His voice quivers slightly. There is no doubt now that they are looking at the Thousand Year Flood here. The Barrier tops out at six metres ninety for the four main gates, rising to seven metres twenty for the smaller side gates. In theory this means that the river will overtop by twenty centimetres. But the model has a built-in safety margin of thirty centimetres. If it holds they should scrape by, just.

Angus scowls. Overtopping of the Barrier, however slight, will be a personal defeat. More than that, even a few inches of water in the streets will inundate the London Underground system and flood thousands of homes. He must prevent it somehow if he can. One option is to over-rotate the central gates, raising their height slightly. The extra freeboard obtained is slight but may suffice.

'What about pinch points?' he asks brusquely. Narrowing of the estuary or sharp bends in the river, possibly combined with a reflected wave off the Barrier, are the principal factors. Over rotating may exacerbate these. Martin scrolls down river to focus on different sectors. 'Tilbury doesn't look so good,' he mutters.

For several minutes Angus studies the computer chart, trying to identify areas at particular risk. The scale of potential disaster is mind numbing. It is hard to remain objective when his decisions will put lives and property at risk. The question is, how to reduce those pinch points and at the same time prevent overtopping of the gates? Would it help to close later? He glances at the clock. It is nine-thirty already. Closing earlier is no longer an option.

Martin has the same thought. 'We could use the undershoot position. Let some of the flow through into the pool behind.'

Undershoot is a step further than over-rotating. In undershoot position the gates are rotated round until water begins to pass between their lower edges and the sills. It is used to equalise the levels upstream and downstream and prevent strain on the gates. It is an idea, Angus thinks. The upstream river behind the Barrier is in effect a great reservoir with water levels as much as three metres lower than downstream. If some of that storage capacity could be used to absorb part of the surge volume, it might reduce levels in the outer river, avoiding pinch points and overtopping.

'Work on it,' he tells Martin. 'I want a plan, fully plotted, within the next half-hour.'

His thoughts churning, Angus returns to his office and shuts the door. Determinedly calm, he unlocks the top drawer of his desk and takes out a file labelled barrier contingency plan. He stares at the cover. This is a moment he has often thought about but never believed would happen. Inside are instructions on what to do in the event of the Barrier failing. He opens the file and extracts a list of thirty-five phone numbers. Head of the list is Dave Wilcox, the Environment Agency's Director of Operations. To Wilcox will fall the task of breaking the news to the government, starting with Lester Gordon at DEFRA.

At North Greenwich underground station, Claire Panton barely has time to take in the stunning architecture. The children storm up towards the surface with whoops of relief. Carried along in the midst of them, she realises her own heart is thumping against her chest. The excitement is catching.

Inside the Dome, the vast translucent tent is bursting with light and colour and sound. Nothing Claire has read or watched on television has prepared her for the boldness of it all, the soaring roof, the crowds, the vibrancy. The Christmas tree of Norwegian spruce must be all of thirty metres high with frosting and lights to the very top. Stewards are on hand to escort the school party to the ice rink. They are friendly but brisk, keen to get the children settled. In a daze, they thread their way along the rows to their numbered seats.

Scarcely are they seated when the overhead lights dim. Spots pan to the centre of the shimmering stage where a single figure, pale as the ice, unwinds her crouching body inside a giant ball of frosted wire. A fairy in a cage of spun sugar. Slowly the delicate creature pirouettes, arms outstretched, in perfect equilibrium. And then the spell is shattered. From every side of the vast rink comes the rasp of skates on ice. Flocks of bird-men, feathered in black, are racing towards the cage, their beaked faces pure malevolence. Shafts of purple light glint off blades and the orchestra shrieks a warning. Claire steals a look at the children. Hands clutch armrests, faces are alive with wonder. This is what we came for, she thinks.

At the Department of the Environment, Food and Rural Affairs, Lester Gordon tells his secretary to hold all his calls. 'And I want you to telephone the Private Office, please. Say I shall shortly be sending up an important note for the Minister that I think he should read at once. You had better have a messenger standing by.'

All ministries have their own traditions. At DEFRA, in the twenty-first century, this is still an established way of transmitting a message up the hierarchy. Even one as urgent as this.

Gordon waits for an acknowledgement, then pulls pen and paper towards him and begins to write fluently and rapidly.

★

The 0900 tide forecast for the Thames estuary, received from the Meteorological Office, based upon the most recent computer model, shows a marked increase in danger levels at Southend for 1320 hours.

While it is not yet possible to predict exactly what level will be reached in the river itself, it appears certain that the defences will be put to a severe test. It is conceivable, though at this stage not inevitable, that a slight degree of overtopping of the banks may occur at a small number of places – pinch points – downstream of the Thames Barrier. According to Barrier Control the places most likely to be affected are THAMESMEAD on the south bank and TILBURY DOCKS on the north bank. The authorities in the districts concerned are being contacted and all riparian boroughs and statutory bodies alerted.

The Environment Agency has confirmed to me that overtopping of the THAMES BARRIER remains theoretical rather than probable. Flooding upstream of the Barrier is therefore NOT considered a threat. The situation is of course being kept under constant and urgent review. Much will depend on wind strengths over the next 4 to 5 hours and on the complex interaction between the surge and the incoming tide. High Water at the Barrier is currently predicted for 1425 hours.

In the circumstances, I feel certain that the Minister will wish to become informed and that the central government response mechanism should be placed on notice. My department is taking immediate steps to alert other Ministries and Departments including the HOME OFFICE and CABINET OFFICE and METROPOLITAN POLICE.

Signed L. Gordon. Head of Department.
Copy to PERMANENT SECRETARY.

He reads through what he has written, then summons his secretary to have it typed up. 'Bring the copies to me for signature and then have the messenger take them up at once. See that they are red-flagged for immediate attention.'

The response comes back to Gordon promptly. The Permanent Secretary will see him in fifteen minutes. Things are beginning to move swiftly.

But by then it will be 10 am. An hour will have been lost since the Met Office computer run became available. The surge peak will be forty miles nearer London and still no warnings have been issued in the capital.

13

It is time to close the Barrier. Such is the power of the hydraulics, it is possible to slam the gates shut in under five minutes but this would send a reflected wave downstream, causing severe flooding in the lower parts of the estuary. As a general rule therefore, closure begins four hours before High Water.

There is also traffic on the river to be considered. With bad weather forecast and a closure due, shipping companies operating on the Thames are anxious to get their vessels up or downstream. Barrier Control is liaising with the Port of London Authority to let as many as possible through. Then there are the waste barges. A great part of the city's rubbish is loaded onto barges and taken to landfill sites down the estuary. This avoids having it trucked through London's streets. If the refuse companies can't use their barges, and rubbish is still coming in, they have to take a decision to divert it onto the roads. It is Barrier policy to be helpful in this matter.

There is a last-minute appeal from the PLA on behalf of the tugs attending HMS *Belfast*. The tug owners intend to detach two of the four vessels now and dispatch them back through the Barrier, but they are forty minutes from Woolwich. Can closure be delayed to allow them passage?

Angus is firm. He has held off from closing the gates as long as he dares. He tells the PLA the answer is no. The tugs will have to remain where they are.

The closure team is running through the checklist. The Barking Barrier and the King George Vth Dock floodgates are confirmed closed and closure messages have been sent to the police, fire brigade, Thames Water, London Underground and other parties requiring a warning. Shipping in the area has been informed by radio and final clearance received from the Port of London. The Barrier navigation lights are switched to close and signboards up and down river illuminated.

Angus checks from the windows that no boats are in the vicinity of the gates. He has a clear view right across the line of steel cowls over the piers to the industrial wasteland of the north bank, backed by an ominous wall of cloud. Through the thick glass comes the distant warble of the klaxons on the piers sounding the alarm for imminent operation.

Closing is carried out by two operators sitting at separate workstations. Each has two monitors, one displaying a diagram of the Barrier with all gates open and the other showing oil-pressure readings for the hydraulic systems. A separate monitor displays the state of the Barking Barrier. All gates can be closed from either station using any one of four screens. The operators begin with the smallest gates, the falling radials at either end of the Barrier. From there they start to work inwards, leaving the main 61-metre gates in the centre till last.

Angus monitors proceedings from his own screen at the rear of the room. Normally the duty controller would handle this but today Angus is taking personal charge and nobody questions his decision. The crew in the operations room are tense but quiet; this closure is critical.

A row of gate displays starts to change as the outer gates slide down into place, one on the south bank and three on the north. When this is complete, Angus gives the order to start the first of the 30.5-metre rising sectors. This is the start of the real closing sequence. The operator uses the mouse to select the gate icon. The only sign that anything has happened is a rise in the display showing the oil pressure in the gate's hydraulic system.

Moving back to the windows, Angus sees the massive yellow rocking beam on the first pier begin to shift. It was lying flat against the pier; now, in response to pressure from the hydraulic cylinders in the motor houses, it is slowly lifting. A connecting link between the tip of the rocking beam and the gate arm transfers the beam movement, making the gate below the water rotate.

Behind him the operator has set the second of the rising sectors on the far side in motion. Everything is going smoothly. On the generator dials the power drain reflects the increased workload. Angus keeps his eyes on Bravo gate. The water between the piers begins to froth and a dark line breaks the surface, a black shape that rises up steadily like the hump of a whale, curving over till the gate reaches the vertical.

'Bravo closed; Foxtrot closed.' It is time to begin on the main central gates. These are the keys to the defence of the river. The operator clicks on the icon for Echo gate and the oil-pressure reading takes a jump as 3,700 tonnes of steel plating begins to lift from its concrete sill on the riverbed.

The strain is telling on the operator, sweat running down his face in spite of the air conditioning and even though he has performed this task many times before. By law, each gate must be raised once a month and the entire Barrier closed once in addition. He is watching the oil pressure and almost immediately he notices an aberration. 'Echo running heavy,' he calls hoarsely. The gate motors are meeting more resistance than usual, causing a rise in oil pressure in the hydraulic rams. There is no reason for alarm. They have exercised this kind of problem. It may be due to a build-up of silt inside the gate. The gate is hollow to allow water to flow in and out freely as it is raised and lowered. Silt collects inside the plating, making the gate heavier and placing extra strain on the hydraulics. The ram motors were designed with this in mind.

The hydraulic pressure continues to rise. 'Echo slowing,' the operator calls out, louder this time. Angus is watching the situation on his own monitor. 'Stop Gate,' he instructs. He picks up the telephone to speak to the duty engineers on the piers. There may be a glitch in one of the engine rooms. There is nothing mechanically wrong that anyone can see. Angus checks the television screen. There are cameras on the piers trained on the gates to watch for obstructions. He can see nothing obviously wrong either. The most likely cause is a baulk of timber jammed between the lip of the gate and the concrete sill. Applying full hydraulic power to the

3,700-tonne weight of the gate would undoubtedly crush the obstruction. Angus prefers to try to work the gate clear if possible.

At a word from him, the operator puts the gate into reverse and the frothing water subsides as the huge half-cylinder returns to its bed. There is a pause while engineers scan the surface for floating debris but nothing is sighted. Angus orders closure to re-start. There are anxious moments as the gate is set in motion again. Pressure is still running high. The operator calls the figures off the screen. The gate continues to rise. It looks as though the obstruction, whatever it was, has been shifted. To everyone's relief the gate breaks the surface and settles into position.

The three final gates give no problem. The Barrier is now fully operational. From bank to bank, a wall of steel seven metres high bars the river.

Upstream, at Canary Wharf Tower, Sophie de Salis's desk is taken up with a bulky freight terminal study. She grabs a bite of a ciabatta roll as she thumbs the pages. Another couple of hours hard reading, then the analysis to write up before the presentation to her boss. Her eye flicks to the time display on the VDU: 12.05 pm; she needs to get this wrapped up today.

Reaching for the telephone, she dials the Binneys' number and gets Harriet's answering machine. 'Hi, it's Sophie. Listen, I'm running late again! Is it okay if Chrissie comes back after school with Jo? I know you've got a dinner thing on tonight and I promise to pick her up by six, okay? That's a big help, thank you.'

It will take her an hour to reach Hammersmith by car from Docklands. At the least. Which means leaving by a quarter to five. She sets the alarm on her organiser and picks up the report again. She is conscious of a buzz of excited chatter in the building but ignores it. Most probably some fresh turmoil in the markets. No concern of hers right now. Ignoring it, she reads on.

Norfolk. Flooding is reported as far inland as Norwich, twenty miles from the coast. Fifty millimetres of rain have fallen in the past six hours and the Middle Level pumping station at St Germans is sucking four million tonnes of water off the Fens. The A47 between Norwich and Great Yarmouth has been closed after the River Bure burst its banks at Acle, and rail services between Norwich and Lowestoft have been cancelled. At Clay in North Norfolk a mile and a half long stretch of sea defences has been swept away.

High Water at Great Yarmouth, chief town of the Norfolk Broads, is forecast for 10.15 am. Already by ten, the sea-level is two metres above prediction. Waves are breaking over the sea wall at Breydon Water into South Town. At Winterton just to the north, the water has cut a hundred-metre gap in the dunes, engulfing the seaward end of the village with thousands of tons of sand. At Gorleston south of Yarmouth, four hundred people, mostly from bed-and-breakfast accommodation, have been taken to local schools after seas breached defences. Across the county border in Suffolk, owners of low-lying properties at Southwold and Aldeburgh are being advised to move to higher ground. And at Harwich, two hours down the coast, where the high tide arrives earliest in Essex, water is lapping ominously near the top of the quay.

14

Horse Guards Parade. A helicopter offloads a trio of officials and lifts off in a spray of water. It circles overhead and disappears. By the archway through to Whitehall, the Lifeguard and his horse stand impassive, staring straight ahead. A group of Japanese tourists in rain capes are taking photographs. The broad avenue is choked with traffic. People still going about their lives as if nothing out of the ordinary is going to happen. When the river overtops, the entire area will be flooded chest deep. And this is Whitehall, the seat of government.

A few paces down to the left, opposite the Ministry of Defence, is the entrance to Number 40, Whitehall. A sign by the door reads Cabinet Office. Inside, the hallway is walled off by floor-to-ceiling bullet-proof glass behind which two security guards goggle like rare fish in a tank.

'. . . potentially the greatest threat the capital has faced since the Blitz of 1940.' Venetia Maitland surveys the meeting. There are sixteen people present besides herself and a stenographer taking minutes.

Triple-C is convened in Cabinet Office Briefing Room A, known as Cobra, a low-ceilinged, windowless basement kept in a state of permanent readiness for the management of emergencies. Adjacent rooms house disaster plans and banks of communications equipment and there are connections to 10 Downing Street and other ministries via the maze of tunnels that run beneath Whitehall. Cobra is a soulless room, grey walls, long table, wooden chairs, but it is away from distractions and the prying eyes of journalists, and participants can come and go unseen.

Members of the committee sit at the table while supporting officials and experts take chairs against the walls to be called upon as necessary. Venetia is at the head. A sign to everyone that the crisis is real. To her right at the table is Lester Gordon from DEFRA. Next to him is Nikki Fuller from the Environment Agency. Nikki is a good choice because she has the heights of the banks at her fingertips and knows the state of the walls up and down the river. With her is the Agency's Emergency Manager for the Thames Region.

To Venetia's immediate left in dark blue and silver uniform is the Police Commissioner, Sir Simon Leeman, commander of the 27,400 officers of the Metropolitan Police. Next to the Commissioner, also wearing uniform, is Chief Inspector Harry Lime from Thames Division River Police. Lime is another good choice; he knows the river as well as anyone.

Down from the Chief Inspector, are the heads of the London Fire Brigade and the Ambulance Service, the Chief Executive of London Underground and the Director of Home Office EPD.

Commander Raikes sits at the foot of the table opposite Venetia. On one side are three more civil servants, representing different divisions of the Department of the Environment, and a medical adviser from the Health Department. On the other, a middle-aged woman from the Storm Tide Desk at the Met Office and two officers from the MOD. A large-scale map of the Thames estuary from Southend to Richmond has been unfolded in the centre.

Mary Lucas from the Met Office is immersed in her file of charts, dreading the moment when she is called to speak. She does not have long to wait. The Minister looks down the table at her. 'Dr Lucas will give us a summary of the Met Office position.'

Mary tries to imagine this is just another seminar. She takes a deep breath, 'My name is Mary Lucas. I work in the Central Forecasting Area of the Meteorological Office. I was on duty last night and have tracked the surge's progress for the past fifteen hours.'

After a brief outline of how surges develop and the threat they pose, Mary continues: 'According to the latest data available, the residual – that is the surge component on its own – will reach two point three metres at Southend, giving a combined tide level of five point six metres.'

Down both sides of the table lips are pursed in thought. Some eyes are fixed on her, others are staring at their own papers and files.

'Five point six metres, that translates into what level in the estuary?' Venetia asks.

Mary shakes her head. 'That's not . . .'

'As a rule you can add half as much again to get

the level at the Barrier,' Gordon interrupts. 'If these figures are accurate. So far we have had half a dozen different predictions from the Met Office, each one worse than the last.'

Before Mary can reply, the Police Commissioner breaks in angrily. 'It was my understanding that the police and emergency services would receive at least twelve hours' clear warning of a major flood alert in the capital. Now we are getting four hours' at most. Just what the hell have you people been doing?'

There are mutters of approval round the table. Hostile looks are directed at Mary.

'Warnings were sent out,' she protests. 'At midnight all regions were alerted that danger levels would be reached. I dispatched the notices myself.'

'My office saw no notice,' says the Commissioner. 'Certainly nothing that warned the Barrier might be at risk.'

Nikki Fuller from the EA thinks the Commissioner has a point. She has a copy of the midnight notice predicting a peak at Southend thirty centimetres above the danger level. Barely sufficient to require raising the Barrier.

Mary tries to explain the problems with the model during the course of the night. That it didn't handle the storm well. That a secondary depression developed and wind speeds increased where they had been predicted to diminish.

The faces round the table remain unconvinced. 'It's another Met Office screw-up. The 1987 hurricane all over again,' the Underground chief says disgustedly.

Venetia exerts her authority, cutting across the argument. 'We are not here to indulge in recriminations. The time for that will come later. Right now we need an estimate of the levels expected in the estuary. Will the defences in London be able to cope?'

Mary Lucas lets Lester Gordon answer this.

'According to Barrier calculations, which are based on the atmospheric model from the Met Office,' he says pointedly, 'and assuming a moderate degree of drop-off, the level at the Barrier will touch 7.3 metres at 2.20 this afternoon.'

Venetia scribbles a note. 'Seven point three is over the Barrier, I take it?' she looks at him for confirmation.

'Technically, yes. But the Barrier tide model includes an error margin of thirty centimetres. Taking this into account, the river will exactly brim the top of the gates.'

Mary Lucas feels a rising panic. Gordon's figures are dangerously optimistic. They are relying on a drop-off that may not occur. 'If the surge does come up the estuary at its full height, it will overtop the Barrier by at least a metre,' she blurts out.

There is silence in the committee room as members mentally picture water a metre deep in the streets. Lester Gordon is looking furious.

'Explain to us please, what is meant by drop-off,' Venetia says crisply.

Gordon clears his throat. 'On previous occasions we have seen large surges come down the coast, only to die away rapidly as they approach the estuary. This phenomenon is due to interaction between the surge and the incoming tide. Tidal forces hold back the onset of the surge.'

'In effect, you are saying tide and surge counteract one another?' Raikes asks.

Lester Gordon nods. '1993 saw a surge reach three metres along the Essex coast only to fall off very steeply. I believe the Met Office was panicky about that one too.'

The 1993 event was very different, Mary wants to say. The winds weren't as strong. Also the surge did not coincide with High Water. She sees Gordon's expression and decides to keep quiet.

Venetia gives her a penetrating look. 'Is it your judgement, Dr Lucas, that drop-off will not occur this time? Please consider carefully.'

Mary flushes. Gordon isn't going to like what she has to say and he is a powerful man in her world. 'Surge-tide interaction is an observed phenomenon, yes,' she replies diffidently. 'But we don't understand the mechanism as yet. And it doesn't always take place. It didn't in 1953.'

'Supposing drop-off does not take place,' Venetia addresses Gordon, 'what are the likely consequences?'

It is Gordon's turn to hesitate. If the tide reaches the eight-metre mark, there will be overtopping of the defences in the Tilbury and Thamesmead areas, he answers. 'We can reduce the level at the Barrier by allowing part of the flow to pass under the gates into the Pool of London behind. Rotating the gates into the undershoot position also adds around a third of a metre to their overall height, thus increasing the protection factor.' The Barrier was actually designed to cope with half a metre of flow over the top of the gates, he finishes.

'So the Barrier will cope successfully even if

drop-off does not occur and the surge comes up-river at its full height?' asks Raikes from the bottom of the table.

'Assuming of course that the Met Office has got its figures right,' Gordon says, with a pointed glance in Mary's direction.

Mary can't let this go. Everything is dependent on wind speed, she protests. 'Far from diminishing, the data coming in shows gales actually gaining strength.' So far they have been talking about a two-metre surge at Southend. If this goes on, she tells the room, it will be three metres. Do the maths, she wants to say. 'Three metres at Southend equals 4.5 metres at London Bridge. Add in the spring tide and you are talking two metres across the Barrier.'

London is going to drown, she is telling them.

At this point the meeting adjourns for Venetia Maitland to take yet another call from the Prime Minister in Australia. CNN is broadcasting news footage of the floods in Norwich. The Prime Minister is growing increasingly anxious. He presses for an update on the situation. Venetia says the position for London is still very uncertain. The experts are divided.

She debates whether to bring up the question of surge-tide interaction but decides not. The situation is complex enough. The Prime Minister is frustrated and resentful. His RAF jet is ready to fly. We don't have that long, Venetia interrupts him. Decisions must be taken here and now.

There is silence at the end of the line.

'Prime Minister,' Venetia says, 'in your absence I must have full powers.'

15

'We are interrupting programmes for a news flash. Good morning, it's 10.55 am and this is Beth Morgan at the London Weather Centre. Within the past few minutes a warning of possible tidal flooding has been issued by the Thames Barrier control room. Storm-force winds in the North Sea are driving an unprecedented surge tide down the East Coast towards the Thames estuary, raising the possibility that the River Thames may overflow its banks. Although central London behind the Barrier is not thought to be in danger, areas down river of the Barrier could see flooding over the walls for the first time in half a century.

'Areas at risk are believed to include Thamesmead, Barking, Dartford and Tilbury. People are advised not to travel into or through these areas. Anyone living or working close to the river is advised to stay put and listen to the radio for further information.

'Local Authorities are making special arrangements for the safety and care of the elderly, disabled and for children at school . . .'

Lauren Khan can hardly believe her luck. All last night she was telling people this could happen and now it has come true. In a few minutes a motorcycle taxi will race her through the traffic across the bridge to Woolwich where she hopes to cover the flood from inside Barrier Control.

Right now though she is conducting an interview over the phone with an expert in the field, Professor Page of University College's Flood Hazard Centre.

'You have to remember,' he tells Lauren, 'the Barrier was designed back in the late nineteen sixties, early seventies, and the heights had been more or less fixed a decade before that. The cost-benefit analysis for the project would fall well below today's standards. In fact, I'm not sure they even undertook one.'

'You're saying the Barrier should have been built higher?'

The professor hesitates before replying. 'With hindsight, yes. But, of course, the designers had little data to go on. Few tide gauge records went back as far as a century. And in 1970 there were financial and physical constraints, which pretty much dictated the level they could build to. In many places the flood defences can't be raised because the land is too unstable. The last study I saw put the risk of the downstream walls at Newham being overtopped at 1 in 300.'

What about Barrier Control's theory that overtopping can be contained within the Pool behind the Barrier? Lauren asks him. The Professor sniffs dismissively. 'Anything that goes over the top of the gates will also flood the walls.'

It is not just a question of probability, he says. There is also the degree of damage that might result. 'Overtopping of the Barrier can be characterised as a "low probability but high risk event." The chances of it occurring may be small but the economic consequences would be catastrophic.'

How much, Lauren asks him.

'In the order of twenty to thirty billion pounds. And that's not taking into account knock-on effects. Claims of that magnitude could bankrupt the insurance industry. With the transport infrastructure destroyed, the financial centre of the City of London might shift permanently to Frankfurt or Paris. We could be looking at national economic collapse, possibly on a global scale.'

Up in Chelmsford, Jenny Pitt, Emergency Planning Officer for Essex County bordering London, is another person who has been up all night. Memories of disaster are long in Essex; the county was hit hardest of any in 1953. Since then the defences have been hugely strengthened. The Met Office's flood warnings go first to the Environment Agency's Ipswich office, where Agency engineers add their own interpretation and allot a risk level from 1 to 9. The lowest is 1 and a 1953 scenario would rate 7 on the scale.

Well before the first alerts went out, Agency press officers were briefing local media that tonight's storm was expected to test the region's defences. As dawn approached with reports of high levels from Humberside, officials were again contacting local radio and TV stations. Red Alerts are in force, the message ran. Flooding is now a certainty and will be severe in places.

At 4 am the Red Alert for Tidal Division 4 was confirmed by the Met Office. Computerised alarm calls began going out to property owners registered with the Agency. Faxes were sent to emergency services and key players in the region – the police and local authorities – had their warnings confirmed by phone.

At Essex Council's Emergency Centre in Chelmsford, the night duty officer takes the call: 'Risk Level 3 for Tidal Division 4 is confirmed.' Tidal Division 4 in Essex extends from Harwich to Southend, a coastline of nearly four hundred miles of which two hundred is protected by sea walls. As well as towns like Ipswich and Colchester, it includes the ports of Felixstowe and Harwich and the beach resorts at Frinton and Clacton.

In a situation like this many different agencies are involved. The Environment Agency is responsible for passing warnings and for repairing breaches to defences; the police have a duty to preserve life and for evacuation; local authorities care for people made homeless. When Jenny reaches the council offices her first action is to check that the warnings have been passed on to district councils within the flood zone.

Instructions to district level vary according to the degree of perceived risk. Maldon District on the River Blackwater, with a long shoreline of marshland and many scattered communities, activates its emergency centre at risk level three or above. Castle Point District, which includes heavily protected Canvey, takes no action till a level six warning is called. This does not happen till after 10 am.

Responsibility for flood protection on the Kent side of the lower estuary falls to the Environment

Agency's Southern Region. Confirmation has come through from Barrier Control that overtopping is now a definite possibility, with best available estimates suggesting river levels reaching half a metre over the walls in the area of the Dartford Crossing. This is a critical point in the national road network where the London Orbital Motorway, the M25, crosses the Thames to join up with the M20 Channel Tunnel link. Originally a road tunnel, Dartford has now been upgraded with a six-lane bridge to carry the huge volume of traffic converging on the river. It is the busiest toll station in Europe, with 157,000 vehicles a day passing through.

Agency engineers from Kent and colleagues from the Essex side hold a joint emergency meeting with the police authority at the Crossing. Half a metre over the walls at Dartford translates to a flood level of just under eight metres and, to allow for a safety margin, the engineers tell their police counterparts that the risk area is being extended to cover everything below the ten-metre contour line. This means that while the bridge approaches are safe, the tunnel entrances on the south side of the crossing are vulnerable.

The police are unhappy. If they have to close the tunnels, halving the traffic flow, it will mean chaos. The engineers shrug their shoulders, it cannot be helped. Keeping the tunnels open is too much of a risk. With the surge due to reach Southend some time after one o'clock, closure will have to be scheduled for no later than midday.

The police implement their contingency plan. The information is passed to motoring organisations and local radio, warning messages start flashing up on road signs, and around the M25 cursing truck drivers prepare to peel off at the next exit and head back westwards. As queues build up at the approaches to the bridge on either bank, the ripple effect of the hold-up radiates traffic misery north and south around the capital.

Meanwhile the warnings are fanning out along both sides of the estuary. There are power stations along the river at Tilbury and West Thurrock on the north bank and at Dartford near the tunnel mouth on the south side. All three will have to shut down at once to give their boilers time to cool before the water reaches them. Then there are the docks and port installations at Tilbury in Essex to consider. The town there is vulnerable, as are Grays to the west and Gravesend and Northfleet on the opposite side. Parts of Dartford too are at risk, but inland Kent is protected by the higher ground of the Darenth hills.

At Thurrock on the Essex shore, east and west of the Dartford Crossing, wharves and jetties line the north bank. It is an area of heavy industry, paper mills, cement works, chemical and lubricant plants and oil terminals backed by acres of massive storage tanks. Hard by the bridge is Truckworld with secure overnight parking and refuelling facilities for three hundred vehicles. The low ground extends deep inland here. A mile back from the shoreline the huge Lakeside shopping centre is below the ten-metre line and will have to be evacuated.

A council official from Thurrock, attending the meeting, questions this last decision. Lakeside is a major employer and ratepayer. This is Christmas week, the busiest period of the year. Closing down the shopping centre will cost the stores there millions in lost takings. Can't anything be done to keep the waters back?

The engineers say no, Lakeside is a gravel pit site, protected on two sides by road embankments but wide open towards the river. Any delay and they could have a massive problem on their hands.

The Thurrock man reddens. 'What about Bluewater then? Aren't you going to shut them down too? Or do different rules apply over in Kent?'

The Smiley family, Stewart, Melissa, daughter Chantal and Stewart's mother, Helen, are heading north from Sevenoaks on the M25. Stewart has taken a day off from his job as an accountant to go Christmas shopping. Melissa has done the same from the estate agency where she works. Chantal is in her university gap year and is free to shop when she likes, which is always. For Helen this is a treat she has been looking forward to.

Stewart has just missed the exit for the A2 but remembers there is another turn-off a mile ahead and eases the car into the slip lane for the A296, the old Roman road to Rochester that runs parallel with the river along the edge of the Downs.

It is bleak up on the ridge today. The land slopes away towards the river. In the distance the immense pillars of the Dartford bridge stand out against the sky. A line of pylons carries electric cables from the power station over at Thurrock across the water to the Kent side. Gusts of wind are sweeping in off the estuary, bending the bare trees of Darenth Wood and hammering the windscreen of Stewart's Land

Cruiser with bullets of freezing rain. Stewart makes a left turn onto the Greenhithe road and joins a long queue of vehicles all headed down for Bluewater.

The car parks are busier than the Smileys can ever remember. Stewart deliberately takes the last exit off the slip road and is directed to an overflow section in the park. It means a long hike back to the shops for Helen, who finds walking painful. Stewart apologises. When the time comes to leave, he will fetch the car and pick the family up at the exit.

Inside the shopping centre, eager throngs of customers are pouring through the galleries in a whirl of frenzied consumerism. Windows blaze with lights and glittering decorations as stores compete in breathtaking displays. Flushed with spending, shoppers shuttle giddily between purchases, festooned with gaudily wrapped packages. The background music, the swift clatter of feet, the yelping voices and the bleep of tills all merge into a steady roar, the irresistible sound of money. Buy! Buy! it says. Quickly, now before everything goes! Forget the cost! You deserve it. You've worked for it. Buy! Buy!

The Smileys' plan of campaign is to split up; Stewart will go his own way while the three women set off together. They arrange to meet in two hours' time, at 1 pm, for lunch in the Winter Garden.

Upstairs, Murdoch Mitchison makes for his office. Originally from Sydney, Murdoch is retail project manager for Lend-Lease Corporation of Australia, the site developer, and as such he is boss of Bluewater. He walks fast for a big man, with long strides that look stately but have his aides scurrying to keep pace. He reaches the door to the management suite half a step in front of an assistant attempting to open it for him. Two men sitting with a tall woman in the reception area rise to their feet.

'These two gentlemen are from the Environment Agency and Dartford Council Emergency Planning,' the woman makes introductions. Her own name badge reads: Rita Yorke – Building Systems. She has palomino hair done up in a French roll.

Murdoch shakes hands briskly. 'The message said your business was urgent. My time is short too so let's get down to it.' He shows them into a small conference room with a cream coloured table and blue upholstered chairs. Before they can start, the door opens again to admit a police sergeant in uniform.

'This is John Grey, who heads up our police detail at Bluewater,' Murdoch explains. 'Now, gentlemen, I understand you say we can expect complications due to river flooding. Well, we're a long way from any river here. Must be, what, a mile to the Thames?' He glances at Rita for confirmation.

Rita stands to unroll a map. 'Three quarters of a mile to the north side of the site, as the crow flies,' she says. Her polished fingernail skims the line of the river. 'The edge of the Downs rises quite steeply off the Thames. According to these contours, the land around Bluewater varies between ten and twenty metres, rising in places to fifty metres. That ought to give us sufficient protection surely?'

The river engineer assents. Agency maps indicate that Bluewater should be safe so far as direct flooding is concerned. 'On the other hand,' the EPO guy points out, 'the site itself is below the height of the river walls. If water were to penetrate inland, through underground conduits or gullies . . .' he leaves the sentence unfinished.

'You're saying we're still at risk?' Murdoch demands.

The EPO makes a wry face. It is difficult, he implies. 'We're talking about a dense concentration of people here. Naturally, we have to give special consideration to the risk factor.'

'You're suggesting we don't?' Murdoch glares at him. 'Customer safety is our number one concern. How long do you expect the emergency to last?'

'We're not sure. Probably in the region of four to six hours. Starting at around two o'clock and persisting until the tide turns again.'

'Let's get something straight,' Murdoch faces the visitors. 'Are you asking us to close down our operation?'

The two men exchange glances. 'Well, that would have to be your decision, sir,' the EPO answers.

'Terrific,' Murdoch growls witheringly. 'You want me to take a decision based on ignorance. You're the blokes with the expertise. You tell me, are our customers at risk?'

'Well, we have advised Lakeside that in the circumstances they should evacuate,' the EPO tells him.

This time it is Murdoch and Rita who look at one another. 'I'm guessing but I'd say Lakeside is lower than us, less well protected,' Rita says carefully.

That is so, the men agree. On balance they feel there is no need for Bluewater to close. Not yet anyway. 'At the levels we've been given you should be safe here,' one of them says finally. 'But the situation could change rapidly, so be prepared to respond.'

The visitors excuse themselves. When they have gone, Murdoch walks over to the window and stares out at the packed car parks. 'We ought to make some kind of announcement through the stores, let everyone know the situation.'

A lot of people have picked up the announcements off the radio and TV already, John Grey, the police sergeant, says. And if the Dartford tunnels are closed it's going to cause traffic chaos. Visitors could face lengthy delays getting home. He suggests posting warning bulletins along with traffic updates.

Good idea, Murdoch says. He has another question. 'For the record, how long does it take us to evacuate?'

The sergeant hesitates. 'Our scenarios are based on fire or bomb threats. Exercises indicate we can get all occupants out of the buildings inside thirty minutes.'

'And how about if we need to clear the site?' Murdoch persists. John Grey looks to Rita. She shakes her head. 'There are no studies for that,' she answers. 'No one ever said anything about flooding.'

16

Real-time satellite images now show the centre of the depression anchored over the Heligoland Bight. There has been no let up in the storm. Winds are gusting to seventy miles an hour, just short of hurricane strength. The rain and sleet has turned to snow and roads are treacherous in many places.

Near Dunwich in Suffolk, the ancient Saxon capital of East Anglia, erosion has destroyed virtually the whole site of the original town. South of the town, the defences fronting the Minsmere nature reserve consist in the main of clay banks. Some of these are ageing and in need of repair.

Minsmere comprises a dozen houses with a few outlying farms. Former wetlands have been drained and shrunk over the centuries and much of the ground is now below high tide level. The sea dyke here is a steep six metres high and wide enough on the crest for four people to walk abreast. Like an ancient fortification it grows higher as you get closer, a grass rampart with a wide water-filled ditch on the landward side from where the spoil was taken to build it. The seaward slope is reinforced with pierced concrete slabs set into the turf. It looks solid enough; over the years though, the crest has dried out and become worn down in places. The closest houses are a quarter of a mile back but the ground between is flat as a pan. If the dyke goes, the village will be lost and much of the country behind.

What are needed are machines: earthmovers, excavators, bulldozers, dumper trucks and JCBs, able to scope out tons of clay at a time, dump it into place and ram it solid. Except that machines are no use in a situation like this. Machines can't climb a steep six-metre dyke wall without breaking it down more. And they couldn't reach this dyke even if they wanted to because of the spoil ditch full of water hard against the foot. So the job will have to be done by men with sandbags.

There are certain basic principles in sandbagging. A thousand bags properly laid are as effective as fifteen hundred dumped anyhow. To be stable, a wall built of sandbags alone must sit on a base at least as broad as its height. Bags should be laid as if they were bricks, in courses, head to tail, the joints overlapped. They must be filled, if possible, with clay or topsoil, since sand is not only heavy but porous and will leach out if the bags are wetted. When the bags eventually rot the remaining sand will spill out and the wall collapse.

This is work that requires its own tools and equipment: shovels, narrow spades for bag filling, wheelbarrows, plastic sheeting, stakes and sledge hammers. It requires large quantities of timber and planking for reinforcement, for running planks and temporary bridges. It requires endless supplies of empty sandbags and clay filler close to the scene. Finally it requires manpower, manpower that must be trained and supervised, transported and fed.

Ever since daybreak, two platoons of the 9th/12th Lancers, from Swanton Morley, have been working to shore up the defences. The sergeant in charge has split them into sections, one section filling bags, the rest chaining them up to the crest of the dyke for laying under the direction of an engineer from the local authority. An hour ago it was decided that the risk to the village was too great and an evacuation was ordered, but transport has been delayed. In spite of the cold and savage conditions, rescue efforts are being hampered by carloads of sightseers. A military ambulance loaded with stretcher cases has been held up for twenty minutes while police search for the owners of vehicles blocking a lane.

The troopers' task now is to hold the line to give the civilians time to get out.

Sandbagging is extremely labour intensive. It takes around a hundred sandbags to fill a cubic metre. A temporary wall fifty metres long, two metres high by one and a half, the base twice the width of the top, will require twenty thousand bags. Since experience shows that a practised team can average seventy bags laid for each man per day, the wall will take the two platoons of Lancers six days to complete. Labouring all day they will be lucky to raise the height of the wall by as much as one foot.

The last house in the village, Golf House, stands on a patch of higher ground reached down a lane running due east to the sea. It is low built with verandas looking towards the coast. In summer it must be a pleasant place, surrounded by rough grazing and marsh to the foot of the dyke; today it is just terrifying. Low cloud is scudding across the sky and the wind has taken on a sustained howl, backed by the drumbeat from the sea to produce a noise the like of which the men have never experienced before.

It is clear to everyone that they cannot hold out here much longer. Waves are pounding the dyke relentlessly and each surge sends the levels higher. The beach has long since disappeared and it is open sea out there. The path along the ridge has been churned into liquid mud by the soldiers' boots and by the spray blown over the crest. A lot of water is coming across in places and streaming down the rear slope. The dyke that seemed so massive from below feels puny and insubstantial on top. Conditions up here are atrocious. The men are frozen, soaked through, and now they are becoming nervous. The lieutenant in charge has gone back to the village in search of a truck to bring the platoon out. He has told the sergeant that if the situation deteriorates he is to pull the men back. The sergeant can't see how things can get much worse than they are now.

He takes a twenty-kilo sandbag from an exhausted trooper at the head of the chain and staggers off along the ridge of the dyke towards the laying section, with the clay sucking at his boots. A burst of spray explodes over the crest, drenching the dyke with water and knocking him to his knees. As he tries to get up, another burst hits him. He wipes his face and stoops to pick up the sandbag again. Looking down he catches sight of something moving downwards on the rear slope. It is a bedraggled looking rabbit. The sergeant watches it slither off the dyke to a crossing point over the ditch and scuttle away into the long grass on the far side. From a nearby burrow two more appear. Suddenly, everywhere the sergeant looks, the side of the dyke is alive with rabbits taking flight.

Downing Street is filling up with official cars. Venetia Maitland has called an emergency Cabinet meeting for later in the day and Ministers are arriving already. For the moment, Venetia is still presiding over Triple-C. The Police Commissioner, the Director of London Underground and the Fire Brigade Chief have quit to take charge of their respective headquarters but they have left deputies in their places and other officials have joined. The temperature is rising in the basement room. Most people are in shirtsleeves and the phones ring constantly.

Nikki Fuller from the Environment Agency is called to speak. Her expertise relates to the river defences. The walls in central London, she states, average 5.41 metres in height.

'So the banks in central London are at least a metre and a half below the height of the Barrier – and lower still at Greenwich and Docklands,' Raikes summarises.

Further discussion on this point is interrupted by a call from Scotland Yard regarding evacuation from Docklands. The Commissioner is concerned the Underground system should not be shut down too hastily. Large crowds still have to be cleared from ExCeL and the Dome.

Venetia switches on the amplifier so the rest of the room can listen. 'That will take how long?' she asks.

'In the case of the Dome, they can clear the building itself in twenty minutes but that's not the point,' the Commissioner's voice echoes tinnily out of the phone. 'It's getting them away from Greenwich. The Dome management reckons they have 40,000 people on site. The Underground can move a maximum of 25,000 an hour; coaches and boats will take some more. So two hours, three to be safe.'

Venetia checks the clock. It's after eleven and the surge is due at the Barrier at twenty minutes past two. Three hours is all they have. That damn tent, she thinks. All politicians loathe the Dome and with reason; it has wrecked many of their careers.

What about ExCeL? Raikes asks. There are 75,000 people there, right alongside the water. ExCeL is less of a concern, the Commissioner tells him. They have the Docklands Light Railway and national main-line rail, in addition to the Jubilee Line. Plus good road access and parking.

Gordon from DEFRA speaks. 'Aren't you forgetting that, even if the Barrier is overtopped, it will still take an hour and a half to raise the level upstream to a point where we can expect flooding across the walls in central London.'

People turn to Nikki Fuller for confirmation. She shakes her head. 'Sure, it will take a while to fill the up-river pool. But there is low ground on the south bank, between the Barrier and the Greenwich Peninsula, which means the water will be able to cut around behind the Barrier and flood the Dome area from the landward side. It could take minutes only.'

Venetia's voice sharpens. 'So we're back to three hours again.'

'Excuse me, Ma'am.' A young man stands up. He wears the uniform of a police constable. 'Tom Branson, British Transport Police.'

Raikes flips down his attendance list till he locates the name. Advisers and technical experts summoned from different departments are sitting around the walls of the room. Branson is from London Underground's emergency unit. A note shows that he has a qualification in traffic systems.

Venetia signals him to proceed. The young man takes a deep breath. 'With respect, Ma'am, we don't even have that much time.' Speaking quickly and to the point, he tells them they cannot run trains into tunnels right up to the moment of flooding. The risk of something going wrong is too great. If 2.20 is the deadline, then the tunnels must be cleared by 1.20 at the very latest.

'Point taken,' Venetia nods. 'Which cuts us down to two hours.'

But Branson is not done yet. Less than that, he responds. To clear the tunnels by 1.20, London Underground will have to start withdrawing services soon after midday. They will switch over from automatic signal control to manual operation and begin running trains out to depots, pulling staff, closing stations. Capacity will drop rapidly with fewer trains, erratic timing and overcrowding. 25,000 passengers per hour at North Greenwich is a peak figure. It relies on a train leaving the platforms every two minutes. Increase that interval to ten minutes and 5,000 are being shifted, not 25,000.

Also, he continues, it won't only be Dome visitors trying to board those trains. 'Once word gets out in Docklands and East London, the stations will fill with passengers trying to get home before the flood. We are talking about ExCeL, Canary Wharf and the Dome all emptying together. The trains that do get through will be full before they even arrive.'

Stunned silence falls in the committee room as people absorb the implications of what the young man is saying. It is Raikes who sums up. 'What it comes down to is, you're telling us we've left it too late.'

Out at Dunwich, the troopers need little urging to pull back off the dyke. They climb down, shoulder their tools and start up the track to the village, glad to be out of the wind and spray at last. The rain seems mild by comparison. Three hours of relentless physical labour has pretty much drained the strongest of them. Wearily, they move along the track in two lines. Trucks have churned the clay into a gooey sludge that clings to boots, slowing progress to a crawl. Looking up the column from the rear, the sergeant can see no sign of the trucks supposed to be collecting them and wonders whether he can stop at Golf House and maybe shelter in the garage till they come.

He looks over his shoulder. The sky is black behind them. Beneath it is a screaming whiteness from out of which great rolling waves thunder. They have got out not a moment too soon. The sea is rising fast. All along the top of the dyke white water is foaming in a single line. The waves are breaking right on the dyke itself now, the crests streaming down the slope in cataracts. They are growing larger and heavier all the time, shouldering their way onto the dyke. Every so often one bigger than the rest flings itself against the defences, swarming over to drench the rear slope with a tumult of raging spray. According to the engineer, the dyke wall has a core of compressed clay 'that will take anything the sea can throw at it'. The sergeant hopes to God it is true or they will be in trouble.

The column has covered a further fifty metres before he looks back again. He is in time to see another wave come over and this one is fearsome because it doesn't break. It simply rolls right on, clean over the dyke wall and down the slope onto the land behind, without pause. It is 'coming over green' as seamen call it. Even as he watches, another follows, burying the dyke and its rear slope in a roaring deluge. Then, as though the sea behind heaves itself up all at once, the entire dyke vanishes under water.

The others have turned to watch too. In horrified amazement they stare at the awful sight. The ocean is rolling forward down the slope unchecked. The sergeant has a momentary glimpse of the bank again as the water spills clear. The former grass slope has been stripped bare of covering by the force of the waves. These are seas that can suck up heavy concrete blocks and throw them hundreds of metres or pound a rock cliff into fragments.

Golf House, the last building in the village, is home to two ladies in their eighties and their seventy-year-old brother. The sisters have been bedridden for the past week with influenza. Ideally an ambulance should be found to bring them out but none is available. Their brother has been following the activities of the soldiers from an upstairs window. He can guess the reason for their retreat and goes to fetch his binoculars. He knows the house is vulnerable but so far the dyke has always held, even with water breaking over. He returns to the window and starts to focus the glasses. His heart leaps into his mouth in shock.

A huge gap has appeared in the earth bank. Fifty metres of the parapet has vanished. Undermined from the seaward side, the footing of the outer face has slid forward, collapsing the dyke's core and exposing a passage for the greedy waves. They surge forward, tearing at the edges of the gap as they come, ripping away the soil, widening the opening. Through the breach, a wall of raging sea, two metres high, roars down upon the house.

The storm is now extending almost the full length of the east coast of England. Coastguard and RAF rescue helicopters are responding to dozens of appeals for help, both at sea and inland, as flooding takes its toll. With all its UK aircraft currently deployed, when the next call comes in, the Rescue Co-ordination turns to Allied military forces. Listed as available to assist in an emergency is the USAF 21st Special Operations Squadron, based at Alconbury, twenty miles northwest of Cambridge.

The 21st SOS operates the Sikorsky MH-53J Pave Low helicopter, still widely known by its Vietnam-era nickname, 'Super Jolly'. This is the largest and most powerful helicopter in the inventory of the US Air Force, four times the size of a Sea King, and able to carry thirty-eight combat equipped troops or twenty-two litter patients, in addition to a flight crew of three.

Since the early hours of the morning the squadron has been placed on enhanced alert ready to assist in the mounting emergency. Alconbury is on the edge of the Fens and the base has already sent men and vehicles to assist in evacuating villagers at Ten Mile Bank near Downham Market. Now word comes through from Suffolk: a sea dyke is down, there are casualties trapped. Help is needed.

A dispatcher's call summons two crews to the Operations Centre and pilots and navigators gather round the chart table. The route is due east to the coast, distance ninety miles. It is a route they have flown before on exercises. The mission is to evacuate casualties back to hospital on the base and bring out anyone else who wants to leave. Inside five minutes they are scrambling into a truck and heading for the hangars.

Special Operations missions usually involve deep penetration of enemy territory in support of Special Forces or combat rescue of friendly personnel using para-rescue jumpers or PJs. Aircraft configured for these missions are equipped with terrain-following radar, infra-red sensors and inertial navigation gear. More often than not, Special Operations are called at short notice and in adverse conditions. If you are flying into the enemy's back yard, it helps to have the weather on your side. Even so, today is about as rough as it can get and still be flyable.

The pilot of the lead aircraft, Pete Sabbich, is coming up for the end of his first year in England

and he has learned to respect the British weather. Mostly on account of its changeability. The sky can close in on you real quick, he tells newcomers. You can take off on a clear summer day and thirty minutes later you're flying blind and every base is socked in with cloud to five hundred feet.

For this trip Pete stays below the cloud cover. The country is dusted with lying snow where it is not sodden with water. A skein of geese passes underneath, inbound from one of the coastal reserves. The helicopter flies over Huntingdon, heading due east till it reaches the sea, and swings north following the line of the coast. From this altitude the breach is visible as an ugly rent with a brown fan of water spilling through onto the land.

A British ground controller guides them in till Pete can pick out the cluster of people drawn up by a solitary house, surrounded by swirling water. Pete circles to the north, takes up a low hover while his co-pilot, Duke Whalen, makes a visual check, then drops down to thirty feet, as close to the house as he dares. Stretcher parties in army fatigues stagger through the spray from the downwash to meet them.

Gorgas, one of the two PJs, slides open the main hatch and winches down a sling to bring the injured up. These are two old ladies, badly shocked and wrapped in thermal blankets. One is in a serious condition, barely conscious; a paramedic is giving her CPR. Gorgas straps her tight on the stretcher and sways it up. Inside, Smith, the other PJ, gets an oxygen mask on and checks her heart.

Duke goes forward to the cockpit to radio for

directions to the nearest medical facility. Gorgas starts bringing up the rest of the survivors. They are all soldiers, filthy with mud, and soaked, but wryly cheerful in the British manner and grateful to their rescuers. Pete and his crew cram in twenty-seven and leave the remainder to the other bird.

British air control comes on with a heading for Ipswich, where a hospital is standing by to receive the sick women. As they wheel away towards the west, the Americans can see the sea raging out beyond the broken dyke. This mission has gone smoothly. They have a hunch that others may not be so easy.

17

Mersea Island, sixty miles northeast of London Bridge on the Essex shore. The tide hits here two hours ahead of the Barrier. There is a long history of flooding all along this part of the coast. Canvey is only twenty-five miles away. The shore is salt marsh, sand dune, and shingle and clay flats. Erosion is a real problem, eating up whole villages like Ithancester, now just a memory. Jagged stumps of old stakes, 'farmer's teeth', projecting above the foreshore mud and ranged in rows, one behind the other, mark the progressive retreat of the defences.

By eight o'clock the bubbler type tide gauge on Mersea Island is indicating 2.2 metres, sufficient to trigger an amber flood warning. A narrow creek separates Mersea from the Essex mainland. The single causeway is only passable to traffic at low tide. At the southeast tip the small town of West Mersea is popular with yachtsmen, the 'yellow-welly' brigade. Inland the country is arable, flat and low lying. Tourist development is confined to caravan parks along the eastern beaches.

It is 8.10 am when the first flood calls go out. A farmer keeps sheep on 175 acres of marsh by the bird sanctuary at Cudmore. The phone alerts him with a pre-recorded message. The Environment Agency's regional office has embarked on an ambitious five-year programme to enhance the warning service. A database of properties at risk of flood damage has been assembled and an automatic voice messaging system installed. The AVM is capable of phoning thirty numbers simultaneously, seventeen hundred calls in an hour. Messages are coded 'flood watch', 'flood warning', 'severe flood warning', depending on the degree of anticipated risk. The farmer's call is just one of hundreds made to landowners, flood wardens, police and local authorities. As yet it is only a warning, level 2 on the scale. The farmer taps in a digit on the phone's keypad to confirm his receipt of the message. If a call is not answered the system automatically redials. All calls are attempted three times. Then he hurries out, whistling to his dog, to round up the sheep and move them inland to higher ground.

Halfway along the island is a mobile-home park located back from the beach. The sea goes out over a wide area of shallows here, Mersea Flats. At low tide you can walk out a quarter of a mile and still stand only knee deep. At high water the spray breaks over the shallow cliffs in rough weather. Huge sums have been squandered attempting to hold back the sea. The beach is littered along its length with the remains of flood defences, house-sized blocks of reinforced concrete, heaved up, toppled and cracked open by wave action, the steel rods rusted out. The new policy is to manage the sea; permit controlled flooding of low-lying land.

Even so, some areas have to be defended. The caravan park near Cudmore Grove is one. When the beach wall was declared unsafe a new berm of shingle and earth, two and a half metres high, was constructed further back. Recently, this too has begun to show signs of wear. Last month, storm breakers undermined the beach in front causing the footings to become waterlogged.

The Agency's regional engineer knows this is the first step to collapse. Ideally he would like to cut out the unstable section, drive piers into the shingle to support the structure and rebuild. This will cost too much and anyway there is no time. The best he can do is shore up outside the weakened section. For the past week he has had two bulldozers at work on the beach side, piling up shingle trucked from inland.

He calls in to the Environment Agency headquarters seeking authority to start evacuations. The berm is already weakened. The ground immediately behind lies below the high water mark. If the sea should break through, then the trailer park behind will be in real danger.

Two hours after the first alarm calls at Mersea, the surge hits the fishing port of Lowestoft. The gauge there jumps right off the scale, triggering panic all down the coast. Felixstowe's gauge is climbing five centimetres a minute. Walton-on-the-Naze is rising fast. Broadcasts go out over TV and radio and the AVM system makes the first of three thousand urgent calls to homes and businesses at risk.

One call is to the Dollar Holiday Camp at Cudmore Grove. The camp holds 208 caravans and mobile homes, evenly split between permanent residents and transients. Almost none of the latter have phone connections. Dot Murray, the owner, a plucky woman in her fifties, routs out her son-in-law Ted Lawless and together they go out into the rain to start banging on doors, waking residents. Most people are co-operative. One look at the water-logged state of the ground is enough to convince them of the need to leave. Some owners start trying to hitch up their caravans but Dot persuades them there isn't time. 'Just get in your cars and drive,' she urges. One pair of honeymooners can't be woken. They don't respond to knocks or banging at the windows. Dot hasn't got a pass-key so in the end Ted puts his shoulder to the door only to discover the van is empty. The couple have done a run without paying. Some cars are stuck already, bogged down in the mud. Other drivers rally round with tows. In the end though, the water comes in too fast; some twenty vehicles have to be abandoned to the floods. Several owners leave in tears.

So far a red alert has not been issued, but down on Mersea beach everyone reckons it is only a question of time. The wind is blowing a full gale, great gusts tearing across the flats, driving the waves before them. Sheets of spray fly across the beach. Jason Webb is working down at the south end, the most exposed position. The sand is too waterlogged now for the trucks to reach him with more ballast. He's just doing the best he can, scraping whatever shingle he can find into heaps and working it up under the berm. The noise of the surf crashing against the timber groins is frightening. It's a continuous thunder, stifling the sound of the bulldozer's engine. Every so often a big burst of spray comes flying overhead, rattling the cab with pebbles. Jason just hopes the windshield holds. He has a CB set with him and he is on the edge of calling in, asking to be relieved.

Jason is just lining up another scrape of shingle when the engineer comes over the air. Conditions are getting too rough; it's time to quit. He is ordering everyone off the beach. Jason thinks about time. He runs the scrape up the beach to the base of the berm; no sense in wasting it. Then he backs off, swings the dozer around and makes for the exit. The wind has really got up in the last hour. When the gusts come the pressure forces a fine spray of water and sand through the door and window seals. The sea is just a dreadful sight. Huge combers leaping and foaming, crashing in over the flats, right up the beach almost to the dunes. At one point, where he has to edge out to pass some rocks, the surf is boiling around the tracks. The dozer is actually driving through the water.

Overhead the sky is grey and full of scudding cloud. There is a squall line closing in, black and angry looking. The engine gives a stutter and starts to run ragged for a minute. He thinks, oh shit, and pumps the throttle pedal. The squall is close now, the shriek of the wind drowning out the sound of the faltering engine. It's a relentless wail like nothing he has ever heard before and it's scary. The darkness grows. It seems to close down over the cab like smoke. He can feel the wind shaking the dozer. Actually shaking a twenty-tonne piece of earth-moving machinery. The doors and windows are rattling furiously.

A lot of things happen at once. There is an explosion of sound, a thunderclap that seems to burst right inside the cab itself, so loud he is dazed and deafened. The nearside door wrenches open or is torn off, it's impossible to say. At the same time the windshield comes away. It just pops right out, sucked bodily into the storm as if punched by an invisible fist and Jason goes right with it. The wind's suction plucks him from his seat and squeezes him out through the gap like something squirted from a tube. His helmet slams against the edge of the roof. Next moment he is outside being dragged over the engine casing. His hands are still gripping the steering wheel and he hangs on for his life while the rest of him flails in the slipstream of the wind. The air is whipping sand and spray. He can't see or hear. He loses his grip on the wheel, falls off the casing and just manages to clutch onto the tracks. Water is surging around him. He feels that waves must be breaking right over the dozer. He's terrified that if he lets go he will be swept out to sea.

As abruptly as it struck, the wind releases him and the water recedes. He claws himself upright in time to see a twisting dark funnel lurch off up the beach in a cloud of sand, then lift back up into the clouds to disappear. Jason Webb has survived a run-in with a tornado.

18

The emergency services have petitioned Triple-C for an hour's grace period in which to evacuate their vehicles from the flood zone, before warnings are issued to the general public. They haven't had it. The airwaves swarm with anarchic radio stations that ignore government directives.

In a disaster, the prime role of the Metropolitan Police is to save life and co-ordinate rescue services. Strategic control below the level of Triple-C is exercised from the Special Operations Room at New Scotland Yard.

Commander Foster Bennett is in charge here, a thickset man with a reputation for efficiency. Commander, in the Metropolitan Police, is the equivalent of Assistant Chief Constable in a provincial force. It is the most senior rank that still carries with it powers of arrest.

Bennett is designated Police Gold Commander. He will liaise directly with Triple-C when decisions are needed at ministerial level. Senior officers from the Fire Brigade and Ambulance Service will join him to provide a co-ordinated response to the flood. An Air Vice-Marshall from the Ministry of Defence is also on his way to represent the armed services.

The Casualty Bureau has been opened up. It has its own switchboard to cope with the rush of calls by anxious relatives that invariably follows the announcement of a disaster. The Metropolitan Police has specialist body recovery and identification teams who will attend mortuaries and casualty clearing centres. Their job will be to record the numbers of dead and injured, establish identities, and see that fatalities are properly labelled using the national body labelling system. Other officers will go to rest centres to take details of survivors and evacuees so as to eliminate them from lists of missing.

Many police establishments, including New Scotland Yard, lie within the flood zone. Vehicles south of the river must be withdrawn to Clapham Common. Those to the north will relocate to Hyde Park. In view of the risk to New Scotland Yard, the Central Command Complex, including the Special Operations Room, will transfer to the Police Training School out at Hendon. Even in normal conditions this would be a massive logistical undertaking.

Off-duty officers, special constables and traffic wardens have been ordered to report in, their immediate task to clear routes for emergency traffic. Police categorise traffic conditions as Green, Amber, Blue, Red or Black. Green and Amber are light and medium traffic, flowing freely. Blue is heavy traffic flowing freely and Red is heavy traffic stationary for up to three minutes. Black is gridlock, a word the police themselves don't use.

Today started out Blue with large numbers of

extra vehicles joining the 140,000 commuter cars normally flowing into the capital. Rush-hour levels have persisted right through the morning, which is only to be expected this near to Christmas. In a traffic system as dense as London's, any hold-up results in congestion. By the time the first warnings of possible flooding begin coming over the radio, large parts of the West End, Kensington and Knightsbridge have moved up to category Red.

The Flood Alert tips an already bad situation over the edge. The closure of the Dartford tunnels shifts heavy traffic westwards into Docklands and the Blackwall crossing under the Thames to Greenwich. There are floodgates fitted at both ends of the Blackwall tunnels as a precaution against terrorist car bombs. Police orders are to close them off, but with both tunnels jammed with vehicles and the approaches solid for half a mile either side, it is asking the impossible.

Next up is the Rotherhithe tunnel, built as a relief to the Blackwall. The police have more success here. They manage to close the floodgates at the Limehouse entrance on the north bank, but only at the cost of diverting traffic onto the bridges. The knock-on effect is dire; within half an hour cars are stationary from the Tower to Blackfriars.

Meanwhile reports are coming in of an accident on the southbound carriageway of the A2 Rochester Relief Road leading to the Blackwall crossing. A coach pulling out into the centre lane causes a truck to swerve and clip an overtaking Mercedes. Other vehicles are following too close to brake in time; the resultant pile-up blocks three lanes and leaves eleven injured. Within minutes cars are backed up for two miles, jamming intersections at Shooters Hill and Woolwich Road.

Paralysis spreads rapidly through the main routes of southeast London. More junctions are blocked, minor roads seize up. The effects ripple through the Blackwall tunnels into Docklands and the City of London, locking up traffic north and west. By midday, London has turned to stone. From Hammersmith in the west to Barking in the east, from Finchley on the north bank down as far as Wimbledon and Bromley, a million vehicles are going nowhere.

'*This train is for Edgware Road only.*'

A Circle Line train moves away from the platform at Gloucester Road, accelerating jerkily up the cutting towards High Street Kensington. The motors are running momentarily out of sync causing a characteristic knocking sound from the line breakers, a common problem on old C-class rolling-stock.

A mile along, the driver swears under his breath and depresses the brake. A red stop lamp is glowing by the track up ahead. As the train wheezes to a halt he eases his hand on the controller lever, the deadman, and waits for the signal to clear. The lamp remains at red and after a minute he shifts the deadman into Hold position and releases it. He stretches his arm and pumps it a couple of times to relax the muscles. The spring on the handle has been renewed recently and the stiffness has given him an ache in the elbow.

The signal is still set against him. This is the third halt in four stations. The emergency is playing havoc with the system. All trains are supposed to run out to their depots by 1 pm at the latest. From the Tower of London to Victoria and South Kensington the track lies close by the river and is crammed with trains escaping westwards. At least this time they are out in the open air of a cutting instead of waiting in a dark tunnel. Above him, either side of the track, rise the backs of buildings. This line was constructed in the days when trains were hauled by steam engines.

The Circle Line, connecting the great main-line railway terminals that girdle the capital, is one of the myths of London's Underground. On the route maps it is boldly marked in yellow; in practice, it doesn't exist. Except for two short sections, Circle Line trains run on track belonging to the Metropolitan and District Lines. Services are slotted between their schedules, making it difficult to timetable and vulnerable to delays.

The train is full with a thousand passengers squeezed into six carriages. In the last carriage a gang of youths is creating a nuisance. A woman passenger finds her purse missing. There are accusations, a scuffle breaks out and someone presses the emergency switch.

The alarm lights up an indicator in the driver's cab. Normal procedure calls for him to stop the train at the next station but the signal is still against him. All he gets over the intercom are confused shouts and screaming. Another light flashes on the panel indicating that someone is attempting to force open the rear door. He tries to contact line control but they can't help. There is nothing for it but to go back and investigate.

The cab connects to the carriage behind so all he has to do is walk the length of the train to the scene of the trouble. But the thought of fighting his way past five carriages and a thousand irritable passengers does not appeal. Instead he climbs out onto the track and makes his way along the side of the cutting, taking care to avoid the rails. Faces stare down at him from the windows as he passes.

When he reaches the back of the train he sees figures struggling at the door. It is probably a crime, but someone could have been taken ill. The driver grips the safety rail and pulls himself up. The door is flung violently open and a youth comes leaping out, hurling the driver backwards. He falls heavily to the ground just missing the live rail. Several more youths spring down from the carriage and tear off up the track.

At Victoria, London Transport Police detect the youths escaping from the stalled Circle Line train on CCTV cameras and immediately disconnect the electric current to prevent an accident. This is one of the most heavily used sectors of the entire system, with District and Circle Line tracks running alongside the Heathrow Express link. A bad stoppage here will throw the evacuation into chaos.

Aboard the Circle Line train there is confusion. People are unclear what is happening. They know there is a flood alert. They have heard a commotion, seen the driver come down to open the door. Now figures are running up the track. The result is a panicky surge for the exit. The driver shouts at them to stay back, but he is swept aside.

Passengers in other carriages start banging on the windows. People outside run along the train opening doors. Soon hundreds are swarming along the tracks in both directions.

Waterloo Station, London. Traffic along the embankment is appalling. Harriet Binney has had to leave her Volkswagen miles from the Eurostar terminal and walk. The train from Brussels has pulled in by the time she reaches the platform and Miranda is cross at having to wait. She can't believe how cold it is in London. Harriet is equally dismayed by the quantity of baggage Miranda has with her. There are no trolleys and by the time they reach the car both women are exhausted.

As they drive off, flood warnings are coming over the radio, along with reports of congestion on the roads. Harriet wonders if it might be better to return to Hammersmith by the south side of the Thames. Miranda is too busy talking on her mother's mobile to offer an opinion, so Harriet heads along Waterloo Road, following the signs for Clapham Common. Minutes later they are sitting in a traffic-jam near the Oval cricket ground.

Cabinet Office technicians have succeeded in patching a computer link from the Met Office to Triple-C. Now the committee can follow the progress of the surge in real time.

The picture is dismaying. Lowestoft is up to record levels. Flooding at King's Lynn shows no sign of abating, more than five hours after first overtopping. Along the Essex coast, tide levels at Harwich, Frinton, Walton-on-the-Naze and Clacton are rising unchecked. Barometric pressure in the centre of the storm is down to 960 millibars; wind strengths are continuing to average above fifty knots from the northwest, hurrying the surge down towards Southend where the gauge is climbing with ominous persistence.

For the estuary the predictions are terrible. By the time the surge reaches Southend it will have swollen to at least three metres. It is moving so fast now that the models show it overtaking the high tide by perhaps a quarter of an hour. When this mass of water is driven up-river, the narrowing banks will squeeze the height to above nine metres. Barring a last-minute miracle, London will experience two metres of flooding across the top of the Barrier.

Twenty-five miles inland from the sea, at the Emergency Response Centre in Chelmsford, EPO Jenny Pitt knows she can't delay any longer. She sits down at her laptop with the modem plugged in and keys in a command. A legend flashes up on the screen – BBC LOW FREQUENCY DATA SERVICE. The sirens are radio-activated via a digital link to the BBC transmitter at Droitwich. Jenny enters a password; there is a short delay before Droitwich responds, then the display changes to an outline map of the county headed TIDAL FLOOD WARNING SIRENS. Jenny now has operational control of all thirty-five sirens in the Essex region. She has already warned borough authorities to stand by. It only remains for her to activate the system.

With rapid fingers she begins, starting in the north with the two sirens at Harwich. Then down the coast to Walton-on-the-Naze, the three sirens at Jaywick Sands, St Osyth and Brightlingsea on the

Colne estuary. Next comes Wivenhoe at the head of the river, two sirens there. On again to the Blackwater, starting with Tollesbury, Heybridge, Maylandsea, St Lawrence Bay, Southminster and the siren on the clock tower at Burnham-on-Crouch. Three more at South Woodham Ferrers, then across the Crouch to the police stations at Hullbridge and South Benfleet. In her mind's eye she pictures the storm-bound coast, the rivers and inlets hammered by the winds and the bleak salt-marsh islands shivering behind their dykes.

She clicks to the last division. Now she has reached the Thames and Canvey Island, the most vulnerable spot on the whole coast, a whole ten sirens here to be activated. Then it is up the Thames to the London approaches and the final pair of horns at the port towns of Tilbury and Grays within sight of the Dartford Crossing.

Jenny sits back. She checks again that all thirty-five sites on the map are selected. Her hand hesitates a moment, poised over the Send button. It is a solemn moment. She is conscious of the eyes of the rest of the room on her. This is no exercise; this is the real thing – the big one they have all prepared for but hoped would never come. A touch of the key will set sirens howling from Harwich to London. Tens of thousands of people are going to feel suddenly afraid and some of them may die.

Repressing a shudder, she presses the key. The map fades to be replaced by the transmitter message – DROITWICH SENDING. It is done. The final warning has gone out.

19

In the south London borough of Southwark, EPO Sandy Middleditch is in his last year before retirement. Talk about going out with a bang, he mutters to his Chief Executive. Sandy has no illusions about the special problems facing his borough. Southwark is shaped like an inverted triangle with the base along the river. The five-metre contour runs across the middle, and the northern sector, from Vauxhall Bridge to Rotherhithe, is very low-lying. Living in the flood risk zone are 160,000 people, a high proportion of them council tenants. According to the old plans these people can expect floods averaging five feet in depth for up to five days.

Southwark's flood zone includes Guy's Hospital, London Bridge station, shopping centres at the Elephant and Castle and Surrey Quays, Millwall football stadium, the Mayor's new offices at Tower Bridge, Shakespeare's Globe Theatre and the capital's most visited tourist attraction, the London Dungeon. All of these have to be sent individual warnings.

Southwark's emergency control centre is located

at the town hall. Sandy's predecessors had the use of the old civil defence bunker but that was sold off, much to his disgust. He has been appealing for funds for a proper communications centre like they have at Hammersmith, but without success. So his first action has to be to wheel trolley loads of equipment into the boardroom.

Once the emergency centre is up and running, Sandy's first thought is for his vulnerables, the old and housebound. Social Services have lists to work from. They also have a small fleet of vans with wheelchair lifts. For general transport the borough emergency plan aims to use the school buses. These can lift five hundred passengers at a go and should be able to ship two thousand an hour to rest centres. Which would be fine if the same buses weren't also required to evacuate the schools.

Sandy rightly reckons that phones are going to be a problem. There aren't enough lines and his mobiles get constant busy signals. There is supposed to be an emergency procedure called Access Overload Control that the Home Office can invoke to block ordinary users from using the mobile network but it is expensive – in the region of £500 per phone per day – and has never yet been used.

In Sandy's opinion two-way radios are more use than phones. The battery life is longer and there is no need to keep redialling, you are instantly on air. Also they do not compete with other users.

In one respect, Sandy is very much an EPO of the old school. He never throws anything away. When a plan is superseded, he date stamps a copy of the old version and stores it away in his archives. And when it came to the Thames Flood Barrier, Sandy never quite trusted the thing anyway. He made sure he kept his old flood map, just to be on the safe side.

The discovery of the map is the first bit of good news Triple-C has had. A police helicopter is ordered to Southwark to fetch it. Sandy Middleditch's name is mentioned as an example of retaining experienced officers in Emergency Planning.

When the copies arrive though, further shocks are in store. The map shows not only the extent of flooding, but also indicates wide areas where water is likely to be trapped behind the banks. It gives figures for the depth of these ponded areas and the average duration of surface flooding, and it becomes apparent that parts of the capital may be submerged for up to three weeks.

'There is also the error factor,' Nikki Fuller puts in.

'Go on,' Raikes tells her.

Contours are subject to a one-metre standard error, Nikki explains. Ground level at the five-metre contour could in fact be six metres or four. 'But that's not all. The standard error is a mean error of a range of errors. In places the contour line could be out by as much as three metres.'

Now they understand. Even a one-metre error could be the difference between life and death, but three metres of possible error means the contours are all but useless in the city.

Graeme Duncan is the Reconfiguration Manager at St Thomas's Hospital, the man in charge of untoward emergencies. In seniority, he is two steps down from the Chief Executive. By the time

Duncan receives notification of the flood from the Department of Health, it is a three-hour warning. Three hours in which to prepare a hospital with eight hundred beds. Duncan has no plan to fall back on. This event was never meant to occur. But he has had experience of a flooding incident at Guy's when a 32-inch water-main burst. The hospital bill was £25 million.

The telephone shrills on Duncan's desk. The Chief Executive is forming a task force drawn from all departments and wants him to head it. The Chief runs through a list of names and asks for suggestions. Duncan adds a couple of engineers to balance the loading of doctors and administrators. They are assembling within the next ten minutes.

Before leaving, Duncan checks with his deputy at Guy's and talks to London Ambulance Control. The meeting has already started when he walks in. The A & E consultant is requesting extra staff to be transferred to his department to deal with the influx of flood victims.

Duncan waits for a pause to interrupt. He has a quiet voice, but it carries authority. 'There will be no Accident & Emergency Department,' he says.

Expressions show how little the implications of the warning have been understood.

'If conditions are as bad as predicted,' Duncan continues, 'we have to expect flooding over the Embankment wall as well as from Lambeth Palace Road. Our lower ground and ground floors will be underwater. A & E will be out, as will the morgue, the pharmacies, most of the sterile units . . .'

The head of the Cancer Directorate gives a groan of anguish. For safety reasons, the Radiotherapy

Department is located on the ground floor. It contains a selection of hugely valuable equipment, including the Trust's linear accelerators. The department will take years to rebuild. 'It must be possible to do something,' he protests.

Duncan details one of the engineers to go downstairs immediately. It may be possible to shift smaller items, but the accelerators will be write-offs.

He moves on to practicalities. Other departments, the operating theatres and most of the wards are second floor and above. The medics are concerned about their power supply. With so much monitoring and treatment computer controlled, even a brief stoppage can be disastrous.

The main generators will be out of action, Duncan tells them. And if the generators themselves survive, the switching systems will be wrecked. But there are a number of smaller generators at higher levels and portables for back-up. They should be able to keep going as long as batteries and diesel supplies last. The kitchens and boilers will also be out. There will be no hot water and only very limited food from ancillary kitchens. Telephones will not function.

'Which means,' the Chief Executive takes over, 'we have to shut down as much of the hospital as we can, straight away. No further admissions, clear and close A & E, cancel operations unless life is threatened. Wherever feasible, patients to be sent home early.'

A query follows about the number of day-case and research beds that can be vacated. The advisability of calling in off-duty staff is considered. There is also the question of patient transfers. This is a possibility if ambulances can be made available. Department heads are asked to list priority cases and a team is set up to negotiate with London Ambulance and liaise with hospitals outside the flood zone.

Further teams are assigned to specific tasks: removal of essential drugs and sterile material to the upper floors; restocking of ancillary kitchens and checking supplies of drinking water; arranging transport and follow-up care for early-discharge patients. The list of things to do is endless. And all of them are vital.

Angus has asked to speak to Venetia Maitland. By Cabinet order, the entire resources of the Met Office are concentrating on the storm. RAF weather planes quarter the North Sea; instrument packages aboard ships, oil platforms and ocean buoys radio back readings on atmospheric pressure and wave heights. As fresh data pours in, Met Office computer scientists are frantically reprogramming their machines to crank out improved forecasts on the surge.

In the Barrier control room, the Tide Defence Manager's desk is strewn with charts and printouts. A grim faced Angus sifts through the data with Martin, as the odds against the Barrier mount. With less than three hours to go till High Water there is still no sign of the hoped for drop-off.

When Venetia comes on the line, he outlines his plans. The key element in the defence is going to be controlled undershoot. The aim will be to reduce the height in the lower estuary by allowing a proportion of the tide through into the pool behind the

Barrier. 'We can rotate the main gates, allowing water to flow over the sills on the riverbed.' Reducing the differential will also lessen the strain on the gates, he adds.

There is a risk of course. 'By partly opening the gates we shall be raising the water level in central London, reducing the margin of safety by up to half a metre.' It is a question of staying in control, he explains. 'Releasing water at the Barrier lowers the pressure downstream. It gives us a chance to manage the river a little longer.'

Venetia hesitates. 'Control, I understand. But surely you're increasing the danger to the capital?'

Are you playing God up there? she is asking. And Angus hasn't an answer.

The midday Cabinet meeting takes place in an atmosphere of alarm and uncertainty. The street outside Number Ten is jammed with journalists and news crews. Ministers arriving by car or on foot refuse interviews and hurry inside.

In the press office, early arrivals crowd round the televisions. All channels are now transmitting footage from the east coast. There are shots of King's Lynn and Harwich showing water in the streets and pictures of evacuees from villages in Suffolk. The breached dyke at Dunwich also features prominently. Interspersed with these are images of the Barrier taken from the air, its gates raised against the expected tide.

Finally, the ministers troop through into the Cabinet Room. Venetia Maitland is already there, seated in the Prime Minister's chair. She has chosen to do this deliberately in order to emphasise her leadership. Last to enter is Hardy Davies, the Environment Minister. Davies is an overbearing man with a reputation for political cunning. The oldest member of the Cabinet, he has until recently seen himself as the Prime Minister's natural successor and bitterly resents Venetia's new status. The Thames Barrier is a part of his fiefdom so he is on the defensive. He has convinced himself in advance that his ministry will be made to shoulder much of the blame for the disaster.

When the doors are shut, Venetia kicks off with a summary of the situation. Everyone present has heard the broadcasts and has a fair idea of what is happening. She makes no attempt to play down the crisis. 'We are faced with a national catastrophe. Unless by some miracle it is averted, the heart of London will be rendered useless for weeks, if not months, to come.'

As at the Triple-C meeting, there is shock that more warning has not been given; several ministers demand a formal inquiry. Hardy Davies interprets this as criticism of his ministry. 'All warnings were issued within the agreed time format!' he snaps. Then he rounds on the Home Secretary. She had no right to convene a meeting of Triple-C without consulting other ministers, he declares. 'There has been no proper security, no control over the press, and wild stories are being circulated that the whole city is about to be drowned.'

Venetia replies carefully. 'The stories, as you put it, were caused by a lack of proper information until it was too late. My department first learned of the risk of the Barrier being overtopped at around 8.30 this morning from a source in the Met Office. This was confirmed by telephone with a senior official at DEFRA shortly before 9 am.'

'A call in which you were advised to wait before acting until the outcome of the next computer run from the Met Office, when the situation could be properly assessed.'

Venetia's tone as she replies is icy. 'In view of the potential threat to the capital and its inhabitants, I took the decision to convene Triple-C at the earliest practical moment. The Committee met shortly after ten, by which time we had confirmation from the Met Office and from DEFRA that overtopping was probable.'

Hardy Davies subsides, still fuming.

The Health Minister, the only other woman in the Cabinet, voices her fears for the city's hospitals. Six major hospitals and at least four private clinics will be seriously affected. Half the capital's accident and emergency capacity will be closed.

Defence follows with details of military equipment and manpower. His attitude is fatalistic. 'Aside from getting people out of the Underground and basement areas, there are no proactive measures. All you can do with a flood is wait until it subsides and clean up afterwards.'

In the silence that follows the sound of police sirens outside is faintly audible through the toughened glass of the Cabinet Room windows.

'Panic measures,' Hardy Davies returns to the attack. 'You've lost your nerve. We should wait, I say. Wait and see what happens. Because I don't think it will be as bad as you make out. Because the risks of getting it wrong, of a false alarm, are every bit as damaging as the real thing.'

Doubt shows in the faces of several ministers. 'But surely,' says Education, 'we must do something to prepare people?'

'Not necessarily. According to the police, evacuation plans are clumsy and ineffective. Left to their own devices people react sensibly. Remember, they live and work here. They have almost daily experience of traffic jams, of bomb scares and flooding mains. They are familiar with their patch. They know the back ways, the short cuts, where the high ground is, better than anyone in authority. If water does come over the walls in places, they'll cope.'

Venetia feels her anger rising but she holds her tongue. Hardy Davies is a dangerous adversary.

Doomsters always exaggerate, he is scoffing now. 'What's the worst that could happen? Water in the streets. Basements flooded, some muck, some mess. So what. If we in government keep our heads, so will the nation.'

'Something in that,' Defence mutters. 'If you tell people they're in danger they become frightened. Let them think it's a nuisance and they'll accept it.'

Other ministers are looking confused. Hardy Davies has offered them the easy way out. Do nothing and hope the surge goes away. How many of them, Venetia wonders, will be prepared to face up to their responsibilities.

She rises from her seat, tall and straight, her hair gleaming under the lights. 'That is a counsel of despair,' she says contemptuously. 'I will not sit idly while this city drowns. The nation has a right to expect more of us. There are actions that can be taken. Lives can be saved.' She pauses. 'I called this

Cabinet meeting because I intend to issue a proclamation under the Emergency Powers Act.'

Hardy Davies half rises in his seat, lips drawn back in outrage. 'You are not Prime Minister. You have no authority. I demand a vote!'

'Very well,' Venetia lifts her chin. Her gaze sweeps the assembly. 'Those in favour?'

Slowly the hands go up round the table. The Foreign Secretary is with her, so are Health and Education. The Treasury Secretary is siding with Hardy Davies, along with Culture, the Chancellor of the Exchequer and the Lord Chancellor. Defence has his hand down and so does the Secretary for Trade and Industry, but Mayhew, the Cabinet Secretary, is for. Transport is another vote for Venetia, so is Social Services.

Venetia counts. Seven votes for, seven against. The Leader of the House of Lords is away sick; the Scottish, Welsh and Northern Ireland Secretaries were not summoned. The Cabinet is evenly divided. Hardy Davies can barely restrain his glee. 'Split vote!' he crows. 'A vote of no confidence, I call it. You no longer have the support of your colleagues. I demand you stand down.'

'Not quite,' Venetia remains where she is. 'You forget, I also have the Prime Minister's casting vote. I exercise that in favour.'

No one has anticipated this. Hardy Davies recoils. 'You can't. You've no right,' he splutters. 'It's unconstitutional. I refuse to accept it!'

Venetia continues calmly. 'I spoke to the Prime Minister by telephone before this meeting to obtain his personal authority.' And received his grudging acquiescence, which he has yet to confirm, she reminds herself privately.

'Authority to use his vote or to take emergency powers?'

Venetia does not flinch. 'He left it for me to decide.'

Such is Davies's resentment, for an instant it seems as if he is about to reach across the table. With a visible effort he masters himself. 'Then you had better pray your flood is coming,' his voice is low and heavy with menace. 'Otherwise on your head be it.'

The room darkens. Venetia's face becomes a pale blur against the blackness outside. A blast of wind shakes the building and rain pelts furiously on the window glass. A phone warbles amid the gloom, then cuts off sharply. As the tempo of the rain increases, someone in the hall below, a woman, judging by the heels, jumps up and hurries away down the corridor. For a minute it seems as though the storm is upon them, then the wind slackens, the drumming rain fades. A semblance of daylight returns slowly to the room. That was only a squall.

20

In the Dome arena, the show has reached its climax. Five thousand iridescent stars glitter and sparkle above the rink. Splayed out on the ice lies the evil queen, her crimson robes like pooling blood. And all around her skaters are spinning, leaping, flying through the air in a final joyous dance, the triumph of good . . .

Abruptly, the music stops. Overhead lights flash on. Performers slither to a halt and stand bemused. Members of the audience start to clap uncertainly but the sound is drowned out by the public-address system.

'Ladies and gentlemen, your attention please. This is an important announcement.' The voice is serious, authoritative. 'Due to the possibility of flooding from the River Thames this afternoon, we are having to cancel the remainder of today's entertainment. All visitors are requested to vacate the Dome by the nearest exit in an orderly fashion. Further information will be made available outside.'

For perhaps twenty seconds after the statement ends there is absolute quiet. Then a child cries and, as if this is a cue, a hum of noise builds. The group from Exeter are stunned. They have come for a Christmas treat; what has the River Thames to do with it? Claire Panton finds herself surrounded by a circle of disappointed faces. 'Please Miss, we don't really have to go now, do we?' 'We haven't looked round yet.'

From the row behind, a colleague echoes Claire's thoughts. 'What are we going to do? If we go back to Paddington now we'll have six hours to wait before the train leaves.'

The thought of four hundred and sixty children on the concourse of a main-line station for that length of time does not bear thinking about. 'Is there somewhere else we could take them? A museum or a cinema . . .' Even as she speaks, Claire realises the impossibility. An entire school, without advance notice, they wouldn't be welcome anywhere.

Another teacher pushes his way through the crush to join them. 'I've just been speaking to a steward. According to him, the authorities want us right away from Greenwich. When the flood comes, this entire area will be under water.'

There is a shocked silence. 'But there must be thirty or forty thousand people here,' Claire says. 'They can't expect us all to get away on the Underground in the next hour, surely?'

The teacher gives her a hard look. 'The guy I spoke to said it's either that or swim out.'

'How could they let this happen?'

Across the river at ExCeL, Bob West, the Health and Safety manager, has just broken the news to his stunned Chief Executive. Both men are shaken as they absorb the implications. The timing of the emergency could not be worse. This is a public day with the media present in strength. Reliability is a crucial factor in the exhibition world. If Docklands is once seen as a flood risk, ExCeL's future bookings will dry up overnight.

What's the point of a flood barrier if it doesn't stop the water? Bob's chief rages. If the Barrier was too low, why didn't they build it higher, for God's sake? They must have known there was a problem. Doesn't anyone in government realise the damage this will do to Docklands, to London? To the entire country?

At least, Bob West tells him, ExCeL's main exhibition floor is raised up five metres, above the flood's reach. 'But the car parks and services are all down at ground level. Power, light, communications, heat, water and drains will be lost. Cars won't start and if these height forecasts are correct, people will be lucky if they can wade out.'

The message is clear: customers must be got away before the roads and railway tracks are cut. The show has to close. Faced with the scenario of having 65,000 people trapped on site for the night, the Chief Executive gives the order and starts phoning the insurance companies.

ExCeL's emergency plans focus on fire or bomb threats. The building's multiple exits and three-lane perimeter roadway make evacuation swift. Exercises have shown that both halls can be cleared in four to ten minutes. Today there is no immediate risk to life and no need for alarm bells. The shutdown is carried out in a controlled manner with the halls cleared in sections at a time. Visitors are told to leave by the same way they came in and make their own way home by car or public transport.

'What about the exhibits?' Bob West's anguished deputy wants to know. Some of the kit here carries million-dollar price tags. The losses don't bear thinking about.

'The halls are secure, or so we're told. If exhibitors choose to remove their stands we will give them every assistance. Anything left behind is at their own risk.'

At the Houses of Parliament, David Leech's official title is Head of Security. At New Scotland Yard he is Superintendent in charge of SO17, the Palace of Westminster Division. In effect Leech has three bosses: the Commissioner, Black Rod from the House of Lords and the Serjeant-at-Arms for the House of Commons.

There is a long history here of flooding from the river. A thousand years ago, Westminster was an island among the fens where, according to legend, King Canute tried to hold back the tide and failed. Westminster Hall has been under water at least five times, most recently in 1928. There have also been numerous fires, notably in 1834, following which the Palace was rebuilt using honey-coloured limestone, in the now familiar Gothic style with ornate turrets.

Leech has 470 police, fire and security officers to cover a beat that extends over eight acres, with eleven hundred rooms connected by two miles of passages. The warning from Scotland Yard comes through to his control post on the first floor at No. 1 Cannon Row, across the road from Big Ben.

He picks up the telephone and dials through to the Serjeant's office, requesting an immediate meeting. 'Yes, right away please. I'm coming across now.'

Pulling on his jacket, Leech heads for Parliament Square. It is a grey day outside. The pavements are jammed with sightseers photographing Big Ben and buying souvenirs. To his left the road rises up towards the bridge. Traffic is heavy; it looks as if news of the flood has broken already. On the far side of the square, busloads of tourists are moving past New Palace Yard where MPs enter. An Opposition spokesman hurries in through the gate, a mobile phone clamped to his head, a secretary trotting after him. Leech stops to let two junior ministers from Whitehall go past in a car.

Up ahead, outside broadcast vans are pulled up on the curb by the Victoria Tower and there are TV crews camped on the Abbey Close, a favourite spot for interviews. The cameramen are bundled up against the cutting wind. It's really cold out today. Leech's pass will admit him through any of the doors to the Palace but it's easier to take the St Stephen's entrance. The guards at the barrier wave him through and he slips between the crowds, taking the granite steps three at a time. He counts twenty-six steps, about three and a half metres at a quick calculation.

Passing through St Stephen's Hall, where the House of Commons met before the building of the new chamber, there are five more steps into a wide octagonal chamber with great arched windows and lofty vaulted stone roof. This is Central Lobby, the crossroads of the Palace. Four arched doorways open off from here: to Leech's left is the corridor leading to the House of Commons; to the right the way to the Lords; ahead lie the libraries and dining rooms and the stairs down to the river front and terrace.

The Lobby is thronged as always with MPs and their researchers, secretaries and advisers, journalists and lobbyists, members of the public up on visits, porters and messengers. Six thousand people work in Parliament, but the debating chambers and offices are only one facet of a highly organised community. There are sitting rooms, chapels, bars and restaurants, art galleries, tea rooms, smoking rooms and rooms for playing chess. There is a florist, a gym, a hair salon and a travel agency, even a rifle-range in the basement. From the beginning, Westminster was designed as a living village in its own right. It has a resident population with flats for officers and staff and state apartments for the Speaker and Lord Chancellor.

The Palace never sleeps. Debates frequently last late into the night, occasionally through into the following day. Dozens of committees are at work at any one time and then there are all the other meetings and social events, receptions, lunches, dinners. And to enable all this to continue there are the battalions of maintenance workers and cleaners and the officials of both Houses, the librarians and IT experts, reporters, clerks, shorthand writers and switchboard operators. There are chaplains and mace-bearers, lawyers and accountants, policemen like himself, doorkeepers and cooks and maids. All these people are now at risk.

News of the flood threat has broken on news

channels and several people try to question Leech, but he makes his excuses and hurries straight through the east doorway to the Lower Waiting Hall. The meeting is taking place in the Speaker's office. His pager bleeps him, showing the number of the Assistant Commissioner for Metropolitan Division 8, which includes Whitehall and Westminster.

The AC wants to know if Parliament has shut down yet. Manpower is desperately short. If the Palace of Westminster can be emptied and closed that will release Leech's men for deployment elsewhere. Leech says he is meeting with the Speaker in a couple of minutes and will call back with the answer.

The Speaker's office is very grand. Black Rod is here, an iron-grey general who will be useful in a crisis, and the Serjeant-at-Arms of the Commons, another good man. The clerks have paged the Speaker, who will be out directly. Meanwhile the Director of Works, the engineer responsible for the fabric of the buildings, spells out the position.

The Palace is on four main levels. The ground-floor houses offices, private dining rooms and bars and the river terrace. The Chambers of both Houses occupy the first or principal floor and much of the second. The remainder of the third floor and the fourth are given over to committee rooms and offices.

In the event of overtopping, there is nothing practical that can be done to hold back the water, he says bleakly. 'Fortunately, the principal floor is above flood level. Which leaves the whole of the ground floor, including ministers' rooms and Westminster

Hall. We shall lose some of the kitchens and all the services: heating and air conditioning plant, telephones, electricity, computer networks.'

Leech asks about access. He is concerned about getting people out.

'The east front of the Palace borders the river. So does Speaker's Green on the north side and Black Rod's Garden to the south. On the west side, New Palace Yard is very low and Westminster Hall has flooded before as we know. The same with Old Palace Yard.'

'In other words we'll be cut off,' Black Rod grunts caustically.

Leech wants to know how deep. Will people be able to wade out? The Director shrugs. That depends how wet they are prepared to get. 'At least a metre, is what I've been told.'

Waist deep on a tall man, Leech thinks. And the water will be cold and filthy. People aren't going to want to wade through that unless they are very desperate. He looks up as the Speaker enters; a rangy Scot dressed in formal wig and gown. 'I don't see that we have any option. I think we should start getting people away now.'

'I shall stay,' says the Speaker.

The Downing Street staff have drafted a proclamation under the Emergency Powers Act of 1920. An official walks it through to the Privy Council Office, which shares the building with the Cabinet Office. In order to take effect, the proclamation must be signed by the Queen at a formal meeting of the Council.

Since the matter is urgent, an emergency session

of the Council will have to be called. Three Cabinet rank ministers are required to make a quorum. Together with the Clerk of the Council they will have to fly to Sandringham in Norfolk, the Queen's country estate where she is spending Christmas with her family. Sandringham is not itself in danger, but conditions on the Wash are terrible.

The Clerk of the Council telephones Norfolk and asks to be put through to Her Majesty's Private Secretary. 'Right away please. Yes, in person. I'll hold.'

The wait is only a few minutes before the quiet voice of one of the least known and most influential figures in the country identifies himself on the line.

'The text is not long, Sir Robin,' the Clerk tells him. 'I could read it over to you.'

The Queen's Secretary is a man of few words. 'Remain on the line,' he says when he has listened to the draft. 'I will speak to Her Majesty at once.'

The Queen is in her study working on government papers. 'If the situation is as serious as they say, Robin, then Cabinet ministers have better things to do than chase about the country to have documents signed. Please order an aircraft at once and inform Mrs Maitland that we intend to return to London to see out this flood. We can call the Council meeting in Buckingham Palace.'

Venetia comes back through the communicating corridor from Number Ten to the Cabinet Office with her Home Office press adviser. Raikes meets them outside the Committee room. 'We need to speak, Minister.'

'Well?' Venetia says.

'The bad news is the traffic. All the bridges are solid, the City and West End as well. Scotland Yard has completed its "black move" out to Hendon. It took almost every motorcycle they have to block off the approach roads to the A2.'

'Yes, I saw the TV pictures. It didn't look good,' Venetia says. Images of the heavily escorted convoy screaming northwards have fuelled fear and resentment among ordinary citizens.

'What about London Underground?' she wants to know. 'Are they clearing people from Docklands?'

Raikes shakes his head. 'I don't know.' It is next to impossible getting through to people and when he finally does he gets conflicting answers. 'Network Control say they are having problems with breakdowns and power outages on some lines but that trains are running more or less normally on the Jubilee. The police are trying to get coaches through to the Dome but the Blackwall Tunnel is jammed solid and traffic is backing up on all the approach roads.'

'What about ExCeL and the Isle of Dogs?'

They at least have the Docklands Light Railway, Raikes tells her. The problem is that all the people are competing for space on the same trains and roads. He lists the figures: Canary Wharf, 90,000 office workers and residents; 100,000 elsewhere on the Isle of Dogs; ExCeL, 65,000; North Greenwich and the Dome, the same; Canning Town, Silvertown, Woolwich and Beckton, 50,000, maybe more. 'Four hundred thousand people? Half a million even?'

If the Barrier should fail, Docklands will be hit first and hardest. Instinct tells Venetia this is too serious to be left to the police and emergency planners. Too many lives are at stake. She looks Raikes in the eye. 'Roland, I want you to take personal charge of evacuations in the Docklands sector. Drop everything else, Home Office Emergency Planning can handle Triple-C, and act as my personal representative. I will sign the authorities myself.'

When Raikes is summoned to Number Ten fifteen minutes later he finds Venetia in the Cabinet Room. A male secretary is just leaving. He nods to Raikes and closes the door, leaving them alone.

Venetia looks up and smiles briefly. 'I've had this drawn up,' she hands him a sheet of paper embossed with the royal crest. 'It is a warrant appointing you as a representative of the Crown and therefore the Cabinet, to act on their behalf.'

The letter empowers Raikes to take any necessary steps to preserve the peace and secure essential services. He can requisition homes and property and require anyone '*to place their person at the disposal of the Crown*'. If they refuse he can order them arrested and detained without trial. Provided he acts honestly and in good faith, his powers are virtually unlimited.

'Keep this safe,' she says seriously, still holding onto the warrant. 'It may cover you later for any actions you have to take if I am not around to defend you.'

At her words, Raikes feels his throat go dry for the first time since the emergency started. She is letting him know that if this turns out badly and disaster falls on the city, then she, Venetia Maitland, will have to answer for it with her career. If the nation's mood is vengeful, conceivably with her liberty.

She is making it clear that whatever he does, she will take the responsibility. His actions will fall on her shoulders.

She stands up, turning to look at him. Under the light, her face is worn, more fragile seeming, the bones finer than before, the eyes deeper, flecked with strain. Only her mouth is as resolute as ever. For the first time he truly appreciates the weight of responsibility she carries. He has a sense of dismay, of abandonment, as if he is leaving her to face her enemies alone.

Her eyes are still on him. Raikes can hear the murmur of voices outside in the hall. He steps forward, draws her close and kisses the straight, soft mouth. She makes a small surprised sound. Her face remains tilted up to his for a moment, an answering pressure, a token of faith between them.

There is a tap at the door. With a gentle sigh she steps back. 'Good luck,' she says quietly.

21

As the sirens shriek their warnings along the storm-battered Essex coast, nowhere do they strike more dread than on Canvey Island. In Basildon and Rayleigh they trigger a panicky dash back to the island by parents and partners working on the mainland. Another stream of vehicles is fleeing in the opposite direction. This, after all, is the site of the single greatest casualty roll in 1953. There are only two roads serving the island, both joining at a single roundabout, and within minutes angry queues build up.

The police station at Long Road has a nominal shift strength of twelve officers. The station is controlled from Rayleigh and even before the sirens sound, the Chief Inspector for the Division begins pulling men off crime teams and traffic to help with the emergency. Officers off shift and support staff are ordered to report for duty, bringing available strength up to forty men and women.

Twenty-two-year-old Constable Lance Harris works the midnight shift from Long Road. Lance lives on the other side of the creek at Hadleigh. He is woken by a call ordering him to report to the local station where transport is waiting. Fifteen minutes later he and eighteen other officers are in a convoy speeding west through lashing wind on the A13 to Basildon. At the Pittsea interchange the convoy turns off southwards and crosses the railway line. A police vehicle blocking a gate pulls aside to let them pass and the convoy enters a track leading out over the marsh. This is the special emergency services vehicle route designed to by-pass traffic blocks in the event of a fire or other incident on the island. It runs down to East Haven Creek, crosses onto the island over a bridge by the barrier there, continues past the landfill site and comes out at Northwick Road. There are more officers guarding the entrance this end and another convoy waiting to travel the route in the opposite direction, carrying elderly evacuees away to high ground.

Down in the town, Cliff Clements has been tensing himself to catch the sirens for the past hour and hoping he won't. Cliff is the master responsible for emergency planning at Waarden Park, a co-ed school with a thousand pupils aged eleven to eighteen. He stands in the main passage as they come surging past him out of dinner, jostling and gossiping and absorbed in themselves as usual.

Cliff Clements is a Canvey Island native. He was born a year to the day from the date his parents moved back to their new house in Sunken Marsh following the 1953 floods. The floodwater washed out the foundations of the old single-storey wooden house, lifted the structure and deposited it in the road. Cliff's parents escaped in their nightclothes to his aunt's house next door where Cliff's father knocked a hole in the ceiling and hoisted the family up into the rafters. At some point during the night the aunt's four-year-old son fell back through the hole into the flooded room below and drowned.

So Cliff knows about floods. The noise of the sirens gives him a sick feeling in his stomach. The school plan for a flood emergency is simple: the school does not open. This is because the plan assumes there will always be at least twelve hours warning. The authorities are so certain of the time factor that they have even designated the school as an emergency centre for vulnerable persons. Cliff received the first warning two hours ago.

What am I supposed to do? he asks the council. Your school has two floors, is the response. Pack everyone upstairs and wait for rescue.

'But we've a thousand pupils here. There isn't room for them all on the upper floor. We haven't the toilet facilities or anything.'

'The building has a flat roof, hasn't it? Put some of them outside on that.'

Cliff looks out the window at the black, scudding clouds. 'You want us to put the children on the roof in this weather? You're not serious.'

'Evacuation is out of the question,' is the chilling response. 'We haven't the resources for one thing. Even if we did, we'd only be moving people into danger. You don't seem to understand, this isn't just Canvey, the whole county is affected. If you're worried you can't cope, try the police. Maybe they can help.'

He rings off. Cliff stares blankly at the phone for a moment. Then he dials Long Road police. All the lines are busy. After repeated attempts he gets through to the station at Benfleet. An officer there promises to do what he can. 'It may take a while but keep calm, we'll bring your kids out. Provided the walls hold, we're told the flooding won't last more than four or five hours where you are.'

Provided the walls hold. Cliff thinks of his own family: his fourteen-year-old son, Kim, here at Waarden; his wife, Lu, who works off-island in a primary school in Benfleet. He tries calling her but can't get a line.

Across Hole Haven Creek at Coryton, Jim Prior, manager of the BP/Mobil refinery, has received the warnings too.

Coryton is the heart of the lower Thames petrochemical industry. For five miles, from Mucking Flats to Deadman's Point, the northern bank is lined with refineries and storage terminals, running back a mile or more into the flat marshlands. Gleaming chimneys stand tall against the sky, hissing plumes of vapour spout from stacks and vents above a thrumming steel maze of cracking towers, boilers and furnaces, pumps, condensers, sulphur units, mixing chambers and collection tanks, linked by multiple levels of branching pipework and spidery gantries. Twenty thousand-tonne storage holders bulge with the products of fractional distillation: gasoline, jet fuel and petroleum gasses, ethane and explosive vinyl acetate. Step outside and the air burns with the raw stench of solvents and exotic petrochemicals bearing alphanumeric prefixes.

Coryton's defences are strong, built to the same standard as Canvey's. The main wall facing the river is a three and a half metre sheer face of reinforced concrete. Four million tonnes of oil and refined products are stored on the four hundred-acre site and its associated chemical plant. Shutting down Coryton is not like switching off a power station. Catalytic cracking is a continuous process, yielding chains of diverse hydrocarbons, ranging from gasses such as butane and propane, through gasoline, kerosene and diesel fuel, to semi-solids like bitumen. Interrupting these processes in anything other than a carefully planned manner is a nightmare prospect. Cooling bitumen hardens like cement and has to be dug out of thousands of metres of steel piping by hand before the cat-crackers can be restarted again.

Prior doesn't want to go down that route unless he absolutely must. He needs a firm yes or no from the authorities. Is there going to be flooding or not? But the answers he gets are ambiguous. 'Over-topping in the Canvey sector is considered unlikely at this stage. There remains however a possibility of localised problems due to wave and spray action.'

None of this is any help to Prior, who has a thousand people on site and a VLCC scheduled to berth shortly. He checks with his jetty supervisors that the floodgates along the sea wall have been closed. Confirmation comes back that all gates onto the jetties are locked off, with the exception of No. 4 where the *Pearl Princess* is due to berth. Over his mobile, the foreman says he is standing on the wall and the tide is splashing up to the level of the walkway, higher than he has ever known it.

The window of Jim Prior's office commands a view over a forest of steel towers and piping, ranks of immense storage tanks, steam plumes and chimneys. The plant is robustly built; it has withstood hurricanes. A bit of spray shouldn't pose too much of a threat.

He decides to hold off implementing the Emergency Action Plan for a while longer.

The Port of London Authority controls navigation on the Thames from its headquarters at Gravesend with radar coverage extending out to a line from Dover to Yarmouth. Every ship in this zone is tagged and its progress recorded until it leaves the area. As the sirens sound on Canvey, anxiety is building over the *Pearl Princess*.

Conditions have deteriorated sharply since the tanker commenced its approach five hours ago. Wind speeds are up to 45 knots and wave heights are hitting 5 metres inside the estuary. Currently the radar trace shows the 340-metre VLCC near the Sea Reach 6 buoy. Four smaller traces close by indicate tugs being sent to meet her. The PLA Harbourmaster is talking to the pilot over the radio, asking him for a condition report. This is an Inner List Berthing pilot brought out by one of the tugs to take over command from the Sea pilot for the final five miles of the journey up-river. It is his job to supervise the delicate manoeuvre of swinging the huge vessel into her berth at the Coryton terminal.

The pilot is nervous. He is short of breath, partly from anxiety and partly from the 120-foot climb up two ladders and six decks from the tug to the tanker's bridge. The vessel is making 7 knots over the ground, way too fast for berthing. The tide is running very fast indeed and with the strong wind astern the ship is extremely hard to handle at lower speed settings. The engine management system is no help; at minimum speeds it overrides bridge settings to boost power. The ship is new, this is her maiden voyage apparently, and the computer needs fine-tuning. In conditions like these, without tugs to hold her steady, he can't risk cutting the engines altogether for fear of losing control.

The ship is inside the estuary, past the pier at Southend and within sight of Canvey and the oil terminals. The pilot squints through the bridge windows at the 275 metres of deck between him and the bows, hoping to see that the crew has gone to stations ready to secure the tows to his tugs. He can't make out anybody at all. According to the GPS readout, the incoming tide is moving them up-river very fast. It is imperative that they shed speed to make the swing at Coryton.

Both pilots endeavour to impress on the captain the need to secure the tugs. Without them the vessel cannot be slowed or swung and it will be impossible to berth at the terminal or to abort the approach. 'Please have the crew stand by ready!' they tell him. The captain repeats the command complacently. 'Yes,' he agrees.

Another quarter of an hour passes. The tug masters come on the radio. They are in position but cannot pass a tow owing to the absence of crew to receive. They ask can the tanker reduce headway? The Coryton terminal is now clearly in sight. The PLA Harbourmaster demands to be kept informed of the pilot's intentions. They are preparing to declare an emergency in the estuary, whether on account of the *Princess* or for more general reasons is unclear. The log readout continues to show the vessel making 7 knots. Strong winds and currents and the narrowness of the channel make it impossible to stop or manoeuvre.

With speed still far too high, the pilot commences rudder cycling, using full helm first in one direction and then the other, with no discernible effect on speed. The pilots discuss going into emergency stop exercise. This will entail deploying anchors with little chance of instructions to crew being understood or obeyed.

The ship's master at last seems to grasp the urgency of the situation and gabbles into a hand-held radio. Crewmembers appear down on the main deck, moving reluctantly through driving spray to their positions. Tugs report that heavy waves are making it difficult to secure. Canvey Island gas terminal is drawing abreast. Finally the tug *Jen-0* reports that she is secure on the centre lead aft. Immediately she is ordered to lean back on the tow. Soon afterwards a second tug secures on the starboard bow. This is the minimum configuration necessary to swing such a large vessel, provided speed can be reduced sufficiently.

On shore in the refinery, Jim Prior has finally had enough. The Essex Catchment Office, which is responsible for this section of the defences, has phoned through with the latest assessment from the Barrier. This shows tide levels brimming the walls downstream, with waves spilling over the crests on exposed stretches. Localised flooding is now a definite possibility. Prior is concerned for his berthing team. The jetty extends out into deep water and conditions on it are fast becoming too dangerous to work, with heavy waves breaking against the pilings, sending sheets of spray bursting over the jetty itself. The foreman says there is nothing now between them and the open sea; they will have to withdraw unless the tanker succeeds in docking in the next few minutes. Prior orders his staff to send non-essential personnel home and prepare shut-down procedures for everything except the fluidised catalytic-cracker units.

The *Pearl Princess* is coming up to Hole Haven Creek. The sea pilot reports from the bridge wing that the two remaining tugs have secured successfully. With the tug aft going full astern with her engines, speed is down to six knots, still too fast to swing. This is the final abort position before the berthing point and the ship is now committed to continuing.

The bows draw level with the big Occidental Jetty in the middle of Hole Haven. There is a smaller vessel berthed here, a North Sea shuttle, her tanks full of gasoline from the Coryton refinery, outward bound and waiting for a tow. The *Princess* is two lengths short of Coryton No. 4 berth. From this distance it is apparent how high the river has risen during the past hour and a half. Waves are slapping close to the top of the jetty with spray breaking across the roadway. There is little time to worry about such matters however. The channel widens here to six hundred metres; it is now or never to start the swing and never is no longer an option. The pilot sends the two forward tugs over on to the port bow and boosts the engines ahead.

The instant he sees the bows are coming round, the pilot centres the helm and rings for full astern on the engines. Wind and tide are working in their favour now, catching the stern and pushing it around. A quick glance at the log – speed is dropping off steeply. As soon as the reading dips below five knots, he orders the tugs to take the bow round to starboard while he holds the engines full astern.

Coryton No. 4 comes into sight ahead as the giant ship completes her turning circle. The log is reading zero. She is stationary in the water now, requiring only a short thrust ahead on the engines to drop her down against the current on to the spray swept berth where the mooring team are clinging onto the steel railings to receive the lines. The immense bulk of the VLCC is moderating the swell to a considerable degree and, sheltered in her lee from the wind, the men hasten to make the ship fast.

22

The black Jaguar bearing Hardy Davies from the turbulent midday Cabinet meeting sweeps round the corner into Whitehall Place. News vans and TV crews are choking the road and, down by the Ministry, a crowd of journalists is camped out on the pavement. A glint of satisfaction comes into the Minister's eyes. Now is the time to get his version of events aired.

The driver noses a way through and brings the car to a halt directly opposite the entrance. The Minister is ushered through the door and straight into the room rigged up for the press conference.

'Channel Four, Minister . . .'

'BBC News, Mr Davies . . .'

Thirty years in politics have taught Davies most of the tricks about handling the media, but today journalists are in vindictive mood. They are cold and wet and this story has caught them napping. Why were there no warnings, they want to know.

Severe weather warnings were issued, Davies replies, sweating under the lights. 'Well within the required time frame.'

'But not for central London, Minister. Nobody

talked about water in the streets or the Underground being closed or . . .'

'Steady,' Davies breaks in. 'The fact is the Met Office had trouble with the computer model. Elements of the surge tide didn't emerge as expected.'

'You're blaming the Met Office then?' a sharp-faced female reporter interjects.

'I'm not blaming anybody. What I said was, the Met Office had trouble with their model. Next question, please.'

'If there is overtopping, how much are we talking about, Minister? What will it mean for central London?'

'I'm getting differing reports. All we can be sure of,' Davies answers, 'is that, whatever happens, Londoners will cope.'

But the journalists are not satisfied. The sharp-faced woman, reporting for Sky News, comes back quickly, 'If there is massive damage to the capital, will you, Mr Davies, as Minister responsible for flood protection, hand in your resignation?'

The trace of a smirk plays on Hardy Davies's lips as he pauses to consider the question. 'The Home Secretary, acting in her capacity as Deputy Prime Minister, has assumed overall control of the emergency.'

Leaving the journalists to make what they will of this remark, he turns on his heel and leaves the room.

The army has a helicopter waiting in St James's Park behind the Cabinet Office, a five-seat army Gazelle that bounces about like an insect in the air pockets as they lift off. Raikes is a qualified pilot and has flown machines off the deck of a frigate in a Force 8 gale, but this is not the time to be taking the controls himself. Peering down through the nose window, he can see the Mall and Trafalgar Square choked with cars locked nose to tail. It is the same story along the embankments. The flood alerts, coupled with the closure of the river tunnels at Rotherhithe and Blackwall, have paralysed the streets. Tower Bridge is solid with queues of stationary vehicles in both directions. Tiny dots of people hurry across on foot. Just downstream of the bridge there is a momentary glimpse of HMS *Belfast* on the river, her tugs in attendance looking like toys from this height.

Then they are over Wapping and Limehouse next with Rotherhithe on the south bank. Beyond, the river takes a great S-shaped double bend around the Isle of Dogs and the Greenwich Peninsula.

Raikes has a map spread out on his knees and he is talking on a portable radio to the military liaison officer at Triple-C. Get on to London City Airport, he tells the officer. Warn them we shall need to use their facilities to base helicopters for the duration of the emergency. Ask if they can lay on extra flights to cope with passengers wanting to leave the area. They may be constrained by noise level and movement restrictions. If so, contact Air Traffic Control and get the restrictions lifted. Make sure everyone concerned understands the need for urgency.

A green light winks from the pinnacle of Canary Wharf Tower to their left. Across the river looms the long roof of the ExCeL centre with the slender line of the pedestrian bridge spanning Victoria

Dock at the western end of the Royal Docks area. Ahead now are the stainless-steel hoods of the Barrier and the black gates barring the tide. The aircraft wheels to starboard, descending over the river, and the yellow masts of the Dome pass underneath.

Raikes's first impression from the air is that the site is overrun with people. Dense crowds are clustered outside the futuristic coach terminal and underground station with more throngs pouring out from the tent to swell the numbers. He catches the upturned faces of children waving at the helicopter and his heart sinks.

Wind sheer buffets the cabin. The pilot shouts to Raikes to hang on and with a lurch they touch down on the pink tarmac of the main square outside the turnstiles.

The administration block at the Dome is on the south side of the site, across from McDonald's. It overlooks the main entrance turnstiles, also the coach terminal and underground station. Beyond McDonald's is the Millennium Pier, where boat passengers arrive and depart. The entire site is secured by three-metre-high, blue painted steel mesh fencing.

'We're not getting people away fast enough,' are Lamar's opening words.

Raikes pulls up a chair opposite Lamar's desk. He urgently needs an accurate breakdown of the evacuation so far.

'The boats have taken off about two thousand. A round trip to Tower Bridge takes approximately ninety minutes including embarking and disembarking. The ferries hope to manage one more lift and bring the total up to four.'

Raikes is jotting down the numbers. The Dome chief continues, 'At a guess around the same number have got away on foot or by bus up to the railway station at Charlton. A few more by coach too, but the traffic situation is making the roads impassable. And North Greenwich reckons another ten thousand have made it out on the underground, but that is also due to close shortly.'

'Leaving how many? Thirty thousand?'

Lamar snorts. 'It's not only Dome visitors, a lot of local residents are trying to get away too. The only hard figure we have is the number going through the turnstiles – just a hundred and eighty short of forty thousand.'

Raikes's pencil strikes a line across the page. Thirty thousand people with no sure means of getting away. Thirty thousand lives in his hands.

London Underground's Network Control Centre at St James's Park station, across the road from New Scotland Yard, is a place few people get to see. The rows of desks with VDU screens and telephones, the high-backed chairs and operators in shirtsleeves might belong in any modern office. Only the wall screen, displaying an illuminated colour image of the Underground, suggests something different. From this room, staffed twenty-four hours a day, every day of the year, NCC computers can call up CCTV images of the entire system.

Harassed staff are struggling to control a situation that is sliding rapidly into chaos. Multiple power shut-downs have brought large sections of the central network to a halt. Winking icons indicating stopped trains pepper the master track diagram.

Duty manager, Hew Thomas, is talking urgently over the phone to Tom Branson of the Transport Police, who earlier briefed Triple-C. Tom has taken charge at Westminster, on the Embankment, where the system is at a standstill. The tunnels here run right alongside the river and unless people inside can be brought out quickly they will drown.

Thirty-six trains operate the Circle Line. Half are stalled along this sector by the river, together with thirty more from the District. The time is now 12.25. In less than two hours the crest of the surge will sweep over the Thames Barrier. Shortly after, water will enter the Jubilee Line at Docklands. The flood will pour westwards along the Jubilee tunnels straight down to the District and Circle interchange here at Westminster, turning both lines into death traps.

Westminster is a newly built station on the Embankment excavated beneath a palatial block of MPs' offices. The ticket hall is a seething mob. Branson forces his way down to the District and Circle level. There are two trains waiting, both packed with passengers, and a harassed supervisor is vainly appealing to people to clear the platforms.

Three trains are stopped this side of St James's Park and another between here and Embankment, he tells Branson. They are evacuating passengers by the emergency stairs. He has no idea how many have been brought out so far or how many more are still in the tunnels.

Four trains, four thousand passengers in the

tunnel, just on this stretch, Branson thinks. And as many again here, waiting on the platforms. And the same picture repeated at every station along the line. The emergency plan calls for the entire system to be run out inside fifty-five minutes. After that they are into danger time.

Half a mile east at Embankment, the next station along, Paul Suter and a team of engineers are attempting to close a floodgate on the Bakerloo Line that shuts off the track running south under the river. The managers hope that sealing it off will slow the flooding of the main network north and give people trapped there longer to get out. It is a faint hope, but they have to try.

The gate dates from the Second World War and hasn't been maintained since the Barrier opened in 1982. It is made from steel plate, reinforced with heavy beam sections, and weighs six tonnes. The gate sits in a recess beside the tunnel, screened from view by metal panelling at the end of the platform. The machinery is filthy and rusted, the electric motors that operate the winding gear frozen solid. There is a handle for use in an emergency, which Paul and his co-workers are having to make do with.

A distant shout echoes up from the station behind. All four men freeze, listening. Everyone is jumpy. This is not a good place to be. They are thirty metres underground with the District and Circle Line tunnels overhead and the river only a road's width from the station entrance. No one on the team knows how long it will take the water to overtop the wall outside and they don't want to be down here when it happens. Paul has his radio with him and he has stationed a man up on the surface to warn in case of trouble.

'It's nothing,' he says after a moment. 'Just the station staff pulling out. Come on, let's get this done.'

The brake van of the battery-powered loco they have ridden down from the depot holds their tools. They spray rack and gears with penetrating oil and apply grease to the sill and the rollers underneath the gate. Four together, they strain at the winding handle; there is a groan from the massive steel plate. 'Again,' Paul calls. This time the gate shudders; a ratchet clicks on the gears and it inches forward a fraction. 'Keep it moving,' he gasps as they throw their weight on the handle. The screech of metal echoes along the deserted platform. A noise like a wheel binding on one of the older Bakerloo carriages. The running gear creaks and rasps and the track below quivers under the weight as the gate grinds outwards.

'Rest,' Paul calls, wiping his streaming face with his sleeve. The gate has definitely shifted which is something. It is a good foot out into the tunnel. They bend their backs to the work again, heaving at the stiff handle. Ponderously the gate rumbles forward another foot. Round goes the winding handle. After a few turns it gets stiffer. Paul orders another halt while more oil is applied. When they resume, the rollers run freely for several turns. The edge of the gate is halfway over to the far side. Then abruptly momentum slows. The men curse and grunt with effort. There is a snapping sound and the handle gives suddenly, pitching them all into a cursing heap on the ground. When they pick themselves up again and try the handle it spins uselessly. One of the cogs has stripped its teeth.

'Bastard thing,' Paul grunts, shining his torch into the mechanism.

Under pressure from the Environment Agency, Angus Walsh has been forced to grant media access to the Barrier. Numbers are limited but, to her relief, Lauren Khan makes the cut. Whatever happens, hers will be an eyewitness account.

In the operations room there is an air of expectancy as Angus returns to his desk. He checks the power supply to the gate piers. All the generators are run up, the power packs functioning normally. 'Right,' he tells the team, 'we'll start with Echo.'

At the desk in front, an engineer double-clicks on an icon. Lauren watches from the window. For a few moments nothing seems to happen, then the furthest of the main 61-metre gates begins inching upwards, the lip curving up and over as it rises out of the water. On the up-river side, the surface seethes as if a giant valve has opened far below. Behind her she hears Angus's gruff voice calling the next gate. In a little over three minutes the manoeuvre is complete; all four central gates have moved to undershoot and water is flooding into the Pool of London at a rate of a thousand cubic metres a second.

23

At Coryton jetty No. 4, the floodgate to the jetty has been locked off and the berthing party withdrawn to the safety of the land. Orders are to de-rig the derrick loading arms that connect the pipelines along the jetty to the *Pearl Princess*'s crude tanks. Discharging oil will have to wait for the weather to ease. The tugs are tied up at one of the inshore berths where there is greater protection.

Up in the plant, Jim Prior's office is in turmoil. A fax has been received from the Environment Agency. It refers to 'a likelihood of several centimetres over the walls'. Jim is aghast. He dials the Agency but can't get through; all the lines are engaged. He tells his secretary to keep trying and hand him the receiver the instant she gets an answer.

He breaks out the emergency plan. There are still almost nine hundred people on site. Some, like those living on Canvey, have been given leave to go home. Now there are forty-five minutes left in which to shut down the complex, and the furnaces alone take three hours to cool. The secretary calls to him and he snatches the phone from her. 'How bad is it going to be?' he demands. More serious than we thought, is the answer. Worst-case scenario is thirty to forty centimetres over the top of the walls at Coryton. 'Forty centimetres! That's near on half a metre! You were talking about a bit of spray an hour ago!' He is staring at the big site map as he speaks. Coryton is shaped like a boot with the toe pointed towards Canvey. There are more than two kilometres of riverbank. Half a metre across the top will drown the entire complex in a matter of minutes.

As alarm bells begin to peal through the plant, engineers knock off trip switches, cut fuel to the furnaces and head for the stairs. Pumps stop, compressors fall silent, steam valves vent to air, the catalytic crackers are shut down. Jim winces when he thinks of what this will cost. The emergency plan calls for moving product around on the site, clearing easily damaged sectors, pumping from plant out to the tanks and from tank to tank. This takes time to set up though and he can't risk personnel being trapped on site. The furnaces will still be hot when the water comes up but there is nothing he can do about that. The big fear at any refinery is always fire. Thank heavens, Jim thinks, in the present situation that is one anxiety he doesn't have to reckon with.

Chaotic scenes on Canvey: the surge has swollen the river, brimming the banks from side to side, swarming up creeks and drainage channels with frightening speed. With the entire island under threat, a Joint Emergency Services Control Centre has been established at Benfleet Police Station. Tactical commanders of police, fire, ambulance and local authority will operate from here. The Chief Constable of Essex has invoked an Access Overload Control order from Cellnet and Vodafone. This cuts off all private and business mobile users in the southeast of the county, reserving available channels for official use. Since many subscribers, reacting to TV and radio warnings, are using their mobiles to keep in touch, the result is widespread alarm bordering on panic.

In 1953, residents sleeping on the ground floor accounted for the majority of deaths. Today 70 per cent of housing is two storey, but this still leaves ten thousand people at the mercy of flooding. These are the flimsiest built homes and the ones least likely to be insured. Then there are the caravans out at Newlands that have no protection at all. Many residents have abandoned their homes, piled their valuables into cars and are frantically fleeing the island. Pavements are choked with lines of plodding pedestrians wheeling prams and barrows or struggling with what they can carry: scenes reminiscent of refugees escaping a war zone. But both bridge approaches are blocked and the police are too busy to help. The big supermarket on Northwick Road has been under siege since the start of the emergency. People fight each other over staples, grabbing water, milk, tinned food. When the tills are closed, they simply walk off with the goods without paying.

The scale of the emergency on the east coast is stretching police resources to their limits. The Chief Inspector at Benfleet has appealed for a 'sky-shout' helicopter to broadcast warnings from the air by loudspeaker, but there are only three machines in

East Anglia and all are already committed. It is the same story with manpower. In previous emergencies they have been able to bring in reinforcements from neighbouring divisions. Today, by the time the flood reaches Canvey, most available reserves have been drawn off elsewhere. Help is promised but it will be too little and too late.

When a strategic reserve of six high-wheeled army trucks from the Shoeburyness artillery range becomes available, the Chief Inspector commits them to Waarden Park School. A hundred and fifty of the younger pupils are packed aboard and brought out over the emergency route. Another hundred or so have been collected by their parents and taken home. That still leaves seven hundred and fifty with nowhere to go; at a pinch the upper floor will accommodate six hundred. The army has promised to return while they can but Cliff Clements knows it is only a matter of time before the routes out are cut. He has been ringing round to other schools to try and get them to take some children, but every school on the island is in the same position. While fellow teachers begin to move those left behind upstairs, Cliff goes out onto the roof.

The rain has let up but the wind whips the door out of his grasp the instant he turns the handle, slamming it back against the side of the building, and it takes all his strength to pull it shut again. It is freezing cold out here, there is no shelter at all and the view is terrifying. Low cloud scuds overhead with dizzying speed. Out in the estuary the sea is huge and ugly, frighteningly close, a mass of chopping waves and whitecaps driving furiously against the island. Down along the Esplanade he can make out gouts of spray leaping above the defences. Another great gust shakes the building. The thought of putting children on the exposed roof seems utter madness. Yet if the sea comes, they will have no other choice.

Southend, at the head of the estuary. It is 12.45 pm and the inshore lifeboat has been launched to go to the aid of a yacht off Two Tree Island: 'WAFI's' – 'wind-assisted fucking idiots' in lifeboat slang. With winds gusting over fifty-five knots and fifteen-foot waves out in the middle of the estuary, this is really a job for the big Trent class boat from Sheerness and not Southend's £71,000 rigid inflatable. But the Trent is out on a call in the North Sea and Southend's boat is handier in the shallows – the crew know these waters so they go anyway. The outward trip, running before the wind, passes without incident and three men are taken off. The coxswain judges that conditions are too rough to attempt to tow the yacht in, so it is abandoned and the survivors put ashore at Bell Wharf, Leigh-on-Sea.

Setting out on the return leg, the lifeboat hits a wave the size of a house at twenty knots and goes airborne. The front end flies up vertically and she flips, capsizes end over end. All lifeboats are self-righting and the crew are strapped in and trained for just this eventuality. In fact this particular boat turned over only two months ago without incident. Holding his breath, upside down under water, the coxswain reaches behind him and activates the gas bottle that inflates the self-righting airbag mounted on the engine roll bar. In seconds the boat has rolled upright. The coxswain checks that everyone is still aboard and restarts the engine.

Nothing happens. All engine parts and electrical equipment are waterproofed, so something must have been damaged. Luckily they are still close inshore and the boat is intact. The Hypalon-coated sponson is built in sections so that if one is punctured the others remain inflated. Wind and tide are driving them back towards the wharf. Unshipping the paddles, the crew steer close enough for someone to throw them a rope.

The lifeboat station is at the end of Southend pier, next to the tide gauge house. Again there are two gauges, an old-fashioned drum type alongside a modern bubbler model. In 1953 the old gauge rang a warning bell fitted in a cell in Southend police station. The new gauge passes its data direct to the Barrier by digital link every fifteen minutes. Southend is the gateway to the river. For the past four hours its readings have been subjected to anxious scrutiny.

Southend's gauge passed the 3.8-metre danger mark for London an hour ago and has been climbing relentlessly ever since. For the last twenty minutes it has been steady at 4.5 metres, slightly below the 1953 record but more than two metres above a normal Spring High Water. At this level the defences will hold – just. Nobody, however, thinks it is going to stop there.

Stretching a mile and a half from the shore, the pier is feeling the full force of the seas driving up the estuary. The railway track and walkway are now less than a metre above the water and are being swept from side to side by waves breaking against the piles. The pier head, several times damaged by fire and rebuilt, has an upper level sun deck. It stands on a mixture of 14-inch greenheart timbers, coated with tar for protection and driven fifteen metres into London clay, and concrete piles reinforced with steel and timber.

In the lifeboat station, the half-dozen members of the launch team and reserve for the inshore boat are watching the gauge closely. With the boat out of action, the pier is their only exit. As conditions stand, the walkway is passable. If they have to, they can escape along it back to the land. But if the sea rises much further they will be trapped. For close on half an hour the gauge has held steady. The men know the safety is illusory, that the surge crest is yet to hit. Instinct tells them to get out while they can, but they hold back, reluctant to desert their post.

The crewman watching the tide gauge comes running back in. The reading has jumped half a metre in five minutes and is still rising. The second coxswain goes up onto the sun deck to look for himself. The wind is so strong he has difficulty in climbing the stairs. The sea is a mass of tumbling crests, white with dense streams of foam, driving furiously up the estuary. The spray is so thick it is near impossible to distinguish the land any more. What alarms him most though are the waves now breaking continuously across the pier.

He runs back down to rout out the others. They need no urging. All are already zipped and strapped into sea gear: thermal body suits, dry suits, boots and gloves, life vests and safety helmets. At a clumsy run they start out back down the pier head and onto the walkway, every man praying they have not left it too late. In single file, clinging to the inner rail, they plunge through bursting spray, staggering to keep their footing on boards already awash ankle deep.

They have made a hundred metres when the swirl of racing sea rises about the coxswain's knees. He struggles on a few more paces but the water is getting deeper with every step. Each time a big wave breaks against the pier he can feel a tremor run through the structure and up into his feet. He squeezes up his eyes to peer ahead but all he can see is raging sea. No sign of the walkway at all. Even as he stares, he glimpses a thirty-metre stretch of the outer railing vanish utterly, torn away and smashed to pieces without a sound to disappear into the water. Another tremor runs through the pier. Safety is still a mile off and heaven knows how high the sea will rise. The strain the pier is under must be terrific. All it takes is one pile to give and the whole structure will start to break apart.

'It's no use!' he shouts, pushing the others back with his arms. 'We won't make it!' Even if by a miracle the pier survives, no man would have the strength to claw his way to land. The only hope is to fight their way back onto the pier head and pray that its timbers can hold out above the waves.

On shore, an anemometer at the Army artillery depot records a speed of sixty-two knots at 12.55 and there are reports of localised flooding. By 1 pm the Marine Parade is under water. Fifteen minutes later, the Western Parade has gone and the Sunken Gardens by the pier have filled with water. At about the same time, water spilling over Eastern Esplanade becomes blocked by the boundary wall of a light industrial zone in Victoria Road. The weight builds and two hundred metres of the wall collapses, sending a man-high torrent pouring through the units. Owners caught still shutting up their premises are forced to take refuge on upper floors.

The Southend Harbourmaster is on the telephone to the lifeboat coxswain when the line goes dead. He assumes it is a connection fault till he gets an urgent call from Clifftown. The owner of a house overlooking the Front, who has been observing the storm through a telescope, reports that a fifty-metre gap has been torn in the pier two thirds of the way along its length. The force of the tide pressing against the railway deck has proved too much for the hundred-year-old structure. The position of the marooned crew is now desperate and a helicopter is summoned. There is an acute shortage of these machines and it will be several hours before one can be released.

On Canvey Island, the tide has reached the top of the Benfleet Barrier, severing the emergency route. The narrowing effect of the river is adding an extra metre to tide levels and water first begins to come over the Tewkes Creek wall, filling the drainage ditch behind and penetrating into the caravan park. Police have managed to evacuate the caravans but with only forty officers to cover the island their task is an impossible one. In nearby Sunken Marsh, Constable Lance Harris runs from house to house, banging on doors, shouting to residents to get upstairs. In a bungalow he finds an old lady who has somehow been missed. The water is ankle deep across the path as he goes in. She is a heavy woman; luckily there is a neighbour to help. Together they bring her out, wading up to their knees. Lance can't believe how cold the water is and how fast it has risen; for the first time he feels afraid.

At Waarden Park, to Cliff Clements's relief, his wife has arrived and picked up their son and a neighbour's boys. Cliff is doing his best to keep a cheerful face in front of the remaining children. Then a man comes running in, shouting that water is flooding down the main road. In the past thirty minutes another two dozen children have been collected by their families. It is now certain that the ground-floor buildings will be flooded. Cliff and the headmaster have appealed again to the county authorities and emergency services to organise an evacuation. 'Pupils forced to spend the night out on a roof in this cold will die!' the headmaster warns bluntly.

Across the creek at Coryton, Jim Prior takes the call he has been dreading. 'Sea pouring over the sea wall near the approach to No. 2 jetty, cascading down the back slope and flooding along the refinery sidings.' A minute later the phone rings again: 'Waves also coming over the wall by No. 6 jetty. Flood depth increasing rapidly.'

At the same time the defences along Hole Haven Creek are causing anxiety. This sector is not exposed to wave action and has been constructed to a lower standard with concrete capping on top of the old earth bank. Prior has ordered a special watch kept on the situation. At 1.14 pm he gets an urgent message. 'Overtopping here is cutting away the inside slope. Defences won't hold for long.'

The rearguard of the engineers are still performing the final shut-downs. Jim can't afford to wait any longer. If the creek wall fails, flooding will spread rapidly across the open ground behind the refinery complex, severing the only road out. He orders all remaining personnel to drop what they are doing. He is just in time. Fifteen minutes later a breach opens in the refinery wall and the sea tears through.

24

From Canvey Island to the Dartford Crossing is twelve miles as the crow flies, seventeen by water. Media warnings of flooding from the river have had no noticeable effect on Bluewater's customers. Many, like the Smiley family, live in the dormitory towns of Kent and Surrey. Others have homes in the suburbs, safe above flood level. Still more come from further afield. Cocooned in the warmth and comfort of Bluewater's shopping malls, they bustle about the business of Christmas.

Along with the other stores, ToyStack has been contacted by the Bluewater management with information on the flood threat in the area. The manager offers to let anyone who lives in a danger zone go home.

When she has a moment, Kerry slips out to have a look at the Thamesometer. On the way she passes the TVs at Dixons. They are showing terrifying shots of the sea somewhere on the east coast. Down at Moon Court there is a big crowd around the black slate tide column. Kerry can't get close enough to read the gauge and she feels a sudden panic. Breaking away, she darts through into Marks

& Spencer, up the stairs and out on to the Upper Mall from where she can look down on to the column.

What she sees makes her catch her breath in shock. The gauge is so high, her first thought is the mechanism must have gone wrong. It is showing over six metres and rising before her eyes. As she stands there, it takes another jolt upwards. A man at her side is saying that at this rate the water will be over the banks within the hour.

His words give Kerry a sick feeling in the pit of her stomach.

Among the customers at Bluewater is Sue Perry Smith. Sue and her husband have recently moved to Greenhithe, where they have converted a former pub to live in. Their new home is in a conservation area down by the river.

Tonight Sue and her husband are giving a house-warming party. Sue still has her Christmas shopping to do as well and, to cap it all, there has been a problem with the living-room carpet. This is cream wool, only down a week, and a fault has appeared in the pile. The suppliers have been very good about it and a replacement was laid yesterday. The carpet extends through into the dining room and cost £9,000. First thing this morning a team came round to Scotchguard it against stains and Sue is praying it will have dried out by this evening. She has told her cleaning woman to keep the windows open to air the room.

While doing up the house Sue has practically lived in Bluewater but she has never known it as busy as this week. Today the queues are worse than ever. The management has laid on a courtesy bus service to ship shoppers in to the entrance halls from outlying car parks.

Sue knows the malls well and she does her shopping in double quick time, slipping through the crowds, leaving heavy items to last. She is passing through Moon Court when she too runs into the packed crowd around the Thamesometer.

Sue recalls catching a reference to flooding on the radio this morning. Even so she takes no notice. She does not even bother to try to look at the gauge. She is not stupid. She simply cannot imagine the Thames ever becoming a threat to her life. Her house is ten minutes' walk uphill from the riverside. On a clear day she can just glimpse the far bank from the upper-floor bedrooms.

In fact Sue's house stands exactly astride the seven-metre contour line and comfortably inside the flood zone.

She finishes her shopping and hurries out to her car. The return journey is easier than the outward trip. All the traffic seems to be heading the other way. Down the hill the roads are almost deserted and the skies are dark as night. The pillars of the Dartford bridge are visible, outlined against the blackness behind. The storm is approaching fast. Sue hopes it will pass over before this evening. It will be such a nuisance if it is raining when the guests arrive. She puts her car in the garage and lets herself into the house. Someone has pushed a bundle of leaflets and some plastic bags through the letterbox. Notices about flooding. As if she hasn't enough to do. Sue puts them on the hall table. There is a strong smell of chemicals from the living room. All the windows are shut. She clicks her tongue in annoyance. 'Brenda?' she calls. 'Brenda?' There is no reply.

Belmarsh Prison, Thamesmead. The main gates are open and a line of inmates is being hustled through, each one handcuffed to two escorting officers. Senior officers bark orders. The inmates are wary and uncooperative. They have been taken out of their cells without explanation and before dinner, and nobody has told them where they are going.

The escort officers are sour too. Their orders came from the Chief half an hour ago without indication of when they could expect to be home. On top of this, they are nervous. Escort duty is normally a soft option: a trip to court or to another prison with no more than a handful of inmates and plenty of police back-up. This is different. The entire high security wing is being evacuated. All of them Category A prisoners: terrorists, armed robbers, rapists, psychopaths. Hard, strong men who spend large parts of each day working out because they have nothing else to do. Many of them warrant a guard of more than two officers each, but the Chief is adamant. He is short staffed as it is. This is the way it is going to be done.

The aircraft with the RAF roundels sitting in the car park looks enormous. A Boeing-built HC2, otherwise known as the Chinook, it is more than fifty feet long and twenty feet high and each of the twin rotors measures sixty feet across. A ramp under the tail leads up to the helicopter's belly, which is large enough to hold two Land Rovers.

The lead inmate pulls up at the base of the ramp,

twisting roughly so that the officers cuffed to his wrists are thrown off balance. The trio behind runs into them and there is confusion and cursing before the officers sort themselves out and force the men up the steps. Inside, red canvas bucket seats are folded down along the sides of the fuselage. Each prisoner has to be strapped in with wrists and ankles cuffed to the frame. Most put up a token struggle, but one man needs four officers to force him down. He is wet with sweat and gagging at the smell of oil and hydraulic fluid. 'What the fuck happens to us if this thing crashes?' he bellows again and again until he is too hoarse to speak.

When thirty prisoners and twenty-five escorts are seated, the ramp is raised. The shrill whine of the auxiliary starter motor spooling up is followed by the blast of the main engines. The slap of the rotor blades overhead gathers speed. The cabin tilts upward and the aircraft rises smoothly into the air. It levels out, holding the hover for a moment, before climbing away rapidly towards the southwest.

As it clears the prison, a second machine moves in over the river to take its place. In all, four Chinooks have been tasked to the operation. Between them they will evacuate 120 of Belmarsh's most dangerous and disruptive inmates.

In Docklands, Sophie de Salis has picked up on the emergency and is watching an Internet news flash of flooding in Essex. Although the warnings are dire, Sophie puts much of it down to media hype. Essex is a long way off. It is hard to imagine the London she knows actually under water. It is the nuisance factor that concerns her. Chaos on the roads means she will have to allow extra time getting home.

Then she catches sight of a map on a BBC channel that shows much of west London in the flood zone, including large parts of Hammersmith. Alarmed, she digs out a guide, which confirms that Chrissie's school is exactly four streets from the river.

She dials the school office but the number is busy. She tries Harriet's number and gets the answering machine again. When she redials the school it is still engaged. Chrissie's mobile is switched off; their use is forbidden at school. Sophie leaves a note on her daughter's message service telling her to call the bank.

There is nothing to worry over, she tells herself. The flood will probably not amount to much and, if there is any danger, the school will see the girls safe. With luck Chrissie will go home with Jo Binney and Harriet will look after them.

If only Harriet would pick up the phone, Sophie would feel happier.

On the concourse outside the Dome, the canopied walkways are small protection from the bitter wind. People hunch together, stamping their feet and shivering. Raikes forces his way through the crowd round the station. People are impatient and bewildered and worried about reaching home. One emotion is absent though. There is no fear yet. They know there is a flood coming but they believe the authorities will get them safely away. It is vital that this trust is maintained if there is to be no panic.

One of Lamar's assistants shows him the emergency stairs to the control room. Inside, the lighting is subdued and a full width glass window looks on to a vast ticket hall, suspended dramatically from the roof by inclined columns, faced with cobalt blue mosaic. This is one of the largest underground stations anywhere in Europe.

A harassed station supervisor greets him. 'We have too many down here,' he gestures helplessly at his banks of monitors displaying images of close-packed platforms and escalators. 'Unless we close the station temporarily there will be an accident.'

On a monitor they observe as a train approaches a westbound platform. Passengers surge forwards as it halts and the platform doors hiss open. But the carriages are already jammed to capacity. Only a handful manages to force a way on board before the train moves off again.

The supervisor's eyes keep straying nervously towards the clock. He is terrified of being trapped down here. The Jubilee is the most vulnerable line on the network. If water comes over the walls, North Greenwich and Canary Wharf will be among the first stations to flood. Raikes understands how he feels. He has seen men crack up on submarine escape drills when the water starts flooding into the simulator.

'How many more trains can you run through before close down?'

The supervisor shrugs, 'Four, perhaps five or six at the outside.'

Six trains, Raikes reckons, seven thousand passengers.

The super points to the system map. The whole

line, from Westminster right up to the depot at Stratford in the east, lies inside the flood zone. Waterloo, Southwark, London Bridge, Bermondsey, Canada Water, Canary Wharf, North Greenwich, Canning Town, West Ham, all of them will flood. 'The only route out to safety is northwards, to Green Park.'

Staring at the map, Raikes grasps his meaning. Even when the passengers make it on to trains they will still have to pass through seven stations and three sub-river tunnels before reaching high ground.

'It's eight miles through the tunnels. Sixteen there and back. Twenty-five minutes for the round trip assuming no breakdowns. If we use the east and westbound tunnels together, we still have to wait for a train to finish its trip before we can dispatch another. Work it out for yourself, Commander. Four to six trains are the maximum possible.'

'That's it then,' Raikes says. 'We'll have to walk the rest out.'

Raikes is back in Lamar's office, a map spread out on the desk. Thirty thousand people are to be evacuated on foot and it is a question of fixing the route. A police inspector is giving advice. 'The most direct way is out from Main Square past the coach park down to Peartree roundabout,' he traces with a pencil. 'At the Marshes superstore they can turn east onto Bugsby's Way, follow that round and over Woolwich Road to Westcombe Park station. Total distance approximately a mile and a half.'

The alternative, he says, is to use the hard shoulder of the Blackwall Tunnel Southern

Approach, but Traffic Division reports that this is littered with abandoned vehicles.

Raikes checks the contour lines. The potential danger point is the patch of low ground across the base of the peninsula. If overtopping occurs south of the Barrier, it is here that water will flood down, completely cutting off the Dome.

He is calculating in his head. East Parkside, the start of the route, is a broad avenue with good sidewalks. Farther on, the roads will be narrower and more congested. Thirty thousand people, walking ten abreast in ranks a metre apart – the column will stretch for the best part of two miles. Servicemen can quick march at 120 paces a minute, but these are civilians of all ages, many unfit and unsuitably dressed. They will be hard pressed to average half as much. It will be forty-five minutes before the leaders reach high ground, twice that for the rearguard to get to safety.

Which may be too long, he realises.

25

The first indication of the true scale of the disaster that is about to unfold comes at Coryton. Ted Turner, master of the tug *Jen-0*, knows there is a freak tide on the way – that's why he has tied his ship up here instead of hot-footing it back to Gravesend. He doesn't buy the flood scenario though. Those walls must be all of ten feet, he says to his three-man crew. Can you imagine the water coming up that high?

Except that now the river is coming up faster than he has ever seen before. The inner berths are sheltered to a considerable extent by the deep-water jetty but the dock alongside is awash. The river is streaming unobstructed over the top of the quay. The speed with which the surge crest climbs over the back of the tide is nothing short of phenomenal. Ted is forty-three, he has done a quarter of a century on tugs but this is outside his experience. It is outside anyone's. His first thought is for the vessel's safety.

Jen-0 is one of the new breed of omni-directional tugs. A tough, stocky little vessel with a heavy bow and a high set wheelhouse with 360-degree windows like an airport control tower. Working displacement is a little over a thousand tonnes and she measures thirty-nine metres overall. In place of a conventional propeller, *Jen-0* is fitted with Voith Schneider propulsion units. A VSP unit looks like an egg-beater and sticks out of the tug's flat bottom. The pitch angle of the blades can be varied to give controllable thrust in any direction, so the tug can go forwards, backwards or sideways and still develop equal pulling power. *Jen-0*'s twin Rushton diesels can jointly deliver almost 4000BHP.

Ted settles himself in the padded chair. Set into the console in front of him along with the R/T for ship-to-shore and ship-to-ship distress messages, are radar, VHF and single sideband radio, satnav and echo sounder. The engine-thrust stick is by his right hand and, mounted next to it, the stalk mike intercom to all crew stations. Fixed to the roof are controls for outside searchlights and the three fire-fighting monitors mounted on the mast platform. *Jen-0* carries Lloyds of London FiFi 1 certification, the highest level obtainable. If a tanker catches fire she can go in with a water screen, pick up the towline and pull the vessel off the berth.

Turner figures the safest course is to cast off the warps and take refuge out in mid channel. Steaming slowly into the wind, the four tugs can ride out the surge. He gets on the radio to the other masters; all three are of the same mind. 'Let's get out of here,' the skipper of *Jen-2* sums up their feelings. Turner punches the buttons to start *Jen-0*'s diesels and shouts to his crew to stand by fore and aft. It is pitch dark and the spray is near solid. Swinging *Jen-0* sideways out from the jetty is almost a matter of guesswork even with the searchlights. Cautiously Turner brings her round onto a bearing for open water.

The exact sequence of events that follows remains uncertain. According to one of the deck crew of the *Princess* (there are no survivors from the tanker's bridge) the vessel rides up on the surge crest so violently that the mooring cables snap. Another explanation is that in the panic and confusion aboard, the cables are slipped deliberately.

Whatever the truth, from this moment onwards the master is limited to a choice of evils. The pilots have gone ashore; he is unfamiliar with the estuary, facing weather conditions exceeding anyone's experience. He speaks no English. The ship is facing downstream, the current forcing her broadside onto the now submerged jetty. Perhaps he can hear the hull grinding against the piers and fears sustaining underwater damage.

In such a position a master's instinct is to start engines and regain control. *Pearl Princess*'s captain may believe that if he could manoeuvre his vessel out into the main channel he would have a better chance of keeping her off the mud. The moment he has power he orders Full Ahead.

A ship on the move pushes water away from itself in all directions. Water flows round and under the ship to fill the space left by its passage. Water is incompressible: in areas of shallow draught, the same amount of water is needed to replace that occupied by the hull, but because of the now restricted space, the water must move faster. Friction and turbulence increase, causing the bow to squat, reducing under keel clearance and degrading steering.

Out in mid-river Ted Turner hears the urgent blasts of a ship's horn. He spins around, poised to take emergency action, expecting to see a vessel bearing down on him out of the storm. But the only craft in sight are his fellow tugs and the VLCC still alongside the deep-water berth. Another succession of horn blasts resounds across the anchorage. The berth and jetty are hidden from view by the tanker's huge bulk but something has changed. The derricks carrying the loading hoses which project high above her main deck are further astern now. The big ship is moving, she is under way. She is sliding forwards away from the dock and he can see already from the angle of her forepeak that the current is starting to swing her bow out to starboard. Turner is witnessing the nightmare contingency everyone who works with ships on the river dreads – a fully laden supertanker out of control.

Even as he is thinking this, Turner is ramming his throttles forward, yelling down the radio to the other tugs. 'Paddy, Sam,' he shouts to the masters of *Jen-1* and *Jen-2*, 'take the stern. Try to hold her steady while *Jen-3* and I secure forward.' Simple orders and the only ones he can give in the circumstances. He is not to know that he has just condemned the crew of one tug to their deaths.

The tanker is sliding off the berth with increased momentum. '*Pearl Princess*! *Pearl Princess*!' Turner tries in vain to raise the tanker and warn her bridge that he is coming alongside. There is no response. '*Pearl Princess*! Urgent. This is tug *Jen-0*. Stand by to receive tow. Acknowledge. Over.'

Still no response. It crosses his mind that maybe he is speaking to an empty ship, that the crew have gone over the side. But he can see the water frothing white under the stern where the screw is biting. Someone must be up there. The radio blares back at him: a blast of static, then a voice, high pitched with fear, jabbering in a foreign tongue. It cuts off abruptly and does not return.

Turner switches to the PLA frequency. 'PAN PAN – PAN PAN – PAN PAN,' he calls, prefacing his message with the radiotelephone Urgency signal that guarantees priority over other traffic. 'This is Tug *Jen-0* at Coryton. VLCC *Pearl Princess* unberthed in channel off Coryton. PAN PAN – PAN PAN – PAN PAN. Tug *Jen-0* at Coryton to PLA Harbourmaster.'

'Harbourmaster to Tug *Jen-0*. Say again.'

'VLCC *Pearl Princess* unberthed and manoeuvring unassisted off Coryton Berth Six. Unable to contact bridge by radio. Self and three tugs on station and attempting to secure.'

'Tug *Jen-0*, your message acknowledged. Will try to contact *Pearl Princess*. Advise no other traffic in your vicinity.'

So the PLA have just checked their radar screens and there are no other vessels on the move. That is a help. Not much but some. *Jen-0* is cramming on speed now and so is *Jen-3*. They are steaming against the full force of the current that is running around ten knots, only two and a half knots slower than *Jen-0*'s best speed. The tanker's momentum is building and she is pulling away steadily. Directly ahead in her path, but submerged by the tide, with only its upper works showing like a half-hidden reef, lies the Occidental deep-water berth. Unless the master takes immediate avoiding action, the VLCC will collide with the shuttle tanker *Solaris* moored alongside. And the shuttle's tanks are filled with inflammable gasoline.

Stunned, Turner watches for the *Princess*'s head to start coming round further. But her course remains inexorably straight. The tide flowing into Hole Haven Creek has her in its grip and is dragging her to portside, negating the effect of her helm.

The master has the supertanker's rudder over as hard as it will go but the ship's head doesn't respond. The strong tidal currents are locking her down. The jetty is less than three hundred metres off, hidden from sight by the *Princess*'s bow but he can see the *Solaris* growing larger and closer by the second. Terror engulfs him at the thought of what will happen if the two ships collide. In desperation, the master grabs a megaphone and screams the order to abandon ship. At that moment there is a shout from his first officer. One of the tugs has secured a tow on aft.

It is *Jen-2*'s tow and how she has managed it no one will ever know. She is hauling in on her winch, setting her 1000-tonne weight and 2600 horsepower against the third of a million tonnes and 30,000 horsepower of the supertanker. The Occidental jetty runs straight out from the Canvey shore then bends eastwards, terminating in an H-shaped head with the *Solaris* on the inside berth. With the unstoppable momentum of a mountain on the move, the *Princess*'s bulbous bow slices into the bent arm of the jetty at a shallow angle, its huge weight effortlessly pulverising the timber and concrete piers. In slow motion derricks buckle, cranes totter sideways, buildings and lighting masts collapse into the foaming river.

Without a check the VLCC ploughs on. Dark streaks of oil in her wake tell of underwater damage from the jagged stumps of the piers. A crewman on *Solaris* throws a life raft overboard and jumps. Another follows but the wind blows the raft away before either can reach it. The *Princess* strikes the shuttle tanker at an oblique angle a few metres forward of the superstructure. Her raked bow slices into the smaller vessel's starboard quarter, cutting through steel plating like a tin opener, screeching and tearing in an agonising cacophony of sound. The crews on the tugs tense themselves, waiting for the spark that will turn both ships into an inferno. Miraculously, it doesn't come. The stricken vessel lurches violently away, pitching over to starboard as water rushes in to fill the empty double bottom space, spilling 30,000 tonnes of high-octane gasoline into the river.

Jen-2 has slipped her tow from the *Princess*'s stern barely in time to avoid being dragged over the jetty in her wake. Her skipper can see bodies in the water, crewmen from *Solaris* desperately struggling to swim clear of the gasoline gushing from the holds of the sinking tanker, and on instinct cuts his speed to go to their aid.

It is a fatal move that places him between the submerged end of the pier and the sinking wreckage of the tanker. He is busy with the rescue when a warning shout from the mate alerts him to the danger. The current has caught the *Solaris*'s bow section and is driving it round onto them. The skipper has sea room behind him, or so he thinks. He waits while the last survivor is pulled aboard, then tries to back out, using his Voith Schneider gear to spin his ship around. But in the confusion he has misjudged the position of the submerged jetty. There is an ominous grating sound under the stern and the tug comes to an abrupt stop. The propulsion gear has fouled on underwater wreckage. Sweating, the skipper reverses the thrust, jockeying the tug from side to side to break free. It is too late. While he is still struggling, the drifting menace closes the gap. It strikes the jetty and at the impact a quiver runs through the hulk. With malign indifference it sways, tilts over and crashes down upon the trapped tug.

Up on the bridge of the *Princess*, her captain is struggling to make sense of what has happened. From where he is standing, six decks up from the main tank deck, he is more than forty metres above the water. Half a dozen voices are screaming to him over the radio but the time frame is too compressed for the captain to sort out the voices, let alone guess what they are trying to tell him. It is as if events have switched without warning into double or triple speed. He can feel the tanker's stern is sliding out from under him, which means somehow the tug has lost its hold. He has no way of telling what underwater damage his ship has sustained but knows he has to regain control and for that he has to have steerageway. In desperation he orders full ahead on the engines. The next jetty is coming up fast but there's a chance he can drive her out of trouble if only he can get the rudder to bite again; he crams on all possible power.

Jen-2's stern is wedged beneath the capsized hulk of the *Solaris*. The river is slick with a film of gasoline and the air is full of fumes. There is a deadly risk of explosion and fire. *Jen-1* is the nearest of her sisters to the scene. Her skipper can see life rafts and men in the water. He turns on the pumps and instantly the tug's powerful monitors deluge the wreck with 13,000 litres a minute of fire suppressant foam.

Ted Turner's attention is still on the VLCC. Dark streaks of oil trail in her wake as she emerges through the wreckage into Hole Haven anchorage. The impact with the jetty has ripped though her double skin, gashing the tanks inside her cavernous belly, and has torn away her rudder. But she is still moving, her bows pointed in the direction of Canvey gas terminal.

Jen-3 is bravely cutting round to leeward, putting his vessel between the tanker and the island. If he can get far enough forward, he should be able to force her bows out into the main channel where she can do less harm. Ted is too far starboard to help. He hasn't the speed to cut round in front of the giant bows and in any case the jetties of the Canvey oil-storage depot are too close for him to risk such a manoeuvre. 'Hank!' he calls over the VHF, 'watch your flank.'

Beyond the oil depot, *Jen-3*'s skipper can see the white tanks of the Canvey gas terminal, with the administration building in front. The VLCC's bow wave is arrowing towards the base of the jetty. Any second the great brute will run hard aground and then God help them all. The *Princess* slides on unstoppably and crashes though the base of the jetty. A fountain of muddy water erupts from the river ahead. It is the foot of the tanker's bulbous bow digging deep into the foreshore beneath the wall. They must be much closer in than he realised. There is a warning yell from the mate up on the mast platform. The tanker's side heels round, looming over them like a cliff, blocking out the light.

The terminal building at the Calor Gas storage facility is fronted by a fifty-metre-wide lagoon. The building itself is constructed from concrete panels and glass. The central portion is two floors high and two rooms deep. The nearest and largest of the ten gas storage tanks in the compound stands across a roadway, fifty metres behind the terminal building and more than twice its height. Immediately behind it are six more large tanks, with the remaining three some distance to the west. The total volume of liquid gas amounts to 25,000 tonnes.

To *Jen-3*'s master, those tanks appear to be getting larger and nearer with frightening speed. *Pearl Princess*'s stern slews round towards the shore and the tug is swept inwards with it. The *Princess* buries her nose in the mud and her engines, now going astern, are sucking her towards the shore. The impact collapses the river wall and a torrent of water ten metres deep pours into the flooded lagoon, sweeping the tug through the gap.

Jen-3's master has a last view of the terminal building hurtling towards him. The tug's reinforced bow crashes through the lightly built façade, pulverising glass and concrete, smashing and crushing everything in its path. Backed by the roaring flood, the tug rampages on, tearing a path of destruction clean through the heart of the building. Water bursts through the other side, propelling the tug unstoppably onwards, across the roadway, through the lines of feeder pipes, into the ranks of towering white tanks beyond.

Jen-0 hears the scream of her sister ship's emergency klaxon and doubles back towards the *Pearl Princess*'s stern. Ted Turner knows something is terribly wrong but nothing can prepare him for the scene of devastation that meets his eyes. Everywhere he looks the river walls are gone, submerged. The tide has overtopped the defences all along the island's frontage and water is surging inland unchecked. It is as if the river has doubled in size all at once.

The tanker has fetched up on the mud, listed over to port. A huge split has opened up in her side, forward where the hull has twisted. Oil is squirting from the gap, spreading out across the water in a treacly lake. The terminal office is a gaping wreck, its centre block torn away, a foaming torrent pouring through the breach. Wedged far into the gap is the smashed and broken hull of *Jen-3*.

Behind the shattered terminal building, a cloud of white mist is mushrooming. For a second Ted thinks it must be smoke, but oil fires give off dark smoke and belch skywards. This is different. It is behaving more like a liquid than a vapour. The white mist pours along at ground level before the wind, flowing in among the tanks of the oil-storage depot next to the terminal. It reaches the head of Hole Haven Creek and streams on out across the water without a check. Then, before Turner's gaze, a change comes over it. As suddenly as it has appeared, the cloud fades and vanishes. Within seconds it has disappeared entirely.

'PAN PAN!' Turner has no time to waste

speculating on the cause of the phenomenon. He is on the radio to the PLA, reporting a tanker collision, the sea wall down and lives at risk, a major pollution disaster. Already crude, gushing from the ruptured tanks, is covering the surface of the river, and the wind and currents are hustling the foul-smelling film upstream. Unless the authorities move fast, hundreds of thousands of tonnes of oil will spread to the upper river.

Turner's immediate concern though is for Hank and his men on the tug. *Jen-3*'s skipper is one of his oldest friends. Spinning the wheel over, he drives *Jen-0* through the stinking mess, as close in to the walls as he dares. The tug has an inflatable pilot boat lashed down behind the bridge house. Turner slackens speed, reversing thrust to hold steady opposite the breach.

The mate signals that they are about to launch the boat. Ted checks from the windows that there is no other hazard nearby. As he glances to starboard he is just in time to catch a fireball rising into the darkening sky above Coryton. A fraction of a second later comes the stunning detonation.

26

The main LPG tank nearest the Canvey terminal office has been split open by debris, releasing 4,000 tonnes of propane to the atmosphere. One hundred litres of liquid propane yield around thirty cubic metres of gas. Propane is classified as an extremely flammable liquefied gas that readily forms explosive air-vapour mixtures.

An LPG leak from a ruptured tank issues as a white cloud. The liquid vaporises and expands so rapidly that it freezes the moisture in the air. As it warms, the gas cloud becomes invisible and therefore more dangerous. It is now highly inflammable and will flash up if it comes in contact with an ignition source.

Canvey's storage tanks are fitted with spray systems designed to disperse an escape of gas and prevent the formation of explosive concentrations. But the controls have been destroyed in the violent impact that ruptured the tank. Four hundred metres downwind of the terminal, the Oikos oil-storage depot holds 200,000 tonnes of hydrocarbon products, mostly gasoline and diesel fuel.

Streaming westwards, the gas envelops the massive oil tanks. The vapour cloud continues to expand until it reaches the banks of Hole Haven Creek on the far side of the site. The wind carries it another six hundred metres across the channel into Coryton.

With the refinery shut down, the gas penetrates deep into the complex before the first explosion is touched off at one of the main catalytic-cracking units. The force of the blast tears the unit apart, ripping open pipework and puncturing a number of holding tanks containing volatile petroleum by-products. In the ensuing fire a series of secondary detonations reduces an acre of plant to twisted wreckage. Gasoline and kerosene, gushing from fractured pipes, vaporise in the intense heat and spread the blaze further.

A refinery complex is a bomb waiting to be touched off. The flames of the primary ignition trigger fire and explosions in neighbouring cracker units. One of these erupts in a 1,000-degree inferno, spewing liquid flame over a pressure vessel containing liquid ethylene, setting off chain reactions that rapidly engulf every sector of the plant. In the same instant, secondary ignition flashes back along the path of the cloud, jumping the creek to detonate among the storage depots on Canvey.

A 20,000-tonne tank bursts apart releasing a river of blazing gasoline. The tank is surrounded by a ditch and earth berm to contain such a spill and prevent it spreading fire to other parts of the site. But flooding over the walls has filled the ditches and submerged the berms. The tanks stand unprotected in the midst of a widening lake. Hydrocarbons are lighter than water and the burning fuel licks outwards towards a neighbouring tank containing diesel oil. At temperatures above 100 degrees diesel forms a flammable vapour; once alight it burns furiously. Within minutes the tank collapses in a sea of flame, the steel walls ruptured and fire spreading. A line of gasoline tanks near the river blows up, one after another, flaring orange fireballs hundreds of feet into the air.

Automatic alarms kick in, pealing their frantic summons to emergency rooms on either side of the channel. But the crews have all evacuated and there is no one left to respond. In a catastrophe on this scale, fire-fighting teams could have put up no more than a token fight anyway. The sea is pouring in over the walls on three sides at Coryton, spreading the burning fuel to every part of the complex, while the wind fans the blaze.

With repeated detonations shaking the tug, Ted Turner wrenches the throttles open, screaming to the crew to take cover. Even as the water froths beneath *Jen-O*'s props, sheets of flame ten metres high are leaping among the oil-storage tanks and racing down on the gas terminal. Turner ducks below the wheel housing, shielding his face. A huge hand seems to pick him up and hurl him against the far bulkhead. The bridge is bathed in a brilliant white light as a stunning concussion sucks the breath from his lungs. The windows burst apart and debris rains down on his unprotected body. He hears the thud of heavy objects striking the cabin. The boat rocks and bounces like a toy and a terrible heat sears his hands and arms and back. Dimly, he is aware of screams and sees a wall of crimson flames roaring overhead outside.

Instinct takes over and he struggles dizzily to his feet, ears singing. His hair and clothes are smouldering and he beats at them as he lurches for the controls to the fire pumps. He punches the switch and sees the button light up. Thank God, the auxiliaries are still working. Over against the bulkhead are the levers for remote operation of the monitors on the roof and mast. Turner wrenches them downward. A rumbling vibration fills the bridge and the flames outside are blotted out behind a hissing wall of spray.

Ashore on Canvey, the primary breach has mostly been contained by the wreckage of the terminal building, but this relief lasts only seconds. Some 250,000 tonnes of tanker slamming into the foreshore at two metres a second has the impact of an earthquake. Shock-waves ripple through the subsoil, snapping pilings, shivering foundations. Parts of the clay bed become unstable and a stretch of underpinning starts to slump outward. The sea wall is already under strain from the suction effect of the water pouring over the crest and, once begun, the movement is unstoppable. To a sound like rolling thunder, three hundred metres collapse in a welter of foam.

The sea floods in through the gap, tearing at the edges of the breach, ripping away the concrete and earth of the back slope. The ground behind is all around two metres above sea-level and virtually unobstructed. The torrent sweeps inland as a roaring white wall, twice the height of a man, carrying everything before it. The nearest houses are on a development only five hundred metres from the terminal and people there have no warning at all.

With flooding already a metre deep across the estate, residents are frantically salvaging possessions when the detonation of the first gas tank pulverises the nearest houses, shattering windows and stripping tiles from roofs like playing cards. Moments later the onrushing mass of water bursts through the flimsy fences of the rear gardens. Survivors will swear afterwards that it was the blast that caused the disaster. In fact the two are unconnected.

The houses stand either side of a U-shaped road whose base runs parallel to the shore. By a miracle three of those homes on the seaward side, which take the initial blast and water impact, are empty. The families have evacuated or are at work or school. The occupants of the others are not so fortunate. The flood strikes with the momentum of an express train. Two houses are destroyed entirely. Walls, floors, doors, roofs swept from their foundations, smashed up and obliterated. The bodies of an elderly couple in one are later found buried under three metres of rubble and silt.

Some people never have a chance. In the first moments of the catastrophe, flood levels surge up to five metres. A young mother is trapped on her stairs with her two-year-old son when the water rises two metres over her head, washing her out through a first-floor window. She manages to swim to another house where she is rescued. Her child's body is never found. A man in his forties dives into the maelstrom to save his widowed mother. She survives but he drowns.

To survivors of the initial surge, battered by debris, swept off their feet by wave after wave of freezing water gushing through shattered doors and windows, death comes easily. Twenty-seven men, women and children lose their lives in this cluster of dwellings. The horror of those minutes is captured on the phone tape of the call to Benfleet emergency control by an unknown voice with the frantic plea: 'For God's sake help us!' before going dead.

Two miles inland, Jim Prior has reached the emergency services assembly point on the high ground near Corringham church, where the refinery's fire-fighting teams have regrouped, and is staring back in horror at the scene of destruction. Even out here he can feel the heat of the flames against his face. The fires have taken a hold among the bulk tanks. The wind up the estuary is driving the flames across the site. Fire and flood, a deadly combination.

As on Canvey, the storage tanks are protected by earth bunds – low dykes surrounding a ditch designed to contain an oil spill and prevent it from spreading. In the event of a fire, bunds are designed to hold the complete contents of a tank plus a 20 per cent margin. While automatic sprays deluge the inner ditch with fire retardant foam to seal off the air and extinguish the flames, underground pumps drain the remaining contents of the damaged tank. Large stocks of foam are stored on site and a fleet of fire tenders with their crews is on permanent readiness.

But all these precautions are helpless in the face of the flood. With the bunds underwater, burning oil spreads unchecked. The foam sprays are inoperable and the trained fire crews can't get their tenders close enough to fight the blaze. The flames sweep from tank to tank. Four million tonnes of mixed fuels and volatile chemicals are going up and nothing on this earth will stop them. Next, the wind will carry the flames on to Shellhaven. The refinery there has closed but its storage facilities are still in use, with at least another million tonnes of petrochemicals to be added to the conflagration.

For a mile and more the entire north bank of the river is a ribbon of flames. Oily smoke boils skywards from a dozen huge fire sites. The air is full of the noise of explosions and crashing plant. A 20,000-tonne gasoline storage tank erupts like a giant firework, spewing geysers of blazing fuel into the air. On the Canvey side, where the gas terminal building once stood, only smashed stumps of wall remain and the big propane tank behind has gone completely, blown to fragments by the explosion.

Down the road behind him sounds the wail of sirens. Fire-engines are on their way to the scene from Basildon and Billericay. The authorities might as well have saved themselves the trouble. From his vantage point, Jim can see the floods have already cut the dual carriageway below him, leaving both Shellhaven and Coryton isolated. There is nothing to be done but watch helplessly until the fires burn themselves out.

It is a mile and a half from the Canvey Island gas terminal to Waarden Park School. The blast of the first LPG tank exploding shatters windows all across the town. Inside, on the upper floor of the school, teachers have drawn down blinds over the windows to conserve warmth. When the glass goes, the blinds trap the lethal fragments, reducing the casualties of what would otherwise have been a slaughter.

The explosions and smashing glass creates panic among the pupils. Only the fact that they are jammed in, almost too close to move, prevents a stampede. Teachers wade in, trying to reach the injured. Bloodied children are helped to the make-shift first-aid point where towels and handkerchiefs are ripped up for bandages. Freezing draughts roar through the gaping panes, sending temperatures plunging. Within minutes children and adults are shivering as well as petrified.

Cliff Clements has been rotating staff and older pupils onto the roof for spells of thirty minutes at a time. Everyone is huddled down low to escape the wind and the hot pulse of the blast passes overhead, followed an instant later by the thud of the detonation. Debris from the shock-wave rains down on the roof and one boy is hit by a flying slate. Above the cries from the pupils, comes the wail of a siren close by. The terminal's fire-alarm system has triggered automatically and is sounding a banshee warning.

'Lie flat! Cover your faces!' Cliff shouts as a second tank goes up, bathing the cloud base in a lurid glow. A waft of choking fumes engulfs them momentarily, creating another wave of panic. 'Stay calm! We're in no immediate danger. The wind is blowing away from us.'

'What if it changes direction?' a woman teacher lying prone next to him gasps. 'What if it blows the gas this way?'

'The gas is alight now. It will burn off whatever the wind does,' Cliff shouts back. As he watches the smoke flaring into the sky over Coryton, he can only pray he is right.

27

The explosions and fire along the river trigger an immediate alert via the Emergency Communications Network to Essex County Emergency Centre at Chelmsford. Jenny Pitt, the EPO, takes the message and her heart skips two beats. There are seven top-tier chemical hazard installations in the North Thames region. An incident at any single one is sufficient to trigger a major alert, involving full emergency services response and possible evacuations. Now the four largest have just been swept up into a single inferno. With fire taking hold on Canvey on top of the flood, the lives of thirty thousand people are in peril.

Jenny doesn't hesitate. Speed is vital. On her own initiative, she issues orders for the immediate evacuation of the island. Every helicopter, boat and amphibious vehicle in the region is directed to the task.

Up in Suffolk, Pete Sabbich of 21st SOS has refuelled after the Dunwich mission. The fresh orders jerk the crew from their dinner. 'Get airborne and head southeast,' the dispatcher tells them. 'You'll receive instructions on route.'

*

Down on the water, the mouth of the estuary is a scene from hell. With every second that passes the gaping tanks on shore vomit thousands more tonnes of blazing fuel into the water. Lakes of burning oil, as much as a foot thick, are reaching out across the river. The entire shoreline, far out into mid-stream, is a sheet of leaping flames. Vast clouds of black, greasy smoke smother the sky and cover the decks of the tugs with sooty particles. On the battered bridge of *Jen-0*, Ted Turner watches the smoke plumes. His ship is blistered and blackened and the furnace heat thrown off by the fires beats fiercely through the shattered windows of the bridge.

Jen-0 and *Jen-1* are manoeuvring upstream of the main body of the fire, attempting to control its spread with their foam monitors. They might as well be pissing into the wind. Both skippers are keeping an anxious watch to port where an ominous red glare indicates that flames are massing. Turner is worried that the wind is backing round to the north and that is bad news. It means the torrents of oil and gasoline leaking from the refinery are pushing outwards from the shore into the aptly named Lower Hope reach. Four miles upstream lie Gravesend and the port of Tilbury. Ted has radioed the authorities there that the fires will reach them in the next half-hour. No, make that twenty minutes, he tells them.

Below Coryton the river narrows as the shores of Essex and Kent close in between Tilbury and Gravesend, squeezing tide levels higher still. Building sea defences along this stretch of coast presents special design problems due to deep deposits of unstable, silty and waterlogged soil. Tilbury is especially vulnerable. The wedge of marshland on which it sits is nowhere more than two metres above sea-level.

The town's main line of defence follows the railway track serving the docks, with steel drop gates fitted into ticket barriers on the station platforms. The floodgate protecting the tidal dock has been closed. The river starts to spill over at around 1.15 pm and, soon after, water rises above dock level in the Tidal Basin, flooding onto the quays.

Fire-engines are called to the sewage works where water is leaking in from the direction of Tilbury Fort. They can't stem the inflow and engineers are forced to switch off the pumps. The power station next door has already shut down its turbines and evacuated all but a skeleton staff. The concrete wall fronting the river is founded on greenheart timber piles, strengthened with reinforced concrete buttresses and ground anchors, but flooding is entering the complex from the direction of the marshes.

At 1.20 a police patrol car radios in from the World's End pub down by the ship. Waves are breaking over a thirty-metre section of the walkway along the river wall and cascading down the bank onto the road. At the same time a phone call to the town hall from a farm inland at Coalhouse warns that Bowaters Sluice has burst its banks and floodwater is streaming across the eastern marshes. A patrol car dispatched to investigate is forced to turn back at Parsonage Common. Officers report seeing the bodies of two horses floating in water at least two metres deep.

Down in the docks the tide is slopping over onto the railway track. The moorings of vessels in the main docks have been slackened off and the ship's hulls tower threateningly over the docks. The port superintendent estimates the water level is three metres above normal spring tide and continuing to climb. He and his assistant are now trapped in their office.

At the emergency centre in the town hall, anxiety is mounting. Floods have cut all roads leading out of town across the marshes. The river is pouring into the town from the north, south and east. The telephones are going down, the sewage system is out, and electricity and gas are failing. Eight thousand people are trapped in their houses by water forecast to reach above first-floor level. Chadwell St Mary, the nearest high ground from which help can come, is a mile away by boat. Gravesend, across the river, would actually be a shorter journey. There are two fast-response lifeboats at the RNLI station at Gravesend but they can carry a maximum of eight passengers each.

And now there is another threat – fire! Jenny Pitt's evacuation order has come too late.

Thirty-five minutes out from Mildenhall and Pete Sabbich can't believe what he is seeing ahead. As the lead H-53 swings in over Benfleet in the teeth of the storm, the horizon is black with the belching smoke of oil fires. 'Jeez,' he hears Duke Whalen call over the intercom, 'it's Kuwait all over.'

Awestruck, the crew stare at the palls of acrid

smoke and pools of liquid flame spreading out across Coryton. The fire has engulfed half the refinery complex and burning petrochemicals are carrying the blaze westwards into the storage facility, driven by the forty-knot surface wind. Burst container vessels gape open, smoking to the sky, and gouts of fire spurt up from ruptured pipelines. A brilliant flash paints the clouds in lurid colour and the helicopter shakes from the detonation of a gasoline storage tank a mile and a half away.

'Mask up,' Sabbich orders, reaching for his respirator. The masks are uncomfortable to fly in but nobody wants to inhale oil fire pollutants. Pete checks through the windshield. They are closing fast with Canvey under a 600-foot overcast. At least he assumes this is Canvey. All he can distinguish are rooftops and trees emerging through water. His earphones crackle suddenly. 'British Army Lynx to our two o'clock one mile northbound, three hundred feet.'

'I have him.' The British have several helicopters working the rescue. Operations in the area are being co-ordinated by an RAF Sentry aircraft. 'Can you locate the target yet?'

'Looks like the school coming up dead ahead. I can see kids standing on the roof.'

Sabbich lowers the collective with his left hand and pulls back on the cyclic with his right. The nose tips down as the angle of the downwash changes and he applies a touch of the left pedal to begin turning to port as the aircraft starts to descend. He has the school in plain vision now and wants to circle round, sizing up the situation for the best approach. As they make the turn, Whalen glances down out of his window in time to catch a glimpse of the blackened and twisted husks of the gas terminal tanks. There are fires burning down there too and not all the tanks have exploded yet. A shift in the wind or a chance spark could see the clustered houses to the east consumed in a holocaust.

The other three H-53s of the flight take up a holding pattern as Sabbich makes a low pass over the shattered roofs of the western side of the town. He can see the children and a teacher huddled together on the school roof, around the stairwell entrance. According to the briefing there are more than seven hundred pupils and staff down there. The helicopter can lift thirty-eight combat-equipped troops; they should be able to pack in at least twice that number of kids.

Pete asks Whalen if they have any communication with the school. Duke shakes his head. Negative. Pete looks down at the roof again and makes his decision. If he can hold a hover directly over, Gorgas and Smith can lower the ramp for the kids to scramble up. The stairwell entrance makes it a tight fit, and the wind is gusting to fifty knots, but he reckons he will have to manage.

If he doesn't, seven hundred children will die.

Down on the school roof, Cliff Clements holds his hands over his ears against the roar of the helicopter's engines. Around him children are screaming with fright as the downdraught of the descending machine tears at them with hurricane strength. Screwing up his eyes against the blast, he can make out the tail ramp winding open and see figures crouched in the gap. The helicopter inches down till the ramp thumps against the roof. A man climbs out, wearing a helmet and flying suit, his face hidden by an oxygen mask. He beckons to Cliff. It is apparent what he wants but Cliff is gripped by a spasm of terror. The thought of leaving the shelter of the stairwell, of being swept off the roof by the down draught, is paralysing.

The man beckons again, more urgently. The children are frightened too. The noise and the fury of the whirling rotors makes rescue a horrifying prospect. They would rather face the night here where they are than step out into the void. The crewman pulls off his mask and puts his hands to his mouth. He is shouting something but his words are torn away.

Cliff clenches his fists. With a great effort he drags himself forward, urging the nearest children with him. It must be possible, he is telling himself, or they wouldn't be doing this. Clutching a boy and girl in either hand, he staggers across the roof towards the ramp. As he reaches its foot, the man there grabs the first child and swings her up into the arms of a second man who is standing in the mouth of the fuselage. In two seconds she has passed from danger to safety. The boy goes the same way.

Crouching to avoid the tail rotor, Cliff turns back towards the group at the stairwell. He finds he can stand after all. He waves vigorously at the nearest children. Now that there is someone between them and the ramp, the trip across the roof seems possible. Several of the larger boys and girls start forward, some holding littler ones by the hand. Cliff passes them on across the roof to where the Americans are waiting to receive them. A small boy stumbles and rolls screaming towards the edge of the roof but Cliff grabs him back, thrusting him, literally throwing him, into the arms of the crewman.

Now they have a line going. Pupils plunge forward of their own accord, tottering clumsily out along the roof, girls clutching at their skirts while the wind whips their hair. Cliff tries to keep a count but he gives up after eighty. And still the evacuation goes on. He can see the faces of children inside the helicopter's belly, waving back to their friends. There is hardly any fear now. The rescue has turned into an adventure.

Up front in the cockpit, Sabbich is sweating into his mask with the effort of holding the hover in the face of the gale. He has to make constant small adjustments with the cyclic to correct sideways drift or movement forwards or back. Any movement of the stick changes the blade angle of the rotor, causing a change in altitude that has to be corrected using the collective. As more children pile aboard, the aircraft is getting heavier and he has to pull up on the collective again to increase power and compensate. The smallest error on his part during any of these manoeuvres will send ten tonnes of helicopter spinning out of control into the school building.

'Okay, that's as many as we can take for now,' Gorgas shouts into his mike. Behind him ranks of children squat, squeezed up together on the floor of the aircraft. He makes a cutting off sign with both arms to the teacher standing out on the roof and points upwards to the other machines waiting overhead. The man nods and pushes back the mob of waiting kids. Gorgas climbs up the ramp, checks that all the children are safe out of the way and presses the switch to activate the lifting mechanism. The beat of the helicopter's engines rises as it lifts off and away.

'One hundred and three,' Smith reports to the cockpit. 'Not bad.'

28

The gathering of forces, ordered by Triple-C, continues apace. Two hundred Land Rovers and medium trucks and a thousand troops, together with pumps and other equipment, are preparing to move out from Warminster on Salisbury Plain in columns of fifty vehicles escorted by police. Included in the move are thirty battlefield ambulances with amphibious capability and a complete field hospital. Estimated journey time for the lead units to reach the capital is three hours. Columns will be directed to strategic points around the M25 orbital motorway to await further orders.

Eighteen assault craft and an unspecified number of inflatable boats have been dispatched from the depot at Aldershot to Richmond Park where they will be held pending instructions. Assault boats can carry up to twenty men and are fitted with outboard engines as well as paddles. More trucks and specialist engineer units with JCBs and recovery vehicles for clearing roads are on their way from Catterick in Yorkshire but it will be six to eight hours before they can be brought into action.

In London, the Foot Guards and Household

Cavalry are at full readiness to move at a few minutes' notice. Hyde Park has been cordoned off from the public for use as a temporary airfield and vehicle holding park. The Broad Walk in neighbouring Kensington Gardens is a thousand metres in length and can accept fixed-wing aircraft. The first plane is due to touch down very shortly bringing the Queen from Sandringham in Norfolk. Buckingham Palace has issued a statement announcing Her Majesty's intention to remain in the capital for the duration.

The need now for emergency lanes into the capital is becoming acute. Venetia Maitland orders that they be given the highest priority. Traffic police are being drafted in from all over the country. A company of Military Police – Redcaps – makes up the first convoy arriving from the West. They are specially trained for keeping routes open in this kind of situation. More are available but are mostly stationed in Northern Ireland. Venetia immediately sanctions their transfer to the mainland. She also authorises the transfer of eight of the province's eighteen Puma troop-carrying helicopters, bringing the total available to twenty-three. These will be used to provide lift from outlying areas to central London.

Venetia's next order relates to the Home Office's Emergency Fire Fleet. The thousand self-propelled pumps, the Green Goddesses, are manned by RAF ground crews and intended to supplement the fire service in the event of war. The fleet has been activated earlier. Venetia wants it brought south as quickly as possible.

'It's in hand,' EPD tell her. 'But it's a hundred and fifty miles from Uttoxeter. Many of the appliances are forty years old. It will be tomorrow at the earliest before they can be brought into action.'

'We don't have to wait for them,' is Venetia's answer. 'We can strip every fire station in the southeast of its fire-engines and crews and bring them all to London. The reserves can drop off to fill the gaps as and when they arrive.'

Raikes is in the air again, headed down river to Silvertown, a spit of land, two and a half miles long and in places only three streets wide, squeezed in between the Royal Docks and the Thames. According to his map, flooding will reach three metres south of the docks. As they fly over the Barrier the long plumes behind the gates, caused by water flowing under, are plainly visible. A mile downstream there is a car-ferry service across the river but the tide is over the top of the jetty and the boats are moored up. The Gazelle banks to avoid the chimney of the sugar refinery and the dishes of the satellite earth station slide past below as the pilot sets down in a car park.

Inside the police post, Raikes finds a harassed sergeant struggling to cope. He is the only officer permanently assigned to the district. Division has sent him forty men in police carriers to help with evacuation but he has a population of twelve thousand to manage, including two schools. The vans are out touring the streets with loudspeakers, reinforcing TV and local radio warnings, while the officers go house to house banging on doors. He has asked for more squads to work the Victoria Dock end but with the entire borough under threat Division hasn't the manpower.

He reckons six thousand people are away at work or have left already, mostly by car. Around four thousand are determined to stay put, no matter what. The majority are on upper floors, so that is their choice. Housing is a mix of tower blocks and low-rise. Some people are actually returning home on foot after driving their vehicles out to safety. Which leaves around fifteen hundred anxious to leave. A fair number of those are without transport. Either the family doesn't own a car or someone has taken it to work.

Borough control has promised buses, but the traffic situation on the north side of the docks is a mess. Gallions roundabout is jammed up and Connaught Bridge was closed for a period to allow transporters to bring out equipment from the Defence show. The bridge is open again but cars are moving slowly and his men are advising drivers to head west through Silvertown. The ferry is cancelled. The rail service likewise. The last train out was half an hour ago and he has been told not to expect another. It's three miles on foot to the nearest high ground.

Raikes radios Whitehall to see if he can have the rail service resumed. One more trainload should do it. After some dickering back and forth, the rail company says it will run the train provided a volunteer crew can be found. Raikes tells the sergeant to pack everyone aboard he can. 'Anyone left over send up to the City Airport and we'll try to lift them out by helicopter.' They should be safe there for a while even if they have to stand on the roof.

*

Up at ExCeL, Lieutenant Yves Besnault, commander of the corvette *Drogou* of the French Marine Nationale, is not happy. His ship is stuck inside the Royal Docks with no prospect of escape until the tide retreats.

Yves has been warned by radio that the British authorities are bracing themselves for serious flooding. Helicopters clatter overhead and the bridges across the docks are jammed with vehicles fleeing north. The French would like to help but when Yves goes ashore he can't find anyone in authority. Time is passing and he returns to his ship to order the warps slackened off in preparation for the flood.

From the ferry pier at North Woolwich to ExCeL is under two miles, but it takes time to obtain clearance from Air Traffic to cross the runway at the City Airport. From five hundred feet Raikes can see planes and helicopters queuing on the apron, among them several military transports. North of the docks long queues of vehicles line the dual carriageways leading to high ground.

The huge car parks at ExCeL are deserted. Raikes is impressed by the way the company is handling the situation. Bob West has got all his visitors away safely. Inside the echoing halls employees are hurriedly dismantling the stands and packing exhibits into waiting trucks. The Stealth Fighter has gone and the helicopters, but the Challenger tank is staying. It's too big to move.

Raikes has seen the French corvette from the air. He runs down onto the dock to find her commander. The first person he meets is a Royal Marine major in charge of a team demonstrating assault boats. It is a godsend. Small craft are badly needed. Get your men over to the marinas, Raikes instructs him, and collect up all the inflatables and small boats you can find. 'You have authority under the state of emergency to commandeer anything you need. There will be people anxious to help. Organise a rescue flotilla if you can. We'll use the exhibition halls here as a collection point.'

Yves Besnault joins them at this moment with his offer of assistance. Co-operation is something all three officers are accustomed to on exercises and it comes naturally now. Yves says if someone can designate an assembly point on the south side of the dock, he will bring his vessel across to embark survivors. That will free up smaller craft to concentrate on less accessible areas.

Raikes leaves them to get on with it and hurries back to the helicopter. He needs to check on the Dome walkout. And he still has Canary Wharf and the Isle of Dogs to see to.

The organised close down of the Underground network is in disarray. And now the problems are being compounded. London Underground Ltd draws its power from the National Grid via transformers at Lots Road in Chelsea, Mansell Street in the City of London and East Ham. In the event of grid failure, battery inverter units installed in tube and sub-surface stations will provide 25 per cent of power and lighting, until an 85-MVA reserve power plant at Greenwich can be activated remotely. This takes approximately fifteen minutes.

Unfortunately the Mansell Street sub-station is temporarily out of service while its transformers are being uprated. This would not matter except that now the East Ham and Lots Road supply points lie within the flood zone, as does the power station at Greenwich.

National Control Centre faxes all line controllers warning them that emergency power from Greenwich will be lost when Grid supply fails, but managers are working under intense pressure and some mistakenly assume that they are facing immediate loss of traction power. In a panic they order trains still running to halt and disembark passengers.

Hew Thomas, the duty manager at NCC, is beside himself with frustration and anger. This is exactly what he has been trying to avoid. Frantic calls go out to the line managers, but the damage is done. There are now passengers in the tunnels and London Electricity cannot re-activate the network until every line is checked and reported clear. For forty precious minutes the evacuation of much of the network has to be halted.

Oxford Circus sits at a junction of three tube lines and delays have built up on the Bakerloo as stock is run out northward through the bottleneck at Paddington. The Bakerloo, originally the Baker Street to Waterloo Line, is running a restricted service, missing out intermediate stops. A north-bound train full of passengers has been waiting at Oxford Street for twenty minutes.

Dean Stacey has given up hope of the train ever moving. It is overfull already but more passengers keep appearing on the platform. There are puzzled looking tourists, families with children and West End shoppers, laden with purchases, all crammed in together. Dean has never known it so crowded this early in the afternoon. He is in the middle section pressed up against a blonde in a pin-stripe trouser suit with a crocodile briefcase wedged between her feet.

With a convulsive rattle the doors slide to a close. Or almost to a close. A plump girl with multi-pierced ears is causing a blockage. She giggles and passengers shift grudgingly to make space. The second time round the doors shut.

The train lurches forwards. They are off at last. Dean is a waiter at Pizza Express in Wardour Street and should be at work but his boss has sent him home early for coughing and sneezing over customers. Just thinking about it starts Dean off again, a dry tickle at the back of his throat. Faces round about give him dirty looks. They don't want colds for Christmas either.

They have left the station now and are picking up speed, bodies bracing as the carriage rocks on the line. The blonde's elbow catches Dean in the ribs. There is a sudden glare of lights as they rattle through Regent's Park station without stopping. Dean lives out at Kilburn. The station there is closed so he will have to get out at Queen's Park. Barring any more hold-ups, he reckons to be home in half an hour.

The halt comes without any warning, a sudden juddering stop that throws everyone off balance. Outside the windows, the tunnel is dead black. 'Not again,' someone groans.

*

'London Bridge tide gauge is reading 4.85 metres,' Martin Simpson, the Tide Defence Manager, calls out, striving to keep his tone matter of fact and hide the nervousness he feels.

Angus Walsh stands by the window in the control room, outlined against the ominous sky. Below him the turbid river waits restlessly at the Barrier, its swollen coils writhing off into the smoking murk of the estuary. Immediately downstream of the Barrier the defence consists of a grass bank with a concealed steel core set back some way from the riverside so as to provide for a promenade walk at a lower level. Already the walkway is submerged with only the top of the railing and a line of lamps protruding above the tide level. Behind each of the main gates, frothing patches of turbulence mark where water is sluicing into the Pool of London at an ever-increasing rate. The difference in levels across the gates is down to 1.5 metres.

A level of 4.85 metres is a fraction over half a metre below the crest of the walls at London Bridge and the maximum permitted level under the Act of Parliament. The trigger level for a Barrier closure is any combination of tide and river flow that appears likely to generate a tide height at London Bridge of 4.85 metres.

Martin repeats himself. Angus shakes his head irritably. 'I heard you.'

'Don't you think the time has come to stop the undershoot?'

Angus scowls. 'When I think it is time to close the gates I'll give the order,' he says crushingly. He sees Martin flush. As a senior engineer the man has a right to speak out.

Angus continues to stare at the river. When the surge reaches the Barrier it will overtop the gates by at least two metres. The strain on the gate supports and bearings will far exceed their design limits. Though Angus hasn't voiced his fears to the team, there is a real possibility that one or more gates could fail. Allowing the pool behind the Barrier to fill will reduce the strain on them.

But will it be enough?

TV images of the Coryton blaze are being beamed back to the capital via a police video link. Chief Inspector Harry Lime of the River Police is preparing to evacuate his Wapping headquarters when news comes over the radio that the surge crest is approaching the Dartford Crossing.

'And Gravesend reports burning oil spreading westwards along the wharves towards the marina,' the officer tells him. 'They are evacuating the hospital and lower town.'

'Gravesend?' That's impossible. Gravesend is a major port on the river, six miles at least from Coryton. How can the burning oil have spread that far? Especially with a storm raging? Slicks break up rapidly in bad weather. Yes, he thinks, but in the protected waters of the estuary, the weight of the oil will damp down the waves.

'Any word on Tilbury?' Tilbury is the busiest port on the river and a major container terminal. It also handles large quantities of timber products and bulk paper. If burning oil spreads to the docks, the conflagration will be devastating.

'Nothing since the power station was reported shutting down, sir.'

'Get on to the PLA. Ask them what they propose to do.'

The Port of London Authority office at Gravesend does not respond. 'Try Woolwich,' Lime says. The operations room there answers finally.

'We're throwing in everything we can,' the voice on the radio sounds badly rattled. 'You're talking about millions of tonnes of petrochemicals, everything from gasoline to crude oil and heavy tars, all moving up-river in a solid mat a kilometre wide and up to half a metre thick.'

'What about fire tugs?'

'There were four in that sector but two are sunk and the others are downstream of the fires.'

The Chief Inspector's mouth grows dry. Two fire tugs sunk is unheard of. And if the others are downstream of the fire front . . . 'But there are other tugs surely?'

'Two, but they're trapped behind the Barrier.'

Lime has withdrawn all but one of his division's boats and the single vessel left downstream is equipped for rescue work, not fire fighting. London Fire Brigade has two fireboats with foam pumps but they are stationed upstream as well. The RNLI has a total of seven boats on the river but two are in action down at Gravesend and the others are west of the Barrier.

Hard on the heels of Tilbury comes Dartford with another fuel terminal and more storage tanks to swell the flames. And beyond Dartford lies Docklands. If the flames once get a hold there, then all London will be at risk. An hour from now the blaze could be licking around Tower Bridge.

29

ATTENTION! THIS IS a police warning. Flooding from the river is expected to commence in the Greenhithe neighbourhood within the next thirty minutes.'

The loudspeaker police car passes down the street and the sound fades out as it turns the corner. Emergency plans call for each home in a danger area to be visited individually to check warnings have been heeded, but there are too few men and not enough time. Every officer that can be spared is down along the river, running from house to house, banging on doors and shouting at people to get out. Up here on the five-metre line they have to make do with the car.

Sue Perry-Smith has closed the windows in the living room again and put on a fan heater to dry the carpet. Twice she tries to call her husband on his mobile but can't get through. She hears enough of the police broadcast to be alarmed and hurries to the front door but by then the car has disappeared from view. Sue looks up and down the street. The acrid fumes are stronger and a pall of darkness is spreading over the sky from the east.

Across the street, a woman in her fifties is

stacking sandbags against her front door. Sue remembers the plastic bags stuffed through her letterbox. Where is she going to get sand though? There was a pile behind the garage left by the builders. She rushes to check. There is still some left.

Twenty minutes of hard work later, Sue has a dozen sandbags filled and is laying them against the sills of the front and back doors. A man from next door has lent her some sheets of polythene and shown her how to wrap them underneath the sandbags to keep the water out. She needs more to do the garage but there are no plastic bags left and she can hardly bare to use pillow cases as it said on the radio. Most of her linen is new, replaced when they moved house. With a shrug of despair, she goes to the cupboard and starts to rip open packets.

Outside, there is a frantic burst of last-minute activity, people checking defences, barricading doors. By the time Sue has finished the garage, sheets of water are spreading across the road. A single car splashes by on its way uphill. Everyone has disappeared indoors. The road is now completely covered and water is spilling onto the path. A puddle has formed in a garden opposite. While she is watching it she realises that she is standing in a shallow pool herself. More water is pouring down behind through the garden.

She hurries back into the house, stepping over the sandbag barrier and closing the front door carefully after her. It feels safe and warm inside. She checks the barricades on other doors. No water is coming through yet but the garden and patio are awash and from the front windows the road is no longer visible. She picks up the phone to try her husband again but there is no dialling tone and when she tries her mobile she can't get a signal.

The leaflet that came with the sandbags said something about drinking water. Sue fills the kitchen sink and goes upstairs to run both baths. The view from the windows is astonishing. There are no roads to be seen anywhere, the whole village has flooded in a matter of minutes. When she comes down again, to her horror, she finds a spreading pool forming in the hallway. She grabs a bucket and mops feverishly. It is hard to tell whether the water is coming under the door or seeping up through the floor. She keeps looking over her shoulder to check the living room. If the carpet gets spoilt, I'll die, she thinks despairingly.

Now the water outside is up to the level of her pathetic sandbag barrier. It is no longer oozing through the floor or under the door; it is spurting through the hinges in little jets. Sue throws down the mop and retreats into the living room. She has the futile idea of barricading the inner doors to keep the flood out somehow. The carpet squelches under foot. Sue gives a cry of dismay. It is changing colour, growing darker, dirtier. The surface takes on a mottled appearance as water emerges through the pile.

Sue takes a hold of herself. Now that what she has been dreading has actually happened, she feels a bizarre sense of relief almost. With it comes the ability to think calmly. Clearly the flooding can't be stopped. The only thing to do is to rescue as much as she can. She begins stacking objects on shelves, carrying the little table that was her mother's up to the landing. The water is up to the tops of her rubber boots. It is freezing cold and filthy.

When the lights fail she abandons her rescue attempts and makes one final slow, splashing trip to the kitchen to gather supplies of food, candles and spare batteries. The water is over her knees on the way out.

Upstairs in her bedroom, she throws off her wet clothes and crawls under the duvet with the cat to keep her warm.

At the Dartford Crossing a few minutes up-river, police and managers at the Kent side control point watch helplessly as the first streams of water pour down the sides of the cutting into the bowl shaped tollbooth area. The twin tunnels have been closed off and crossing managers have made an attempt to protect them with sandbags but it is wasted effort. The volume of water funnelling into the approaches becomes a flood that gushes down the slope to the tunnel mouths. Within minutes both tunnels are filled and the level mounts steadily, submerging the tollbooths in an expanding lake.

The bridge is still secure and the control block, but they have lost the truck park, where oversized and dangerous loads are held to await police escort, and tailbacks stretch nine miles to the M20 junction. Police are monitoring the situation anxiously; they are concerned for the twenty or so road tankers parked up on the hard shoulder either side of the bridge, waiting to be allowed across. They are too close to passing vehicles and pose an accident hazard. It is agreed to stop traffic temporarily to allow them onto the bridge.

Other drivers petition to join the convoy. Steve Moran is one of them. His truck carries twenty tonnes of liquid chlorine in a pressurised container emblazoned with Hazchem warning decals. The gas is destined for a water treatment plant in the northeast. Steve needs to be across the bridge by 2 pm if he is to make delivery before the plant shuts down for the weekend.

At Purfleet on the Essex side, there is heavy industry all along the river frontage, with jetties and wharves running out into mid-stream. Defences mainly take the form of a concrete crest reinforced in places with sheet piling; the pressure of the flood tearing over the top of the wall is too great to be sustained indefinitely.

The first breach occurs near the Thames Terminal; the water bursts into the site, rushing through storage sheds towards the railway behind. A police patrol on the London Road sees a wave of floodwater charge along the tracks into the Esso terminal, sweeping a three-metre mound of debris before it. A 4000-tonne storage tank is lifted off its foundations and washed a mile away. At Thames Board Mills hundreds of bales of paper, weighing three and four tonnes each, are carried right out of the site onto adjacent marshland.

At the same time, water is also spreading westwards along the same tracks from the direction of Tilbury and Grays. With incredible rapidity the entire industrial sector is cut off from the high ground behind. In the Oliver Road section, east of the Dartford bridge, fifty trucks are trapped and overwhelmed. Across the area in scores of factories and depots, workers slow in evacuating scramble for safety, wading or swimming through water as much as four metres deep.

It has taken less than half an hour for the tide crest to travel up-river from Canvey to Dartford. At a quarter to two Murdoch Mitchison takes a call from the borough engineer warning him that flooding has reached Greenhithe and is up to the eight-metre mark. 'But you should be secure where you are. The water won't climb beyond the railway track.'

Murdoch and Rita Yorke examine the map. The railway runs parallel with the river, three-quarters of a mile from Bluewater at its nearest point. Between the two is a belt of high ground rising to fifty metres. 'I've checked with our surveyors,' Rita says. 'There are a couple of low spots where roads have been widened but nowhere below twenty metres.'

The margin of safety sounds ample till Murdoch remembers that Bluewater lies below sea-level. He has a mental image of the quarry turned into a lake, with the rooftops of the drowned arcades sticking above the surface.

What the engineers have overlooked is that the hills are formed of chalk and chalk is porous. There are streams and watercourses here that never see the light of day, carving out channels far below ground. The northern slopes have been mined since Palaeolithic times. Modern man has continued the process, enlarging seams, sinking shafts, cutting roads and excavating, leaving the hillsides fractured and drilled like old teeth.

The first sinkhole appears in a patch of scrub woodland on the railway line outside the village of Stone, a quarter of a mile from the river. The ground is sodden from days of heavy rain. As the flood rises, a cavern in the chalk that has never been detected collapses inwards. The inrush of water scours out a path for itself, following fissures till it breaks through into an ancient river course. This develops into the main conduit but there are others, many of them, ranging from trickles to torrents several feet across.

Two Bluewater service engineers are working to clear a drain in one of the outer car parks. The steep walls of the quarry screen the palls of smoke rising to the east, but it is bitterly cold, with a fierce wind, and the distant thump of a blast from down the estuary seems like a peal of thunder to go with the darkness of the sky. The younger man is first to notice the stream running down the cliff. I don't remember that before, he says. Must be all the rain we've had, his companion remarks, unconcerned.

As they watch, the stream broadens out into a small cataract that plunges clear of the cliff face to splash onto the roadway below. Another stream spouts outwards in a milky white jet. The whole quarry wall is trickling with water. A lump of chalk breaks away from the cliff and tumbles down, bringing a small avalanche with it. Out of the gap spews a chalky cascade. More chalk falls from higher up and another spout is added to the first. The two men start to back away, alarmed. Before they have gone a dozen metres there is a rumbling sound behind them. They turn in time to see a fifty-metre section of the cliff face crumble and slide forwards into the roadway. As though a dam has burst, a foaming torrent pours down through the gap.

*

Melissa Smiley is trying on a cocktail dress. They are meant to be looking for something for Chantal to wear to a dance on the twenty-third, but Melissa's eye has lit on a little red silk number on special offer. So while Chantal is checking the racks with her grandmother, Melissa slips into the changing room. She is just pulling the garment from the hanger when the lights go out.

Typical, she thinks. It is pitch black in the cubicle and she can't see her hand in front of her face. She waits patiently for the lights to come on again. Except that they don't. Melissa waits and waits but nothing happens. She can hear other women blundering about and raised voices but she can't make out what is being said. There seems to be a lot of noise, it almost sounds like screaming. Melissa begins to grow worried. Suppose it's a fire? She sniffs but can't smell smoke.

She fumbles round in the darkness trying to find her clothes again. What she definitely does not want to do is run out into the shop half naked and have the lights come on. It is very annoying and she is getting cold. The floor feels freezing under her feet.

She reaches down a hand and lets out a gasp. The carpet is sodden; she is standing in a pool of water. There must be a leak from somewhere. But the water is getting deeper; it is up to her ankles and icy. And then suddenly she remembers about the flood and fear grips her.

30

The fire at Coryton, coming on top of the flood, has thrown the emergency services into chaos. In Chelmsford, Jenny Pitt is frantically trying to co-ordinate. She is thirty miles away from the scene and she can sense an air of detachment creeping over her team, a sure sign, she knows, that events are slipping beyond control.

Local Control at Benfleet is pleading for helicopters and boats and high-wheeled trucks to evacuate people trapped on Canvey. There are twenty aircraft operating over the island, including Chinooks of the RAF, with more promised. But finding machines means taking them from somewhere else and every sector on the eastern seaboard is under pressure. The RNLI boats are already fully committed.

London is screaming at everyone to do something to halt the fires moving up-river. The scale of the disaster on the estuary dwarfs the worst scenario the emergency services have ever envisaged: a VLCC aground, a gas terminal explosion plus a refinery, chemical plant and two oil-storage depots ablaze. The tugs are helpless in the face of millions of tonnes of inflammables pouring into the river on top of the tide. There is a real danger that Tilbury and Gravesend will fall to the flames. On top of that Jenny has just learned that the Lakeside retail centre is still evacuating.

There are so many different agencies and commands competing for resources that it is hard to keep track. Prioritising evacuations is next to impossible with all the people at risk. First Jenny was told that the danger zone for flooding included all ground below the five-metre contour. Later that was changed to ten metres. Now there is talk of withdrawing personnel up to fifteen metres above sea-level. Some groups of refugees are having to be evacuated for a second time. The sheer numbers needing shelter are overwhelming. With the loss of Tilbury sewage works, a quarter of a million residents in the Thurrock area are left without lavatories or drinking water. Emergencies are in force the whole length of the Essex coast. Every school in the county is on standby to receive evacuees and Jenny has alerted the authorities in neighbouring Bedfordshire that she may have to call on them.

There is a desperate shortage of transport. It is not just people that have to be moved, they need blankets and bedding, food, clothing and medical supplies. Road conditions are abominable. Commuters are stampeding out of London, desperate to get home before the floods strike, and traffic is at a crawl on the county's main roads. Emergency centres face an impossible task to keep track of what is where. The police have been forced to lift their ban on mobile phones in order that coach drivers can give their positions.

*

Heroic efforts by lifeboats at Tilbury have succeeded in bringing out the port superintendent and others cut off in the port buildings. Tide levels in the port area are three metres deep in places and much damage is being caused by bulk containers and storage tanks floated off and carried along by the floods. In the oil bunkerage section a pipeline has become dislocated and fuel is leaking out. The first intimation of the approaching fire comes as a stench of oil on the wind, followed by choking billows of dense smoke cutting off the sky. An angry glow develops, moving in from the east, and, before long, red tongues of fire appear out in mid-stream, creeping up-river. In advance of the main mass of flames, an incandescent cloud of fiery particles envelops the waterfront in droplets of blazing gasoline.

Before long, the few ships' crews that have held on find themselves threatened by fires breaking out at a score of different points. Abandoning their vessels, they take to the boats. They are the last to escape. Behind them patches of burning oil are pushing into the tidal basin, setting light to buildings at the southern end of the docks. Efforts have been made to clear the quays but there has been too little time and immense stocks remain to stoke the conflagration.

Someone has left a webcam on a windowsill, trained across the harbour. God knows how it still functions; it must be running on a back-up battery. Power in the port has been out for the past half-hour. While it remains on air, images of Tilbury's agony are beamed around the world. A 30,000-tonne Dutch vessel at the Roll On-Roll Off dock can be seen surrounded by a sea of fire. She has been unable to discharge all her vehicles, some of which carry chemicals in bulk. As flames lick upwards into the superstructure, the ship's cat is visible cowering in a ventilator moments before a titanic eruption from the vehicle deck literally splits the vessel in two.

On the northern quays, eight-wheeled straddle cranes stand abandoned beside stacked ranks of twelve-metre containers. A bulk tank holding thirty tonnes of cooking oil catches alight and explodes, touching off four others in a chain reaction. The explosions devastate a cold store crammed with butter and margarine, and the melting fats will feed the blaze for the rest of the day and night. Beyond the warehouses are the timber yards. Burning fuel spreads in among the pallets of laminates and the flames leap from stack to stack until the heat is so intense that it melts the steel security fence around the compound. Sparks carry on the wind towards the railway where eighteen rail tanker cars of grain alcohol destined for a distillery stand marooned.

The infernos at Tilbury are mirrored on the Kent shore. Wharves and jetties fall to the flames. Riverside Gravesend, including the hospital, has been evacuated, but terrible damage is done to buildings in the ancient part of the town. West of Tilbury, the Thames takes a double loop around the opposing promontories of Broadness and Stone Ness. Here at Dartford an immense industrial concentration has sprung up at Thurrock and Purfleet, either side of the Crossing.

*

As the burning slicks move down on Purfleet, Ted Turner peers through the smoke with red-rimmed eyes at the bridge ahead. *Jen-0* and *Jen-1* are hemmed in to starboard by sheets of flame. Both shores on this stretch are lined with piers and jetties, some extending almost halfway out to the centre line of the river. To avoid running into them the tugs must somehow blast a path with their monitor jets right into the heart of the fires.

He signals *Jen-1* to follow and they swing out in line, *Jen-0* in the lead, her monitors sweeping in front and to port, *Jen-1* a cable's length astern, warding off the flames to starboard. Turner's stomach heaves as gusts of poisonous smoke sweep through the shattered windows of *Jen-0*'s wheelhouse. Half blinded, he ducks and weaves his head, vainly trying to scan a course through the murk. Directly in the tug's path stands a pontoon and jetty serving the freightliner terminal on the Kent shore at Dartford.

With both hands Ted wrenches the wheel round, spinning *Jen-0* on her stubby beam. Flames leap up on every side as the tug ploughs gallantly into the cauldron of fire. The hull sprays are on but the temperature is so great the water explodes into steam on contact. The stench and fumes are unbearable, Ted's head is swimming and he is terrified he may pass out. No ship can survive in the midst of such an inferno; they must find clear water or perish.

The pillars of the Dartford bridge are dimly visible through the flames and smoke. He scans the river ahead for a sign of the pontoon. At the speed the current is driving them, a collision will split the hull. The smoke parts and for an instant Turner glimpses a flaring wooden structure sliding past right alongside. He has just time to throw himself against the deck as flames fill the cabin.

At the Dartford Crossing the authorities are in trouble. They have been congratulating themselves on keeping this vital road artery open through the flood when warning comes of fires on the river. Clearing the bridge of more than two thousand vehicles at short notice is impossible. Worse still, the two convoys of road tankers sent across under escort in the past half-hour have made such slow progress that the majority are still on the bridge. From the crest there is a clear view down the estuary and drivers lean out of their windows to watch the smoke columns rising from Coryton's blazing refineries.

The appearance of the flames at Tilbury causes panicky alarm. Escape lanes are already blocked by drivers trying to beat the jams. The wind blows the smoke towards the bridge, filling Steve Moran's cab with fumes. He closes the ventilators and switches on the air-conditioning. The vehicles in front shrink to dim shapes as a cloud of smoke drifts over the bridge. Somewhere up ahead emergency sirens are wailing. Over the CB radio other truck drivers are discussing what to do. Steve reckons sit tight, they are safe on the bridge and if people start abandoning vehicles, no one will get out.

Minutes later he is changing his mind.

The effect of the current running under the bridge is to throw a mass of burning oil against a shoreline choked with fuel terminals and storage tanks. There is nothing the emergency services or local authorities can do to stem the onslaught. By 2 pm the first of three major terminals is ablaze and shortly afterwards the flames round Stone Ness opposite Greenhithe. Directly in their path, and unprotected, lie the jetties serving the mighty Van Ommeren oil terminal. This is an officially listed top-tier chemical hazard site on a par with Shellhaven. The tanks here hold mainly gasoline and diesel fuel, 300,000 tonnes of it for distribution throughout the southeast. On receipt of the first flood warning the company has activated its emergency action plan, shutting all valves and exchanges and closing down its jetties. The company fire-fighting team has been evacuated and placed under the orders of the local brigade. In the face of disaster on this scale they are helpless.

Mesmerised by the spectacle, people on the bridge can only watch through the smoke and fumes as relentlessly the tide of burning oil invades the terminal. Many have left their vehicles to get a better view, even bringing cameras to record the sight, when the first 20,000-tonne tank blows up two hundred and fifty metres from the foot of the piers.

The bridge stands sixty metres above the surface of the river and the cone of flame blossoms into a monster fireball that engulfs the northern carriage-way. Two hundred metres back Steve Moran feels the heat on his face as he leans out of the window of his cab. For a single instant it hangs suspended in space, a pulsating cloud of liquid fire that flares from red to vivid orange against the writhing smoke, while hideous death rains down on the nearest vehicles. The blue tarpaulin covering a trailer up ahead shrivels and flakes away. Fire spouts from the trailer, licking at the tyres. In another instant the entire truck is a mass of flames. The fuel tank explodes, setting light to vehicles alongside. A car door opens and a figure stumbles out, clothes on fire. The truck is carrying paint or some other inflammable liquid. It burns with a deep roar like a gas jet, drowning out the screams of people running through the smoke.

Steve selects reverse gear. There is a gap over to his right and he tries to squirm the truck's rear towards it. Next to him is a coach with windows full of terrified faces. There is a *whoomp* sound from up ahead and the pressure wave of a second blast rocks the cab. He flicks his gaze back in time to see another fireball boil upwards from the centre of the bridge. That must have been a petrol tanker. Flames are leaping everywhere. A woman blunders into the path of a van trying to reverse between lanes and is dragged screaming under the wheels. And now Steve is truly frightened.

The bridge control manager has a fire-engine on stand-by in case of trouble. It goes haring up the ramp to the bridge, only to be stopped by vehicles reversing back down the slope. From the control post the manager can see smoke billowing up from the centre of the bridge, coiling around the eighty-metre pylons which carry the steel cables. Amid the thuds of more detonations and the crackle of flames can be heard the desperate braying of car horns. Figures are streaming back down the carriageways. The smoke is now so thick it is near impossible to make out what is happening on the bridge itself, just a swarm of blackness shot through with lurid gouts of fire, like a scene from hell.

A police officer comes running in, wild-eyed and hatless. 'Littlebrook power station has gone up!' he shouts. The manager goes white. Behind the officer, across the widening lake covering the tunnel entrances, yellow and red flames are sprouting. Littlebrook stands on the near shore. Its oil-storage tanks are only a few hundred metres off. If they catch and the fire spreads to the viaduct then the thousands still on the bridge will be trapped.

Steve Moran doesn't know what to do. Around him many people are leaving their vehicles and running back down towards the Kent side, away from the flames, but Steve can't bring himself to abandon his truck, not yet. All the far side of the bridge is burning fiercely and the Essex shore, east and west for as far as he can see, is one vast conflagration. Looking down through the smoke at the river he can glimpse patches of oil ringed by fire.

There is a banging on the cab door and a fireman appears in the window, helmeted and clutching an axe, eyes and teeth gleaming in his oil blackened face. 'Are you hurt?' he shouts. 'Well, get the hell out, for God's sake. There's a lorry load of gas cylinders two in front of you.'

Even as he speaks another violent blast shakes the bridge. Flying fragments whang against the cab's skin and the windscreen cracks suddenly into a starry maze. Steve jumps out onto the road. Broken glass and wreckage are strewn everywhere. The heat and fumes are unendurable. Coughing and retching, he stumbles blindly through the smoke. The fire crews have brought up hoses to connect to hydrants along the bridge and are working their way up to the crest, dousing vehicles with jets of foam.

There is a blinding flash. A giant hand lifts him up and hurls him against the ground. The whole bridge shudders beneath him. He can't think or breath, it is as if the air has been sucked from his lungs. His hair is singed and his ears filled with roaring noise. He clutches at the step of an artic's cab to pull himself up, then snatches his hand away with a scream. The cab is red hot.

Acrid fumes sear his throat. Yellow smoke is billowing across the central barrier. Fresh terror grips him. Yellow smoke means chlorine has escaped. An explosion must have cracked the pressure vessel on the truck. Any second now clouds of poisonous gas will roll down the bridge asphyxiating everyone in their path.

Gasping for air, Steve staggers past the cable stays of the back span and down on to the south viaduct. Terrified figures loom up in the smoke, some burned and blackened, clothes scorched off, sobbing with pain. Steve can make out the helmets of more firemen up ahead and hose jets arcing outwards, and amid the smoke an ominous ruddy glow . . .

The flames have reached the Kent viaduct – they are trapped on the bridge.

31

For some people the flood means good business. Right now, every disaster recovery firm in the country has clients in the flood zone screaming for emergency office space. One such company has first call on a complete mirror-image dealing floor over in Dublin. A major bank desperately needs two thousand square metres to put its foreign-exchange operation. Dublin will suit perfectly but the dealers are stuck in Docklands; they will have to be flown out.

The regular airlines have stopped flights into the City Airport but money talks and a charter outfit comes up with a British Aerospace 146 jet at Stansted. It can reach London in forty minutes and load and be off again in another fifteen.

The unique situation of London City Airport demands special skills to make a landing. The runway, constructed on the pier between the former Royal Albert Dock and King George V Dock, is only twelve hundred metres long and the heavily built-up surrounding area imposes a sharply steeper descent pattern than normal.

The BA 146 lines up from the east at an altitude of 3,500 feet over the river. Like a dive-bomber, the aircraft's nose tips down in a 6-degree glide path that throws the crew forwards against their harnesses. Descending so steeply means that the plane is accelerating and the pilot has to apply his air brakes if he doesn't want to slam into the ground. He has to judge speed, height and altitude to a fraction in order to flare out at the correct moment and land on the end of the runway, allowing maximum distance for the aircraft to come to a halt.

Taking off, particularly with a full load of a hundred passengers, requires the length of the runway and a steep ascent to clear the buildings by the dock gates. Today the fierce winds and low cloud make both operations considerably more hazardous.

Down under the Embankment Paul Suter and his team have repaired the shift mechanism on the Bakerloo floodgate, but the gate itself is still locked solid and refusing to move. They have given up and are preparing to see what success they can have with the one at the southern end of the tunnel when Paul's radio beeps. It is Hew Thomas at NCC. A Bakerloo train is immobilised south of Baker Street. The driver says the motor is dead and thinks there must be a short circuit. Hew wants Paul to take a couple of men up the tunnel with him, sort the problem out and get the train running again.

'On foot?' Paul can feel the crew's eyes on him as he says it. The ERU usually travels to the scene of an incident by truck. He listens with half an ear to Hew telling him about traffic conditions on the surface.

Mentally he is calculating the distance to Regent's Park along the tunnel. A mile and a half? Two miles? Twenty minutes' brisk walk, carrying their tools with them. Quicker than driving probably.

'What about the job here?'

'Leave half the team to see if they can get the other gate closed off. When they're done, they can make their way up to the surface and go to Charing Cross.'

Paul doesn't answer. It is something that has to be done. He is the senior engineer, the obvious person to send. The only question is, who to take along? It occurs to him that if the crew left behind fail to get the gate closed before water comes over the walls, then anyone still in the tunnel will have very little time to get out.

Dean Stacey has undone his coat. In spite of the air-conditioning it is hot inside the train and the air is getting stuffier by the minute. Musical plinkings chime up and down the carriage as passengers vainly try their mobile phones. Hardly anyone seems to get through. The woman in the business suit standing next to Dean is listening to a CD player with her eyes closed, her head swaying gently. Her slim left wrist grips the handrail of a nearby seat. She wears a black crystal Rado wristwatch that must have cost more than Dean earns in three months. So far they have been stuck here for twenty-five minutes. During that time there has been a single announcement over the public-address system to the effect that the train is halted 'due to a fault'.

★

Operation Exodus, the evacuation of the Dome, is under way. The first columns of pedestrians have reached the railway station at Charlton and more are arriving at the rate of two hundred a minute. Now there is a fresh problem: where to put twenty-five thousand people?

'No chance of getting them away by rail?'

'None at all,' the Inspector tells him. 'All services into Waterloo and London Bridge are stopped and the eastbound line is already cut by the floods at Dartford.'

Raikes studies the map a moment. 'There are the old Royal Artillery Barracks up on the heath at Woolwich. They're no longer used and you could put an army there, literally. They have kitchens and lavatories, everything. The distance is what . . .?' he measures. 'A mile and a half from the station. Another forty minutes' walk.'

'We can take them through the park. Easier than going by the road.' The Inspector is catching on fast to Raikes's way of doing things. 'I'll get them started.'

'You should have checked with a higher authority before making commitments,' a general at Northwood tells Raikes blandly, minutes later. 'Woolwich Barracks have been pre-empted for military use. There's no question of civilians getting a look in.'

'The Barracks are already activated?'

'That's what I said, Commander. They have been pre-empted as a vehicle assembly point and helicopter base.'

'That's excellent news, General. Please tell them

to send all available transport at the Barracks to Charlton Station on Woolwich Road, where I have twenty-five thousand evacuees waiting.'

'Evidently I did not make myself clear, Commander. Woolwich is unavailable and I will not authorise . . .'

'General,' Raikes cuts in crisply. 'I am acting under the direct mandate of the Deputy Prime Minister.' Unfolding Venetia Maitland's letter, he reads it out over the line. 'By virtue of this authority, General, I am directing you to make the facilities at Woolwich Barracks available to my refugees with immediate effect. You will, additionally, instruct the Logistics Corps to provide food and shelter as may be required until further notice and to see that medical personnel are on hand should they be needed. Do I make myself clear, sir?'

The general gulps. No naval commander speaks like that to an officer of his rank. Unless that commander is totally sure of backing from the very highest authority, in which case . . .

From all across Kent, fire crews and ambulances are converging on the Dartford-Gravesend area. The first appliances to struggle through the M25 tailbacks tackle the oil fires at the bridge approaches. It takes twelve pumps using foam retardant to clear a path through the flames onto the Kent viaduct. Blazing fuel from the Van Ommeren terminal continues to spill into the river, repeatedly threatening to cut off the firefighters. East of the bridge on the Dartford side a huge freightliner terminal has caught light, adding to the chaos. It is as if the whole world is ablaze.

Even when fire crews do succeed in gaining the viaduct ramp, they find the carriageways choked with burning and abandoned vehicles that must be dowsed and dragged away before the hoses can be brought to bear on those beyond. Gas and chemical contamination are deadly hazards, hampering rescue work.

From the viaduct, Steve Moran sees a huge chimney belonging to the power station sway in the smoke and collapse like a child's toy. He and others are clustered around the only fire-engine still to survive on the bridge. The heat from the river fires below has turned the carriageways red hot and the hydrants on the bridge are out of action. Bodies are strewn about, burned, mangled by explosions, suffocated by smoke and heat. The firemen are saving what remains of their precious water supply to damp down a road tanker further up the bridge. If that should catch light, exploding its thirty thousand litres of petrol, everyone present will die a hideous death.

Steve Moran's lungs are sore from breathing the fumes from burning tyres. Every gasp is like sandpaper. Something hot splashes onto his hand, making him yelp, a burning liquid. A bulk tanker containing liquid sugar has caught fire and is spewing its cargo across the roadway. Tongues of burning sugar, spitting and bubbling from the heat, are leaking down towards where he is crouched, like rivers of fiery lava. Suddenly a frightful screaming erupts nearby. A human torch drops from the cab of a truck. The figure writhes on the ground pleading for help. Before anyone can reach him, the man staggers to his feet, stumbles blindly for a few paces, then pitches headlong into the morass of boiling sugar and is swallowed up.

Steve's stomach heaves. They have to get out of here before the fires claim them all. 'Come on!' he shouts. He spots a momentary gap in the flames and seizes his chance, followed by two or three others. They don't get far, barely a dozen metres, before the flames close in. A car explodes right beside them and a man gasps and staggers, his face and hands cut to ribbons by a storm of glass shards. Dimly through the flames Moran thinks he glimpses the helmets of firefighters. Wrapping his coat over his head for protection, he breaks into a lumbering run.

At fearful risk to themselves, the Kent fire crews are trying to open a corridor for paramedics to bring out the injured. As the flames roar around him, Steve slips and falls. He feels his skin burning and opens his mouth to scream when a blast of high-pressure water blasts the pain away. Strong arms pull him up and drag him to safety.

'. . . *one hundred and twenty very seriously injured at emergency dressing points on both sides of the river with more being brought out by the minute. Many with 80 per cent plus burns to the body . . . desperately need helicopter transport to get patients to specialist units as rapidly as possible . . .*'

Over at Number Ten, Venetia Maitland is preparing to speak to other world leaders when the telephone shrills. It is the Chief Constable of Kent almost incoherent with fury. The MOD has refused his appeals for Chinooks to evacuate badly burned victims from the Dartford bridge.

'And Northwood won't help? We'll see about

that,' Venetia says.

An MOD liaison officer attached to Number Ten is already scrambling to contact Northwood. 'Ma'am, three squadrons operate the Chinook HC2, all based at RAF Odiham, but 27 Squadron is currently deployed out of the country on exercise in Norway. It is due back in two days' time. Of fourteen operational aircraft available, ten have been tasked to the mouth of the estuary for rescue operations on Canvey Island. The remaining four machines are transferring prisoners from Belmarsh at the request of the Home Office.'

For a second Venetia can't believe what she is hearing. Too late she remembers officials telling her the MOD was evacuating the Category A inmates. She hadn't thought to ask how, just ticked it off mentally as one item less to worry about.

She curses herself for her stupidity. Hardy Davies's cunning is stamped all over this. He and Defence are old cronies. They have deliberately committed the Chinook fleet to make it appear that the Home Secretary is putting prisoners' safety ahead of innocent lives.

'Where are the Belmarsh helicopters at this moment? Radio the pilots and tell them to off-load at the nearest prison or military base. Give this immediate priority!'

White faced, the MOD officer lifts the telephone again. A minute later he is shaking his head. The four Chinooks are dispersed over the country, one destined for the Isle of White, two to Dartmoor and the fourth on route to a prison in Wales. To off-load, refuel and return will take a minimum of two hours.

They can't pull machines out of Canvey and the

Sea Kings are fully stretched. 'What about the Americans?' Venetia asks, but the answer is the same. The Americans are helping all they can, but even their resources are finite. Every available US aircraft is already tasked to an emergency response.

Venetia is angrier than she has ever been before but anger makes her brain work faster. She remembers something from her briefings as Home Secretary. 'Doesn't one of the Odiham squadrons maintain a flight on immediate readiness for the SAS Counter-Terrorist Unit?'

'Yes, ma'am, the Special Forces flight. Two aircraft on permanent 24-hour stand-by but they are blocked . . .' his voice trails off.

'Unblock them. I want them airborne within fifteen minutes and heading for Dartford. Do it now. And get me the station commander at Odiham on the line. I want a full breakdown on all other machines not carried on regular squadron strength or listed as unavailable. If there is a Chinook there capable of flying, I want to know.'

Five minutes later, a group captain in command at Odiham has been brought to the phone to assure the Home Secretary personally that nothing is being held back. 'The only flyable aircraft not already tasked are two machines attached to the Operational Conversion Unit, our training flight, which have had their Airworthiness Certificates suspended.'

'Are they incapable of flying?'

'Not incapable exactly. They are older D models some of which, in other parts of the world, have been discovered to have fatigue cracks so they have been grounded pending inspection.'

'In other words they are flyable. Get them into the air and down to Dartford.'

'Minister, I can't do that, their Certificates have been suspended by the . . .'

'Group Captain, I don't care if the Angel Gabriel has personally condemned those machines. There are over a hundred casualties at Dartford who will die unless they receive help within the next sixty minutes. You are to get every aircraft that is capable of flight airborne immediately. Do I make myself clear?'

'Yes, yes, I understand, Minister. Immediately, right away.' Out in Hampshire the officer's protests wither before the Home Secretary's icy fury.

'How in hell's name did this happen?'

Murdoch Mitchison is on the top level of the multi-storey car park outside the John Lewis store. Behind him are several hundred customers and staff. In the ten minutes since the quarry wall collapsed and the river burst through, the flood has not slackened. If anything, it has increased with fresh sections of cliff crumbling and new torrents breaking out along the northern chalk face. Already the north lake is overflowing, the perimeter road skirting the cliff is impassable and floodwater is pouring into the east roundabouts. Soon those will be submerged and when that happens escape will be cut off.

Rita is on her phone. 'That was John Grey. The police have closed off the Bean Interchange to stop traffic entering the site.'

'Get on to our contractors,' Murdoch orders her. 'Tell them to send machines up there and block off that damn inflow. Call the fire brigade and have them bring in pumps and sandbags.'

'I'm trying to raise them now.' She speed dials another number. 'This is Rita Yorke. Yeah, I can see what's happened. I'm looking at the thing now. What are you doing about it? Well, what machinery do you have?' There is a pause, a long one, while Murdoch fumes with impatience and his aides try to keep the crowd back out of earshot. 'Yeah, yeah, I understand,' Rita is saying. 'Get some men on to the job then. Dig a ditch, throw some earth up, build a dam, anything, just keep that water away from the buildings.'

Rita shuts the phone with a snap. 'We only have one JCB on site, would you believe? The others were requisitioned by the Council earlier and sent down to Greenhithe. He's trying to get them released but . . .' she shrugs.

Murdoch doesn't need her to spell it out. Even if he could get the machines released they would never reach the site in time. Bluewater is on its own. He can sense dismay rising among the crowd. It is vital now to keep their confidence.

'Call up the Council,' he tells one of his aides quietly. 'Find out from them how long this is going to continue.'

The young man glances towards the cliffs. 'Long enough to lose the cars, I guess,' he answers uneasily.

Faces go pale as people recall that they are standing in a bowl, fifty metres below the surrounding hills. The aide who has spoken licks his lips nervously.

Rita interrupts. 'Look at the gap again,' she says. 'It's what, fifty metres wide? How deep is the water? A metre, wouldn't you say, if not more?'

She has their attention. Everyone turns to look again at the torrent gushing down the hill.

'Two hundred and fifty cubic metres a second,' Murdoch estimates, 'over a 97-hectare site. If flow continues at the present rate we'll be dealing with water half a metre deep over the entire area in half an hour's time. Too bloody deep for people to wade through. Too bloody deep for cars to ford either.' Bracing himself, Murdoch faces his team. 'We haven't time to lose. We have to start getting customers out of here now.'

32

Above Purfleet, past Rainham marshes, the river changes where the Thames meets London at last. The earth and clay banks of the lower estuary give way to a frontage of wharves, warehouses, factories, power stations and treatment works. Tall timber piers and steel piles rise from the water and concrete walls present a barricade against the river.

At 2 pm the tide starts overflowing onto Frog Island at the mouth of Rainham Creek. The creek is running high – all the Thames tributaries are in spate today – and floodwater backs up under the bridge carrying the new A13 road and spills over into Dagenham sewage works. Almost the whole of Barking and Dagenham lies below the ten-metre contour line and the borough engineer phones the police the warning that 75,000 people are now at grave risk.

With ten miles of river-frontage, including the courses of Barking and Rainham creeks, the authorities face an impossible task. Many people living two miles inland seldom set eyes on the river or give its existence a thought. Heavy rain has fallen earlier. Creeks and streams and flood-relief gullies, unable to discharge into the swollen Thames, are backing up and overflowing all along their lengths. Water spews up from road gutters, inundating whole streets at once. Inside ten minutes the flood edge has raced a mile from the banks. In some places it covers ground faster than a man can run. Behind the sewage works, water chases a police patrol car ahead of it into South Hornchurch and a man trying to escape through the subway under the main road is trapped and drowned before anyone can help him.

Marie Ryan has heard the news warnings on the radio and is driving back to her home in Castle Green after picking up her son, Michael, from his school. Two hundred metres from her front door she notices a puddle in the road and pays no attention, doesn't even associate it in her mind with possible flooding but puts it down to all the rain earlier. Fifty metres farther on and the water is suddenly all across the road and running fast. She brakes, wondering what to do.

'Go on! Go on!' her son shouts to her. Marie jerks forward and they make another twenty metres by which time the water has risen to bumper level. Michael is urging her to 'keep going, don't stop whatever you do', but she is nervous and the car stalls. She tries to restart it but nothing happens, maybe water has got into the electrics or the air filter. Trickles are coming in through the door seals. 'My Game Boy!' Michael shouts, scrabbling around on the floor. A large white object goes sliding past the windscreen. It is a mini-van toppled over on its side and being swept along on the flood. The car gives a quiver and rocks as if it is about to go the same way. Marie panics; she grabs her purse, forces open the door and scrambles out, pulling Michael after her.

The water is knee deep in the road. Its coldness makes Marie gasp as they splash towards their front gate. A neighbour's dog barks frantically and a four-wheel-drive jeep goes roaring past, sending up a wash that drenches her to the waist. An old man up ahead has been knocked off his feet; Marie last sees him struggling to swim as the current drags him past the corner.

They reach the house. Marie's husband is home and has barricaded the door with sheets of plastic held down with bricks. He sees them coming and pulls up the sash window for them and they scramble through into the living room, soaked to the skin, frozen and terrified. The entire episode has lasted hardly more than a minute.

On the south bank it is less than five miles from the Dartford Crossing round Coldharbour Point to Thamesmead. Already the floods have penetrated up the River Darent into the heart of Dartford New Town and the fires have swept on to torch the waterfront at neighbouring Erith and forty hectares of industrial park including a paper mill and a borax factory.

Beyond Erith lies Thamesmead and the immense sewage works at Crossness. Thames Water engineers have isolated electrical equipment at the treatment plant and opened sluices to permit free discharge from the main interceptory, but there is nothing more that they can do to save the works that serve the whole of south London. The surge bursts over the banks along the entire frontage, submerging the filter beds and settling tanks. A million residents now face disruption and bacterial contamination of floodwater will pose a major health problem for the authorities.

At Belmarsh prison, half a mile to the west, the atmosphere is knife-edge. Inmates have access to TV; they know about the flood; they have watched the newsreel footage from Coryton and Dartford. From the upperfloor windows they can see the smoke plumes at Erith barely three miles away. They are frightened of being trapped and with good reason.

Early on rumours were rife: all prisoners were going to be evacuated, or released, or both. Then came the sound of the Chinooks overhead and news spread fast that the Category As were being taken out. When the engine noise faded, fear set in.

Jock May is an officer with eight years of service, but even he is feeling the pressure. The cons on his wing are up to something. For the past half-hour they have been holding a meeting in the recreation room and the Chief has sent word it's to be broken up. Governor's orders.

The central area of the wing is eerily empty. No orderlies bustling about or queues of inmates outside Welfare. All the non-uniform staff, the psychos and probation and social workers, left long ago. Lucky bastards, Jock thinks. He lives in prison housing on the other side of the road, but appeals to be allowed home are a waste of time. Right now his wife will be carting furniture upstairs. He just hopes the kids are safe.

He joins the group of officers waiting outside the recreation room, four Seniors like himself and the rest young ones. Key chains are jingling, a sure sign of nerves. They are all worried for their families too. 'What about cars?' asks one abruptly. 'Will the insurance pay up, or is flooding an act of God?'

The group tenses. There is shouting from inside then a thump and a crash. Jock barks a command. Two officers put their shoulders to the door and heave. Something big is barricading it on the other side, a table maybe. The men take a step back and heave again. This time the door gives and a blast of warm air hits Jock in the face, stale with tobacco and sweat.

Inmates near the door jeer as they enter. The room is full, with a crowd gathered round the TV screen. Jock's stomach churns. Before it was just flood, now aerial shots of the river are showing vast areas on fire. Raging, uncontrollable flames. He turns away, shaken. No wonder the cons are on edge.

A scuffle breaks out towards the back. Jock and other officers push through, their paths hampered by solid, surly men. The fight is savage by the time they get there. Bloody noses, ears torn, a heap of cons on the ground beating the hell out of each other. There are yells of encouragement from the sidelines and more and more bodies piling in.

Jock sees the flash of a blade. He forces a way in, grabbing the nearest con, twisting his arm and kneeing him in the back to slip on the cuffs. He makes for another man, getting him by the scruff this time and wrenching him round. A knife clatters to the floor but before Jock can get it a balled fist connects with his ribs and he doubles in pain. It is all he can do to shove the two cuffed men towards a colleague. 'Bang them up,' he croaks. The next moment he is in the thick of it again, pushed and thumped, trying to keep an eye on the blade. There is not another officer anywhere near. A punch glances off his shoulder and he spins to see a blood-streaked face leering close to him. Hands tear at his jacket and reach for his keys.

Jock doesn't hear the shrilling of the alarm or the pounding of booted feet from the other wings. The first thing he knows is that he is being pulled to safety. There are uniforms everywhere all of a sudden and cons being grappled to the ground and led away. Gasps of pain and groaning are followed by an unnatural quiet. Jock feels a chill down his spine. They have been a hair's breadth away from full scale riot. Out there on the river smoke plumes are spiralling towards the prison. Tension is not going to ease.

'*Will owners of four-wheel-drive vehicles please come to the roof car park by the House of Fraser entrance.*'

In the Bluewater car parks hundreds of drivers are starting their cars and tearing for the exits in a race to beat the floods. Among them are the Smileys. Melissa has had a bad fright. Her shoes are ruined, her clothes soaked. Half their purchases are with the Concierge and will have to be left behind but she doesn't care any longer. All she wants is to get home.

Water is coursing through the car parks, licking around kerbstones and collecting in depressions. They reach the Toyota and bundle inside. 'Look out!' Chantal screams as they pull away. A people-carrier has reversed straight out in front of them. The driver hardly spares them a glance as he shoots off down the exit lane.

Stewart swings right, heading round to the east side of the complex towards the only road out that is not yet under water. Twice he has to brake sharply, once to avoid a wildly driven vehicle and the other time when a frightened pedestrian runs in front of him. Long before they get near the ramp up to the roadway the Land Cruiser is caught up in a mass of other vehicles all with the same intention.

From the crest of the hill leading down into Bluewater, John Grey, the sergeant in charge of the centre's police contingent, can only watch helplessly as the car parks below descend into chaos. With all but one road off the site blocked by flooding, the only hope of carrying out an orderly evacuation of the two hundred thousand customers and staff depends on keeping tight control of traffic. By turning both sides of the approach road into a one-way system, Grey reckons that up to seven thousand vehicles an hour can make their escape. Even so it will take eight hours to empty the centre.

Meanwhile water is continuing to filter into the car parks. In spite of appeals from the management to give the jam time to clear, customers are scrambling for a way out. Many head for the northern exits only to find the approach to the upper level roadway blocked by mudslides. Two or three articulated trucks do succeed in fording the water that has pooled in the dip at the northeast exit, but the level is coming up fast and soon that way out is cut off too.

Before the police can get into position, large numbers of cars converge on the roundabout and are forcing their way up the gradient. Traffic on the main road at the top is heavy, making it hard for vehicles to join, and within minutes vehicles are stalled all the way back down the hill.

It's Stewart Smiley who inadvertently provides the catalyst that turns the situation into a disaster. The slip roads onto the roundabout are jammed solid and water has begun oozing under the wheels of the cars. He looks up the hill with its lines of stationary vehicles and gauges the angle of the slope. He is driving the toughest off-roader in the world, he thinks; now is the time to make use of that capability.

'Hold tight,' he tells the family, turning the wheel and bumping over the kerb.

Close to, the slope rises precipitously. There are squeals of dismay from the back as Stewart selects low ratio and steers ahead. The trick, he remembers, is to keep going straight up, not be tempted to cut the diagonal. 'Dad, I don't think I like this. I'm scared. I want to get out!' Chantal pleads as the nose of the car rears skywards.

'Keep calm. I went up worse than this on that cross-country course two years ago.' The going is soft but the Land Cruiser's wide tyres provide plenty of grip. Stewart estimates the slope as about 1 in 4. Steep but not dangerous. He is confident of making it.

And he does. In a matter of minutes the Toyota's nose pitches down again as the front wheels reach the hard shoulder of the approach road. Drivers stare in astonishment as Stewart takes off along the verge past them, spewing mud and gravel. Up at the top he cuts in front of a furious BMW and thirty minutes later they are through to the M25 and heading for home.

'I bet a lot of others will be trying that now,' Chantal crows with relief. 'But we thought of it first. Clever old Dad.'

That is exactly what happens. In fact, before the Smileys have reached the top of the slope, the first of dozens of off-road vehicles is following in the Land Cruiser's track. The next up is a Range Rover, which takes the hill effortlessly. But the rain of recent days has left the ground sodden and as vehicle after vehicle claws its way to the top, the surface quickly degenerates into a morass of churned mud.

Not all drivers have had the benefit of proper off-road training either. As more and more vehicles struggle up the slope, there is a tendency for them to avoid the worst ruts by cutting away to the side, with the result that, as they approach the crest, they are poised perilously over the roadway.

John Grey runs down from the Interchange in time to see a huge American Chevrolet Suburban starting its climb. He is horrified by the state of the hillside. Access is restricted by the slip road at one end and at the other by a concrete watercourse draining the site. In the confined space, five or six vehicles are grinding their way upwards with others jostling for position at the foot of the slope. The air is loud with revving engines and angry hooting from drivers impatient to get through the mass of ordinary cars jamming the roundabout.

By now parts of the roadway are covered in water and occupants of smaller vehicles are starting to panic. Several try to cut across the verges and become bogged down. One big estate sinks up to its wheel arches, clouds of smoke spouting from its exhaust while the family stands around wringing their hands helplessly.

The Suburban is growling up the slope, lurching in the ruts left by earlier vehicles. In an effort to find firm ground the driver is being forced further and further out to the side until he is at such a shallow angle to the top road he is almost travelling horizontal. The hillside looks like a battleground now; Grey can see the mud flying from the wide wheels as they struggle to keep a grip. Then to his amazement two more 4x4s begin moving up on the inside, apparently trying to slip round past the lumbering American. Grey can't believe the lunacy he is witnessing. Don't any of these people realise the risks they are running?

And now the Suburban is in trouble. Its wheels have lost their grip and are slipping sideways down the hill. The slope falls away steeply at this point and the cab is visibly tilting. The driver tries frantically to halt the slide, but he is inexperienced and instead of turning into it and regaining control he twists the wheel the opposite way. The rate of the slide increases, then before Grey's horrified gaze the ground seems to give way under the outer wheels and the heavy vehicle topples slowly over onto its side.

Screams erupt from the cars below as it slithers down the hill through the mud. For a moment Grey thinks it is going to career right down into the mass of vehicles jammed at the foot of the road. The other two off-roaders are roaring their engines, frantically scrambling to get clear. The Suburban comes crashing down on them like a falling tree. Its rear end catches the nearest by the bumper and flips it over. From then on things happen too fast to see clearly. All three vehicles roll together, pitching down onto the road in an avalanche of thundering metal that seems to go on and on. The silence that follows afterwards is the worst of all.

And now the last escape route out of Bluewater is blocked.

33

'ATTENTION,' a voice blares over the public-address system at St Thomas's Hospital. '*The staff kitchen will be shutting down shortly. Anyone wanting a hot meal is advised to head immediately for the canteens. This will be your last chance until the emergency is over.*'

Melanie Sykes hasn't eaten since coming on duty at eight but she is too busy to take a break. The Respiratory Unit is being moved from Ground Floor level up to the sixth floor where a ward has been cleared next to Intensive Care. Many of the sixteen patients on the unit have severe disabilities and require mechanical breathing assistance. Intensive Care has its own generator for ventilators to connect to.

Jenny is a polio victim, a survivor of the 1950's epidemic. Much of her early life was spent in hospital and, though she now lives at home, she is still respirator-dependent. Last week she was readmitted with an acute chest infection and is temporarily back in one of the unit's iron lungs. Before she can be moved, the battery back-up system has to be connected and the alarms reset.

Upstairs, tinsel and holly still decorate the wards.

There are Christmas cards on bedside lockers and trees with artificial snow and presents underneath. To Melanie there is a mad air of make-believe about it all. Like being on the *Titanic* after it hit the iceberg. People pretending they have the situation under control, while all the time water is rising around them.

Downstairs again, she shivers. Already there is a noticeable drop in temperature. The basement boilers have been off for nearly two hours and the buildings leak heat. Showers are locked and managers are posting signs ordering everyone to conserve water. Nurses run up and down stairs with supplies while porters load oxygen cylinders into the lifts. Two doctors Melanie doesn't recognise hurry past talking about 'battery power for twelve hours minimum'.

Accident and Emergency has officially closed. Ambulance control is diverting emergencies to hospitals outside the flood zone but a trickle of patients continues to arrive. Only a handful of cases is urgent enough to warrant admission. There have been a number of ugly incidents where people have been turned away and security guards have had to be called in.

The hospital's rumour-mill is in full swing. Tales of explosions and dreadful casualties down at the river mouth, of tube trains trapped in tunnels and thousands drowned at the Dome. Someone else claims to have heard that the surge tide has been reflected back by the Thames Barrier after all and the emergency will shortly be declared over.

At half-past two Melanie gets an urgent call on her pager. Jenny's condition has suddenly deteriorated and she has been moved to Intensive Care. Melanie hurries upstairs. There are thirty-four beds in the unit, rows of patients tended by winking monitors, with tubes snaking out of their bodies. Jenny lies still, only her chest moving as it rises and falls to each click and wheeze of the ventilator.

Normal operation of Intensive Care requires twenty-four nurses on duty each shift. If those ventilators cease working, then patients will die. Every member of the medical staff has been pressed into rotas ready to work the machines by hand in that event. How long for, is anyone's guess.

Paul Suter leads his two engineers up the northbound track of the Bakerloo Line in single file. The tunnel lights are on so power to the lines is off; the blackened brick walls unfold ahead of them. They have left Oxford Circus behind and are approaching Regent's Park. They walk in silence broken only by the steady tramp of their boots on the sleepers and the clink of the tools they shoulder.

Paul glances at his watch. So far they have been going twenty minutes. As they round the bend the tunnel becomes brighter, they have reached Regent's Park. The platforms here are lit, but the station is deserted. Paul calls a halt and the other two perch on the platform resting while he unclips his radio to call NCC. If the information they have given him is correct, the stalled train should be just up the tunnel from here.

Over at the NCC, Hew Thomas is struggling with a network that is disintegrating under him. Thousands of passengers are still being evacuated in the triangle between Sloane Square, Notting Hill and Earls Court. There are trains stuck in tunnels on the Central Line and other black spots at Liverpool Street, King's Cross and Baker Street. With power to many sectors cut off, supervisors are closing stations on their own initiative and sending staff home. Hew needs to get the stations reopened urgently. He has asked for Transport Police to be sent at once to Baker Street to help bring passengers out.

Now, in addition to his other troubles, communications are breaking up. He has lost radio contact with the engineers sent to the Bakerloo Line.

Paul Suter shuts off his radio in disgust. Trust these devices to go down just when they are most needed. But the train can't be far and the three set off again.

They have come a third of a mile before they see the rear lights of a carriage up ahead. Soon they are close enough to make out the passengers inside. Paul finds a phone receiver from among his tool kit and clips it to a pair of copper wires running along the side of the tunnel. By this means he can talk to the driver in the cab. The man has no idea what could have caused the breakdown. Paul will have to go and see for himself.

He tells the two others to wait where they are and swings himself up into the rear cab. The door to the coach opens inward, which is awkward because the coach is jammed full. Inside, he is bombarded with questions from passengers: '*What's the matter? How much longer are we going to be here? Why is it taking so long?*' Paul tells them he won't know till he has looked at the problem and he pushes through into the next car where he meets the same questions all over again.

There are seven cars in the train; it takes longer to reach the head of the train than it did to walk up the tunnel from the station. He raps on the door of the cab and the driver unlocks it to let him through.

At least the radio in here is working. Paul calls up NCC to tell them he has reached the scene. The fuse giving trouble is located in a distribution box up the tunnel and he is going out to take a look at it now.

There is a door in the front of the cab and Paul steps down onto the track again. He has taken only half a dozen steps when he stiffens. He listens carefully, ears straining through the gloom. There are the clicking sounds given off by the train's running gear cooling down and the gurgle of the air-conditioning pumps under the carriages, but they are in the background. What is bothering him is a different sound, something that is out of place. It is the splash of running water gushing over stones.

He shines his torch up the wall of the tunnel. Water is trickling among the ballast supporting the track. He stoops to touch the stones. His hand comes away wet and when he takes a step, water splashes up under his boot. He is standing in a puddle, a large one.

Paul stares at the water, wiping his hand on his jacket. He can't understand how it has got so wet down here. There shouldn't be that much seepage coming in.

He fetches out the train driver, an old hand whose name is Winston Charles, and together they walk along the tunnel with their flashlights. After fifty metres they come to the source of the trouble: water is bubbling up from a drain conduit. A long pool glistens blackly on the bed of the tunnel. It has collected at a low point until it is deep enough to short out the live rail. Winston says there have been problems with seepage here before. 'The power outage must have killed the pumps.'

Paul is thinking that the power has only been off a short while. The water shouldn't be building up this fast.

On Canary Wharf, the authorities are keeping an anxious eye on the river level. When the docks were first constructed, the excavated material was used to raise the level of the quays. So even if flooding does occur, there is a good chance Canary Wharf itself may escape. The buildings are linked to the Docklands Light Railway and by elevated roads and walkways; evacuation will remain possible even after flooding has started. There is general agreement that people will be better off staying put than adding to the confusion on the roads.

The facilities manager at Canary Wharf Tower is Barry Singleton, forty-one years old, married with two children. Barry takes his orders from the management office in the South Colonnade. The first warnings reach Barry around midday and his immediate action is to call the borough emergency centre. It is not easy getting through; all the lines are busy. When finally Barry speaks to someone, the initial response is reassuring. Any overtopping will be downstream of the Barrier. Even a worst-case scenario will see flooding confined to the five-metre contour, presenting no threat to Canary Wharf. Barry instructs his building supervisors to be on alert nevertheless.

Within an hour, though, the picture is blacker. Conditions are plainly deteriorating but Barry is having difficulty in getting positive information. The people at the borough centre seem to know no more than he does. They suggest he try the police.

Canary Wharf has its own security force, commanded by former police officers. Their contacts at New Scotland Yard are mainly with the Anti-terrorist Branch and related to bomb threats. Barry is advised to talk to C-11, but the unit is in the middle of moving to Hendon. First the lines are down and then they too are busy. By this time television is carrying dramatic pictures from Southend and Canvey. But Southend is a long way off, surely?

Barry speaks to his managing director. They discuss evacuation plans. It is not clear this will necessarily be in the best interests either of the company or its clients. 'We could be evacuating people into danger,' the MD points out. 'They might be safer staying put.' Several tenants with dealing rooms have intimated they will only accept orders to leave from the police. They promise legal action for loss of revenue if they are forced to vacate unnecessarily. These are no idle threats; claims could run into millions.

Lauren Khan's editor, Archie Watson, intends to remain at his desk at One Canada Square. The paper's printing works is at Millwall down by the water and likely to be flooded and Archie's board is trying to arrange an emergency print run with a Scottish or Irish group. Meanwhile, from his office in the tower he has a clear view eastwards across the City Airport to the Thames Barrier. The river appears swollen and heavy, charged with menace. Away to the east dark palls hang in the sky, ominous and threatening. And less than a mile away sits the Dome, 'like a flattened breast', as a woman writer once described it. Archie has three people over there covering the evacuation. He hopes they will bring out some good copy.

Up on the fortieth floor, Sophie de Salis takes a call from her husband in Boston.

'Are you okay?' Randal is shouting into the phone. 'My God, I can't believe what we're seeing on the television. It looks like the whole city is on fire!'

'That's way down the estuary, twenty, thirty miles off. We don't even have flooding here. Not yet anyway,' Sophie tells him, pretending to a confidence she does not feel.

'What about Chrissie? Is she with you?'

'She's at school. It's one o'clock in the afternoon here, honey.'

The truth is, Sophie is growing increasingly frightened. Not for herself but for her daughter. For the past hour she has been continually on the phone, dialling and re-dialling every number she can think of. But lines into the school remain blocked by several hundred equally frantic parents; Chrissie's mobile is still turned off and on Harriet Binney's number all she gets is the answering machine.

Meanwhile the pictures on TV are growing ever more alarming. Flooding has reached the edge of London and everyone knows it is only a matter of time before the city goes down. Public transport has stopped and the roads are jamming up.

Suddenly Sophie decides she can't stay here any longer. She must make sure Chrissie is safe. Swivelling to the computer, she fires off an e-mail to her boss: *going to rescue my child – don't wait up*. Maybe he will see the joke, maybe not. Sophie doesn't care. She jumps up, grabs her coat and runs to the lifts.

Down in the lower level of the car park there is a spooky feel to being deep underground now. The attendants and security guards are nowhere to be seen and there's no sign of Larry and his gang either. A handful of cars are left and the BMW is there, sparkling clean under the lights. It is only as she draws close that Sophie notices a black pool spreading across the tarmac.

There is an internal telephone on the wall. A voice answers. 'Security.'

'There's water running over the floor on the third level car park.'

'That's Canada Square?'

'Right. Looks like a drain backing up.'

'Okay, we'll tell maintenance to check it out.'

'London Bridge is showing 5.10 metres.' Martin injects a note of grim finality into his voice this time. The wall at London Bridge stands at 5.41 metres. There are just thirty centimetres of freeboard, the height of a sheet of A4 paper, left before over-topping, hardly sufficient to contain wave action in a stiff wind.

Angus has not moved from the window. For the past half-hour he has maintained his brooding watch, oblivious to appeals, while the river rises and smoke palls shroud the city. Observing the scene, it crosses Lauren Khan's mind that Angus may actually be willing to accept a limited amount of water on the streets of the capital as a price for maintaining control of the river. But at last, to the palpable relief of the rest of the team, he turns to face the room.

'Return all gates to defence position.'

Martin takes a deep breath. 'Close Bravo,' he orders, 'Close Golf.' The controller is anticipating the command. A click on his screen sets the yellow rocker arm of the nearside 30.5-metre rising sector gate in motion. 'Close Charlie, Close Delta . . . Echo . . . Foxtrot. Fasten all latches.' One by one, the 3,700-tonne behemoths rotate smoothly back into the upright position till their lower flanges are once more resting in the concrete sills on the riverbed, choking off the flow of water passing under the Barrier. One by one the churning millraces on the upstream side slacken and cease. Tension among the team eases.

The Barrier is closed once more.

34

From his office, Murdoch Mitchison watches the bright yellow helicopter orbit Bluewater before heading off to hospital in Maidstone. It has taken an hour to reach them. The tally from the débâcle on the slopes is eleven customers hurt, four with serious crushing injuries, and one dead. Hundreds of other drivers and passengers have abandoned their vehicles and retreated back to the buildings, shocked and cold.

In the half-hour since the accidents, the chalk pit in which Bluewater is sited has become a lake. Water is a metre deep, more in places, and the access road impassable now even for four-wheel drives. Foot evacuation is out of the question.

Murdoch reckons he has between 150,000 and 170,000 customers marooned, herded onto the upper levels of the complex. John Lewis is one of Bluewater's prestige department stores, but now the scene is like a refugee camp in some war-torn corner of the globe. Every metre of space is taken up with huddled groups of people, camped out like nomads and surrounded by piles of dripping, oozing garments. It is the same at House of Fraser and again at Marks & Spencer. All three have been commandeered by police for the duration.

Thousands were caught on the lower malls when the floodwater came in. Everywhere, people are soaked through and filthy. They have grabbed whatever they can to wrap themselves in, clothes, bed linen, soft furnishings, but there is nothing like enough dry stuff to go round.

It is cold too. Until the generators packed up the stores had heating and light, but all the power has been off for some time. In the cavernous interiors only a little daylight filters through and that is fading fast. Younger children are growing tired and frightened and the sound of fractious crying fills the halls.

Back out on Guild Hall a stench of drains is rising from below. The upper walk is crowded, although the shops along it are closed against looters. People jostle for sitting room on the floor or hang over the balustrades and watch the floodwater. Guild Hall is the classiest of the malls and the filthy brown lake is lapping outlets like Kookai and Gap. Its surface is scummy with all manner of trash. Murdoch doesn't even want to think about insurance claims.

He stops by the concierge desk to check with the staff sorting out missing persons, families who were split in the initial chaos and wound up in different parts of the complex. It makes sense for Bluewater to operate a central register rather than have people running round in circles trying to find one another.

When he returns to the office, Rita is rapping her fingers on the desk. With the phones down, communications have to be relayed through John Grey's radio net on the outside and it is driving her mad with frustration. She needs to know what evacuation plans the police have. When the call finally comes, she snaps a 'Well?'

Murdoch leans over the desk. They can land helicopters on the car park roofs, he indicates. But Rita shakes her head at him. She clicks off the radio, her face pale.

'They can't help,' she says quietly. 'No resources. We have to sit it out until tomorrow, maybe longer even.'

Murdoch's heart sinks. How is he going to tell this to the customers?

In the Barrier operations room, Lauren Khan's attention is on the screen covering the sixty-metre drop-gate barrier at Barking Creek. As she watches, the red line of the tide level intersects with the limit mark on the display and a warning buzzer sounds. Beside the monitor, a phone rings urgently. The tide is overtopping at Barking. The surge has come another step closer.

With Barking's barrier down, an immense area of the northeast London suburbs lies open to the flood. The water here makes its deepest penetration yet, extending four miles inland up the River Roding into Ilford. The North Circular Road is cut as well as vital rail junctions at Barking and East Ham.

Near Mayes Brook, a man on his way to put flowers on his parents' grave meets a flood coming in so fast that the water is unable to escape under a low bridge. The brook spills out onto the roadway and he is wondering whether to take off his shoes and socks and roll up his trousers when in the space of a minute the level surges to his chest. He holds the flowers over his head, unable to recognise the path or any of his surroundings and terrified to move in case he falls into the brook and drowns. He is rescued by soldiers from the Territorial Army depot.

West of Barking Creek, the first casualty of the flooding is the giant sewage works at Beckton, the counterpart of Crossness on the south shore. The torrents then thrust on through Beckton into new housing on the border of the Docklands redevelopment zone. Twenty years of construction effort and a multi-billion pound investment on the former flood plain are now threatened with destruction.

Over in Docklands, the brokers scheduled to join the Dublin flight are boarding the airport bus. Judith Tang is part of the team and she is late. She has stayed behind trying to phone her partner to tell him she is leaving the city. The telephone system is breaking down. It is impossible to get a line and when you do finally get through every number is engaged. Giving up, she sprints for the lift. It is five minutes coming and she reaches the front door to find the transport gone.

Her boss will be livid. He will think she did this on purpose. Outside it is icy. It has stopped raining but the wind is ferocious. An articulated truck loaded with immense rolls of newsprint paper stands abandoned across the street. Half the people in the building have left early and the rest are off somewhere getting drunk. It is no use trying to go home because the roads are jammed and the underground has stopped.

Finally she succeeds in cadging a lift on a motorbike from a photographer off to get a shot of the last plane departing from City Airport before the flood closes it.

The ride to the airport is freezing but mercifully short. The terminal is full of people demanding flights out but there is no sign of her group and none of the harassed staff on duty can help. The photographer has wandered off and she goes to the upper level to look for him. The windows face north across the dock to the flat ground of Beckton: row upon row of small houses with treeless parks and tower blocks rising like totems against the darkening sky. There is a lot of helicopter activity, much of it military machines. Rumour is that mass evacuations are under way.

The photographer reappears. The plane is about to take off and he has secured permission to photograph it from the end of the runway. A service truck is taking him out. Judith grabs at the chance of a ride. She hopes she might be able to get aboard somehow, even at this late stage.

'KGV gatehouse reports water coming over the top of the locks.' The terse reports crackle across the Barrier operations room. 'Indicators on Gates Charlie and Foxtrot showing 6.85 metres.' On the computer screens the red line marking the surge's progress is just touching the Barrier.

Lauren joins Angus at the windows. From here the river seems immense. Where it meets the Barrier, great eddies churn the muddied water, swirling about the piers in sullen anger. Choppy waves whipped up by the wind splash against the tops of the gates, slopping over down the back faces. On the upstream side the level is sharply lower, almost two metres. The flood is straining against the Barrier, its weight growing by the minute. How much longer can steel and concrete withstand such pressure?

Docklands is already going down. Nothing can save the capital now.

At North Woolwich station the volunteer train crew is jumpy. Water is brimming the walls on Pier Road fifty metres away. Earlier they brought out a thousand passengers from the locality and agreed to return for one more trip. Now they wish they hadn't. The moment the train sounded its approach a crowd stormed the platform. Hundreds of people are forcing their way aboard the already jammed carriages.

The sweating police sergeant is shouting at those inside to move down to make room for others when his radio bleeps. It is the WPC he stationed outside to watch the river. He has to strain to catch her words. 'It's the Foot Tunnel,' she is shouting. The Woolwich Foot Tunnel is a three-quarter-mile pedestrian link running under the river to the Charlton shore. The entrances on both banks have been locked off since the start of the emergency. In a flood it is as good a death trap as you could wish.

Leaving the station, the sergeant runs outside. The WPC is signalling to him down by the cupola-shaped entrance to the stairs. A mob broke open the doors with bolt cutters and crowbars, she says. When she tried to interfere, they pushed her out of the way.

The sergeant doesn't know what to do. If he locks the doors again it will only trap those already in the tunnel. Across Pier Road, water is pouring over the river wall and running across the pavement. Another group of people appears, making for the tunnel entrance. The sergeant blocks their path. If you want to commit suicide, go jump off the pier, he yells at them.

There is a hooting sound from the railway. The train is about to pull out. The sergeant turns on the WPC. How many went down? he wants to know. She shakes her head, she didn't have time to count. 'Come on,' he says, plunging inside. Together they clatter down the spiral iron stairs round the lift-shaft.

'Charter 146 to Tower. What's the hold-up?' Out on the apron the pilot of the charter jet is impatient for clearance. His passengers are aboard, he has fuel and he is growing edgy as the minutes tick by.

'Charter 146 this is Tower. We are still checking the runway.'

'Well, get a move on, for God's sake. I'm all set to roll.' The pilot has personal money tied up in this plane; he wants out of here before the flood comes.

In the tower, the controller gnaws at his fingernails. The civilian jet should never have been allowed to land. Flooding is imminent, power could cut out any minute and the radar screen is filled with helicopter traffic that hasn't filed flight plans. The entire situation is teetering on the edge of calamity. And all so that a bunch of dealers can go on racking up their profits.

⋆

It is colder still out on the runway. The wind sweeps off the dock and cuts through Judith's coat, setting her shivering. They have stopped by a set of approach lights at the far southeastern tip of the runway. Out on the open dock an ugly swell is sending waves splashing against the stone blocks of the old quay. To the east vast smoking plumes mark the approaching fires, much nearer now. The driver of the service truck says the floods have reached Thamesmead.

The photographer focuses his telephoto lens on the jet sitting out on the apron. The driver's radio crackles. It's no go, he says. They've cancelled the flight, passengers are being disembarked. The photographer wants to know why. He is angry at missing his shot. The driver says it's too dangerous. Flooding has begun; the river is pouring in over the gates at the dock entrance behind them. It's time to go.

The photographer wants to wait. They can get back in no time and a few good shots of the flood coming up might compensate for missing the plane. Judith rubs her arms to keep warm and tries to control her nervousness. Gusts of wind are tearing at the swell and there is a lot of spray on the concrete already. All at once she notices water trickling through the grass at her feet. At the same time the driver gives a shout and points to the runway where dark tongues are starting to creep across the concrete.

The train pulls slowly out from North Woolwich station. The engineer has the throttle lever hard over, trying to build up speed, but there are ten carriages, all of them grossly overloaded. They grind slowly along next to Connaught Road, alongside the last few vehicles racing for the bridge.

The train rattles into the mouth of the underpass beneath Albert Dock and tilts down the slope, gathering momentum to carry them up the far side. They reach the bottom clocking forty on the indicator and hammer along the dip. The reverse slope begins. It seems endless. 'Come on, come on,' the engineer urges under his breath, peering through the windscreen. The exit mouth comes into sight round the bend. All at once he narrows his eyes again. Something is gleaming in the light up ahead beside the rails. Water from an overflowing drain is trickling down the slope.

His assistant has seen it too from the footplate. That was close, he says as the engine climbs out into the open air again. The water will be collecting in the dip at the bottom. Soon it will be over the rails and deep enough to halt a train. A few minutes later and they would have been trapped.

The lights in the Foot Tunnel have been switched off. The stairs wind down dizzily into darkness. The sergeant and the WPC reach the bottom and halt uncertainly, shining their torches round. The tunnel is three metres in diameter and lined with off-white glazed tiles scrawled with anarchic graffiti. It smells damp and dirty. They are fifteen metres below the river.

Sounds of distorted voices boom off the walls. A light appears in the distance where the tunnel dips to the mid-point. 'Come back,' the sergeant shouts. The light approaches, bobbing and wavering. A middle-aged man materialises from the darkness, stumbling towards them, half carrying an exhausted woman.

The two police break into a run. The man waves them back with his free arm. 'Get out,' he gasps. 'Get away, the water's coming.' The couple's clothing is streaming, the horror of what they have been through written in their faces. 'Are there any more of you?' the sergeant demands. The man slumps against the wall. Eight or nine, he thinks. Their party was halfway up the rise at the far end when the water started coming in. It rushed down the slope so fast people lost their footing and were swept away. 'We were at the rear. When we tried to turn back the level was up to the roof. We had to swim for it.' He doesn't know what became of the others.

The sergeant shines his torch up the tunnel. The beam glances off a black lake rippling menacingly over the floor towards them. A single glimpse is enough. The WPC slips a shoulder under the woman and the sergeant takes the other side. In desperate haste they retreat to the north shaft. More water is splashing down from above, pouring over the stairs as they clamber up to the surface and out through the doors. They are only just in time. Outside, the road is already awash.

The river is spilling down over the walls by the ferry pier, pouring into the yards of the sugar refinery. In places here the land is three metres below the defences. In moments floodwater is sluicing through the drab streets, across the railway track and onto the main road. The two police and the couple with them wade back to the main road where a police carrier is sloshing along, water halfway up the hubcaps. An officer slides back the side door and all four scramble thankfully aboard.

Even now the photographer will not come away. He snaps obsessively while Judith and the driver plead with him and the water spreads over the runway. Finally the driver says he is leaving anyway. He climbs back into the truck and Judith follows, terrified of being left. There comes a blast of engine noise from the direction of the terminal. The photographer swivels, staring down his lens, trying to make out what is happening in the gloom of the storm. 'Is it taking off?' he shouts.

Up in the tower the controller is wondering the same thing. 'What's the idiot think he's doing?' He flips the radio button. 'Charter 146. Abort take-off and return to terminal immediately. Runway is under water, do not, repeat not, attempt take-off.'

'I can do this,' the pilot snarls back. 'Let us go.'

Before the furious controller has a chance to repeat his order, the main lights in the terminal flicker suddenly and a warning alarm sounds in the tower. 'Generator failure. Switching to mains alternate,' a computer synthesised voice articulates.

London City's generators are situated at ground-floor level and are vulnerable to flooding. The back-up supply consists of two independent main feeds, each with an estimated failure rate of once in ninety years. Unfortunately both feeds are also located at ground level. All three power sources short-circuit within seconds of each other as the water reaches them.

'I'm taking her up,' the pilot of the charter jet shouts into his radio.

In response there is a blast of static. 'What the hell is that?' the co-pilot says.

'I don't care,' the other shakes his head grimly. 'We're getting out of here before they change their bloody minds.'

The truck driver revs his engine; the photographer can stay if he wants, he is pulling out now. There's a lot more water about all of a sudden. It's hard to see now where the edges of the dock are. Waves are riding over and spilling unobstructed towards the runway. Even the photographer looks surprised by the speed at which things are happening. Down the runway Judith can make out the jet's tail swinging round till its nose is pointing towards her.

'It's coming this way. It's taking off!' the photographer shouts as the jet begins to move. Gathering speed, engines bellowing under full power, it hurtles up the runway towards them, spray bursting from beneath its wheels as it comes. The photographer crouches, his camera snapping. Closer and closer the plane races; Judith clenches her fists, willing it to lift off.

'The water's too deep!' she hears the driver gasp. 'It can't get speed up.'

He's right. Judith can hear the scream of the engines straining to break the water's grip on the wheels as the plane tears towards the end of the runway. It's almost level with them now but the tail is up. The main wheels lift and bounce on the waterlogged surface. Beyond the concrete flarepath there is only the grass perimeter where they are crouching in the truck. Then comes a narrow strip of water joining the two halves of the dock and on the far side of that the gleaming new campus buildings of London Docklands University at the dock entrance.

Almost to the last moment it seems as though the pilot won't succeed. The plane crosses the very end of the runway, its wheels skimming the grass. The shadow of the wing flashes over the truck and the ground shakes with the deafening thunder from turbojets passing feet above them. As it zooms clear there is a heavy double thump behind. Judith cranes her neck round in time to see a burst of spray as something huge and black bounds out over the dock to bury itself with a terrific splash in the frothing water. There's a last glimpse of the tail fin beyond the bridge over the dock gate and then the plane vanishes away up-river.

'What was that?' she gasps to the driver.

The driver has let in the clutch and is racing back along the runway as fast as the truck will take him. His face is white as paper as he fumbles at his radio to try to call the control tower. 'That was the wheel assembly. It tore off on the bridge and was thrown back onto the runway. It hit right behind us.' Another few feet and they would all have been killed.

Judith turns back in horror after the plane.

A mile down river the jet is in desperate trouble. Ripping off the wheel assembly has also damaged the tail control surfaces. The crew felt the thump and know the aircraft has sustained damage, but they've no way of telling what or how bad. Either the linkages have been cut or the elevator has been smashed, the pilot hasn't time to figure out.

Warning lights are flashing over the instrument panels and hydraulic pressure is falling. The plane is wallowing around the sky like a wounded duck and the pilot thinks the rear elevator controls are out. The co-pilot is flipping through his manuals to try and reconfigure the hydraulics and recover tail stability. They are flying through intermittent cloud and smoke on a southeasterly heading with the river visible a thousand feet below.

Five miles down river, a Chinook from Odiham is airborne from Dartford with a load of burns victims, destination the John Radcliffe hospital in Oxford. Helicopters operating over the estuary have been warned to stay below 2,500 feet to allow a 1,000-foot separation between the 3,500-foot minimum for civilian air traffic over the London area. The Chinook is flying at 1,500 feet to reduce risk of collision with other machines engaged in rescue work. Amid thick smoke, the radar operator detects the 146 jet rising up from the airport at Docklands. They are on converging courses but the airliner is climbing and should rapidly transit the low-flight zone.

Thirty seconds later the jet has started to level out at 2,500 feet. It is still on a converging course and has picked up speed; it is now two and a half miles west and closing at an estimated 300 knots. The Chinook operator advises his pilot to make a 15-degree turn to south. With a thousand feet of separation there is still no anxiety.

Without warning the jet's nose drops suddenly, accelerating it into a dive at 400 knots. At the same time it veers to starboard. The two aircraft are now converging again at a combined speed of ten miles a minute. Horizontal separation will shrink to zero in just seven seconds. 'Break right!' the Chinook's radar operator screams into the intercom. The pilot pulls the collective to maximum power, rams the cyclic forward and stamps on the right pedal. The Chinook's huge blades scythe the air as the helicopter peels away in a violent banking turn.

Over Dagenham and Thamesmead the sound of aero-engines is terminated by a violent explosion that stains the clouds crimson for several seconds. A fireman at the Ford works observes 'a great red ball like a mass of flames descending through the smoke towards the water'. A barge tow moving up-river to escape the oil fires records 'burning wreckage tumbling out of the sky . . . splashing into the water astern'.

London Air Traffic Control, over at West Drayton by Heathrow, sees the charter jet and the helicopter disappear from their screens and calls a mid-air collision. Due to confusion, it is uncertain exactly which helicopter is involved. But they know it has to be a Chinook and a message confirming the loss is passed to Triple-C.

35

The Barrier is overtopping. The wave crests that have been splashing down the backs of the gates for the past twenty minutes are now pouring over unchecked. The thunder of water plunging into the pool can be heard up in the control room. Photographers crowd the windows, eager to record the event. From bank to bank the piers stand like concrete islands on a giant weir across which the river foams unhindered. At their stations, the closure team can only watch powerless as the upstream tide gauges record the unfolding catastrophe.

'Millennium Pier indicating 4.8 metres.'

'West India Dock 4.9 metres.'

Minutes tick by. Beyond the windows, a helicopter appears, skimming upstream like a brightly coloured insect. It hovers noisily over the Barrier, close enough to make out the cameramen inside, before peeling away in the direction of the Dome.

A moment ago they saw their first body, an adult in a yellow life jacket being whirled past in the current. Impossible to tell if it was man or woman.

Word is that a plane has gone down in the river somewhere, perhaps more than one.

Beneath the smoke plumes darkness is approaching and away to the east the sky is stained with an angry red glare reflected off the huge fires burning on the river.

Aboard *Jen-0*, Ted Turner squints through the tug's shattered windshield. His face feels as if it has been scraped raw by the fierce heat. His eyebrows and lashes have been singed away, half his hair is gone and he is bleeding from cuts everywhere. Every window on the bridge has been blown out. Broken glass and debris cover the deck. Steel fittings are buckled or torn away; the paintwork blistered as by a blowtorch; and every surface is blackened beneath a coating of soot and grease.

Visible now on the north bank are the chimneys of the 300-acre Ford Motor plant. Two million diesel engines are turned out here each year, a quarter of the company's entire world production. Directly opposite on the Erith marshes lie the settlement tanks of Crossness sewage works. In between them a line of flames flickers on the water, spewing inky smoke against the sky. Ted grits his teeth as he pushes the throttle forward against the stops. The cabin deck throbs under him. The strength of the surge is so great the vessel is barely making headway. According to an army spotter aircraft overhead, the oil has passed Frog Island and is approaching the engine factories.

A hundred metres still to go till *Jen-0*'s monitors are within range of the flames and already the heat is scorching. Turner orders the sprays turned on to cool the vessel down and cuts the speed. The burning slicks are bearing down at eight or ten knots. The monitors are just within range now and begin to play on the forward edge of the flames. Ted tries to see if they are having any effect but it is hard to tell.

Jen-1 joins in alongside. Only one of her monitors is working. Between them the two tugs cruise back and forth in front of the advancing flames, trying to keep them away from the factory. It is a dangerous task because the current keeps sweeping patches of burning oil past them up-river. When that happens the tugs have to pull back or risk being cut off and surrounded again.

Pumping at full power, the monitors sweep great swathes of the oil clear of flames. Turner can hear the hiss of steam as foam and water deluge the red-hot surface. He puts the helm over a trifle, bringing the tug's head round to let the monitors play on another section. *Jen-1* is plugging away alongside. If only they had more tugs. Turner has been on the radio repeatedly, pleading with the PLA for support.

'We're doing what we can, but the other fireboats are stuck behind the Barrier. The flames must be stopped at all costs.'

So critical is the danger that the PLA seeks permission from Triple-C to assign a Puma helicopter to stand by for immediate rescue of the crews. Venetia Maitland sanctions the order personally. No crew, however courageous, can be expected to risk being burned alive with no possibility of escape.

'What do we do if we can't halt the fires at Dagenham?' she demands of the Committee. 'I want a contingency plan drawn up ready for immediate action.'

The rest of the room looks back at her stunned. What can we do? Harry Lime wonders. He has a wild thought of opening one of the Barrier gates to let the tugs through but dismisses it instantly. The idea is hopeless. The difference in river level across the gate must be of the order of two metres, a metre and a half at the least. No tug could get through the gate against such a flow.

There is no other way. The fires must be stopped at Dagenham or not at all.

They might just do it, Turner thinks. *Jen-0* is forging ahead against the tide, her blunt bow cutting through a lake of smouldering oil from which the flames have been killed. If only they can keep this up till help comes or it starts to rain.

A lot of oil has moved past them but none of it so far has been alight. The crews are exhausted and both ships are starting to run low on fuel but for the moment at least they are holding the line.

Once more he squeezes up his eyes to stare at the shore. There is still a lot of smoke boiling up from out there. He is worried in case patches of burning oil may be working their way round by the banks. He has asked the spotter plane to keep a watch but with the smoke so thick it is hard for the pilot to see and he doesn't have a thermal imager.

A squawk from the radio jerks his attention back. 'Ted, check astern to starboard. Looks like trouble.'

Turner whips around to see more smoke

erupting from off the river. All the oil astern is supposed to have been extinguished so this has to be a spontaneous re-ignition. It has been happening; the oil is still very hot and the air is full of sparks and incandescent droplets. He puts the wheel over and opens the throttle; the outbreak has to be dealt with fast before it spreads. With both tugs operating deep inside the oil slicks, an ambush from the rear is a deadly peril.

The water froths greasily under *Jen-O*'s stern as her twin Voith-Schneider units beat the filthy mix of hydrocarbons and the tug pirouettes round to face the threat. As she does so another voice crackles urgently over the air. It's the pilot of the helicopter, who has spotted a second flare-up.

Ted sees it too. A patch of fire immediately behind the first. If the two should link up the situation could turn ugly very quickly. The wide clumps of doused oil are still hot and seething with volatile vapours that can spark off at any time. They have been foolish to venture in so far, but there was no choice.

Both tugs are retreating at full speed and, as if in response, a savage gust sweeps up the estuary fanning the fires behind to fresh intensity. Before the tug crews' horrified gaze, streaks of red flash across the water, leaping from slick to slick. In seconds both ships are trapped in a blazing girdle, a noose that draws tighter as they watch.

Ted doesn't hesitate. The speed of the current combined with gale-force winds is driving oil upriver too fast for the tugs to outrun. Any second now another of those vapour clouds will fry them all alive. Either that or the stinking mess smothering the surface of the river will foul their engines' cooling inlets, leaving them helpless.

He reaches for the radio, screaming for the helicopter.

From 4,000 feet the pilot has already spotted the danger. He swoops in like a hawk, the Puma's rotors beating back the flames in a wide circle as he hovers over the encircled tugs. *Jen-1* is first, her crew clustering round the lowered hoist to be lifted to safety. Aboard *Jen-0*, the engineer comes scrambling up from below. 'I opened the cocks,' he shouts. 'She'll go down in a minute.'

They can hear the helicopter thrashing the air as it comes in above them. The men on the monitor platform go up two at a time. Ted and the engineer climb onto the roof of the wheelhouse. The line comes down again. They grab it and cling on for dear life. As they lift off into the air he sees a fireball erupt over the land.

Damn, Ted thinks savagely, and we so nearly had it licked.

The fires on the river have reached Dagenham, igniting the storage tanks of the fuel depot. The machine shops with their stocks of volatile compounds are next to go up. The flames are visible ten miles away in central London. Clouds of poisonous fumes descend over neighbouring streets prompting urgent broadcasts warning residents to close all doors and windows and stay inside.

A fire crew from the New Road station has been trying to rescue passengers of vehicles trapped on the elevated section of the A13 that runs through the heart of the plant, only to be forced back themselves by the rising water. Now they are trying to check the flames from spreading across the dual carriageway into the residential streets beyond.

To the crew chief, the factory resembles a scene from hell, the ferocious heat given off by blazing fuel tanks setting up an incandescent whirlwind that rages through the site, exploding buildings and freight cars in violent fireballs. Amid the steaming inferno, gas cylinders detonate like rocket bombs, looping skyward in flaring trajectories, spewing out a hissing rain of red-hot fragments. The power station burns from end to end, flames and sparks spiralling upwards through clouds of debris swirled aloft on the super-heated air.

'It's no use,' the chief shouts into his radio. 'A mass of burning stuff has broken through past the highway. You'll have to start evacuating!'

This is the confirmation the local emergency centre has been dreading.

At the City Airport, Judith Tang can't believe how fast the water is rising. Before they are halfway back to the terminal building it is up around the truck's hubcaps. The flight path has gone, submerged beneath the river. They are driving through open water and it is no longer possible to see the edge of the dock. The force of the waves buffeting the vehicle makes it hard for the driver to hold a straight course. All three of them are terrified of veering off into deep water.

The truck begins to labour and choke. 'Keep going,' the photographer hisses. 'Whatever you do don't stop, for God's sake.'

The driver doesn't need to be told. He clutches the wheel, his eyes riveted on the terminal building.

Spray is flying up over the bonnet. There is water inside the cab now. The front footwell by Judith is awash. She tucks her feet up under her on the seat and clenches her fist, willing the truck to keep moving. She has just seen the aircraft with all her colleagues aboard vanish and now she could die out here on the runway. She is striving to keep her mind off that.

Then the truck gives up. The engine cuts out and they come to a swishing halt. The photographer recovers first. 'Get out,' he says, winding down his window. 'No, not that side!' he yells to Judith as she struggles with her door handle. He forces his own door open. Water rushes in, swamping the cab. Judith scrambles out after the driver.

'Link hands,' the photographer tells them. The flood surges round Judith's knees and the cold makes her cry out. The two men put her between them and together they wade towards the terminal. It looks to be at least 150 metres and the water is swirling more deeply around her legs with every step.

The Governor of Belmarsh has just learned that neither buses nor helicopters are available to take off his remaining prisoners. News bulletins show fires consuming the Ford engine works at Dagenham, less than two miles off across the river, and he has run out of alternatives. Outside, smoke swirls past the windows. If the winds keep up, flames could spread to Thamesmead within the next half-hour. Is he going to risk these men burning to death? He grabs the telephone and punches through to the Chief Officer.

'Inform all the remaining inmates that they are to be released at once on extraordinary parole.'

It is left to him personally to operate the electronic bolt to the main gate. The Chief has refused to perform the deed without a written instruction and there is no time for that. Western Way, the dual carriageway, is already awash and water is lapping round the walls of the jail. A news crew is on hand to record the prisoners splashing out to freedom. Tipped off, the Governor reflects bitterly.

Behind them the flood rolls on through the new housing estates of Thamesmead West, where prison officers' families are vainly trying to barricade their homes, till it reaches the ridge of the Southern Outfall Sewer. Checked here all along its front, the water level behind starts to rise quickly.

Hunched against the blast of the wind, Judith Tang plunges on towards the terminal building. The effort of battling the swirling water is exhausting. Her feet are numb and she has to tense them at every step to keep her shoes on. The driver is the oldest of the three; he's finding the going hard and the photographer has dropped back to help him.

Enormous volumes of water are building up in the streets of Silvertown and North Woolwich. Under pressure, walls collapse, debris and obstructions are pushed aside. At approximately 2.15 pm, a metre-high wave is seen to sweep outwards across King George V Dock and over the runway.

Judith has just time to shout a warning to the men before she is hit by a wall of water. Its crest is higher than her head and the impact is like being smacked by a car. She is hurled backwards off her feet, rolled over and washed along, choking and gasping for air, battered and tossed in the flood like a piece of rag. She struggles to touch the ground but there is nothing there, only darkness and a freezing depth of water.

The back surge rips into her as her head breaks the surface. A heavy weight drags her under again. Her sodden winter coat is weighing her down. She tears frantically at the buttons with numbed fingers and suddenly she is swimming free. She searches round for bearings; far off on the tossing swell an aircraft wing rears up for an instant canted dizzily skywards but she can't see the terminal at all. There is an iron post sticking from the water and she kicks out for it. Clawing desperately, she finds her fingers clutching a metal chain. Her feet touch solid ground and with her final shreds of strength Judith manages to drag herself onto land. The post and chain are part of a line of bollards fronting the quay. The surge has washed her off the airport, right across Albert Dock onto the Beckton side.

Of the two men who were her companions, no trace remains.

On the Thames Barrier loudspeakers crackle urgently. Angus is calling from the operations room. He wants all personnel off the piers. It is getting too dangerous. Peering down from the tower, Lauren Khan can see water rushing down the ramp and cascading over the main entrance gates below. Those same gates Lauren came through earlier; she remembers them as being at least twice her height.

From a window on the main stairs Angus watches the flood advance up the quayside. The water streams over the concrete to the doors of the generator plant. Angus has ordered the turbines shut down and the operating staff withdrawn to the control block.

This is failure, he tells himself. This is what he promised could never happen.

'Port of London Authority have called in. Water is penetrating their building and they are starting to lose power,' an assistant's voice breaks in on his thoughts.

Angus's glance takes in the radio mast of the PLA's Docklands control centre visible above the power station roof. Only a few hundred metres separate the two buildings. 'What's the status of our high-tension feeds?'

'Functioning normally so far. Andy is watching the high-voltage board.'

Loss of electrical capacity is Angus's chief worry. With its own generators down, the Barrier is totally reliant upon the National Grid for power to operate the gates.

He looks back at the forecourt. The water is perceptibly deeper already. At the end of the line of cars a green Rover is in trouble. The wash underneath is lifting it and jostling it towards the ramp. The power of the flood is incredible. That vehicle must weigh close to a ton, he thinks.

The Rover moves closer and closer to the edge of the ramp. The water is tearing down like a millrace, dragging the car with it. At one point it bumps against a light pillar and seems to stick but waves off the river are sweeping unhindered across the forecourt. The Rover lurches forwards again, the nose dips down suddenly and in another instant it is gone, sucked down into the depths of the gate level. Angus turns away.

Immediately west of the control tower, across Westmoor Road, is a truck park and delivery depot. Warnings have had little effect here; drivers can see the Barrier and assume that because they are upstream of the gates they are safe. The flood pours round the walls of the Barrier compound. A wooden fence gives way under the weight of water and within moments the trucks are up to their wheel arches.

Drivers leap for their cabs and those that can start their engines head for the exit onto Riverside, but it is a sharp turn out onto the road and the site is flooding fast behind them. The driver of a big Scania rig has discharged his load earlier. As he wrenches the wheel round he feels the empty trailer start to slide out from under him. He pumps the brakes but to no effect. The truck slews across the road and the driver scrabbles for the door handle as the cab tilts. Too late. The flood has the trailer off-balance and its weight flips the cab over. Water rushes in through the shattered side window. The driver has just time to kick the windshield out and climb through onto the upturned trailer. Around him the water is five feet deep and rising by the minute.

It's just under a mile from the Barrier to the base of the Greenwich Peninsula. The ground is much lower behind the walls and the water runs rapidly downhill into a maze of small streets and light-industrial premises, where the first indication that something is wrong comes from the ringing of burglar alarms as power supplies short out. The pressure behind grows until the flow breaks through onto the main road. The ground is higher to the south and the natural fall of the land leads westwards into Greenwich.

36

Bluewater. The entire sky to the east is a pulsating orange hue from the glow of fires at Dartford and Greenhithe. Murdoch flicks his office blind to check outside and straightens up in shock. He had no idea it was so bad over there.

Rita is beside him, her mouth tight. The conflagration is less than a mile away as the crow flies. The wind has got up too; clouds of smoke are billowing and swirling around the buildings. They watch mesmerised as a fragment of debris is carried comet-like towards them, only to dive and fizzle in the flooded car park. 'That was lucky,' Rita mutters, but even as she does so a further shower of sparks splutters against the window.

Murdoch has his radio out, calling maintenance. He wants fire-fighting teams up on the second-floor car parks right away.

Out on the rooftops, the sky is alive with flashes of fire. There are close on a thousand vehicles parked in the open and thousands more underneath. Acrid smoke taints the air. The fire crews could do with masks, but much of their kit lies awash down below.

And the pressure in the hydrants is playing up, which is an irony given there is so much water all around.

The incendiary that starts the damage lands on the A10 zone, between the back ends of a battered Ford people carrier and an Audi estate. It is no bigger than a football and might have burnt itself out if the vehicles were not so closely parked. As it is, the intense heat starts to sear the rear tyre of the Ford, causing the rubber to melt. Fanned by a blast of wind, flames curl greedily along the rim. Inside the half-empty fuel tank, pressure builds.

When the blast comes, the nearest fire crew is twenty metres away and to a man they hit the floor.

The upper east entrance of John Lewis abuts A10 and its reinforced glass doors implode in shattered fragments. People nearby stumble backwards, crying out in pain and shock. Outside, the two cars are a roaring inferno and black smoke billows into the store. Coughing and choking, disoriented figures battle to get away, only to find their escape blocked because crowds nearer the centre have no idea what has happened. In the dark and confusion people trip and fall. There are shouts of 'Fire!' Children caught up in the crush start to scream. Panic builds.

The mass of bodies bursts out of the mall entrance and funnels along Rose Gallery towards the stairs. Those in front are carried along helplessly by the pressure behind. Ten steps from the bottom their feet hit water. It is freezing cold. They pull up, shocked, but behind them the crowd surges on. Screams and shouts echo through the hall. A man is forced in and then a woman. They have to swim; it is too deep to wade. Within seconds, twenty or thirty heads are bobbing on the surface of the flood and more people are toppling in to join them.

The crowds in Marks & Spencer have heard the explosion and some can see the blaze across the Winter Garden. Smoke is billowing through the galleries and alarm bells are pealing. Those nearest rush out into Moon Court and meet people charging down the stairs. The sound of screaming swells till it fills the centre. Kerry Rosin and the staff from Thames Walk are sheltering in Moon Court. They have been trained in what to do in the event of fire and they know the emergency exits. Without stopping to question, they act. Customers are led to the stairs and hurried down. Kerry is first to take to the water; somebody has to set an example. She plunges in, feeling icy bands of cold squeeze her chest.

Outside, Sergeant John Grey runs out onto the bank above the access road. The once grassy slope is churned and scarred like a battlefield. Ruts criss-cross and swerve and there are great hollows where wheel spins have gouged the soil. Down at the flood line it is a morass of mud.

The last words he hears from Rita before she goes off air are, 'For God's sake, get us out of here!'

Fires are still burning Dartford way and the shower of blazing debris shows no signs of easing. Bluewater's upper car park is blazing fiercely, vehicles exploding one after another like bombs, and flames are being fanned across the site by the wind. Already burning fuel has spread the conflagration to the second-floor level too and dense smoke is boiling into the sky. There is no possibility of outside assistance and unless crews get on top of the situation quickly, the entire complex will be at risk.

A fresh chain of explosions lights up the scene. John notices what seem to be flailing dots in the water over by the Winter Garden entrance. He stares at the spot. The street lamps are out and light is failing fast; it's hard to be sure what is happening.

Two constables come running over with hand lamps. They slither to a halt beside him, playing the powerful beams out across the water. Now John can see. The lake is alive with splashing figures fleeing the burning buildings like rats.

Reaching the water's edge means sliding down twenty metres of glutinous mud. By the time John makes it, the first survivors are lying heaving and gasping on the bank. A woman is floundering a short way out. He yells at her to stand, the water is not deep here, but she is too traumatised to hear. Bracing his feet, John stretches out to grab her, but his hand is slippery and the woman falls back again.

He shouts to the sergeant above him to call Control. They need reinforcements, more men and medics, urgently.

John is in the water now, taking the woman bodily and heaving her onto the bank. She is too weak to help herself so he drags her, half crawling, half scrambling up the muddy slope. It is about ten metres high and the incline is steep. Long before they reach the crash barrier at the top both are unrecognisable. After what seems a lifetime, the woman is lifted off him by helpers from above.

Bedraggled survivors clamber past him as he

returns to the water's edge. Clothes are plastered to their bodies and their teeth chatter. Hair and faces smeared with mud. Even so, John recognizes Kerry Rosin from Thames Walk. She is pulling a woman and child up with her. Near the water again, John reaches out to grasp desperate arms stretching up to him. People stagger and slide, falling on top of one another. For many the mud churned bank is the final hurdle that proves too much. Sounds of uncontrollable weeping mix with the choking and retching of the half-drowned.

John spits the mud from his mouth, but it won't go away. Out on the water the bobbing heads are coming over faster than before. Thousands upon thousands of desperate men, women and children swimming for their lives.

More police arrive and he hears the Super barking orders. Ropes are thrown down to act as handgrips and teams of men formed into human chains to pass people up the bank. Volunteers wade out into the water to rescue stragglers. And still the panicking rush from the buildings continues. Terrified swimmers are thrashing and kicking for their lives towards the shore. Not all will make it; among them are figures no longer moving, bodies that float face down in the dark waters.

John's uniform is soaked and so caked in mud he can hardly move. It takes him a huge effort to plunge back into the icy lake once more. But he does, again and again, till he is so tired and cold he no longer cares. And still they keep on coming.

Across the water Murdoch Morrison has taken personal control of the firefighting crews and slowly he is managing to bring the situation under control.

But there are hundreds of burns victims desperate for treatment. In all, around 150,000 people will need shelter and medical attention if they are not to die.

At Kent Police Headquarters, John Grey's radio message triggers a fresh emergency response. There is no choice now. Bluewater's survivors will have to be evacuated. Even in normal conditions this would be a logistical nightmare. Schools and reception centres as far as the Channel coast are placed on immediate alert and every bus and coach in the south of England requisitioned.

Carol Hayes, a WPC stationed at Westcombe Park covering the Greenwich Peninsula, has been detailed to help clear the Blackwall road tunnels. Carol is fresh out of training, and this is her first real emergency. The tunnels are a mile and a quarter long and each carries two lanes of cars, with a three-foot walkway along one side. Police have been unable to shut the floodgates for fear of trapping people inside. There are two thousand vehicles jammed in the tunnels and only ten uniformed officers to get them out.

Carol works her way down the lines, rapping on windows. 'This tunnel is about to flood. All the exit roads are traffic blocked. Leave your vehicle *now*, and make your way out on foot as quickly as you can.'

Some occupants refuse point blank to leave. Carol argues and pleads, but it is no use. They have seen jams before, this one will clear eventually, they say. They have got valuables in the car that might get stolen; every kind of excuse. When I see water coming up, then I'll think about leaving, sums up the attitude.

Drivers are running their engines to keep warm and, as Carol goes deeper in, the fumes make her head ache. To complicate matters further, pedestrians have started using the tunnel as a footpath under the river between North Greenwich and the Isle of Dogs. There are not enough police to stop them.

No one has foreseen the sheer time needed to evacuate a tunnel system like Blackwall. Carol is spending less than ten seconds with each car and even so it has taken her twenty minutes to reach the middle section of the tunnel. Stuck among the vehicles down here is a double-decker coach and Carol climbs up to tell the driver to disembark his passengers.

'You've got to be joking, luv,' the driver answers. 'There's not one of them back there under eighty. They couldn't manage fifty yards on their own, and you're asking them to walk to Greenwich?'

Brian Honey has paid £120 to bring his wife, Gayle and their two children, Kylie, nine, and Darren, ten, up from Bristol to see today's show and he feels badly let down. Okay, so there is a problem with the river but the Dome management must have had advance warning, he thinks. They should have cancelled the show and posted notices at stations to stop people coming. As it is there has been chaos. First spectators were sent down to the Underground to wait on platforms for trains that were too crowded to get aboard, then the trains were cancelled and everybody was ordered up to the surface again. Now it seems he is expected to walk his family out.

'Act cheerful,' his wife hisses, elbowing him in the ribs. 'You'll upset the kids. Anyway, it's better than hanging around here all afternoon. If we've got to walk, then let's get on with it.'

The column is spread out across the roadway, a dense mass of people, all flowing in one direction like a crowd leaving a football match, with an occasional trapped car moving slowly among them. Snatches of song and of Christmas carols start and then fade. The darkness of a winter afternoon is closing in and the first streetlights have come on. A few local youths jeer at the trudging column. 'They'll be laughing on the other side of their faces when the flood starts,' says Brian sourly.

A short distance beyond the crossroad the column grinds to a halt. 'Now what?' Brian grumbles as a commotion breaks out ahead. A man next to him springs backwards with a curse, 'Watch your feet, there's water here!'

A drain gully in the bottom of the dip is gushing water and already a shallow pool has spread into the roadway. People scramble onto the pavement or press back up the hill the way they have come. Other drains along the road gurgle and start to spew up their contents. Soon the pool has become a torrent streaming down the road towards the Blackwall Tunnel approaches.

'Keep moving! Don't stop!' a police officer pushes through the crowd. 'Come on,' he calls, striding forwards and ignoring the water streaming about his feet. 'It'll be a lot worse if you give it time to get deeper.'

Reluctantly the marchers edge closer. A few people with solid footwear splash confidently out towards the far side. Given a lead more follow. 'Come on,' Brian says grimly. Kneeling, he unlaces his trainers, removes his socks and rolls up his trousers. Darren follows suit. Gayle hesitates a moment. To hell with it, this is no time for modesty. Reaching under her skirt, she strips off her tights and stuffs them into her shoulder bag. Her shoes follow; father and son string theirs around their necks by the laces. Kylie hangs back. She is a nervous child; the thought of stepping into the murky water in bare feet terrifies her. 'Here, love,' Brian reaches down and scoops her into his arms. 'Darren, take your mum's hand.' Gayle grits her teeth. It's only a road, she tells herself.

Nothing has prepared her for the cold though. She has to keep from crying out as her feet touch the water. She holds her skirt up above her knees with her free hand. Other women are doing the same. A camera clicks, catching the scene, and a man swears at the photographer. After the first few steps Gayle's feet go completely numb. Her son squeezes her hand. 'We said this would be a day to remember and we were right,' she says to him.

They reach dry ground again and shake the water from their feet. The wind feels colder than ever. The road lies uphill now, Gayle sees with relief. But more water is streaming down the gutters into the low patch behind them.

'The rest of them aren't going to have it so easy,' Brian says as he sets his daughter down. 'They'll be lucky if it isn't up to their knees.'

Lucky, Gayle thinks ruefully contemplating her filthy feet, her best skirt splashed and muddied. Is that what we are, lucky not to be drowned?

By the time the Exeter school reaches the area the flood is a moat a hundred and fifty metres across and approaching a metre deep. It is not a question of rolling up trousers any longer; people emerge on the far side soaked to the waist and traumatised.

'We can't put them through this,' Colin Gynn says.

The other teachers agree. The younger pupils are plainly terrified at the thought of entering the filthy, freezing lake. Any attempt to herd them across against their will would be madness.

There is no shelter out in the middle of the peninsula and the screeching wind is sending temperatures plummeting. Claire takes a moment to try phoning home again. Her fingers are almost too frozen to work the buttons. Anyway, it seems impossible to find a signal and she gives up, afraid of running down the battery.

It is growing darker too. The afternoon is fading as dusk approaches, sucking the colour from the landscape. As the school trudges dispiritedly back to the Dome with other refugees, a row of street-lights on the motorway behind goes dim suddenly. Some of the children set up a wail of fear. Water has penetrated the circuit somewhere.

Claire tries to keep a cheerful front, bantering with the children, but she is acutely anxious. 'If the roads are cut and the Underground is shut, how are we going to escape from here?' she whispers to Phil.

'The Head talked about boats and helicopters.'

Claire looks around at the people left. There must be a thousand at least cut off here. They are going to need a lot of helicopters, she thinks.

★

Emma Albery is seventeen. It's her birthday and she's sick of waiting out in the cold and gloom. She's wearing a light fleece top over a skimpy skirt and her nose is red and her limbs are frozen. She doesn't want to go to Woolwich. She lives in Notting Hill on the other side of the river.

Now her boyfriend, Tim, is telling her a bunch of people are planning to break out through the Jubilee Line. Apparently they have found a way to climb down inside an escape shaft. The tunnel comes out at Canary Wharf on the north bank. It's a bit of a risk, Tim says. Is she up for it? Emma shrugs, anything to get out of the wind.

The way down begins under a concrete bunker, terraced with plants, that flanks the Dome Main Square. 'See that vent sticking out the roof?' Tim says as they slip through after the rest of the party. 'That's the air shaft. There are stairs inside.'

The shaft is an echoing concrete funnel with a steel stairway that winds around a central well. Draughts of warm moist air rise up out of the shadowed depths. Emma clings tightly to the handrail as she follows the others down, her feet clattering on the metal steps. One of the girls trips on her platform shoes. Bursts of nervous laughter bounce off the walls.

The shaft goes down and down. Just when Emma thinks it is never going to end she finds herself stepping off in some dark place underground. She clutches Tim's hand, 'Where is this?'

'We've reached the tunnel. They're just checking which way to go.'

Raikes's radio bleeps. It is a message from Triple-C. At last it is good news. One of the big river ferries is on its way back to the Millennium pier. She has taken all this time to off-load her passengers and fight her way back downstream against the gale. Her arrival will be a huge bonus. Raikes had almost given up hope of getting significant numbers away by river.

He speaks to the emergency control room in Newham. The Emergency Planning Officer says police have established a rescue collection point at ExCeL and boats are ferrying survivors into the exhibition halls. Approximately a thousand people are gathered there and a train is on its way down from Stratford to pick them up from Custom House station.

His greatest worry now is what to do if fires spread to the Royal Docks.

The SS *Orion Trader*, a 20,000-tonne coastal tanker registered in Rotterdam, entered the estuary on the morning tide, her tanks loaded with seven thousand tonnes of gasoline destined for the Esso terminal at Purfleet. By the time she made Dartford, Esso was shutting down and the PLA instructed the master to moor until the surge was past. Then came the explosion and fire at Coryton.

Now the *Orion Trader* is steaming up-river as fast as she can go, her hull shaking with the vibration of her machinery, in a race to stay ahead of the pursuing flames. Her master is Erich Hausser from Hamburg, an experienced officer who wonders how much longer he can keep this up. Erich knows the lower estuary well as far as Purfleet, but these are unfamiliar waters; legally he shouldn't be here at all without a pilot. As it is, he is steering off the chart by dead reckoning. All landmarks for navigation are gone and he has to judge the position of the banks as best he can from derricks and buildings sticking above the water.

He thinks he can make out the tanks of Beckton sewage works away to starboard. Canary Wharf Tower lies almost dead ahead. Over to port is the light on Tripcock Ness. Woolwich Reach will be coming up next, according to the chart, and with it the Thames Barrier. Once they sight the Barrier there will be no more room left to run. Erich has a half-formed plan of dropping anchor alongside and taking the lifeboats across to the piers. Assuming the British will let them on board.

The radio operator comes hurrying onto the bridge, waving a fax. Erich skims it. The heading is from the Port of London Authority. 'Do not, repeat not, enter Woolwich Reach in any circumstances. Your cargo poses serious risk to other shipping in area. Anchor off Barking Point and wait further instructions.'

Erich reads the message through again. A glance at the chart confirms the ship has already left Barking Point behind. What do they expect him to do, wait here passively to be overtaken by the fires? Even if they take to the boats, where can they go? The river has swollen to a lake four miles wide.

The radio operator is waiting nervously for an answer. Erich puts a reassuring hand on the young man's shoulder. 'Inform the British I will stop the ship when they send a helicopter to remove my crew.'

At the PLA's request a helicopter is tasked to lift off the tanker's crew. The authority's operations centre is in the process of shifting its location for the second time during the emergency. Radar coverage of the upper estuary has lapsed and in the confusion the helicopter is directed to the wrong sector. It searches for fifteen minutes but fails to locate the vessel. So many machines are airborne over the river that when the pilot radios requesting fresh instructions, the dispatcher misunderstands and lists the task as completed.

37

A Met Office team is plotting the extent of the smoke plumes. Using wind forecasts they are producing models showing how the pollution will spread. Already the ominous dark pall hangs over the estuary and across London as far west as Heathrow Airport. Fine droplets of oil are precipitating out as a foul smelling drizzle, leaving yellow smears on windows and metal surfaces.

Closer to the heart of the flames, clouds of noxious gases are travelling at ground level. Already hospital emergency departments north and south of the estuary are filling with cases of respiratory failure. The stench of the burning oil can be detected twenty miles away. The RAF has sent up a reconnaissance plane equipped with infra-red cameras capable of penetrating the smoke and the first pictures have been received at the Met Office. They show Coryton's fires still raging, with hundreds of thousands of tonnes of fuel escaping out into the Thames. From Canvey to Docklands the river is a continuous ribbon of fire.

The meteorologists scan the data into their computers and transmit the projections to the Cabinet Office in Whitehall.

*

An alarm buzzer sounds in the Barrier Control room. The strain gauges on Echo gate are jumping off the scale. Angus checks the screen worriedly. With the tide almost up to the decks of the piers, all gates are loaded way beyond their design limits.

Angus suspects collision damage. There is a lot of debris coming upstream on the current. A waterlogged barge, a sunken container, could have knocked the gate out of true, causing it to deform under the weight of overtopping and vibrate. He is puzzled though. Even if the gate is damaged, the Shift and Latch mechanism ought to be damping out any movement.

I'll go out and take a look, he says.

The only way to reach Echo is by the sub-river tunnel. Angus takes the stairs down to the subway level. Water is leaking into the tunnels, but it's nothing the pumps can't cope with. His rubber boots ring dully on the metal gratings as he moves past the rows of pipes and electrical cables.

Walking briskly he passes through door after door. At the exit for Pier 6 he halts. The sill he is standing in is a 10,000-tonne concrete block. Usually it is silent as a tomb down here. Now though, he can detect a low, throbbing vibration running through the tunnel walls. The sound of the river coursing over the gate above.

He climbs the metal stairs to the main deck level. Stepping out onto the pier into the wind is a rude shock. Beneath the low scudding cloud the dismal winter light reveals a chilling expanse of heaving grey chopped with white foam. Darkness is fast approaching under plumes of smoke and away to the east the sky is stained with an angry red glare. Angus clutches at the handrail, his eyes squeezed up against the ferocious wind blasting up the estuary. Waves surge against the pier, sending up sheets of icy spray, drenching the concrete. The tide is so high that the walkway is almost awash. The gates themselves are completely under water.

'The rocker-beams and hydraulics are functioning normally but they can't control the shaking. The problem must be with Shift and Latch. I'm going forward to check now.'

Up in the operations room the rest of the team are following Angus's progress on the CCTV, communicating with him by radio.

What is Shift and Latch? Lauren wants to know.

The mechanism for locking a gate in position, Martin, the Tidal Defence Manager, explains. A steel arm latches onto pins around the rim of the gate end. Angus thinks the latch on Pier 6 may have worked loose.

'What will you do?'

'According to the manual the procedure is to lower the gate one notch so the latch engages onto a fresh pin. But attempting to move the gate in these conditions is a desperate course. There is a risk we might lose control.'

'And if the gate stays as it is?'

Martin shakes his head. Overtopping is putting tremendous pressure on all gates. If Echo continues to vibrate it could start to twist or buckle. 'In an extreme event we could be looking at a gate failure.'

*

On the bridge of the *Orion Trader*, Captain Erich Hausser peers into the murk upstream. The light is failing and drifts of smoke obscure the shore. The nearest blazing slicks are less than half a mile off. He is trying to confirm the GPS plot against visual landmarks but the swollen river makes it impossible. He estimates his position as somewhere off Gallions Point, by the entrance to KGV dock. In fact the ship is already moving down Woolwich Reach, barely a mile from the Thames Barrier.

He also has underestimated his speed. The log shows the tanker making four knots through the water but the current is running at seven knots. When the Barrier does come into view he will need to react very quickly indeed.

WPC Carol Hayes has returned to the south entrance of the Blackwall Tunnel seeking help for the pensioners aboard the coach. The local Inspector contacts Greenwich Emergency Control and arranges for stretcher teams and wheelchairs from the nearby hospital to give assistance. Carol hurries back down the tunnel again to prepare the passengers.

One of the women offers Carol a piece of chocolate. Her name is Enid, she says, and she is eighty-six.

'Enid, can you manage the steps up to the walkway?'

Enid shakes her white head. 'Oh no, dearie. I couldn't leave my Bill,' she indicates a dozing figure in the window seat next to her. 'His legs give him trouble and I couldn't leave him here. Or my friends,' she adds looking round at the other passengers. She sees Carol's face fall. 'Never mind, dearie,' she says brightly. 'We'll come through all right in the end, you'll see.'

Carol waits but there is no sign of the expected helpers and the driver is becoming nervous. Finally, Carol returns to the entrance to find out what is causing the delay. She discovers that the hospital party has reached the scene but another policeman has mistakenly directed them down the wrong entrance.

Flooding has reached Bow Creek by the western end of the Royal Docks where the River Lea, the last major tributary east of Tower Bridge, enters the Thames. Evacuation continues after overtopping has begun using boats from the water sports centre and yacht marinas. The French corvette *Drogou* brings out over two hundred. A few people are rescued by jet ski. Still some obstinately remain, prepared to sit out the flood on upper floors. Among them are residents of fifteen hundred homes in a newly opened urban village on South Quay, now submerged by the river. The authorities have no powers to compel them to leave.

Against the gathering darkness, the Dome glows fantastically, lit from within by greens and blues. Wind is driving spray off the river and the air is filled with icy particles that lance exposed skin like a million needles. Wave crests shoulder against the tops of the walls, slopping over in places. It is past 3 pm on a winter's evening approaching the shortest day of the year and, with the coming of the smoke, dusk has descended. The lamps shine weakly in the murk and water streams across the site. Anyone not on urgent business has taken shelter inside the great tent, leaving the concourse awash and abandoned.

Raikes is standing by the pier, his eyes on the ferry as it rounds the point. He watches anxiously as the bow begins to turn. The river is narrow here. If the skipper misjudges the turn he won't be able to manoeuvre the vessel into position for a second attempt before the peninsula floods.

Slowly, the cumbersome craft comes round, wallowing through the water. On deck, the berthing crew are standing by.

'Wait inside, please. You'll be told when it's your turn.'

News of the ferry's approach has spread through the Dome crowd, prompting a crush towards the exits. The police and Lamar with his remaining staff are striving to keep control. The Exeter school is formed up ready to board first. Claire and the other teachers push the pupils into groups, with older ones on the outside and youngsters in the centre.

The river is coming up fast. Waves are driving into the coach park on the eastern side of the compound. Glass doors have been closed across the entrances to North Greenwich station.

Outside the tent, water is running across the concourse past the turnstiles. When Lamar gives the signal to let the Exeter party out, Colin Gynn takes charge. 'Right, follow me,' he calls, striding into the flood. Nervously the front ranks of the column push through the doors after him. Wind sweeps spray blindingly in their faces.

Waves are surging high around the pier. A lattice steel bridge, ninety metres long and resting on cast-iron caissons, runs out to a floating pontoon where the ferries dock. The pontoon rises and falls with the tide and right now, with the river surging against the top of the caissons, it is up level with the main landing stage.

The pontoon is heaving on the heavy swell and the ferry-master has to make several attempts before he succeeds in docking. The whole pier is protected from the weather by stretched fabric awnings but, with the river running so high, waves are deluging passengers with spray. Down on the pontoon, they huddle together under the lights, half soaked, teeth chattering, one thought only in their minds, to get aboard that boat and out of here.

'I can take five hundred and twenty,' the ferry-master tells Raikes over the radio. 'That includes the upper deck. Any over and I lose my licence.' He is nervous and with reason. His vessel is a strictly fair-weather craft, hardly more than a self-propelled barge. It was pitching badly on the way down.

To hell with your licence, is Raikes's response. If you double up on the lower deck we can cram in twice that number. 'We are running out of time here.'

The pupils scramble out along the bridge and onto the pontoon where crewmen pull them aboard the ferry. There is a real urgency now. In a space of minutes the first section is safely below.

For Claire Panton the worst part is waiting in line. Out here the river is a terrifying sight. By the time she reaches the pontoon, water is sweeping the decking; ferry and pontoon pitch sickeningly up and down with each wave. Claire has the children link arms and clutch the safety rails.

The queue shuffles forwards and it is her group's turn. It is a huge relief to step onto the solid boat. A seaman in oilskins directs her forward to the open hatch. Claire could hug him from sheer relief. Hundreds of Exeter pupils are thronging the deck up ahead of her. She is virtually the last of their party to board.

The next column arrives on the pier and begins filing onto the bridge. These are family groups of mixed ages so the pace slows. Raikes has been keeping a rough tally and reckons they have embarked close on four hundred so far.

More people are splashing out from the Dome. There are worried faces among them and many have been soaked on the way. On the bridge a woman stumbles, causing a blockage. There have been mercifully few such incidents, but time is precious and it is slipping away.

A gust of bitter wind sweeps in off the river. To the east the skies are darkening to night and with the darkness comes a sound like thunder.

38

'Release lock on Echo!' At the Barrier, the atmosphere is tense. Angus has opted to re-set the Shift and Latch. Almost immediately the attempt runs into trouble. When the lock on Pier 6 is released, the gate starts to oscillate violently in the current. Angus, who is directing operations by radio from the pier, has to call for full power on the hydraulic rams. Two technicians are handling the controls from workstations, while Martin monitors the strain gauges. Lauren watches from the windows but amid the gathering dark it is hard to make out what is happening.

Behind her in the operations room there is another flurry of radio exchanges. It seems the latch mechanism is failing to engage with the new pin. Angus and Martin are divided over what to do. Angus wants to return the gate to its original position; Martin thinks they would do better to leave it where it is.

At this moment the lights of the *Orion Trader* come into view.

The tanker's captain has just had his first sight of the Barrier. All he can see are the tops of the piers submerged up to the stainless-steel hoods. The gates are completely invisible under water. The tide barriers he is familiar with have been of the drop-gate type. The light arrays that indicate gates are shut are under water. No helicopter has arrived and the fire is at their backs. The ship is a mile away, travelling at ten knots. Stopping is no longer a possibility. In the circumstances it is understandable that all aboard should assume that the Barrier has opened to let them pass.

He selects Delta gate between Piers 6 and 7 and lines the ship up. According to the chart the gap is sixty-one metres; from up on the bridge it looks horribly narrow. The tanker is making too much speed but cutting power to the engines will reduce the bite of the rudder and cost him steering control.

The look-out stationed in the bow calls out that he can see turbulence. That is only to be expected, the captain thinks, with the current funnelling between the piers. He is trusting to the speed and weight of the ship to carry them through. At this rate they will draw level with the Barrier in the next two minutes.

The radio officer comes running onto the bridge. He has been trying to raise the PLA on VHF. The captain pushes him away. He needs all his concentration now. They are close enough to the Barrier to see a figure waving to them from Pier 6.

Up in the operations room, Lauren witnesses the unfolding catastrophe, transfixed with horror. The swirling smoke has concealed the tanker's approach until now it is almost on the Barrier. Martin is the first to recover. Snatching the radio mike, he screams a warning over the pier tannoys.

*

Angus has seen the ship too. He knows it is too close to stop or turn away. There is just one chance left. He yells into the radio to control to drop Delta. Without waiting for an answer, he runs down into Pier 6 lower machinery room to knock off the latches.

Martin freezes. He grasps Angus's meaning; if they can lower the gate enough in time, there is a chance the ship will skim over without striking it. But to engineers the Barrier is a sacred charge. Their duty is to defend London against a surge, a duty backed up by Parliament. By law, anyone opening gates without authority is liable to fourteen years' imprisonment.

The rest of the team gape at him. Beyond the windows the tanker is closing the gap, water foaming under its bow. Above the wind comes the sound of its horn. The whole room hangs on his orders.

Martin takes hold of himself. Angus is right, a smashed gate is no use to London. His arm goes out, snapping his fingers to the technicians on the gate controls. 'Unlatch Delta. Full power on all hydraulics. Start emergency opening countdown!'

The room leaps into action. Martin picks up the direct-line phone to Agency Headquarters, praying it still works and he doesn't have to try the radio. To his relief there is an answer. In seconds he is through to Dave Wilcox. 'Warn Triple-C that a main gate is going down now!'

He hears a gasp. Then, 'Once the ship is through, can you raise it again?'

'Negative,' Martin replies. He is watching the screens on the desk opposite wishing that Angus was here. The latches are off and the power packs showing ready. The technicians catch his eye. Does he really mean this? Martin gestures to them. Go! Go!

Listen, he tells Wilcox. The gates are being strained beyond all limits as it is. We'll be lucky if they don't all shake themselves to pieces. Once Delta's down, it has to stay down.

'Delta lowering!' a voice interrupts.

There is no more time to argue. Martin drops the phone and darts to the windows. His heart sinks; the tanker is right on the Barrier. It must strike the gate in seconds. Water is swirling between the piers. As the gate descends the increased flow is sucking the current through, actually pulling the ship faster towards it.

'Delta point five of a metre off top,' the voice calls out again.

The gate is dropping, but it's not fast enough Martin realises with a sickening sensation. The tanker's bow wave has reached the piers. As he tenses for the impact, he sees the prow rear up suddenly and the whole vessel shudder. An instant later the boom of the collision reaches the control tower like the sound of a heavy wave breaking against a sea wall.

It is a tribute to Erich Hausser's seamanship that the *Orion Trader* hits Delta gate exactly on the mid-point. The tanker has a deadweight of 20,000 tonnes fully laden and draws five metres. When it strikes the gate it is travelling at approximately six metres per second. Its momentum is such that the point of the bow rides up over the sloped hump of the gate. The gate leaf is constructed from strips of

5-centimetre steel on a box-girder frame. With the strain of overtopping it's already supporting twice its design pressure of 9,000 tonnes.

As the tanker ploughs on, piling its enormous weight onto the gate, the inner frame crumples, bending inwards. The gate is supported at either end by massive disks, weighing 1,100 tonnes apiece, that rotate around trunnion shafts, short stub axles set into the piers. The force of the impact wrenches the gate end on Pier 6, twisting it violently inwards and jamming the bearings. The trunnion shaft is a forged steel billet bolted to a flanged steel pipe embedded in concrete and running right through the pier. Shaft and bearings are designed to support a hydraulic loading in excess of 5,000 tonnes. The shaft withstands the collision but the strain shears the bolts connecting it to the support structure. With a ringing crash that jars right through the pier, the gate end rips clean away.

On the tanker's bridge the force of the crash has thrown every man to the deck. As the captain staggers back to his feet he can feel the ship judder violently, corkscrewing and twisting all along her length. Sounds of tortured metal, tearing and scraping against the hull, reach his ears. The bow of the ship pitches downwards and for a moment he thinks they are holed and sinking. There is another hideous shuddering, from astern this time, followed by a second heavy impact that rains debris on the decks. The after section of the tanker's hull has rolled into the side of Pier 5, sending a two-metre wave cascading across the concrete deck.

And still she ploughs onwards. A throat-gagging stench of raw gasoline envelops the bridge. The twisted wreckage of the gate must have punctured the double hull forward. Smoke billows through shattered windows. Bells and sirens are shrieking. Toxic gas alarm, radio short alarm, main fire alarm, every whistle and klaxon goes off. The bridge is filled with panic noises. The captain grasps the microphone and stabs the button for the engine room. 'Stop all engines! Evacuate below decks! Execute CO_2 drench!'

With sparks filling the air it is vital to snuff out any fire before it can take a hold. The ship is more than halfway through the Barrier now. Her bow plunging down at so steep an angle that the entire forward section of the tank deck is completely buried for several seconds. Then she starts to rise again, but slowly, listing over to starboard as she does. At that moment a very strong vibration runs through the ship and the whole rear accommodation structure whips like a springboard. The lights go out and power failure leaves the instruments and controls useless.

Up in the control tower, Martin is frantically trying to raise Angus. Alarm bells are sounding here too. Delta is down; Echo is in trouble and now red lights are flashing on the monitors covering Charlie gate. Staring down at the scene, he sees the ship slide clear of the piers. It looks to be down at the bow and listing badly, surrounded by an iridescent patch of leaking fuel. The gate has disappeared completely, the ends torn bodily away, leaving the surge foaming triumphantly through the gap.

Martin relays the news to a stunned Dave Wilcox. Grimly he spells out the facts. Delta is gone, smashed in the collision. The strain gauges on the bearings for Charlie gate are jumping off the scale and the controls for the Latch mechanisms don't respond. Echo gate is in bad shape and they can't reach Angus.

Before Wilcox can answer, pandemonium breaks out around the monitors.

'Pier 6 Shift and Latch has broken. Echo is swinging free!' a technician shouts.

Lauren is at the windows. The black lip of the gate rears above the water for an instant then dives again. The river is thundering around the piers, water breaking confusedly across the gap. There are cries from behind her. 'The bearings have gone!' Through the gloom Lauren glimpses a huge object like the humped back of a whale. The gate has broken free at one end and rotated up to the surface. Another violent commotion ensues and it disappears from view.

The Cabinet Office Briefing Room swarms with officials. Messengers run in and out. Most people are in shirtsleeves and the phones ring constantly. Thick rubber power cables snake over the carpet. Army signallers have brought in radio sets and laid on extra phone capacity but they can't keep up with demand. Venetia sits at the head, with permanently open lines to the emergency services strategic control rooms – Police, Fire, Ambulance and Military – in front of her.

Thirty men and women are squeezed in around the main table, which is half buried under laptops and binders, directories, heaps of files. Down the centre runs an immense map of central London and the Thames estuary out as far as the Dartford

Crossing. Two assistants are marking the surge's progress with coloured flags: blue for flooding; red for fire; black for an incident involving loss of life. The blue flags extend all the way up-river as far as the Thames Barrier, indicated by a broad band of yellow. North and south of it, the flood is shown engulfing Woolwich and the City Airport. Now Mary Lucas watches as an assistant leans over to plant a blue marker at Canning Town on the western end of the Royal Docks.

There are other markers indicating evacuation centres, troop concentrations, receiving hospitals and emergency control centres. Most ominous of all, though, is the line of red flags advancing westwards along the river towards Woolwich that marks the vanguard of the burning oil slicks.

Into this comes an urgent call from the Environment Agency. It is Dave Wilcox for Venetia Maitland. 'Two gates down at the Barrier?' her voice cuts through the babble around.

The entire room freezes. All eyes go to the map. Then frantic activity breaks out. Conversations are broken off in mid-sentence. Hands grab for phones and radios: 'Stand by for urgent message!'

Nikki Fuller scribbles calculations. Each main gate measures 61 metres by 20. The tide is moving at six knots. With two gates down, 7,000 cubic metres of water will flow into the upper pool every second.

Greenwich and the Isle of Dogs will be swamped and fifteen minutes from now the tide will be half a metre above the walls at London Bridge.

The enormous volume of water released from the Barrier moves upstream in a hump that spreads out across the banks at either side. Torrents pour through Charlton down towards the Greenwich Peninsula. The force of the flood washes containers from the truck park beside the Barrier into neighbouring factory premises, collapsing walls and bringing down the roof. Half a dozen employees are trapped inside and drowned.

The flood rushes between the business parks on the south side of Woolwich Road, sweeping all manner of wreckage before it. A gang of youths who have been looting among the warehouses flee across the sports ground and only escape drowning by scaling the fence around the tennis courts. Along Bugsby's Way the level rises five feet in the space of two to three minutes. In the Millennium village, ground-floor residents take refuge on their kitchen worktops with water chest deep around them.

Out on the Dome pier a hundred or more have yet to board and the handful of Dome staff by the entrance are struggling to maintain control. Frightened people are jamming the long narrow bridge and the pressure is forcing those further along onto the pontoon. The ferry's crew is doing its best to get passengers aboard quickly but it's not easy with a high sea running and the deck of the pontoon awash.

Raikes radios Lamar to send reinforcements and sprints over to take charge himself. There is jostling and shoving by the gate. Children are crying and punches being thrown. Idiots, Raikes thinks. This is what he has been trying to avoid. He shoulders into the mob and is trying to reach the gate when a seventy-knot gust comes tearing up the estuary.

The wind catches the back slope of a wave,

whipping it up into a lashing grey mountain, driving it onwards against the peninsula. The two-metre avalanche hits the crowded pontoon broadside on, swamping it from end to end. Those passengers waiting to board by the ferry's gangway have no chance. There is not even time for a warning shout before they are waist deep in surging water.

Raikes hears the screams and forces his way to the edge. The breaker has swept the pontoon clear like a broom. The safety rail at the rear has broken away, crushed by the weight of bodies piled against it. A few fortunate ones were close to the toe of the bridge and have managed to cling on, but the rest are gone, washed over the side. Raikes can see heads bobbing in the river. A woman in a red jacket has a child strapped to her back. Her arms flail the water in a desperate attempt to get her head above the surface but the weight of the child keeps forcing her under. Before anyone can reach them mother and child sink out of sight. There is a glimpse of the child's white face straining upwards, then the water closes over them.

Pandemonium breaks out on the pier. People are screaming with horror. Among those on the bridge there is an ugly rush back towards the shore. There are screams from the ferry too; quantities of water have poured in through the open hatch, drenching the passengers inside and causing panic in the cabins.

Raikes unclips a life preserver fastened to the rail and throws it in the direction of the nearest survivors. He gets on to the radio and sends out an urgent distress call, trying to count the number in the water. It looks like twenty plus overboard but in the poor light the victims are hard to track. One or two have managed to swim back to the pontoon and are being helped aboard. Seamen from the ferry are pulling some out too. But others are being swept under the pier or are drifting out of reach into midstream. They will drown quickly in the freezing water if they aren't rescued.

The people still on the bridge are stumbling over one another in their haste to reach the bank again. Raikes pushes past them and fights his way down onto the pontoon. The ferry-master knows his business; he has an inflatable in the water and another being made ready. More shocked survivors are being pulled out to collapse coughing and retching on the deck. Raikes climbs down a ladder into the water to go to the help of a woman. She is holding a child in her arms; a boy of six or seven, so limp Raikes fears he is dead. But when he lays him down the boy vomits copiously and starts to wail. Raikes hauls the mother out and she falls on her son, weeping hysterically.

He rescues another man who is gasping under the weight of his sodden overcoat. It is astonishing how heavy people are. Raikes himself is soaked through to the skin. He takes another quick headcount. Twelve have been definitely saved so far and one of the boats is heading back with figures huddled in the thwarts. More have been pulled onto the ferry. Rescuers are giving CPR. Overhead there is a thudding of rotor blades; a helicopter has picked up the Mayday call and joined in the rescue.

There is no time to count the dead. The last passengers are herded aboard without ceremony and the warps cast off. Raikes watches anxiously as the ferry backs away from the pier and turns broadside on to the wind and current. With over a thousand aboard she lies deep in the water, the spray breaking over the glassed-in superstructure. Her bows come round, the wake froths under her stern as the engines are put ahead and she disappears northwards into the gathering dark.

Raikes stumbles away from the pier, wading back through the flood into the Dome. The wind tears at the steel rigging, filling the tent with an eerie droning sound. Spray rattles on the sides and roof, water is streaming in under the doors. There is no sign of life. The lights are failing and the vast arena is deserted. It is a strange feeling being the only person left.

Water is running knee deep out in Main Square. His helicopter is waiting on the roof of the administration block, its rotors turning. He scrambles aboard and it lifts off, wheeling away across the swollen river.

39

The Barrier is down! From Triple-C urgent messages are being dispatched to TV and radio stations with fresh warnings to be broadcast to the population. Along the hardened circuits of the government's emergency communications network alerts flash to police and borough emergency control centres, setting evacuations in train.

For many the warnings will come too late.

With the Barrier gone, hard decisions have to be faced. Whitehall itself is in imminent danger. Flood levels will shortly submerge the heart of government and Triple-C must relocate or be trapped. All around, people are grabbing up maps and briefing books and preparing for evacuation.

Venetia Maitland leads the way. She carries herself defiantly, her head thrown back, shoulders straight. The others follow her out through a rear door, emerging into the bitter wind onto Horse Guard's Parade. The famous square is filled with hurrying people and vehicles. Orders are shouted and radios crackle in the frozen air. An urgent military operation is under way to evacuate hundreds of civil servants. A soldier directs Mary Lucas to a waiting Land Rover. Nikki Fuller from the Environment Agency squeezes in the rear beside her. They are hardly settled when the engine starts.

Preceded by a motorcycle outrider, the convoy moves off westwards along the Mall. At the Palace it swings right. Traffic is backed up along Constitution Hill. The driver of the lead truck selects low-ratio and plunges off the road onto the edge of Green Park. The rest follow, churning a broad trail up the slope. At Hyde Park Corner, police and soldiers struggle to clear a passage between queues of traffic from Piccadilly and Park Lane. It takes several vital minutes for the convoy to force a way across to the park and onto the South Carriage Drive.

Hyde Park is an astonishing sight. The whole area inside the railings has been sealed off and turned into a military base. The scale of the relief operation is enormous, with helicopters landing and taking off and vast stores of material being assembled under the glare of floodlights. Everywhere Mary looks there are bulldozers and bridging equipment, trucks unloading inflatable boats, fire-engines and military ambulances. Beside the Serpentine a canvas city is springing up, with long lines of shelter tents and a 200-bed field hospital under construction.

'Where are we headed, do you know?' she whispers to Nikki.

'Knightsbridge Barracks, I heard someone say. We must be almost there.'

At the Barrier, the last phone links have been lost. Martin is using the radio to contact Dave Wilcox.

Charlie gate can't hold much longer, he warns him. The shaft support for the gate axle must have been damaged when Delta tore loose and the gate end is shaking itself apart.

There is still nothing from Angus. Martin takes one of the technicians down to the subways in search of him. There is a lot of water below now. It swirls about their boots as they wade along the tunnel with lamps strapped to their helmets. 'Where's all this coming from?' the technician wants to know.

He gets his answer soon enough. At Pier 6, it is cascading down the stairs in torrents.

We can't climb up there, Martin says. We'll have to try the upstream shaft.

The other stairs are wet but passable still. They climb five storeys to the machinery rooms. There is a lot of damage here. The forty-tonne hydraulic rams that work the rocking beams have been jarred from their concrete beds and the floor gleams with pools of viscous green fluid. Martin radios back to the operations room to report. Charlie is still holding, his junior tells him. But they had better hurry.

The two-tonne arm from a fallen crane blocks the exit onto the deck. Outside, the pier is a shambles. The massive yellow rocking-beams are gone, wrenched bodily off their bearings when the gates were torn away. The railings have disappeared and strips of steel cladding to the machinery houses flap in the storm. There is no sign of Angus.

Picking their way through the wreckage, they reach the downstream machinery house and take the stairs down to the Shift and Latch room. This is where Angus was heading for when contact was lost.

Abruptly they stop, staring in shock. The way is blocked. There is a huge hole in the wall of the pier and the river is surging in through it. Below them, the Shift and Latch chamber is choked with smashed machinery and broken concrete. The roof has given way and the whole end of the pier has been torn apart as if by high explosive. The technician nudges Martin and points silently. Protruding from under a tangle of reinforcing bars beneath the water on the far side of the chamber is the arm of a yellow plastic jacket.

Martin clambers down into the water. Up close it is clear there is no hope. Angus's body is trapped beneath the surface, crushed under tons of concrete rubble. Martin crosses himself and murmurs a prayer. At least, he thinks, it must have been quick. And Angus would not have wanted to live with his precious Barrier destroyed.

Sombrely, the two retrace their steps to the subway. They are passing Pier 7 when there is a deep booming sound overhead; a violent tremor shakes the tunnel and the hammering of steel on steel echoes off the concrete walls.

'That was Charlie!' Martin shouts. 'Run!' And they plunge along the flooded passage to the tower stairs.

And now a third Barrier gate is down.

At Canary Wharf Tower, Barry Singleton has been calling the police, asking for guidance. If they can give him an order to shut down, then the building's owners will be covered against legal action. We can't do that, comes the answer. The police only have power to order compulsory evacuation in the case of bomb alerts. Barry next speaks to the borough emergency planning officer. The EPO says if Canary Wharf isn't safe, then nowhere is. 'Official government advice is to move upstairs.'

The board of directors is in session; the head of security assures them that evacuation drills are in place and, if necessary, the entire complex can be emptied in minutes. Members decide to defer action until the situation becomes clearer. Barry's office begins ringing round tenant firms, urging them to start sending home non-essential personnel.

Then comes news of disaster at the Barrier.

What nobody appreciates, including Barry, is that the flood is already infiltrating the district from the rear. A mile to the east the River Lea is in spate. Prevented by rising tide levels from discharging into the Thames, the river has burst its banks near the former gas works at Beckton and is pouring through South Bromley. Floodwater is flowing rapidly through the drainage system, causing surcharges and back-ups on a widening front as much as a mile ahead of the main threat.

The surge invades the Dome unopposed all along the shore, sweeping across the banks adjacent to the coach park in a solid grey wave that rolls unchecked over open ground past the superstore by the gas-holder and onto the Blackwall Tunnel approach road. It has picked up an immense amount of gravel and silt in its passage and this mass of material gathers speed as it flows downhill in an avalanche of liquid mud. By the tunnel portico a small party of police and rescue workers are still frantically trying to get people clear. None of them stands a chance. The torrent engulfs people and vehicles in seconds, burying them alive and sweeping onwards towards the mouths of the tunnels.

In spite of all the warnings, drivers in the Blackwall tunnels are still refusing to abandon their cars. Some have been stuck underground for more than four hours, tying handkerchiefs round their faces against the exhaust fumes. Now, with a tide of lethal mud swirling about their feet, courageous officers tear along the lines of stationary vehicles, screaming to the occupants to get out.

Before they can cover a third of the distance, frantic alarms burst from their personal radios. Hendon's cameras have detected a fresh danger: the floods spreading through Canning Town on the opposing bank have reached the tunnel's northern portals. On the operations room monitors water can be seen running down the slopes into the tunnel entrances.

With death cascading in at both ends, panic breaks out in the tunnel. The flood is coming in so fast people cannot open their car doors against the pressure and the screams of the trapped echo off the white tiled walls. Police wade in, smashing windows with their truncheons and helping people scramble onto the raised walkway along the inner wall.

Even up here, though, the respite is temporary. Hundreds are jamming the narrow ledge, with more struggling to claw their way up, and escape in either direction is next to impossible. The emergency lighting has failed, leaving all but the entrances in darkness. In the chaos several people fall back over the edge or are pushed into the water below. Fighting erupts, with police desperately striving to restore order and calling for assistance over their radios.

The tunnel is now filling rapidly; in the middle part it is up to car roof level. A frantic woman struggles to free a child caught up in its seat belt. Both drown before help arrives. People are climbing onto their vehicles to escape the rising water. In the darkness and confusion families become separated, children are carried away by the torrent. People trying to swim clear become trapped between vehicles, their shrieks choked off by the relentless water. Near the tunnel exit a terrified truck driver tries to bulldoze a way through the cars in front, crushing dozens in the flood.

Even out at the entrances people are no longer safe. Huge volumes of water are pouring off the land and rushing down the ramps into the tunnels. The flows are so great that water starts to back up in the approaches. Before long, levels are rising rapidly here too.

With water surging around her chest, WPC Carol Hayes fights her way back towards the coach. The door is closed fast. Carol hammers on it to get the driver's attention. Peering through the glass, she makes out a figure slumped on the floor by the stairwell. The driver has collapsed. One of the ladies is leaning over him. She twists round and her gaze catches Carol's, distorted with fear. Carol bangs on the glass again, mouthing at her to open the doors, but the woman is too shocked to move.

The rear emergency door opens from outside. Carol struggles round the side of the coach but before she can reach it the lights go out, plunging the tunnel in darkness. The screams of the trapped become frantic. Carol fumbles for her torch, loses her footing and feels the water close over her. The current is swirling furiously between the vehicles. All she can think of is keeping her head above the water. Another figure clutches at her in the dark and they go under together. For a terrifying spell she is whirled about in the blackness, unable to breathe, crashing against unseen objects, while the blood roars in her ears and her lungs scream for air. Then, just as she thinks she must pass out, her hands find a purchase.

Gasping for breath, she pulls herself upright. To her relief she sees a beam of light. Someone up on the walkway is using a torch to guide survivors. Carol holds onto a car roof-rack with the current rushing past. She can't see the coach any longer. Everywhere people are struggling and crying for help. A hand clutches at her in the water. With horror she realises somebody is trapped inside the car, trying to get out through a window. She grasps hold and pulls out a terrified girl.

Carol pushes her up onto the car roof. Another hand follows; a second person is attempting to escape. Carol helps this one clear too. It is the child's mother. She is scratched and bleeding; the electric locks on the doors and windows have seized up and she had to break the glass to get the two of them out.

'Get onto the walkway,' Carol shouts. She finds her own torch and switches it on. Thank goodness it's working still. Together she and the woman carry the girl over to the safety rail and onto the walkway. The water is now nearly level with the foot of the railing. Looping the torch round her wrist, Carol scrambles up to safety and collapses exhausted on the ledge.

The flood is two metres deep in this part of the tunnel and those still trapped inside cars are beyond saving. A few are struggling in the water and, using her torch, Carol guides them to a point where she can pull them up.

'Walk against the flow!' she shouts to people. 'Head uphill.' It is a hard thing to do. Instinct tells them to run away from the inrushing water. Shivering and terrified in the near total darkness, clinging onto the handrail with freezing water surging around their knees, they stumble in the direction of the entrance.

Carol follows, trying not to think of Enid and her husband and all their friends left behind in the coach.

40

Across the river at Canary Wharf, following Sophie de Salis's telephone message, a maintenance engineer has been dispatched to the car park beneath One Canada Square. By now there is a foot of water on the lower level. It is coming in so fast that the engineer assumes there must be a burst main. He hunts about for the source of the influx but can't locate it, so he loops a chain across the ramp to warn people to keep clear and goes back to telephone the local authority.

In the meantime, a fresh indication of trouble comes when a woman shopper collecting her car from underneath Cabot Square, next door, discovers water welling up from a manhole there also. She is sufficiently concerned that when she reaches open air she stops the car and returns inside the building to inform security.

The officer who takes the call in the complex's central monitoring post checks his screens, but the basement lighting is dim and it's not possible to make out clearly what is happening. He contacts the nearest operative on the ground and asks him to investigate. Security staff are stretched to their limits by the emergency and some fifteen minutes elapse before this guard can get downstairs. Fortunately he is wearing rubber boots because, on reaching the lower basement level of the car park, his torch reveals water a foot deep at the bottom of the ramp. He is about to radio confirmation back to the control post when his attention is caught by a rattling noise from a service door in the far wall. The door leads to a passage containing utility ducts and is kept locked. It is rattling as if someone is trying to force it open from inside.

The guard wades over. The door is shaking furiously and to his horror he notices that water is spurting out through the keyhole and round the hinges. The passage inside must be flooding and whoever is trapped inside will drown unless he acts swiftly. He doesn't have a key but there is a fire emergency axe in a glass case on the wall and he doesn't hesitate. He smashes the glass and grabs the axe inside. He forces the blade into the wedge of the door and throws his weight against the haft.

The guard's first heave on the axe has no effect. He pulls back, gathers himself and throws his whole weight against the haft again. With an echoing boom the door explodes outwards under the pressure and an avalanche of water erupts into the basement, hurling him backward. He struggles to his feet and tries to force the door shut, but the pressure of the torrent coming through is like a dam burst. He slips again and the flood hoses him across the floor, sliding and slithering till he fetches up against the wall, with water swirling all around him. He has lost his radio and his torch. When he picks himself up to try to make for the exit ramp he stumbles into a pillar and falls again. By the time he recovers himself this time, the level is over his knees. The noise and the surging water in the darkness are terrifying. He has lost sight of the ramp and now he is too disoriented to find his way out.

Fear of drowning panics him. Half swimming, half wading, he blunders blindly across the basement until he is caught against a vehicle. It is a heavy four-wheel drive and in his terror he climbs onto the bonnet. The water is pursuing him; it is splashing against the sides and in desperation he crawls up onto the roof. There is just room for him to lie flat under the basement ceiling.

The last thing that he remembers as the water rises is an indicator light glowing over one of the lift doors.

At 3.50 pm, with the light fading, Canary Wharf security receives an urgent message from Tower Hamlets emergency centre. 'The Barrier is down! Repeat, the Barrier is down! Rapid flooding is expected in all parts of the borough!'

Barry Singleton is in the Tower's lofty ground-floor atrium. He has just heard word over local radio that overtopping has commenced in the region of Blackwall Basin. Barry has detailed one of his own people to go down to South Quay and monitor the situation. Now he tries to contact the man, but can't raise him. Exasperated, he hurries outside to check for himself.

Up in the control post, the duty controller is trying to make sense of what is going on at Cabot Square. The lights have failed in the basement; he can't see anything on the video screen and the security guard he sent down there doesn't answer his radio any longer. Now a water-detection alarm in the car park is flashing and that is worrying because the sensor is fitted on the ramp leading down from the street.

He tries the car park control booth but gets no response there either. The attendants on duty have been withdrawn for safety. He phones down to the ground-floor desk to find out what has become of the guard. No one has seen the man and they can't spare anyone to look for him.

'He's probably on his way back up to you to report.'

'Then why doesn't he answer his radio? And why have I got an alarm signal showing up here? I'd go myself but I can't leave the post.'

'Okay, okay. Stay where you are. One of us will go down to take a look.'

Reports that flooding has begun have had a galvanic effect in Canary Wharf Tower. There is a sudden late surge of people quitting their desks and making for the elevators. On the twelfth floor a lunch party has broken up in the private dining room of a firm of investment advisers. The twenty or so merry revellers spill out onto the landing, cracking jokes about 'wading home' and 'hailing a gondola' as they wait for the lifts to take them down.

One floor below, Archie Watson and a bunch of other editors have also picked up the radio report and are on their way down to see for themselves the onset of the flood. Archie intends to have himself photographed smoking a cigar on the steps of the building with the water lapping at his feet.

*

Barry has just reached the piazza overlooking Export Dock, where the Underground station is situated. This is one of the Jubilee Line's showpiece structures, designed by architect Norman Foster, and, by an astonishing feat of engineering, actually sunk inside the former dock. From the vaulted concrete and glass entrance canopies, five parallel sets of escalators lead down into a ticket concourse the length of an ocean liner.

Except that now that concourse is a terrifying sight. The dock is brimming over, the level climbing visibly before Barry's gaze. Records will later show the river rising at the amazing rate of thirty centimetres in every minute. At one point the automatic gauge records a near vertical jump of 1.52 metres before going off the scale. Water spills down over the dock wall and gushes up from the steps. Already there is a river running across the open pavement of the piazza and under the canopy. There are barriers here, waist-high steel gates that close off the entrance, but the centre sections are still open to let people escape and the flood is cascading down the banks of escalators. The ticket hall below is a sea of bursting foam. To Barry's horror there are figures visible down there. He sees one poor devil, clinging to the side of an escalator, half buried in the torrent, lose his grip and tumble backwards into the maelstrom.

Back at Cabot Square, the employee dispatched from the ground floor to check the basement takes the stairs down to the promenade level. The shopping mall extends right through under Canary

Wharf Tower and Canada Square. Altogether there are more than a hundred and twenty stores, with underground parking for nine hundred cars on three levels. The guard is passing through the mall when he hears a disturbance. The glass doors fronting the piazza have been locked and businesses are now being advised to close, but this is Christmas and many are slow to obey the order.

'What's the matter?' he asks some girls running towards him.

'There's water piling up outside the doors down there,' one of them says, pointing back in the direction of the piazza.

The man pushes past them. He runs through to the cross passage under the Tower. To his left are the service lifts, to the right an arched tunnel leading out to the Underground station. More people come hurrying back in alarm, skipping out of the way of a rapidly spreading pool of water. All of a sudden a booming concussion rings through the mall. The glass double doors at the end of the tunnel have imploded, releasing a man-high torrent into the crowded eastern mall. A second crash follows from the other end of the mall as a service door near the Canada Square entrance bursts open. Trapped below ground, with water rushing in from two directions and already surging around their knees, a frantic mob fights for the stairs.

Up in the Tower, the first group of the party from the twelfth floor has reached the main foyer. All the elevators are busy, with occupants squeezing up to make room for more at each floor. When a service lift stops there is a rush to scramble on board.

Fourteen people are crammed inside when it sets off. Freight elevators are not supposed to carry passengers but the building manager is understandably anxious to evacuate occupants as quickly as possible.

On the thirtieth floor another service lift has just started down. Among its passengers is an actor dressed as Father Christmas, two strippers who have come to the wrong floor by mistake and are trying to find the office they are supposed to perform in, and a twenty-year-old girl named Alison delivering a basket of sandwiches.

Barry Singleton reaches the main entrance and pushes past Archie and his colleagues, shouting orders over his radio as he goes. The fifty floors of the tower are served by thirty-two passenger lift-shafts divided into four banks, all contained within the building's central core. In addition there are two freight lifts and two others reserved for fire emergencies. The service engineer in charge at once initiates the shut-down sequence. This is a safety procedure whereby all escalators are halted and lifts brought down in a controlled manner. It is standard practice for any serious emergency where power may be cut off and the intention is to prevent occupants becoming trapped.

The uproar on the lower promenade level has not yet spread to the main foyer upstairs. The entrance area is thronged with people and all four banks of lifts are in operation. Inside the freight elevator from Floor 12, the light dims and a recorded voice announces, '*For security reasons this lift will proceed directly to Ground Floor Level without intermediate stops.*'

A man squeezed up by the control panel swears under his breath. He still has to fetch his car out. He presses the Basement level button and holds it in all the way down. Whether this action overrides the safe shut-down sequence and is repeated by impatient passengers in other cars, or whether there is a flaw in the program itself, will never be known. The lift-shafts are fitted with detectors to alert controllers to the presence of water but it may be that the flood comes up too fast for them to react. Either way the consequences will be catastrophic.

Down below, their friends in the lobby watch the indicator wind back to the Ground Floor mark and continue on past. 'Going down to the basement,' observes a fat man holding a bottle of champagne in each hand.

'Someone wants to fetch their car.'

'Left it a bit late, haven't they?'

The indicator has stopped at the B2 level sign.

'Taking its time,' observes the fat man after a minute or two. The lobby is filling up with people. A sound of confused shouting comes from the lower level.

Someone cocks an ear, 'What's all that noise about?'

'Just another rowdy office party.' They chat among themselves while they wait but the indicator hand does not move.

'Oh come on, this is boring,' the fat man says. 'Press the tit somebody. I want to go home.'

Up in the engineer's control room a row of red lights begins to flash on the screen monitoring the elevators. The engineer scowls as he peers at the display. Several lift-cars have descended to the promenade level and appear to have stalled there. They are supposed to stop up in the atrium. Something has gone wrong and he wonders belatedly if it's to do with the water down there.

He switches over to the emergency movement system. This is designed to bring cars safely down in the event of power failure and operates by automatically adjusting cable counterweights. It has worked in the past in exercises and he prays it will now.

It does. As he watches on the screen, the car indicators on the remaining lifts wind slowly back up to main level. With a sigh of relief he clicks the Operate All Doors button.

The lift doors operate on a system of hydraulic pistons; in the circumstances it is surprising how resistant to damage they are. The marble colonnade between the elevators is thronged with people waiting for friends and colleagues. As the lights go on over the doors an expectant buzz runs through the crowd.

Barry Singleton has climbed the steps past the coffee house on his right and is threading his way towards the central lobby. Behind him, Archie Watson has given up on his cigar and is following him back inside. The two are no more than five metres away when the doors of the nearest elevator crack open.

Things happen so fast, from that moment time appears fractured – a kaleidoscope of images and sounds. He is aware of the champagne bottles flying from the fat man's grasp to shatter on the white marble floor. Of the bursting wine foaming in a wave, exploding outwards from the lift; of the screams of the crowd as water envelops them from both sides, as if the colonnade has suddenly become a bathing pool, with cascades pouring from a dozen doorways. Of a young woman's lips, scarlet against the white foam spewing from her bloated mouth as she slides by him on the floor. Of wondering how there can be so many bodies slithering and slopping in the water at his feet like stranded fish. He is aware of averting his eyes to shut out the awfulness of the gaping lift-cars with their mounds of heaped dead. Of the horror in the shrieking faces pushing past him, fleeing from the scene of so much death. And the slowly dawning apprehension that this dreadful thing is somehow his doing.

41

There are two police stations on the Isle of Dogs: at Canary Wharf and another by Millwall Park at the island's toe. Since midday, Sergeant Damien Furst of the Millwall station has been banging on doors in the new developments, telling residents to get upstairs. Now he is making the rounds again, but this time the message is stark: '*Get out. Leave the building while you still can. Take whatever clothes you can carry and make your way out on foot. Follow the elevated track of the Docklands Light Railway north through Canary Wharf.*'

Damien is turning the corner into Barnsdale Avenue, by the health centre, when he meets people fleeing towards him. The water has come over Millwall outer dock and is pursuing them down the street. Damien shouts to them to follow him back along to the DLR station at Mudchute. They have gone a few paces when they meet more water flooding across the road in front. It is knee deep and running fast. Damien is the only one wearing rubber boots. He hears a woman scream and snatches her little boy up in his arms as he is about to be swept away, and together they struggle through to the station.

Damien deposits mother and child on the stairs to the track and turns back to help the rest of the party. He sees an elderly woman struggling in an alley between two buildings and wades in after her. Within seconds the torrent is round his waist. He manages to catch hold of the woman's hand, but her wrist is so thin and frail it slips through his grip and she slides under. A heavy object cannons into Damien from behind, knocking him down. Flailing to recover his footing, his fingers close on the collar of the old woman's coat. She is pinned underneath a steel waste bin that must have been carried down on the current. Damien attempts to heave it clear but the thing is filled with silt and water and weighs a ton. Another man wades in to help and together they haul the woman's body to the surface but as they wipe the water from her face her head flops over. For this one, rescue has come too late.

The man looks stricken. She is his mother. Damien can't think of anything to say. He is trying to recall the emergency arrangements for the handling of bodies. There is supposed to be a temporary mortuary at the fire station on Ship Road but when he tries his radio to ask for transport to convey the body it doesn't work. In the end he and the son carry the old lady up the steps to the station platform and lay her out on one of the benches. The man says he will stay with her till she can be moved.

Damien wades back to the station to report the death and pick up a replacement radio, knocking on more doors along the way. He meets a party of firemen towing a boat with a family of four aboard complete with dog. They tell him that more water is coming in fast through Island Gardens. The school there is cut off and help is urgently needed to get people up onto the rail track.

On the map at the re-established Triple-C, the blue marks that indicate flooded ground are overrunning the south bank through Greenwich to Deptford with devastating speed. Venetia watches Nikki Fuller bent over the table with a marker pen, tracing out the ten-metre contour. From New Cross Road in Deptford the line extends due west through Peckham, Stockwell and Clapham as far as Wandsworth.

This is the river's ancient flood plain. Men built walls to contain the flow of tides, drained the marshes and made homes for a million inhabitants. Now the river is reclaiming its lost territory.

Pam Eaves, head teacher at St Olav's Church of England School, Rotherhithe, is growing increasingly anxious. Pam has called the council emergency number a dozen times in the past hour but the transport promised still hasn't arrived. Nor is it going to, she tells herself. The school is close to the Rotherhithe Tunnel approach road and even before the first official broadcasts, traffic in the surrounding streets was locked solid. Now the police have closed the tunnel to vehicles so there is no escape that way any longer.

Around half the pupils have so far been collected by family or friends. That leaves 311 remaining at the last count. The phones ring constantly with worried parents wanting to know what will happen to their children. Pam tries to reassure them, but it is difficult to sound convincing. The television pictures from down the estuary are so ghastly that she has had to order the sets switched off.

Rotherhithe is all low-lying former marshland and docks. The flood will run deeper here than anywhere. Pam is a woman who has always trusted her instincts; she has a bad feeling about today. She knows she has to get the children away. It has crossed her mind to walk the school out, but it's nearly three miles to Tower Bridge and police are appealing to Londoners not to add to congestion. Better to remain in the buildings than be caught on the streets when the river comes over, she thinks.

Rotherhithe station, on the other hand, is only minutes away. Pam has begged London Underground to help bring the children out. 'We could all squash into a couple of carriages easily.' But she has waited so long for the council transport that the line has already shut down by the time she makes her appeal. 'It's only a few hundred metres under the river. If there isn't a train free we could do it on foot. We could lead the children through if only you'd let us,' she pleads, but to no avail. The line is closed, the station locked up and the staff withdrawn. Looking after themselves, Pam thinks bitterly.

And now, from the direction of the river, comes a wind bearing black smoke.

In the tunnels below Baker Street, the evacuation of the Bakerloo Line is progressing slowly. At least, thinks Paul Suter, the lights are working. They are on a separate circuit from the track and are a godsend.

He has radioed the Network Control Centre to

tell them his decision to head east but reception is so bad he is not certain they have understood his reasons. A few inches of water doesn't sound much but the thought of trying to drive this lot to wade through a pitch black lake, ruining their shoes, and quite possibly falling and injuring themselves, doesn't bare thinking about.

NCC keeps goading him to get moving. 'Have you started yet?' is all he hears over the radio. 'There are five of us here to manage two thousand passengers. What do you expect?' Paul snaps back. 'Can't you send station staff up the track to meet us?' The radio crackles in response but the voice is indecipherable.

The controllers are growing jumpy, Paul suspects, and are trying not to show it, which only makes it worse. It seems to have taken ages getting everybody out of the carriages and formed up ready to march. Most are behaving sensibly but a few are neurotic or genuinely terrified. Orders and instructions have to be explained to them repeatedly. Agitated tourists babble at him in different languages while Paul searches vainly for anyone who can translate that the electric current is off and there is no danger from touching a rail. More minutes are lost arguing over which way out to take. A trouble-maker demands to know why they aren't making for Marylebone. Paul has to explain about the water and that it is continuing to build up in the tunnel. This in turn causes more alarm.

'Stay calm,' he repeats over and over. 'It is only drains surcharging because the river is high and the pumps aren't functioning.'

*

At the NCC in St James's, Hew Thomas's problems are multiplying. Floods are overwhelming Canning Town, Canary Wharf and North Greenwich. They have lost the emergency generating station and the inundation of central London is only minutes away. London Underground's headquarters opposite Scotland Yard, which includes the NCC, lies inside the danger zone and will have to be abandoned.

Technicians are striving to restore radio contact with Paul Suter. Hew has pleaded for more police to be sent up the Bakerloo tunnel to help but all available manpower has been deployed along the river. Baker Street has its own control centre but it has closed down and the operators transferred to Neasden. Hew is at his wits' end; there are more than two thousand lives at stake and he is powerless to intervene. Emergency lighting in tunnels and stations will run on back-up batteries, but for how much longer?

At Westminster station, on the Thames embankment, Tom Branson has been ordered down to check the Jubilee Line platforms for stray passengers. The stations in Docklands have been abandoned and all communications lost. With the river pouring in at numerous points, a torrent of water is flooding through the tubes towards central London. Westminster is where it will reach the north bank first.

The concourse is eerily quiet as he passes through and the barriers in the ticket hall stand open. The control room is empty; the stationmaster and staff have retreated to the surface. Inside, the phones are dead and when he tries the CCTV the screens come up blank. On the far wall is a fire emergency cabinet containing breathing apparatus for use in case of smoke. He verifies the pressure on the air cylinder before slipping the harness over his shoulders. He hunts out a helmet flashlight and spare battery and clips another hand torch to his belt.

The escalators are stopped now. At peak periods fifteen thousand passengers an hour pass through here. Branson runs down the steps from flight to flight, the air tank thumping on his back. Once he pauses to listen for a minute, thinking he detects a sound of splashing, but it is only his imagining. Images of water pouring down from above crowd his mind. The splash and roar of the flood echoing under the cavernous roof. Torrents rushing down the escalators, spilling off the edges of the overhead floors, streaming down the concrete walls. He pushes them away and hurries on.

This is one of the deepest holes in London. Fifteen metres below street level a concrete bridge was constructed to support the platform and tracks of the existing District and Circle lines. Then the ground was excavated down to forty metres, creating a vast open-plan escalator well with twin running tunnels stacked one above the other.

Branson forces himself to take the westbound tunnel, the lowest level of all. This is where flooding will appear first. The main lights are out down here, leaving only the emergency lamps burning. It feels like descending into the bowels of a ship. He is more than thirty metres below ground, the equivalent of a seven-storey building.

At the bottom a short passage gives onto the

westbound platform. The only sound is his own footfall. The long platform is deserted; the sides and roof, faced with grid-patterned metal plating, curving away in the dim light. Steel and glass transparent screens at the platform edge shut off the empty track. The air is still. Only a faint ripple of shadow hints at movement beyond the tinted glass. Branson peers but can't at first make out what it is.

Then he stops and stares, the pulse beating loud in his ears. What he is seeing beyond the glass doors is water. The track area on the other side of the glass has flooded and the water has reached nearly to the roofline of the tunnel. The water is sand coloured due to light reflecting on particles in suspension and it is running fast, with bits of dirt and debris whirling by in the current.

All this Branson takes in at the same time as his brain is telling him that any second, surely, the internal pressure will shatter the glass walls and the flood will burst through onto the platform. And then he freezes again.

Out of the eastern mouth of the tunnel a figure emerges, a girl in her late teens or early twenties. Limbs outstretched, long hair trailing, she slides along the glass panels, her body twisting and rotating with a macabre grace. The white face stares, dull-eyed with gaping mouth, and then she is gone, drifting away up the platform towards the black maw of the farther tunnel entrance.

As if a spell has been broken Branson turns and flees for the stairs. As he leaps up the steps he hears behind him the crash of breaking glass and the tidal-wave thunder of the flood bursting in below.

42

H ERE AT LONDON'S Tower Bridge the Thames is now brimming the walls. It is only a matter of time before the river starts spilling over into the streets by this great symbol of the city . . .'

The river is brimming the walls in central London. In the shadow of the Tower, transmitter vans point their satellite dishes at the sky and arc lamps pierce the dusk. Nervous news crews jostle for space along the promenade, intent on recording the moment when overtopping begins here. Others have set up on the piers of Tower Bridge itself, within sight of the RNLI station, both of whose rescue boats have been dispatched to Docklands to aid in the evacuations.

Public transport has shut down and the roads are clogged. Refugees are streaming across the bridge in both directions, desperate to reach home before the floods trap them. Everyone has the same questions. How did this happen? Why weren't there proper warnings? Wasn't the Thames Barrier supposed to protect us?

Half a mile upstream at London Bridge, City of London police are at last having success in imposing order on the chaotic road system. Traffic in the capital's financial district is already tightly controlled under 'Ring of Steel' anti-terrorist provisions. Under existing legislation police are empowered to impose pedestrian cordons and set up roadblocks, using armed officers to stop and search vehicles. Now, with army help, they have closed off the bridge approaches and are sending in convoys of ambulances to evacuate patients from Guy's Hospital across the river to St Bart's at Smithfield.

Andy James is a qualified A & E driver, trained to D2 standard, meaning he can hustle a 5.7-litre, V8 Chevrolet 350 pick-up truck-based ambulance, eight feet wide and weighing two and half tonnes, through London's narrow streets at high speed. In twenty years, though, he has never known anything like this. Cheapside, one of the principal thoroughfares in the City, has been turned into a clearway. Abandoned vehicles, and any that refuse to comply, are being ruthlessly cleared by squads of soldiers. Drivers trying to break through the cordon find their tyres shredded by spike barriers. There is a clear run now past the Mansion House, down King William Street to the bridge.

The authorities are lucky in that both hospitals have big student contingents. Plenty of willing hands and strong backs to manhandle patients off beds and onto trolleys. A decision has been taken to risk using the lifts up to the last moment. It is the only possible way and now twenty ambulances are running a shuttle service between the two hospitals.

Andy pulls up, joining a queue of other ambulances waiting to load. Police are routing incoming empty vehicles round the rear of the building and departing ones out at the front. It's the loading that takes the time. The Intensive Care Unit at Thomas Guy House has thirteen beds. It takes a specialist ambulance with five trained staff to move a single IC patient, drip, portable respirator and resuscitation kit. This trip Andy is taking a post-op cardiac case. He has to be accompanied by a nurse in case there is trouble between here and Smithfield.

The lightweight aluminium stretcher is slid inside, taking care not to disarrange the tubes and drips trailing from the sedated patient. Nurse and paramedic climb in after and run swift checks to make sure the equipment is functioning. Barely four minutes elapse before Andy hears the doors shut and gets the off sign.

The Limehouse Link Road from the Isle of Dogs to the City is closed and Sophie de Salis has to take the A13, the old Commercial Road. At first the traffic is not too bad but at Stepney it comes to a total halt. A girl on roller-blades zips past, weaving in and out of the cars. Sophie looks for a turning off; the northbound streets are clogged so she points the BMW down to the river and heads south for Shadwell.

She crosses another main road, loses her way in a maze of little streets, crosses a canal that is alarmingly full, takes a left turn and finds herself by St Katharine's Dock with the Tower dead ahead. The police have made Tower Bridge into a one-way system, with four lanes heading north, in an effort to clear the south bank. Sophie fights her way into the traffic stream through convoys of ambulances and coaches carrying school children and cuts round Tower Hill, darting past a startled constable attempting to stop her, and into Lower Thames Street.

Traffic is lighter here alongside the river, almost ominously so. The road passes under London Bridge and Cannon Street. Southwark Bridge has been closed to divert traffic off the Embankment and three hundred metres on the BMW enters the Blackfriars underpass and comes to a halt again.

Five miles to the west in a quiet residential street in Hammersmith, Jo Binney and Chrissie de Salis are lying on Jo's bed watching TV. The school term is finished.

Jo cocks her head. 'Hey, listen. That's Mum's key in the lock. She must be back.'

Two floors below, Harriet Binney shoulders open the front door and thumps a suitcase in the hallway. Miranda pushes past her into the living room to collapse in a bedraggled heap on the sofa, her shoes leaving filthy prints across the carpet.

'Mum!' Jo's head appears over the banister. 'Mum, guess what? I'm back early and Chrissie's here. There's a flood or something and the school sent us home early.' She pauses and looks at her mother curiously. 'How come you're in such a mess? Where's Miranda?'

Harriet sinks down onto the stairs and starts to massage her feet. Her navy tights are wet through and spattered with mud and her hair is hanging limp about her face. 'We've just walked all the way back from Barnes Common.'

'Barnes Common?' Jo and Chrissie repeat, uncomprehending. 'That's the other side of the river.'

'And the drains were overflowing,' grumps Miranda from the living room, 'and it was wet and cold and dark.'

'The traffic is awful. All the roads are seized up,' Harriet explains wearily. 'I've never known it so bad. It took us two hours to get from Waterloo to Barnes and then a policeman told us there was no chance of going any further tonight. It was a choice of sitting there until tomorrow or coming home on foot. So we left the car – and most of Miranda's luggage which will probably be stolen.

'The road was jammed solid; even ambulances couldn't get through. There were hundreds of people waiting to cross. Pools of filthy water everywhere . . . my shoes are ruined.'

'The roads were worse in Hammersmith,' Miranda adds. 'There was like this huge army convoy on the flyover blocking it.'

'Poor Mum,' Jo says comfortingly. 'Shall I make you some tea?'

Harriet manages a weak smile. Her younger daughter is not a teenager yet. 'Hello, Chrissie,' she says. 'Does your mother know you're here?'

'Yeah. Well, kind of,' Chrissie tells her. 'There's a message from her on your machine. She sounds real worried. I tried calling back but the lines are busy. I'll stay here with you if that's okay?'

Harriet buries her face in her hands. She's too tired to think clearly. It occurs to her that there is very little food in the house. She had been meaning to go shopping after bringing Miranda home. Then came the emergency and the chaos drove it out of her head. How are they going to survive?

The two younger girls offer to go to the corner shop on their bikes. It may still be open. Harriet scribbles a list and tells them not to be long. Then she plays back the answering machine. The messages are all from Sophie de Salis. The first is the one that Chrissie mentioned. After that come two more, each increasingly anxious. Is Chrissie with you? Can you confirm you have Chrissie safe? Please call. Please call at once.

Harriet dials Sophie's office but gets an unobtainable sound. She checks the number in her book and tries again, with the same result. No luck either with the mobile. She hopes Sophie is all right.

There is nothing to be done until the girls return, so Harriet makes a pot of tea. Taking a couple of mugs through into the sitting room, she slumps down wearily on the sofa with Miranda.

At St Olav's school in Rotherhithe, a young policeman bangs on the main door, demanding to see the principal.

'Are the children ready to leave?' he asks Pam Eaves. 'I've orders to take you across the park to the station at South Bermondsey. A train will carry you on from there. I don't know where to, but they'll tell you.'

The railway station is a mile to the south by Millwall Club football stadium. On the radio they were saying that all the overland trains had been stopped. Now, according to the constable, selected stations have re-opened for emergency evacuations.

Teachers are hurriedly writing labels for the

children to tie to their clothing, giving names and home addresses. The police have insisted on this. 'In case anyone gets lost.' Pam suspects it is to provide a means of identifying corpses but she keeps the thought to herself. Her biggest worry is communication. Pupils come from disparate ethnic backgrounds and many have limited English. Route directions must be issued in seven different languages. Former refugees need reassuring that their families will be able to find them again.

The constable's relief is palpable as the leaders file out through the playground. He has a colleague waiting with a motor bike. It weaves between the cars, blue light flashing. Much of Rotherhithe to the east appears to be blacked out. With a shock Pam realises that flooding must already have begun there and it dawns on her that they are in danger. Once across Jamaica Road, she organises the children into a column four abreast and they enter the park.

It is darker still here; there are few street lamps. Away from the buildings, the storm whips the branches of the trees and tears at the children's clothes. It needs all the encouragement of the staff to keep them moving.

Other people are crossing the park in different directions. They push impatiently through the unwieldy column causing confusion and distress. After each incident it is necessary to gather up stragglers and re-form the line. The police radio crackles and they step up the pace. They are nearing Surrey Quays. Four hundred metres away, through the darkened streets to their left, lies Greenland Dock.

*

It is not just St Olav's that is at risk. Southwark is shaped like an inverted triangle, with the low-lying wide end against the river. The five-metre contour runs across the middle of the borough towards Peckham Road and there are thirty-six schools in the sector between Tower Bridge and New Cross Gate. With so many demands, priority has to be given to those most in need. All across the borough troops of children, shepherded by anxious teachers, stumble through wind and darkness in hopes of finding safety.

At the end of the park, Pam can see the lights of the Tutin estate tower blocks in the distance and the brick arches of a railway viaduct crossing the road ahead. Another file of children comes into sight up the street, moving in the same direction. They turn right, pass under two sets of arches, along beside some railings and there is the station at last.

And then, suddenly, water is everywhere. It doesn't come at them down the road or from any single direction that Pam sees. It is as if it just appears out of the ground. One moment they are walking along dry pavement, the next they are standing in a freezing stream that is already leaking into their shoes. The children squeal in fear and hop about, scattering across the road. 'Stay together,' Pam shouts. 'It's only water, it won't hurt you.'

Ruthlessly she and the other teachers push them back into line against the railings. 'Keep moving,' Pam orders, ignoring the cries. At all costs, they must stay together.

They herd the school on into the station forecourt. It is crammed with children of all ages, squeezed onto a patch of higher ground out of the water. On every side Pam can hear teachers calling the names of schools from the borough, Alwyn, St Josephs, Alfred Salter, Southwark Park. Anxious local residents are being kept back by police, among them old people and families with young children of their own. The police commander is urging them to walk out south to the safety of higher ground at Peckham, but they refuse to heed him.

Under the lights Pam organises a swift head count. A shout goes up from the crowd; a train is approaching up the track. Agitation increases and there is a surge towards the entrance. The police link arms to force people back. Pam hears the officer calling for assistance. His men are outnumbered and the situation is growing ugly.

St Olav's turn comes to climb the stairs to the platform. The crowd is pressing tight about the entrance, the police sweating to keep a path open. It is a struggle to get through. Someone shoulders Pam in the back and a woman with pink hair spits at her as she brings up the rear. She is the last at the steps and a harassed officer reaches out an arm to bar her passage. 'Schools only, lady.'

'This is my school, St Olav's. I am the principal.' In spite of herself Pam has a momentary twinge of dismay. She is aware of angry calls in the crowd behind and feels terrible. This is what it's like to be a refugee.

'Sorry, Ma'am,' the man signals her to proceed.

For the first time in her life Pam is thankful that she looks like a headmistress.

*

With three gates down on the Barrier, ten thousand cubic metres of water a second are sweeping upstream. Environment Agency engineers fear the surge will come up so fast that the walls will be unable to take the pressure. They predict widespread collapses. Venetia Maitland gives the Police Commissioners power to order residents from their homes and has ordered regulations prepared to enforce compulsory billeting of refugees. According to Nikki Fuller, flooding on the south bank can be expected to extend two miles inland along a line westwards from Rotherhithe, through Clapham to Wandsworth Common.

The RNLI have seven rapid-response lifeboats on the river, including those manned by volunteers. But two are stationed down at Tilbury and two more from Tower Bridge are already committed, alongside the River Police boats, to evacuations in Docklands. The remaining trio are pitifully inadequate to handle a catastrophe on the scale now approaching.

The Culture Secretary is pleading for help. Some of the nation's most treasured heritage is in danger from the flood. Experts are especially anxious for the new Tate Modern at Bankside, opposite Blackfriars, and for the Gilbert Collection at Somerset House, half a mile upstream on the north side. Both stand right on the river and loss of their contents will be a national catastrophe.

Venetia Maitland orders troops to be sent to both locations. No one has any illusion though. The soldiers will do what they can but meanwhile frantic Gilbert curators are racing against time to carry eight hundred priceless gold and silver artefacts to safety.

*

At Tower Bridge, anticipation grips the ranks of waiting journalists. In the past minutes the tide has come up very fast. Under the glare of spotlights commentators pose on the drenched footpath, with waves splashing against the crest of the wall behind. Everyone knows this is only the prelude; the main event is yet to come.

There is a momentary lull in the wind. The chatter of the crowd falls still. Against the glowing sky a helicopter appears, racing up from the east. From its belly the long beam of a searchlight stabs downward at the tossing water. Then, with a roar, the storm resumes. A howling gust blasts up the estuary, raking the bridge with icy hail, lashing the bare trees into frenzy.

Shrills of alarm break out on the bank. Out of nowhere the surface of the river seems to swell up in a dark hump overhanging the land. Horns sound and truck engines roar into life. News crews snatch a last shot at the long black wave cascading over the wall and run for their lives. The foaming deluge breaks on the pavement, bursting among the cameras, overturning light arrays, scattering onlookers and drowning out their cries in one continuous peal of destruction and noise.

The flood has broken through into central London.

43

Andy James swings the ambulance out from Guy's hospital carefully so as not to shake the patient in the back and makes the right turn onto Borough High Street. The way is clear in front and he pushes on past the looming mass of London Bridge Tower, the world's sixth tallest building, under the railway viaduct and towards the river. A hundred metres up, the road divides, with Duke Street curving away right to London Bridge station, while straight ahead the road angles back west for the approach to the bridge.

He is drawing level with the cathedral when a policeman leaps out in front of the ambulance, waving his arms. Beyond the viaduct, Duke Street is vomiting water into the roadway like an opened sluice. Andy has seen something like it once before when a main burst on the north circular. To hell with this, he thinks. He is damned if he is going to stop now.

The ambulance lurches forwards again as Andy floors the Chevrolet's big throttle pedal. He has a fleeting glimpse of the constable's astonished face as he jumps back out of the way, and he grins to himself. Just before the water, Andy eases off the speed a trifle and drops down a gear. The flood is deeper than it looks. He can feel the current dragging against the wheels, pushing them over towards the left.

He changes down again. He is in first gear, working the throttle to keep up momentum. Thank God for four-wheel drive. The torrent is a good foot deep now; the swish of water against the underside is alarming. Andy knows that twenty inches, half a metre, is the most the ambulance can handle before the engine gives out. He presses on. There is an agonising moment when the engine starts to splutter, then at last the bonnet is lifting again and the drag easing. They are on the bridge approach, moving uphill between tall buildings and clear of the water.

Andy wipes away the sweat that is running down his face. They are through. The road on the far side of the bridge is at a higher level. We did it, he tells himself proudly. We beat the flood.

Over at Blackfriars, Sophie de Salis has been stuck in her car at the exit to the underpass for the last fifteen minutes, trying without success to get through to Harriet on her mobile. The mouth of the underpass is fifty metres further up, but a pedestrian walk runs along the inside lane and there are gaps in the side walls giving glimpses of the Thames. None of the vehicles in front are moving and a few drivers have left their cars.

Sophie tries her phone again but still can't get a signal. Frustrated, she gets out and threads her way between the cars on the inside lane. Reaching the pavement, she has a shock. The tide is up to within inches of the top of the parapet. It is an alarming sight. The river is so swollen that occasional wave splashes are actually slopping over in places and water is trickling down the wall onto the pavement.

Craning out to see upstream, Sophie gets a vivid indication of just how much the river has risen. Tied up alongside the embankment two hundred metres up is the hospitality ship, HMS *President*. Sophie has been to receptions on board. The freak tide has lifted the hull so that it towers threateningly over the parapet, its waterline bobbing on a level with car roofs. For the first time she feels frightened by the power of the river.

Sophie is starting to feel cold. She returns to the car to get her things. The radio is carrying reports of flooding at Lewisham. Lewisham, she knows, is on the other side of the river. Where exactly, she is unsure.

When she looks out the window next, water is running in the gutters beneath the underpass, streaming downhill from the street up ahead and gathering in a fast expanding pool at the low point. The drain there is either blocked or simply can't take the volume. Sophie registers a shaft of fear. The pool is spreading right across the roadway. It is not just being fed by surface water off the road. Water is bubbling, spurting from the gully into which it is supposed to be draining. Already it is lapping the pavement, flowing around the shoes of pedestrians. Within another minute the flood is too deep to cross. It is creeping up to the level of car doorsills.

Motorists in front are abandoning their vehicles.

It dawns on Sophie that she is going to have to do the same. Hurriedly she checks what to take. There's a pair of running shoes in the boot that will be more practical than her Italian heels. She scrambles over into the rear and pulls down the split seat to reach them. She grabs the car's papers from the glove compartment, along with a flashlight and street map too. She hesitates over her laptop. It is an added weight but it holds all her files from work. If it goes missing it will be a catastrophe.

A man runs past, banging on car windows, shouting to occupants to get out. Sophie buckles her coat tightly around her. When she opens the door water gushes in. The cold makes her cry out. It is like stepping onto a block of ice. She locks the car and starts wading towards the mouth of the underpass. Other drivers and passengers join her. The flood is flowing fast and feels as if it is growing deeper and colder with every step. A cyclist holds his machine above his head. A woman struggles to free herself from a jammed seat belt. It gives way, precipitating her into the water with a splash. Sophie and another woman help her to her feet and all three stagger to the opening.

The relief at reaching open air is tremendous even though they have to splash on for another twenty metres to gain the ramp leading up to Queen Victoria Street. After a dozen paces Sophie steps thankfully onto dry pavement. Behind them, the river is spilling over the embankment in a steady stream. There are cries from people still wading out. The flood is getting deeper, making it harder to force a passage against the flow.

Two policemen come running down the ramp

from above, shouting at people to clear a path. Without hesitating they plunge into the underpass. A handful of other men follow their lead. One re-emerges carrying a spluttering woman. He hands her over to the people on the ramp and ducks back inside. The water is up to his waist as he disappears again.

The river is now completely drowning the wall. The foaming current picks up cars in the nearside lane, crashing them into one another. The lamps on the wall are still burning. Other people are shaking the water from their shoes and making light of their escape. Meanwhile passers-by have come down to gawp; at least two are using video cameras to capture the incident. The water level creeps further up the ramp, forcing the crowd to retreat. Sophie's teeth are chattering with cold and her trainers squelch with every step. The water is above the roofs of the cars now and no one else has come out. The watchers fall silent. Sophie feels sick suddenly. Shouldering her bag, she heads off up the hill in the direction of St Paul's to find a taxi.

It is a mile and a half from London Bridge to Westminster. Normally it takes the tide peak eleven minutes to travel up-river between the two. Today that time is cut to no more than six minutes. For practical purposes, overtopping occurs simultaneously all along the south bank of the Thames from Tower Bridge to Vauxhall.

There is so much wind-blown spray and wave action across the walls that it is hard to pinpoint the exact instant when flooding begins. Water is running in the roadway along Bankside and Queen's Walk from 4 pm onwards. In the minutes that follow, the river seems to heave itself up all along its length and spill over the defences in one continuous wave. The land behind the walls is well below the five-metre contour and the flood rushes unobstructed into the heart of the built-up area along a six-mile front.

At Tate Modern, water surges over the river wall, funnelling down the wide ramp to the lower floor level. The gallery is closed and staff and troops are busy moving exhibits upstairs from the vast Turbine Hall. Floor level down here is four metres below the crest of the river wall.

The suddenness of the flood catches everyone unawares and there hasn't been time to lower the steel shutter on the ramp. Two women are carrying armfuls of books from the study centre when they are startled by a crash from above. A window facing across the embankment path has just given way and the flood is barrelling through the second level café. They glance left and to their horror see water mounting outside against the 21-metre-wide glass doors of the ramp. Within seconds it is above head height and jets of fine spray are spurting around joints and hinges.

The glass creaks under the strain. There are shouts and the sound of feet running on the upper floors. The women gape at one another fearfully. Small trickles of water are snaking down the ramp. Carefully, as if frightened of triggering a landslide, one of the women sets down the books she is holding on a nearby exhibit stand. In the same instant the doors at the top of the ramp implode one after another like dam gates bursting and a cataract thunders down the slope into the hall.

The women's cries are lost in the roar of water. They turn to run, but instead of making for the stairs in front of them leading up to the bridge at second-floor level they run back the way they have come.

It is a fatal mistake. The tidal wave rips the length of the hall, inundating the two information desks, sweeping up and scattering chairs stacked alongside. It catches the women, bowling them over like dolls and hurling them against the glass wall of the lower floor. The ramp has become a spillway with thousands of tons of water spewing down to fill the lower floors. In seconds it is up to the tops of the doors. More windows crash upstairs as renewed flooding sweeps in from the river front. Within minutes the second floor is under water too and the main hall lies drowned to the six-metre mark.

Moving west, the flood engulfs the London Television Centre and surrounds the concrete terraces of the National Theatre and the Royal Festival Hall. The spectacular drum-shaped Imax cinema, set in the middle of the Waterloo Road roundabout, is submerged to first-floor level when water bursts open the glass entrance doors. This is a major road junction, criss-crossed by subway tunnels. Scores of terrified pedestrians are caught in underground passages, with torrents pouring down from all directions. A woman from Fulham is trying to reach the north bank with her six-year-old daughter. She drops her Christmas parcels as water rises over the little girl's head, floating her hat off up the tunnel. Mother and daughter swim for their lives, staggering out at the King's College entrance minus their shoes.

Just a short way on, Colombo House, owned by British Telecom, is one of two principal telephone exchanges in central London. Six hundred employees work here around the clock. Main phone cables are laid in tunnels for protection: the latest fibre-optic cables with their ultra high capacity being particularly vulnerable to breakage. From junction boxes located beneath the Imax cinema the cables radiate across the capital. At Colombo, they enter the cable chamber at basement level and terminate on the ground floor at distribution frames.

Frantic activity is taking place to prepare the building against the flood. Non-essential staff have been sent home and sandbag barricades laid across entrances. Down in the basement beneath the road, a crew of engineers led by Ryan Tees is testing gas pressure in mains cables when a look-out stationed on the stairs shouts that water is coming in.

'Right, everybody out,' Ryan orders. The crews start gathering their tools together. Ryan pauses to screw back the cover plate of an injector pump. There is another shout from the stairs and a gush of water floods into the chamber. Everyone piles towards the exit but there is no panic. Ryan is the last to leave; the water is coming down very fast, it is gurgling round his knees in the passage outside. He tries to pull shut the door to the cable chamber, but the flow is too strong.

'Come on,' one of the others shouts from above. He wades over to the stairs and starts to climb. The force of the torrent pouring down is frightening. Twice he loses his footing and only saves himself by clinging onto the rail. He reaches the street level exhausted and soaked just as the lights go out.

No lives have been lost, but the building is dead. The emergency generators are located in the basement. Without power, the gas injection system will no longer work, allowing water to penetrate the cables. On the upper floors switchboards and computers fall silent. Across the capital four million phone and fax lines die. At a stroke, London has lost half its exchange capacity.

Crisis teams in three boroughs are tracking the flood's progress via street cameras. The images coming onto their screens are horrifying. At Jubilee Gardens between Waterloo and Westminster the water is spilling down off the walls and through the Shell Centre into Yorke Road at an estimated ten metres a second, faster than a fit man can run. In Yorke Road it meets more water flowing in from the other end. The only way it can go is ahead down the taxi ramp to Waterloo International, the Eurostar Terminal. Some of the flow goes down the ramp but the roadway is too narrow and the rest is squeezed up and over the edging wall. With so much volume pressing on from the rear, the flow becomes a torrent, then a wave.

The entrance front of the Eurostar Terminal is constructed of glass and there is a limit to the weight it can stand. An abandoned car is swept along on the flood and with a crash that echoes through the main station overhead, the glass front shatters and the torrent rips through into the terminal.

West of the Eurostar terminal, Yorke Road joins Westminster Bridge Road, passing under the main-line railway tracks leading out from the station.

Unlike the north bank, the tracks on this side of the Thames are carried on massive raised embankments that run parallel to the river. These embankments pen up the flood, channelling the waters along main roads. As levels rise behind the embankments, the force of the current through the gaps increases in proportion.

There are a lot of vehicles still on Westminster Bridge Road, abandoned at the first sign of overtopping. As the expanding river finds its path blocked by the embankments, it deepens dramatically. Ten minutes after the first assault, a wall of water two metres high smashes across the junction with St George's Road.

Vehicles, pieces of timber, even paving stones sucked from their bedding by the force of the current are seized and borne along in an avalanche that crushes and destroys everything in its path. A man tries to outrun the torrent, is caught and clings for his life to the railings of the Imperial War Museum park. One hand is later found caught between the iron uprights; the rest of him is too badly mangled to be identified. A car is pitch-poled through the window of a ground-floor office where staff are belatedly trying to salvage equipment. Miraculously all inside escape.

A hundred metres to the east the flood tearing down Waterloo Road meets another torrent coming from the direction of Blackfriars at St George's Circus. The combined flows then funnel into London Road along one side of the triangle containing the campus of South Bank University. The lower ground levels of the main buildings here are used for lecture rooms, offices and canteens.

The university runs a number of winter programmes. Windows fronting the road are double-glazed but that counts for little. As the panes go black and burst inwards, screaming students stampede over one another to reach the exits. Many are still unfamiliar with the layout of the buildings. With the flood enveloping the campus on three sides, the lower regions have become death traps. Lost in a maze of darkened corridors, with water surging towards the ceilings, the end for most victims is mercifully swift.

Twenty-four-year-old Juan Romero is with a party of Spanish students on an English familiarisation course in one of the seminar rooms. The session has just wound up and members are beginning to drift out into the corridor in search of the canteen. Juan has to hand in some forms at the front desk and he nips upstairs. 'Wait for me,' he tells his girlfriend, Paola. She blows him a kiss. It is the last time he will see her.

He hears the crash of the windows imploding downstairs at the same time as the street doors burst inwards into the foyer and a deluge of water sweeps him backwards over the desk. All he can think of is Paola. With the flood surging around his legs he fights his way to the stairs. He can hear the cries of the other students trapped down there. The water is pushing up around his chin by the time he makes it to the bottom. Standing on tiptoe he somehow finds the doorway and ducks under. When his head breaks the surface again he is in total blackness. There is a tiny air gap against the ceiling, only a few fingers but sufficient to breathe – just.

'Paola!' he shouts. 'Paola! Where are you?' There

is no answer, only the sucking sounds of water slopping against the walls. The flood he is standing in clings to him, thick as treacle, viscous with dirt and mud picked up on its course inland.

'Paola!' he calls again, but his voice booms hollow in his ears. Juan will spend the rest of the night searching vainly through the basement, calling her name. He will bring out three other people alive, all of them strangers, earning a medal for bravery, but not Paola. Her body and those of thirty others will later be found entombed in silt. Of the entire class in the seminar room that evening, Juan is the sole survivor.

And the flood is not done yet. Vast amounts of water are being channelled into the network of streets, squeezing levels higher still. Along St George's Road the speed of the racing torrent sucks windows from the fronts of buildings, the shattered glass fragments adding to the destructive violence of the flood. Customers in a fast-food restaurant are drowned at their tables when water sweeps in to engulf them without warning. A clutch of families returning from a shopping trip are caught in the open and overwhelmed, fourteen lives erased in the blink of an eye. At 4.29, after travelling a mile in three minutes, the cataract spews out into the Elephant and Castle.

This is one of the ugliest spots in London, a brutal concrete mess of gigantic roundabouts, three-lane highways and high-rise council blocks. In spite of regeneration efforts by successive urban task forces, it remains a dead area, a place where visitors stop for as short a time as they can and often that is too long. Arterial roads from eight of London's principal bridges come together at the traffic junction here. Almost every main route south of the river passes through Elephant and Castle and the gyratory is permanently monitored by cameras of the police Traffic Division. Appalled officers out at Hendon can only watch helpless as the screens show the river pouring down six separate roads all converging on the same spot.

With a million people living and working in eight square miles, local services are hopelessly overstretched. There has been too little time to carry out more than a fraction of the evacuations needed. Traffic congestion has been at gridlock since before the first public warning and, in spite of the obvious danger, police even have to turn away sightseers.

Stuck in the heart of the system is a minibus containing six teenagers with learning difficulties and their two teachers. The bus is shuttling evacuees away from the London Bridge area and there is no other way to go. They are trying to reach Walworth Road, the shortest route to high ground. Unfortunately, right now, so are twenty thousand other people.

The floods drive before them walls of debris: paving stones, timber and scaffolding, smashed furniture, vehicle parts, iron railings, street signs, corpses and mud from the river, mixed with rubble and shards of glass. This mass of wreckage bursts upon the stationary traffic with the momentum of an avalanche. The vehicles nearest stand no chance. Crushed, overturned and shattered by impacts, windows stoved in, doors jammed, they become instant coffins for their helpless occupants adding to the debris driven along by the flood.

Within the space of seconds the flood is up around the doors of the minibus. A quick-thinking police cadet seizes the rear door and tries to wrench it open but the force of the flood pins him against the vehicle. In desperation he draws his truncheon and hacks at the windows to break the glass. The teacher in the passenger seat is struggling to get out, but the door on his side was damaged in a minor collision earlier in the week and is stuck. When the driver forces his door open water pours in, filling the inside to seat level. The screams of the youngsters redouble. They tear at their belts, flinging themselves against the seats, kicking and fighting. A lad of sixteen grabs the teacher in front around the neck and hangs on in sheer terror. The driver pushes the side door back and drags out the nearest boy. A careering baulk of timber cuts him down before he can reach the next and the screams inside the minibus are choked off as the water reaches the roofline.

Other disasters are to come. A maze of subways under the central island links the different streets and the shabby red shopping arcade on the east side. Pedestrians have continued to make use of these in spite of attempts to stop them. Now disobedience exacts a terrible price. The flood pours in on trapped victims from a dozen different entrances. A photographer snaps a searing image of bloodied hands scrabbling despairingly at an air grating as the water rises.

Between the Elephant and Castle shopping centre and the Underground station runs a lane used by market traders. Len Hecht rents a stall here where he deals in bric-à-brac. He has seen the flood warnings but this is Christmas; the money he makes this week will see him through the next two months. Besides, how bad can it get right down here? The other traders share his attitude with just one difference: Len operates from a wheelchair so for him the risk is much greater.

Trade is busy this evening and the confined space of the lane means the only warning of danger is a roaring sound from the direction of the roundabout. It grows so loud that Len reckons it must be a jet airliner about to crash. It is almost the last coherent thought he has.

The lane narrows at the bottom and the flood pours in from the north, rising in seconds till it is over people's heads. Len has swung his chair round to reach an object behind him when the water strikes and that probably saves his life. The water closes over him, swirling him around like washing in a machine. He thrashes with his arms and bobs up to the surface. He can see nothing, feels himself sinking again, strikes out with all his strength and hits his knuckles painfully against a wall. There is a pipe running down it and Len grabs that and hangs on. It is as well he does because in another instant the backwash comes tearing back down the opposite way. The strength of the pull almost sucks Len out with it. He clings on, dimly aware of people and stalls being washed past. When the flow slackens the level drops and he slides down the pipe. His chair is gone, so is everything else. The water is round his chest still and he has to hold himself up by his hands. If he once lets go, his legs can't support him. He will be submerged and drown.

Len can hear noises not far off in the darkness. He guesses they are from the main thoroughfare. He tries calling for help but nobody comes. He keeps on calling until he is too hoarse and cold to go on. He wedges his fingers in behind the pipe and lets himself hang there, waiting to be found.

He will wait fifteen dreadful hours. Not until eight next morning will a rescue party investigating the alley stumble on his half-drowned form huddled against the wall. Doctors still don't understand how he survived.

44

A flash of brilliant light turns the evening momentarily as bright as day, followed an instant later by an earth shattering concussion. At Beckton, on the north bank, flames have touched off the first of six gas-holders on the edge of Docklands. Moments later a second fireball explodes into the air, while overhead the sky pulsates with the tremendous afterglow as 50,000 cubic metres of gas burn off in seconds.

Along the north bank the fires are working their way overland on the flood causing a panic evacuation of Beckton's housing estates as the flames spill down through the Royal Docks.

'*Fire has reached KGV dock and North Woolwich is burning.*'

The staccato radio message comes from a spotter aircraft that has just flown low over the scene. Raikes can see its lights from the cockpit of the Gazelle, climbing away through the smoke. A vivid orange flash illuminates the murk down river. A half second later the thud of the explosion bounces the helicopter.

'City Airport has a jet-fuel farm on the southwest end of Albert Dock,' the Army pilot tells him. 'That was one of the tanks going up.' As if in confirmation, a second fireball blazes upwards through the smoke, followed by another rumble.

When Raikes calls Venetia there is a hiatus. The surge has broken into central London and every circuit is jammed with frantic controllers appealing for aid. It's several minutes before she comes on air. The situation is desperate. They are still bringing people out from the tubes and there has been heavy loss of life. At least a million are trapped on the south bank. No one believed the Barrier could fail and the emergency services are helpless against the speed and scale of flooding.

And there is worse to come, Raikes tells her. From Woolwich eastwards, the Thames is alight. He is passing over the Barrier now. He can see the tide coursing through the shattered gates. The Royal Docks are lost; fireboats can't get in to fight the flames. The Isle of Dogs will be next and from there the fires will spread to Wapping and Rotherhithe.

Roland, she says, you've done much but I need more. It will be an hour before the water bombers can reach the capital. The populations of Lambeth and Southwark are threatened. You have to buy us time.

It is at the Barrier that they must fight the holding action, Raikes tells her. He asks for fire crews to man the piers, helicopters to bring them in and boats with monitors to break up the burning slicks.

Whatever it takes, Venetia replies. You have the authority – use it.

*

At North Woolwich a fire crew has been rescuing people trapped on Connaught Road, only to be forced back themselves by rising water. Now they are trying to check the flames from spreading past the sugar factory into the residential streets beyond.

To the crew chief the factory area resembles a scene from hell. Giant silos lean drunkenly, vomiting burning molasses and sickly sweet smoke. An incandescent whirlwind rages through the site, exploding buildings and freight cars in violent fireballs. Gas cylinders detonate like rocket bombs, looping skywards in flaring trajectories, spewing out a hissing rain of red-hot fragments. Flames and sparks spiral hundreds of feet upwards through clouds of debris swirled aloft on the super-heated air.

'It's no use,' the chief shouts into his radio. 'The oil has broken through. You'll have to start evacuating!'

Fire and water: the combination the emergency services have been dreading.

Fire Officer Charlie Sanger's chest waders reach up to his armpits. They are heavy and cumbersome, hell to walk in, especially with water waist deep all around. Charlie is twenty-four years old and has been with the Fire Brigade eight months. This is his first major incident, his first experience of flooding. The unit's appliances have withdrawn beyond Beckton, and Charlie and the rest of Blue Watch are going from house to house in the inundated Silvertown, west of the City Airport, banging on windows, telling people to get out ahead of the fire.

'There are trucks coming up the street now. The moment you see one, you wade out and climb aboard. Bring your pets, but nothing more. If you're not there the trucks will go without you. If you miss the trucks, don't wait around, there won't be any more coming. Head west on foot for Canning Town.'

The householder stares at him round-eyed with dismay. He wears a roll-neck sweater and a turban. Everyone reacts the same way, they can't believe that they are being evicted like this at no notice, that the Brigade can't protect them.

'But what about our stuff? Our clothes or . . .?' the man's family cluster round, crying and pleading. 'Give us five minutes to pack,' the man begs.

'There's no time. The fire is two blocks away. You have to leave right now.' Charlie feels like a tyrant as he says it. At a stroke his orders have stripped away their home and all that they have worked for and turned them into refugees.

The fire gives no choice. The smell of its hot breath is all around them, smoke eddying up the street even as they hesitate. One at a time the father hands the family out through the window – wife, three daughters, two sons. An old woman is last, bundled up in shawls. She shrinks back, terror in her eyes. The father says something curt in her own language and pushes her out onto the sill. 'My mother does not walk well, we must carry her to the truck.'

It's not so easy. The old woman is hard to get a grip on. Charlie has to show the father how to link arms to support her. For a little old lady she weighs a lot. A truck filled with other residents is outside in the road, a huge earthmover with man-high wheels. The family has waded out and are already helping one another aboard. Grunting with effort under their burden, Charlie and the father stagger towards the front gate. Behind the house the sky is a hideous black, shot through with flickering red. The air is hot and dry in their throats and they can hear the pop and crackle of the flames growing closer.

The driver of the truck leans out from the cab, shouting to them to hurry it up. He is nervous being so close to the fire front. He has been told to pick up as many as his truck will hold and get the hell out before the flames cut him off. It takes the combined strength of Charlie and the father, assisted by other people in the truck, to haul the old lady up. The father turns back to Charlie, one hand on the rim of the truck tailgate. 'Thank you,' he says.

The driver revs the engine impatiently. The man makes a spring, gets his middle over the lip and is dragged inside by his family as the truck moves off. From the back the children wave to Charlie. He waves back, tears starting in his eyes.

At ExCeL, Bob West has twenty odd guys left to fight the approaching fires. The rest have quit to look after their families. West doesn't blame them. He would do the same in their position. The main exhibition floor is still above water level and for the moment he has pressure in the pumps. He has set up sprays to cover the north and west sides. The halls have firewalls and sprinklers but they are designed to suppress a blaze occurring inside the building. No one envisaged a conflagration on the scale bearing down upon them from outside.

From where he is standing on the three-lane truckway around the main building, tongues of flame are visible creeping across the water. The nearest slicks are two hundred metres off and the air is full of sparks and hissing fragments. Two boats emerge from the smoke, laden down to the gunwales with refugees, the men at the oars pulling frantically for the building. As fast as they get people away more arrive.

The thud of another explosion rattles the walls. A fuel tanker or gas tank going up most likely. West ducks as debris whizzes overhead. There's a terrific crash behind him. His radio squawks, 'Charlie X-Ray!' His call sign. Wreckage from the blast has fallen through the roof into the north hall. He runs back inside. Smoke comes billowing to meet him. Alarm bells echo through the empty halls and flames sprout along the ceiling as more debris showers down. He hears orders shouted and men in helmets run past. Several stands are burning. Sprinklers cut in, drenching the scene. Another fire party hurries up. Jets of water lance out as the blaze is dowsed.

West's radio shrills again. It is the police sergeant at the main entrance. He has got six hundred refugees on his hands, packed into the banqueting rooms. Smoke is pouring in from the main boulevard and they are starting to panic.

'Can't you walk them over the footbridge to Silvertown?' West shouts back.

'Are you mad? Silvertown is burning. I'd be sending them to their deaths.'

Another voice cuts in on the frequency. Fires have taken hold on the truckway at the Prince

Regent end. Vehicles are burning and hose teams can't get close enough to bring them under control.

West has no illusions; the battle now is not to save the centre but to hold the flames off long enough to give those trapped inside a chance to escape.

Over at Silvertown, the corvette *Drogou* has just embarked a load of refugees. With the wind gusting above sixty knots, the ship ploughs back across the dock towards ExCeL. Lieutenant Besnault can make out the red glare of flames reflected in the glass frontage. His men train their hoses on the fires closing in around them as they steer into the densest part of the smoke. Radar is useless for this kind of operation, the quayside is only metres away and burning oil is moving up to cut them off. From the entrance by the footbridge figures are visible signalling desperately. Anxiously he gauges the tide level. The water is nearly up to the level of the truckway; too deep for those inside to wade out. And the ship's small gangway is too short to span the quay. He calculates quickly. The depth over the quay must be almost four metres. The *Drogou* draws 3.2 metres. Enough just, perhaps.

'Slow astern.' Besnault tenses for the collision as the vessel noses in. He remembers there is a railing along the edge of the quay. With luck the bows will scrape over, forcing it down. 'Starboard rudder.' The building is very close now and with the wind on the beam it is all he can do to hold her steady. A crowd of refugees watches anxiously. If the ship goes aground now they will all be trapped.

The crew are hastily hanging fenders over the bow. But her momentum is dropping. She is steadying. The jar when it comes is still a shock though. Besnault grabs at the bridge rail. 'Stop engines,' he calls. His men leap ashore with lines to make fast. The *Drogou* rests with her bow against the truckway. The waiting refugees surge round. Besnault is aghast at their numbers. He has two hundred passengers already and there must be three times that queuing to get aboard.

His mind is working with brisk efficiency. The elderly and children among the refugees must be taken below. All others must find what shelter they can on deck. In the meantime a great tide of burning oil is moving unstoppably up the dock, cutting off escape southwards. To get out now he will have to take the ship under the footbridge spanning the western end of the dock. A hasty check of the chart confirms his fears. Clearance beneath the central span is just fourteen metres. The *Drogou*'s mast stands twenty. He sends for his chief engineer, an imperturbable Breton. 'Jacques, take a party of men up the masthead with cutting gear. I want everything above thirteen metres height sawn away. Hurry – you've five minutes.'

Inside the exhibition centre, dazed by heat and fumes, Bob West and his fire crews are fighting a rearguard action against flames advancing down the central boulevard. Burning oil has spread through the truck marshalling yard to the rear and set light to stores stacked on the access ramps. Intense heat has melted steel roof trusses, collapsing ceilings and knocking out the sprinkler system. As they retreat past the studios of the media centre, a glass wall disintegrates with a crash. Inflammable gas leaking through cable conduits has detonated inside. The two-storey panels explode outward in balls of fire. One man goes down screaming, cut to ribbons by a blizzard of razor-edged shards.

So many people are cramming aboard the *Drogou* that some have had to be accommodated on the bridge. Others have been squeezed inside the corvette's 100mm-gun turret. And still exhausted survivors continue to stagger up the gangway into the bows. From overhead come showers of sparks and a crashing of steel; the engineers are cutting away the mast supports, ruthlessly jettisoning priceless electronic gear over the side. 'But our radars, our satellite systems,' the warfare officer protests. 'Would you rather stay here with it and burn?' Besnault counters witheringly.

Ashore, the entrance hall is empty as Bob West's men stumble through the smoke, dragging their injured with them. An urgent blast of the corvette's siren drives them to one last spurt outside onto the truckway. The *Drogou* is marooned in a ring of fire. The last refugees have reached the deck. West hurls himself up the gangway and the sailors haul on the winches. Besnault rings for power and backs cautiously away from the quay. Her searchlights probing the smoke, the *Drogou* sets out on her final journey.

Beneath the arched glass roof that spans Canary Wharf station, ten thousand people jostle for space on the platforms.

The elevated track of the Docklands Light Railway crosses West India Dock on a concrete viaduct to bore through the heart of the development at second-floor level. Normally the spans that carry the track stand eight metres clear of the dock; today flooding has cut that to just over three metres.

Seven-year-old Johnny Foster doesn't understand what is happening. He and baby sister Carrie came up today from South Kensington with their mother to see the Christmas tree in Canada Square and meet Johnny's dad for lunch in the mall underneath Canary Wharf Tower. When the flood warnings came, his father didn't want them to travel back on the Underground. They would be safer staying in Docklands till the river went down again, he said.

So they went shopping and the next thing Johnny knew water was coming into the malls and people were rushing about and screaming. Johnny was frightened then, though he tried not to show it. Mum hurried them along to the Tower to find Dad, but bad things were happening there too and they had to wait by the entrance for him to walk down from the forty-third floor.

Now they are upstairs in the station. It is dark under the glass roof and the smoke smell is bad. Mum has Carrie in the papoose against her chest, fending people off to protect her in the crush. Policemen are shouting orders Johnny doesn't understand and he holds onto Dad's hand tightly as they step to the edge of the platform. His father climbs onto the track and lifts Johnny down beside him.

'It's an adventure,' he says. 'We all have to keep together and be brave.'

It is strange to be walking along the railway where the trains go. They can look down on boats floating in the streets below and see firemen rescuing people from cars. Helicopters whirr overhead. They reach the station at West India Quay and follow the track round to the left. The tracks divide here causing confusion and delay. Johnny is getting tired. It is dark and exposed without protection from the buildings; the rail-bed is hard to walk on and the wind makes his eyes sore.

He gazes up in wonder at the trails of glowing sparks flitting through the sky. 'Watch where you're going,' his father warns. There is a whizzing sound like a rocket overhead and screams erupt close by. Pieces of burning hardboard, carried aloft by the gale, have fallen back onto the viaduct. A wave of panic runs along the track. The crowd surges against them. Johnny and his father are forced backwards and Johnny is knocked off his feet.

'Dad!' he shrieks. In the confusion somebody stumbles over his small figure and falls on top of him. Another follows and then a third. People are squeezed against the railing and, terrified of falling through, fight back fiercely. Johnny is panicky. He is pinned under half a dozen bodies and the weight is suffocating him. He is lying across something hard and cold and the pain in his back makes him cry out. 'Dad!' he screams again feebly. 'Help me!'

'Johnny!' his father's voice sounds faint and far away in the darkness. 'Johnny, where are you?'

Canary Wharf Tower has state-of-the-art fire protection with detectors throughout the building, sprinklers on every floor, automatic smoke shutters on airshafts and an addressable alarm system. There are four fire stairways and every tenth floor has a fireproof survival area where trapped occupants can hold out till rescue reaches them.

But flooding has cut off electrical supplies to the building and the stand-by generators are drowned in the basement. There are back-up power plants to provide emergency lighting and communications, but these have a limited life and the drain on them is already considerable. The phones are down too. Security still have their radios but batteries are running low and coverage is patchy.

Monitoring equipment in the lobby and service bays is supposed to keep a constant record of who is in the building, but the computers have crashed with the flood and no one knows how many people have ignored advice to leave. So every floor has to be individually checked.

Barry Singleton climbs the fire stairs in the tower. He is never going to use the lift again, never. So long as he lives he will take the stairs. That scene in the lobby is etched on his retina like a too bright light.

The lift-cars must have wound all the way down into the flooded basement and stopped there while the water poured in. Those poor people trapped inside . . . clawing at the walls of their steel box with the level rising . . . the last screaming gasps of air before their lungs burst and they drowned.

A sense of impending dread grips him. From the windows he looks down on a vista of submerged streets. The dock basins have swollen monstrously, leaving the towers of Canary Wharf rising out of a lake, surrounded by the all-conquering river. In the past few minutes the smog too has grown worse, thickening and pressing ever lower against the buildings. By the time Barry stops for a rest on the tenth floor he is surrounded by clouds stained yellow and brown and shot through with greasy droplets. Beckton is burning and the wind is fanning the furnace through Canning Town. From this height, the fires in the Royal Docks seem terrifyingly close.

45

The battle of the Barrier has entered its final phase. It is only minutes since the first streaks of oil appeared on the water swirling through the burst gates. Oil laced with fire that seems to dance across the surface, advancing and retreating. The wind pelts the piers with a constant fiery hail, from burning droplets to clumps of blazing tar a metre across that splash like incendiaries on the stainless-steel hoods of the engine rooms.

A fire tug patrols behind the Barrier, the jets of its powerful monitors arcing over the piers into the lake of oil moving upstream. On the piers teams of firemen and engineers man hoses coupled to the Barrier's own fire mains. Where the foam jets strike the oil, clouds of steam spout from the surface. As fast as one patch is extinguished another bursts into flame again, the oil bubbling and blistering in the fearful heat, vomiting up coils of stifling smoke. The hiss and roar of the burning slicks drowns out the storm and the red glare of the fires beats upon every surface. Even the air is burning, pockets of flammable gases igniting in vivid fireballs that touch off chains of explosions across the river.

Each pier has two two-man fire parties and a third resting. The heat is so great, no one is allowed more than fifteen minutes outside. Everyone wears breathing apparatus, with heavy protective gear and lifelines. Crews work in pairs, watching each other's backs, ready to turn a hose on a partner if the flames get too close.

Lauren and some other journalists have waded along the flooded tunnels. Wrapping wet towels round their faces, they climb into the smoke-filled upper engine rooms to witness the struggle first hand. Lauren meets an exhausted Martin slumped in the stairwell, his face soot grimed, hair plastered with sweat.

'We're holding our own, just,' he says in answer to Lauren's query. 'According to the helicopters, oil is piling up in a solid mass downstream. If we can keep spraying foam over it to cut the oxygen off, then with luck the temperature should fall below the vapour flash-point.'

'If we can keep spraying?'

Martin shrugs, 'To make foam you need concentrate to inject into the water. Water on its own is useless against an oil fire. It falls straight through into the river underneath. Our hoses are gulping a thousand litres of foam concentrate a minute and the tanks won't last forever. At this rate they'll be sucked dry in under an hour.'

'This is an appeal to boat owners in the London area. There is an urgent need of small craft for rescue purposes. The Commissioner of Metropolitan Police requests members of the public owning or having charge of inflatable dinghies or rowing boats in or around the

capital to contact the nearest police station or local authority emergency centre with details.'

The public radio and TV appeal is Chief Inspector Harry Lime's idea. 'What you want for rescue work is a boat you can tow behind you up a flooded street and put people into to bring them out,' he tells Triple-C. 'Anything with an engine will be more trouble than it's worth.'

Harry is more worried about fire than flood. The fuel spreads flames across the water where fire appliances can't follow. 'Up to now, we've been telling the population on the south bank they are better off staying put on upper floors. If we don't start getting them out, they will be trapped and burned alive.'

At Knightsbridge Barracks, overlooking Hyde Park, Triple-C is installed in the dining room of the Officers' Mess, which has been cleared to accommodate them. Army signallers have fitted up additional communications. The Mayor for London and his deputy have joined civil servants and ministers around the table. The RAF and Navy are looking into the possibility of dropping retardant from helicopters, but high winds make operations of this kind extremely difficult. The Germans are rushing over C-130 Hercules aircraft equipped for water bombing forest fires.

Venetia turns to Mary Lucas. 'Rain would help. What are the chances?'

Mary is scanning her charts. 'For the next three or four hours, not good. The main band of rain-bearing cloud looks to have passed over. The best we might see is a light shower. Nothing that's going to extinguish a blaze.'

'What other assets have we on the river?' Venetia asks the Fire Chief.

'The Brigade has two fireboats, both have been tasked to rush teams to help defend the Barrier. There are also two tugs equipped with monitors for fire fighting.'

'What about the helicopter bombing device?'

The Chief shrugs, 'It's called a Bambi Bucket. A canvas sling on a long line. The helicopter dunks it in the river to fill, flies over the fire and releases the valve. Royal Navy has one at Plymouth. They say two hours to bring it into action. There is rumoured to be another in the Scottish Highlands and we're trying to track that down.'

'Brilliant,' says the Mayor sarcastically. 'We're a nuclear power and we have to scratch around to find a canvas bucket to save London from a firestorm.'

Across the river by Lambeth Bridge, the river is spilling over the walls by the London Fire Brigade pier. A chain of men passes equipment up from the embankment onto two red-hulled launches that rock on the swell. Air cylinders, breathing sets, impulse extinguishers that shoot bursts of water droplets into the heart of a fire at half the speed of sound. Last of all come the firefighters in their bulky orange suits and helmets, picking their way along the gangway, a team of five to each boat.

The launches are new to the river; low freeboard, rapid-response vessels fitted with a powerful monitor and a bow ramp for speedy embarkation of personnel and equipment. Their twin jet drives are specially designed for use in shallow water.

Commanders check that all equipment is safely stowed before the craft pull away. Out in mid-stream, crewmembers tighten the harnesses on their suspension seats as the helmsmen open up the throttles. The river is coming up so fast already they can only just scrape beneath Westminster Bridge. Water creaming in their wake, the launches slam through the waves at twenty knots, racing for the Barrier.

'Descendez! Descendez! Plus en bas! Go low! We see more.'

Five hundred feet over Docklands, a Eurocopter 2000 from Biggin Hill, on charter to a French TV crew, descends into the darkness. The pilot is English; he picked up his passengers fifteen minutes ago at Gatwick with instructions to fly them out to the Barrier to film the overtopping. Now they have heard radio reports of a fresh disaster at the Royal Docks and are demanding to be taken there.

The helicopter follows the line of the river westwards. Half a mile ahead, huge columns of smoke belch furiously into the sky. Black smoke, dark and greasy, pierced by infernos of orange flame that flare and flicker amid the darkness.

The pilot levels out at two hundred feet and the journalists cease their jabber, peering tensely from the windows. The smoke grows thicker, darkening the cabin. The pilot eases back his speed till they are creeping ahead. Radio static crackles in his earphones; rescue aircraft are working in the vicinity. Suddenly the journalists let out a shout. Through a hole in the smoke they have just glimpsed water.

A moment later the full horror of the scene becomes visible. They are over Silvertown. Between burning docks on either side flows a torrent of fire. From the shattered storage tanks at the City Airport, streams of inflammable fuel spew out unstoppably to swell the slicks from Coryton. Whipped by fifty-knot winds, flames leap in an unbroken wall whose ends are lost in darkness. There are boats down there, rescue craft crammed with terrified passengers caught up in lakes of burning oil.

On the north side, flames have reduced the huge ExCeL exhibition centre to a mass of twisted wreckage. In the centre of the dock a slender footbridge provides a last exit for hundreds cut off by encircling flames. The fifteen-metre-high cable-stayed walkway spans the length of a football pitch. Pylons shrouded in drifting smoke, it seems to hang in space above the fire-filled dock. Blazing oil licks around the glass-walled lift-shaft on the north side. Further escape is impossible and the people on the bridge itself are now trapped.

The heat beats on the windows of the helicopter and the cabin is filled with a lurid glow. The journalists are jostling with their cameras, shouting at the pilot to take them closer. Flames are leaping up almost level with the footway. Someone on the bridge is climbing the cable stays to escape the flames. The helicopter's occupants stare, transfixed by the figure's desperate antics. The cables must be red hot. The person clings on for a few more seconds, then suddenly falls back, tumbling like a fly into the inferno below.

The French are jabbering at him again, but the

pilot has no ear for them. For some minutes they hover at a distance, observing the spectacle. At last, a rescue helicopter swoops out of the smoke. Even the journalists hold their breath as they watch the orange-suited winchman being buffeted by the gale, swinging among the pylons and cable stays. One survivor is lifted off and the winchman comes down for another. The process seems agonisingly slow. What the poor devils on the bridge must be enduring is unimaginable.

A second Sea King appears on the scene and commences operations at the northern end of the bridge. One person is swayed up, unconscious from smoke or heat. The fires have spread to the far end of the dock and the entire scene is illuminated in a hellish red glare. A line of brick warehouses burns, flames spouting from the windows, clouds of sparks flying up as the roof caves in.

The first helicopter lifts away so heavily laden it wallows in the sky. Another machine moves in to take its place. In the cabin of the Eurocopter the radio chatters again. Air Traffic control wants the pilot to move further out. Before he can comply there is a gasp of horror from the passengers. A sudden gust, or the savage updraught of the fire, has caused the tail rotor of the newly arrived Sea King to snap against one of the bridge pylons.

The helicopter slews sideways and for an instant looks as though it will fall clear of the bridge. Then the body of the aircraft tilts and the main rotor blades disintegrate in a whirl of snapping cables. The Sea King cabin rolls over on its back onto the bridge's central boom, dragging pylons and rigging with it. The bridge sags and the shattered helicopter disintegrates in a blinding fireball of vaporised fuel, its ruptured tanks showering flaming debris over the walkway.

The English pilot sits frozen at the controls of his machine. The bridge flexes, twisting along its length, spilling tiny figures from the footway. A gap opens in the centre, the pylons crumple, and the whole burning mass collapses into the inferno below.

Archie Watson, Lauren Khan's editor, is walking out along the Docklands railway with a group from the *Telegraph*. The wind howls over the viaduct, flaying the huddled marchers. Archie scarcely notices. He can't rid himself of the horror of those deaths in the lifts. An image from his childhood keeps returning in his mind. The family cat had littered half a dozen kittens. A kid of seven, he wasn't supposed to see when his father scooped four into a sack, weighted it with a stone, and dropped them in the canal. He hasn't thought about that in forty years.

At West India Dock the pace slows. Another track is joining from the right. It is choked with fleeing refugees coming up from Beckton, many of them soaked from wading through deep water. Up till now they have been walking mainly in silence, with the occasional curse as someone stumbles. Now Archie can detect words in the darkness. A woman's voice, desperate, pleading over and over, 'Please, be careful . . . my boy is hurt.'

One of the journalists with him has a torch. 'Stop a minute,' Archie says. Maybe it is the newspaper man in him, the instinct for a story, or perhaps it is something more compassionate. Whatever the truth he cannot walk on past, he must find out what is wrong.

He squeezes in beside the woman. She holds a baby against her chest. For a moment Archie imagines the problem is with that, then he makes out a man crouched over a figure on the ground.

'Are you a doctor? Our boy's hurt his back and can't move his feet,' the woman struggles to hold back a sob.

'No,' Archie says. 'I'm not a doctor. Has anybody gone to fetch one?'

The boy's parents don't seem to know. They are desperate and confused, overwhelmed by what has happened and daren't leave their son.

The boy moans softly and grips his father's hand. His eyes are closed. Archie dials the emergency number on his phone but can't get a line. 'I'll find a doctor for you,' he hears himself say. If he doesn't help this family he will never be able to live with himself. He slips off his coat and lays it gently on the boy.

'Try to keep him warm till I get back.'

The smoke in Woolwich Reach is so thick, the fireboat crews can't even see their bows. Somewhere in the murk ahead, less than a hundred metres off according to the radar, are the central piers of the Thames Barrier. Burning oil is moving through the open gates to cut the boats off.

'Fireboats! Fireboats!' It is the Barrier control tower on the radio. The firefighters have seen the flames breaking through and are calling urgently for help.

Aboard the boats, sweat streams down the crews' faces inside their breathing masks. The helmsmen are steering blind on radar, terrified that if they take their eyes off the screens for an instant they will become disoriented. The intense heat, the fumes and dense smoke rob them of all sense of direction. And close up to the Barrier, radar will be no guide.

The smoke parts for a moment and a pier looms ahead. The lead boat has visual contact with the Barrier. The skipper pushes the throttle forward and the boat throbs under him. The vessel is barely making headway against the fierce currents. Twenty metres to go till the monitors are within range and the heat is blistering the paintwork. The skipper orders the sprays to be turned on to protect the crew and moves in closer. The monitors begin to play on the forward edge of the flames.

The second boat joins in. They cruise back and forth in front of the advancing flames. It is dangerous work because the current keeps sweeping patches of burning oil past them up-river. When that happens, the boats have to pull back or risk being cut off.

Raikes's helicopter is equipped with a thermal imager but with so many fires burning it is hard to make out patterns. One thing is becoming clear though, confirming his worst fears. Flames have broken through the Royal Docks and are spilling back out into the main river again opposite the Dome. Raikes uses the radio to order his precious fireboats back up-river before they are cut off. For now the Barrier will have to look after itself. Unless the boats can regroup promptly, all London will be lost.

46

WE HAVE LOST contact with the Barrier control tower. Flooding must have broken in somehow. The first we knew was when water began pouring down the lift-shafts. We have closed the watertight doors and the tunnels are secure – for the present.'

An arc of fire half a mile wide engulfs the Barrier. Lauren Khan, who is dictating into her tape machine, has lost count of the number of times she has seen the oil in front of the piers doused with frothing retardant only to burst into flames again. The constant heat, the glare and roar of the flames has a deadening effect upon her mind. The men on the piers are exhausted; they handle the hoses like automatons.

The north bank is all aflame. The control room on that side has had to be abandoned, the engineers and firefighters escaping down the tunnel under the river. Lauren met them a short while ago staggering back, haggard and filthy. Several are badly burned, tears running down their faces with the pain. A first-aid post has been established in the stairwell of Pier 7.

According to the firefighters, the flames in the Royal Docks have broken through onto the

Greenwich Peninsula. If the rumour is true then the river is cut behind them, in which case the only way out is by helicopter. Lauren gets this from another journalist who heard it confirmed on the radio. The depleted press pack is grouped on the stairs below Pier 8, where Lauren dictates notes for the story she might never live to finish.

'You have done all that brave men could. It is time to leave now!'

The message over the radio is addressed to Lieutenant Besnault from a Royal Navy helicopter circling overhead. For the past forty minutes the *Drogou*'s crew have fought on against the flames. Her hull and scrambling nets are caked with congealed oil, the once spotless decks blackened and scorched. There's no tally of how many survivors the seamen have pulled from the water. Their medical stores have long ago run out and they can do nothing to ease the sufferings of the injured. As fast as the helicopters lift them off, more are brought aboard.

Relentlessly the flames have driven the corvette back into a corner of the dock. Her hoses are powerless against fires on this scale. Still the tricolour flutters defiantly amid the smoke. Only when flames surround his ship on all sides does Besnault finally admit defeat.

The first crewmember to be lifted off the deck carries the ship's cat. Besnault is the last to leave. He has one final duty to perform. The magazines have been flooded and anchors let go fore and aft. While the crew is evacuating to safety he descends to the now silent engine room and opens the seacocks. As he climbs back up the clattering steel ladders, water is blasting inboard through the open valves below. It is the most he can do for her, he thinks sorrowfully. At least this way she will not be burned out.

Via satellite, the whole world has watched the *Drogou*'s gallant fight. She has saved more than five hundred lives and her crew are heroes. When Besnault steps off the helicopter at a British military base, a waiting crowd breaks spontaneously into the 'Marseillaise'. Fêted wherever he goes, he will be honoured by the Queen and receive the freedom of the City of London. The Royal Navy will name one of its own vessels *Drogou* in tribute. For Yves Besnault though the night will always remain one of sorrow. 'If only we could have saved more,' he says.

At Canary Wharf the shopping malls and passages below the tower are still inundated; flames have spread to the inner basin. Smoke is pouring from buildings along Trafalgar Way. Tongues of fire can be seen moving past South Quay and the crowds on the footbridges are mad with fear. As the flames edge closer people leap from the parapets into the water in desperate attempts to swim to safety.

The burning slicks have torched the famous Christmas tree in Canada Square. Barry Singleton can smell the smoke as he runs down the stairs of the tower to the lobby. He is the last person to leave. The rest of his teams have departed already. He has climbed more than four thousand steps since the emergency began and he is long past exhaustion, but nervous energy drives him on.

Pools of water reflect back in his torch beam. The

stairways are awash. Smoke drifting upwards has triggered sprinklers on every floor. Barry's shoes and clothing are soaked but he no longer notices. On the last flight of stairs a gust of boiling smoke greets him. Holding a handkerchief to his mouth he plunges blindly through. Down in the lift hall the heat is sweltering. The splash of water echoes hollowly under the lofty ceiling. The sprinklers are in action here too but the flow is tailing off; with half the upper floors drenched, the roof tanks must be nearly emptied.

Barry's torch plays round, briefly illuminating the bodies from the lifts, still lying where they fell. Spirals of vapour hiss from the gaps around the doors. Barry puts his hand to one of the metal panels and jerks it back. The steel has blistered his skin. And the floor is hot too; he can feel it through his shoes. There is steam rising from the pools around his feet. His heart starts to beat fast: flames must have penetrated into the shopping malls underneath him. The building is on fire.

The glass doors at the end of the hall are soot blackened and scorched. Barry kicks one open and the heat hits him like a wall. Shielding his face with his arm, he edges along the passage towards the mezzanine entrance. Yellow flames are belching up the circular stairwell. An inferno is raging down there among the shops and stores. A terrific concussion shakes the floor, throwing him to his knees. Glass and debris rain down as a blast of flaming gas explodes along the passage towards him.

Scrambling to his feet, Barry dives back through the door to the hall, pulling it shut behind him.

There is no escape to the DLR track that way. He is cut off. There is nothing for it but to retreat back the way he came – up into the tower.

A Sea King HC4 helicopter of the Fleet Air Arm swings in low over RAF Manston in Kent. Aboard are twenty-three disaster victims plucked from the flames in the Royal Docks. They huddle, shocked and silent, wrapped in survival blankets, as the helicopter touches down. Ambulances race out across the floodlit apron to meet them. A tender draws up alongside and starts pumping fuel into the belly tanks. The base is operating at full battle tempo. RAF ground crew help the passengers out and toss aboard fresh blankets and medical packs, bottled water, fruit juice and candy. Canteen assistants scramble through to the cockpit with hot coffee and Big Macs for the crew.

The co-pilot speaks to the tower. Orders are the same as before: return to Docklands; pick up survivors. As fast and as many as you can.

Refuelling is complete. Mechanics snap the latches shut. A ground controller gives the high sign and the Sea King lifts off into the night, curving away northwards back towards the river.

The military response ordered by Venetia Maitland is moving into high gear. A dozen Puma helicopters from RAF Benson are among the latest units to reach the capital. Venetia wants them tasked to the evacuation of St Thomas's. The Chief Medical Officer protests. He wants the aircraft sent to St Bart's where a thousand patients transferred from Guy's are lying on mattresses in corridors.

The problem with evacuating hospitals is where to put the patients being transferred. Even in normal times, 90 per cent of the 109,000 NHS beds in England and Wales are occupied. In winter the rate can rise above 100 per cent, more patients than beds available, with admission cases waiting on trolleys for hours at peak periods.

'At the latest tally, we have 322 major burns cases and an equal number of general trauma victims,' the Chief Medical Officer tells Venetia. 'So far we have had to close six hospitals and approximately forty health centres. All elective surgery in the country has been cancelled. All non-urgent admissions stopped. Where possible, patients are being sent home or transferred to the private sector or to general nursing homes. Before the flooding started, the Health Service was struggling to cope with influenza admissions. As of this morning there were 478 beds empty, or due to become so, and a further two in Intensive Care Units.'

'That's in London?'

'In the whole of England and Wales,' the CMO says. 'Even assuming the fires are checked, we anticipate at least another two thousand injury and resuscitation cases. I am talking about the very sick here; people who will die without prompt treatment at a major hospital facility. Specialist burns units are already turning patients away. We are even having to send victims to places like St Thomas's, inside the flood zone, because there is nowhere else that can take them.'

He continues: 'The eastern sector of the country is starting to see a wave of admissions from hypothermia. A majority of these will be elderly or sick who have been trapped in cold houses and will die without immediate care. Their numbers will rise sharply during the next few days unless power supplies can be restored in blacked-out areas.

'We don't have the beds available. Even if we did, we don't have the surgeons, trained nurses or specialist trauma teams. Put bluntly, the nation is simply not equipped to handle casualties on anything like this scale.'

'What about our European friends, can we get help from them?'

'The Germans, Belgians and Scandinavians are offering aid. The French have cleared an entire hospital in the Pas de Calais region. Eurostar trains manned by French medical teams will bring casualties directly out through the Channel Tunnel and the Armée de l'Air is sending helicopter units to RAF bases in the Home Counties. The Germans are also offering helicopters in addition to boats and amphibious vehicles. Then there are the Americans . . .'

Down on the Bakerloo Line, engineer Paul Suter plods on towards Baker Street station with his thousand passengers strung out behind him in a stumbling, exhausted column. Progress is terribly slow. The tunnel is only three metres in diameter and the arched roof and four-rail layout of the track make it impossible to walk more than two abreast. Obstructions like junction boxes and signalling equipment reduce this to single file in places.

The tunnel lighting is growing dimmer and, as the darkness increases, the walls seem to close in. Passengers are now extremely frightened. Dean

Stacey has stripped off his coat and still he is sweating. Somewhere behind him a foreign woman sobs quietly and persistently. She is getting on his nerves. Dean's coat is heavy, the dust in the air is making his throat tight and his ankles are sore from repeated knocks on the rails. Children whimper and complain, parents doing their best to comfort them. Baby buggies lurch and overturn on the uneven gravel of the track ballast. Other people are burdened with suitcases or packages that they refuse to discard. There is one young man on crutches.

Stoppages are growing more frequent. Many of the women are wearing light shoes and when one trips on a broken sleeper, another two or three go down. The delays ripple back along the column which is now stretched out over a third of a mile. Paul makes his way up and down, exhorting and encouraging. 'Only another few hundred metres,' he repeats as he goes.

'You keep saying that, Mister.'

It is true and Paul is increasingly worried. With power to the ventilation fans switched off and no trains running to provide air circulation, the ambient temperature underground is approaching 30 Celsius. At the same time, with so many people in the tunnel, oxygen levels are falling.

He checks his watch by a torch. Twenty-five minutes and still no more than halfway to Baker Street at an optimistic estimate. The stuffiness of the tunnel is becoming unendurable. An overweight woman sets up a wail. Her husband cannot go on. He has a heart complaint and the strain is killing him. A message is passed up to Paul. Wearily, he goes back to see. The man's face is pasty white and running with sweat, his breath coming in painful wheezes. The woman is near hysterical.

The man is too heavy to carry. The only course is to leave them behind. If only they can reach the station there will be a stretcher there. The woman gives Paul a piteous look as he turns away. Feeling terrible, he hurries back to the head of the column. Behind him, the remaining passengers shuffle off along the tunnel, averting their eyes guiltily from the couple as they edge past. The journey is turning into a nightmare without end.

Up in Notting Hill, Sophie de Salis clambers over her fellow companions in the back seat and flips the door catch. The Samaritan who has given her the ride is apologising for not taking her further. 'Don't even think about it,' Sophie tells him. The guy's car is crammed full of desperate people and he has come far out of his way to drop her here.

Standing on the pavement by the Gate cinema, with people pushing past in both directions, Sophie tries to orient herself. Somehow she must get south and west but there's not a taxi or a bus in sight and the traffic is locked solid all the way up to the traffic lights and beyond. No point in trying for a ride then; her only option is to walk. At the Shepherd's Bush roundabout there's a chance she might get lucky again.

Sophie strides out, fast and purposefully, trying to exorcise the terrifying images of the Blackfriars underpass that come seething back into her brain. She has an urgent need to see and hold Chrissie, to know that she is safe. Taking out her mobile, she tries the Binneys' number but can't get a line.

The craziest thing is that all around her life is going on as normal up here. The supermarket across the road is busy with evening shoppers, girls are fingering the racks in the fashion stores, pubs and cafés are filling up with post-work trade. Don't they know what is happening to their city? Sophie wonders. Don't they care?

Past Notting Hill, she heads along Holland Park, with its plane trees and expensive houses set back from the road. Smartly dressed women stare. Sophie's trainers and legs are wet and muddied and her suit is a mess. Let them, she thinks furiously. It is the traffic she cares about. It is worse than ever here. Drivers are abandoning their cars, just leaving them in the middle of the thoroughfare, and it looks to be the same all the way to the roundabout. In which case, Sophie realises, she will be walking home to Hammersmith. It will take her forever.

If she hadn't been passing the showroom, she would never have had the idea. But Sophie has always grabbed at opportunities. Pushing open the double glass doors she flashes her credit card. 'I want a scooter and I want it right away.'

NBC Studios, Washington, DC. The bulletin is coming through live from London, from one of the bridges upstream of the Docklands fires. The reporter is being jostled for space by other camera crews and by pedestrians hurrying across. His face is flushed and his speech rapid – whether from excitement or fear, it is impossible to tell. In the background the sky is a throbbing orange, wreathed with funnels of smoke, the glow reflected on the surging waters of the river below. Helicopter engines and the constant wail of sirens punctuate the piece.

'. . . *and it's not only the thousands of homes that are being lost. We're talking finance, infrastructure, telecommunications. Forty per cent of Internet service providers use servers located up in Docklands. Half of international telephone exchange capacity, two of the country's four satellite earth stations. First flooded out and now an inferno . . .*

'. . . *the building burning like a torch behind me is Canary Wharf Tower, symbol of the regeneration of the docks. The European headquarters of five multinational banking groups, four of them US corporations, are sited here, as well as countless other major businesses. Damage to this area alone is going to be catastrophic. In London as a whole, devastation on a truly unimaginable scale . . .*'

The anchorwoman's earpiece is yapping at her. 'Can you give us some indication of how the firefighters are handling things?' she interrupts. 'Do they have a strategy for holding the line anywhere?'

A brief pause and then the reporter speaks, but now his words are distorted. The image scrambles.

'He's breaking up. Shit! We're losing him.'

A flash and the screen blanks. The production team goes into overdrive.

'Brad, Brad, can you hear us?'

'Testing negative.'

'Check the signal with Goonhilly.'

'They say it's the London feed. Nothing they can do.'

'Marcia, we have to cover. Cut back to studio.'

'*I'm sorry, we're having problems with that live report from burning London. We'll get back to it as soon as we can. Meantime, for an expert opinion on the situation over there, we have former US Ambassador to Great Britain . . .'*

At the White House, an aide switches off the television with a finality not lost on the group watching. The Secretary of State is here, members of the military, the President's National Security Adviser, the Chairman of the Federal Reserve. All summoned when news of the disaster started coming in at dawn. Styrene coffee-cups and plates of half-finished doughnuts litter the table. The military are liaising with Europe on the immediate aid package. The Chairman of the Federal Reserve is talking quietly with members of his team.

'What's the latest?' the President asks them.

A young woman checks her screens. 'Sterling is in free fall, Mr President. Everyone is dumping it. The markets are very, very jittery. The Dow opened down three hundred points and has dropped a further seventy-three. Same story on the Nikkei. It's the lack of hard information. No one knows for sure what's going on over there.'

'Least of all the Brits by the sound of it,' adds someone else.

The President nods. None of the sources are giving a clear picture. The Ambassador in London called in an update from Venetia Maitland thirty minutes back but it is out of date already. He addresses the team again. 'And for the long term?'

'If there is a long term.'

The dead dry response comes from the Chairman. It provokes an uncomfortable stirring round the table. The President looks at him searchingly. 'Meaning what? That the UK could go under?'

'Consider the scenario,' the Chairman answers. 'We have a capital city that will have lost most of its infrastructure: its public transportation system, telecommunications network, power grid, maybe even something as basic as its water supply. A million or more citizens are homeless, hundreds of major corporations are without premises. People can't get into work or, if they can, they'll have no place to work in. How long is that going to take to repair? One year? Five years? Ten? Big business won't wait that long. They'll relocate to Frankfurt, or Paris or New York.

'The insurance industry is facing claims running into tens of billions. Unless the government steps in, it will fail entirely and pull the rest of the financial sector down with it. And where's the British Government to find the money? Institutions like banks, real estate companies, investment and pension funds will be bankrupt. Millions of ordinary Britishers are going to find their life savings wiped out. Recession and mass unemployment in the middle of winter, lack of heat and light and food – it's an explosive mix.

'Against that we have a trillion dollars worth of investments in the UK, the majority in London and the southeast. Roughly 13 per cent of the nation's GDP is in American ownership. It's a big sum to write off.'

The President looks confused. 'You're saying we should leave them to it – cut Britain loose?' His voice registers shock. 'Surely that would drag us all down?'

The Chairman, characteristically, takes time to frame his response. 'I can give you the figures, Mr President,' he replies dispassionately. 'What you chose to do with them is beyond my brief.'

47

The ferry bringing survivors from Greenwich is approaching Tower Bridge. Conditions on the river are atrocious with winds gusting to eighty miles per hour. The banks are submerged. Darkness has fallen and the lights along the walls have failed. Visibility is down to a few metres. The vessel is pitching badly and the captain radios that waves have broken in the doors to the passenger cabin and they are taking in water. By the time the bridge comes in sight, Tower Pier is flooded and docking is out of the question.

Moored opposite the pier is HMS *Belfast*. The plan is for the ferry-master to pull alongside and, if necessary, transfer his passengers to the cruiser. River police are on hand to assist in the rescue. One of their precious launches is standing by and searchlights are rigged on *Belfast* to guide the ferry in. But her skipper has misjudged the situation. He is positioned too far out into the river and ferocious wind and currents carry the ferry on past the cruiser. She is riding low in the water and the master is afraid she will founder if he attempts to put about.

Now the ferry's lights pick out London Bridge coming up fast. He steers for the centre arch and the low-built vessel slips freely under. Only two hundred and fifty metres away, on the far side, stands the gaunt structure of the Cannon Street rail crossing.

Penned in by buildings on both banks, the surge here has swollen almost to the tops of the piers. Visibility in the darkness and spray is still very bad and only at the last minute, as they close on the bridge, does the ferry-master realise there is no chance of scraping through this time. In a panic he rings for hard astern on the engines and puts the helm over to try and bring the vessel alongside. But enormous volumes of water are flowing upstream. Unable to fight the current, the ferry loses way and turns broadside on. At the last instant, the helpless vessel's bow swings back into the flood and it slides stern first into the northernmost arch.

Down on the lower deck, the Exeter school children are seasick and frightened. It is dark outside and there is so much spray hitting the windows that people have only a vague idea whereabouts they are on the river. Claire Panton hears the sudden roar of the engines going astern and the boat starts to swing round. There is a warning yell from the stern; something huge and black fills the windows aft. Before she can brace herself, she is jolted violently backwards in her seat. Then a second collision shakes the boat, throwing her into the aisle. Lights go out, glass shatters and grinding sounds fill the cabin. Children are shrieking, people are screaming and crying out in terror.

A blast of freezing spray stings Claire's face. The salt taste in her mouth is blood. She is shaking all over but she doesn't cry. She is too frightened for that. The ferry lurches again with another grinding crunch. Water bursts through broken windows. The screams redouble and a rush of feet tramples Claire to the deck. She rolls herself into a ball and squirms against the seats. Another cascade of water comes crashing in. Horror of drowning grips her and she fights herself upright. The hideous grinding sounds continue and bodies slam into each other in the darkness.

A searchlight snaps on, illuminating the scene with a blinding glare. The commander of the police launch has kept his head. The glass roof of the upper deck housing has been crushed against the underside of the arch and the stern section of the vessel is wedged in under the bridge. He calls in a major incident, giving the location and numbers involved – up to a thousand, with many injured. The ferry appears badly damaged and could be forced under if the river rises further. He can see figures struggling in the water and they are his first priority.

With light restored, a semblance of sanity returns inside the cabin. Dazed passengers pick themselves up, feeling for their injuries. The children's cries fade to whimpers; older ones are pale but quiet. Many of them have been badly knocked about. A boy near Claire is bleeding profusely from a gashed head. Automatically she reaches in a pocket for a tissue and tells him to press it to the wound. She wants to get nearer to help, but the cabin is listing to one side making it hard to move across.

A crewmember comes staggering through. He tells everyone to sit down and put life vests on. Claire is trying to find enough to go round when something wet splashes on her hand. A scarlet droplet that trickles stickily over her fingers. She stares blankly at it. Her brain seems to be working very slowly, as if she is moving in a fog. Another drop follows and another. She looks up. Children shrink back with cries of horror. A thin stream of blood is showering down between the planking overhead.

Just up the track from the bridge is Cannon Street station, which has been designated an emergency assembly point by the City of London Police. COLP is an independent force responsible for policing London's financial district between Blackfriars and Tower Hill. The area is experiencing only limited flooding and has resources to concentrate on a river emergency.

A superintendent and a chief fire officer run along the track onto the bridge to assess the situation, forcing a path through the horde of people picking their way across from the Southwark side. It is evident at once that the incident is extremely serious, with potentially major loss of life. Storm-force winds and driving spray make a rescue attempt using boats difficult if not impossible. Heavy equipment will be needed to bring survivors up and get medical help to the injured. The superintendent orders part of the bridge cordoned off to give access for cranes and ambulances.

A rescue tender is brought onto the bridge and officers descend over the side on ropes. They find appalling scenes below. The glassed-in roof on the stern has been ripped off three feet above the deck and the seats are jammed up under the bridge. Many injured are trapped in there. Cutting gear and pneumatic tools will be needed to reach them.

The first priority is to remove the uninjured passengers. The bridge side is too high to put a turntable ladder over. Efforts are made to pierce an opening in the decking between the tracks but the thickness of the girders renders this impossible. The officer in charge orders a truckload of scaffolding to be brought up. In the freezing night, with a storm raging overhead and the surge tearing at the piers, emergency crews set to work constructing a ramp over which to bring the passengers out.

At Embankment underground station by Charing Cross Pier, a young line manager, Matt Holyfield, is standing lookout for the engineers working on the floodgates twelve metres below. The river level is coming up fast and twice Matt has pleaded with the team leader over the radio to bring his men up. The tide is brimming the wall now, wave crests splashing down onto the pavement. Police are running along the lines of traffic, ordering people out of their vehicles. Matt is the only person left on this side of the road and he is terrified.

He hears a shout and jerks his head round. What he sees transfixes him. He is looking left, down river, towards Waterloo Bridge and Somerset House. Between him and the river a line of globe lanterns on bronze shafts tops the Embankment wall, illuminating an astonishing sight. A row of fountains has sprouted down the centre of the broad pavement. Up at Blackfriars, overtopping has sucked the manhole covers off a service tunnel running under the Embankment.

Even as Matt stares, unable to move momentarily for surprise, the leaping jets come racing towards him. A metal grill at his paralysed feet emits a gurgle and gushes water. He jumps back drenched. In the same instant the river rolls over the wall in a glittering wave. Matt turns to run for the station, slips in the racing water and crashes against a car. The radio flies from his hand. Frantically he scrabbles for it but now the water is up to his waist. He struggles to the station entrance, shouts a despairing warning down the escalators and runs for his life up Villiers Street.

The three men below ground have reached the Circle Line level when the water bursts in on them. One is hurled back down the escalator and never seen again. His companions link arms and make for the emergency stairs, but the flood races after them, trapping the two men in a side tunnel. Water surges over their heads, then suddenly drops again leaving them gasping in total blackness. Groping along the passage, trying to remember the layout, they find a ventilation shaft and manage to crawl inside, only to find escape blocked by a grill. Using a pair of hand pliers in pitch darkness, with water rising about their chests, they cut a hole large enough to squirm through and climb sixty feet of iron rungs to safety.

Unseen beneath the city streets the flood spreads northwards through the Underground tunnel system. Like the spearheads of an invasion, water is racing along the tracks into the heart of the capital. Already it has penetrated beyond Green Park and is lapping the platforms at Bond Street.

So far the damage is being contained. At the Green Park interchange the Jubilee tunnels pass under the Piccadilly and Victoria lines, preventing the flood from entering other parts of the system. But half a mile north of Bond Street lies Baker Street where the Jubilee intersects with the Bakerloo Line.

In Trafalgar Square, gusting wind is blowing spray from the fountains, soaking the pavement where tourists are feeding the pigeons beneath Nelson's Column. All at once a deafening report sends the birds scattering in alarm. A cast-iron manhole cover has been blasted free by pressure in the drain below. Another blast follows and a second heavy metal disk tumbles back with a ringing crash. Murky liquid spouts from the shafts, spreading across the paving stones as pedestrians scurry out of the way.

Four hundred metres away, down by the river, the pleasure steamer *Tattershall Castle* has been torn from her mooring by the storm and swept onto the Embankment. A twenty-metre section of wall gives way, releasing a torrent up Northumberland Avenue, past the deserted DEFRA building, into Trafalgar Square. Along the way it picks up a Mercedes coupé, whose owner is defying instructions to clear the area, and launches car and driver through the plate-glass window of a bookshop on the corner.

Policemen run ahead of the advancing water, chasing sightseers and photographers out of the square. The flood foams against the fountains and surrounds the tall Norwegian spruce that has been a Christmas gift to the capital from the people of Norway since 1945. With undiminished momentum it thunders down the subway under the Strand, the street that once marked the old foreshore of the river, into the underground shopping centre at Charing Cross, which has fortunately been cleared.

On the north side of Trafalgar Square, the National Gallery is in turmoil. Director, Dame Susan Crawford, has been advised the building is not in danger. The ten-metre contour passes through the square and the road behind is sharply higher. The gallery has been closed to the public and staff told to remain on duty. The core of the collection is displayed on the first floor in four main wings, but lesser works are housed at lower ground level and these could be at risk. A decision is taken to move as many as possible upstairs.

The gallery maintains a special team of dedicated picture handlers. Works can measure six metres across and weigh half a tonne. Moving them requires ropes and lifting tackle. And time. It was midday when Dame Susan's office received the first warning and four hours later only a fraction of the paintings have been transferred to the upper floor. Everyone in the building is engaged on the task when the lights fail. Drains backing up in Panton Street have flooded a crucial electricity sub-station twelve metres under Leicester Square in theatre land.

South and west of Trafalgar Square the flood pushes inland, flowing along Whitehall, with its massive government ministries, and under Admiralty Arch into the Mall. The evacuation effort in Horse Guards Parade is still continuing and the inrush of water triggers a mad dash by civil servants desperate to escape through St James's Park. Within minutes flooding has reached the forecourt of Buckingham Palace at the far end of the Mall, where soldiers are aiding footmen and equerries in a race to save the basement treasuries and more priceless works of art from the Picture Collection.

From a ground-floor window in the bleak white fortress of the Ministry of Defence, Juliet Chambers watches the road. Other ministries have shut down, with only skeleton staffs left behind. Juliet and a dozen others at the MOD are camped in the main entrance with the contents of their offices piled about them, awaiting transport up to the department's Holborn building.

Outside, Whitehall is eerily deserted. There is not a person or vehicle in sight. Even the wind seems muted temporarily. The flood is expected any minute now, according to the TV. Directly opposite, Juliet can see the sandbag barricade protecting Downing Street.

A sudden small movement catches her eye and her stomach tightens. A shiver seems to run across the road for an instant. She looks again and blinks. The pavement on the opposite side of the street has gone. The tarmac has moved right up to the railings. Except that it is not the road she is staring at but water. The suddenness of the flood's onset is shocking. One minute the street is dry and the next the river is lapping at the Cabinet Office steps.

Other colleagues crowd the windows. Everybody in these circumstances reacts differently. For the first time since the start of the emergency Juliet experiences a sharp sense of dread. Her first thought is for Nicholas, her husband. Has he made it home to Bromley from the Treasury? Suppose suburban trains aren't running? A few of the younger employees are excited. At last something is really happening.

A guard opens one of the main doors to look out, holding it firm against the gale. The flood has swallowed the grass lawn along the road and is rising up the steps. The wind whips up the water in strange eddies and the surface has a greasy sheen that reflects the glow of the street lamps. Where these have failed, the water takes on a sullen blackness that gives no hint of depth and looks cold and menacing.

'Hey! Look,' someone calls suddenly. 'Here come the trucks.'

Everyone stares as headlights appear from the direction of Trafalgar Square, ploughing slowly towards them. Surely this must be the transport come to take them out? Then the lights swing away and their spirits flag. 'It's turned into Horse Guards,' Juliet tries to keep the disappointment out of her voice.

The door is shut again. The water is almost up to the top step. Sandbags have been laid to hold it back but before long pools appear inside, leaking across the marble floor. Another guard comes running up from the basement with news that water is entering the citadel, the five-level underground bunker beneath the building. Juliet shrugs. Right now that is the least of their problems. They lug their kit back up to the first floor, wandering dismally along corridors filled with signs of hasty evacuation: gaping filing-cabinets, desks strewn with papers, trolley-loads of equipment abandoned outside lifts. Some sections were given only minutes' notice to leave.

A sudden buzzing sound makes Juliet jump. A telephone is ringing. More than one. The noise grows to deafening intensity. Every phone in the building is pealing with sustained urgency. People stare at one another. Then as suddenly as it started the ringing ceases. Silence returns as the echoes die. 'Water must have reached the switchboard,' says somebody nervously. 'The power will be next.'

They have reached the south side of the building overlooking the river. The embankments, usually spangled with lights, are dark. As Juliet watches she can see fingers of blackness creeping inland, plunging street after street into night, as circuits succumb to the flood. A blast of wind shakes the windows. In the distance a red glare stains the overcast. Juliet shivers involuntarily; they are watching London die.

Within a short time the entire centre of the capital has been paralysed. Cars are stranded, lights vanish. The inhabitants have fled or taken refuge in buildings, where they huddle with torches, drawing what comfort they can from news broadcasts on portable radios. Outside the stillness is broken only by the lapping of water and the moaning of the wind. Faint across the city come the wail of sirens and the thudding of helicopters as rescue work continues.

The flood spills between the railings of Whitehall

and down into the basement areas of the ministries. As the pressure builds, windows give way and water pours through into the rooms beyond. All these buildings have several levels below ground. Over the past half-century, successive governments have excavated bomb-proof citadels hidden away from public gaze. Connecting these underground warrens is a network of secret tunnels whose true extent can only be guessed at.

Now, as Whitehall floods, the underground world floods too. Soon water is spreading out beneath the streets northwards and west. Within minutes it is drowning the nuclear bunker beneath the Home Office at Queen Anne's Gate and working through the cellars of New Scotland Yard in Victoria, knocking out electricity and communications. Across the road at Broadway the screens at London Underground's National Control Centre flicker and go blank as the power dies.

48

With the NCC down and the Underground stations along the river flooding one by one, closed-circuit television surveillance of the network has collapsed. It is no longer possible to monitor how far water has penetrated along the system. Rescue crews from several stations are searching the tunnels for Suter's column, but without communications there is confusion over their whereabouts. Teams at Oxford Circus have been forced back by floodwater.

The first firemen to reach Baker Street find the street entrance gates locked. They rattle the grills, trying to attract the attention of anyone inside, while the chief officer radios for instructions. The station controllers have evacuated to Neasden and there is no one else with the keys. The fire crew break the locks and enter the station.

Baker Street is one of the most complex interchanges of the Underground network. Five separate lines run through here, served by eight different platforms spread over four levels, interconnected by a warren of stairs and passages. The station is completely blacked out, with no lighting below ground and no power to escalators and lifts. The firemen have no one to guide them and no idea even which line the stranded passengers are trying to escape from. They check the platforms of the Hammersmith and Circle lines without result and descend to the next level to search the Jubilee and Bakerloo.

Here they encounter signs of flooding. Water is running chest deep in the north and southbound Jubilee tunnels. The platforms are awash, and water is spreading through the link passages to the escalator hall and from there onto the northbound Bakerloo platform. The layout on this level is confusing. The Bakerloo Line tunnels are stacked vertically, with the southbound track running underneath the northbound.

Water is streaming down the escalators connecting the two platforms and it takes a lot of courage for the fire crew to climb down to the lowest level. There is a further flight of stone steps at the bottom, leading down to the southbound platform. The water level here is frighteningly deeper, almost up to the roof of the passage. The chief officer wades in, his helmet light glinting off the white brickwork, but one look onto the platform is enough. Both tunnel entrances are under water. Any passengers inside will have drowned by now.

They are retreating back up the escalator when there is a shout from above. It is the driver from the train, sent on ahead by Paul Suter to raise help. He has reached the station and seen the firemen's lights. At last they know where the passengers are, but the station is flooding fast and there is very little time left in which to bring them out.

⋆

Across the river from Whitehall, the flood pouring down into Waterloo has isolated County Hall, the former headquarters of the disbanded Greater London Council. The colonnaded riverside development contains hotels, a health club, the London Aquarium and the booking office for the London Eye which is directly in front of the building.

The aquarium has closed early, on police advice, and evacuated staff. Situated on the ground floor, it opens directly onto the embankment and is one of the largest of its kind in Europe. There are two main tanks. The Pacific descends through three floors and holds a million litres of filtered water, supporting over a hundred species of fish including Sand Tiger and Nurse sharks, groupers and jacks. The Atlantic tank is similar and features conger eels and dogfish. Other tanks are home to exotic types such as sea horses, jellyfish and piranha.

The river rises rapidly above the level of the main doors, but it is a plate-glass window that gives way first, possibly as a result of impact by debris. Water crashes through, flooding the ground floor up to the tops of the tanks. Life support-systems have been set to automatic, removing waste, cleaning and re-oxygenating the contents of the tanks every thirty minutes. As floodwater spills over the glass walls, temperature, salinity, pH and oxygen levels go haywire. Fish go into violent shock at the sudden changes and the contact with chemical pollutants. Desperate to escape, they surge out from their tanks in search of clean water.

Behind its elegant classical exterior, County Hall is a warren of courtyards and blocks connected by passageways and staircases. Many of the occupants are visitors to London and only vaguely aware of the crisis engulfing the city. The health club in the basement has closed but a party of Australian students find an unlocked door to the swimming pool. Their frolics alert security but by then it is too late.

It seems a joke at first when the power fails. The emergency lights are just bright enough for a game of tag. For many it will be the last they ever play. The flood has taken a little time to penetrate the inner regions of the building. Once it does however, the courtyards fill rapidly. A security guard from the lobby is on his way down to warn them when the first outer door gives way. He is knocked down and driven back, barely escaping with his life.

The basement passages become underground rivers. Intent on their games, in the dim light, none of the swimmers notices the dark tide building against the double doors to the pool area. There is no warning. Surprise is total. One moment they are playing in clear water, the next instant a filthy torrent bursts in, swamping the pool. Dismay turns to fear as the flood pours in unstoppably. The swimmers scramble out and grab their towels. Already the floor is awash and the water over their ankles. In thirty seconds it has reached their knees. Two youths charge the emergency exit and force it open against the flow. The passage beyond is a black river, rising fast. Hurry, they shout to the others.

Four plunge through; the next, a girl, screams suddenly. A huge fish has surfaced close to her, its rough skin scraping against her shoulders. It is a three-metre white shark from the aquarium, floating belly up, near dead from toxic shock and rapid changes in water temperature and salinity, but in the half-light it sparks panic. Some struggle back into the pool room, pulling the doors shut. They are never seen alive again.

The others owe their escape to one of their number, who yells at them to grab hands and move against the current. In freezing water up to their necks they fight their way to the stairs where hotel staff hear their cries.

On the other side of Westminster Bridge Road it is the turn of St Thomas's Hospital. Overtopping begins on the river walk below the hospital wall at the same time that the first serious flooding appears on York Road from the direction of Waterloo. Minutes later a torrent sweeps in from the opposite direction along Lambeth Palace Road. Volunteers have erected a barrier of sandbags across the entrance to the basement car park but there are too many entry points and not all are well secured. As the level in the river rises, water streams in through the cast-iron gate by the bridge and across the gardens.

Graeme Duncan and his Emergency Reconfiguration Group are managing the crisis from the second floor of Riddell House on the southwest corner of the site. It is their understanding that they have at least thirty minutes before overtopping commences. Though they have access to radio and TV, they are too stretched to follow the situation down the estuary closely. Consequently they do not immediately pick up on the significance of the gate failures at the Barrier.

The speed of the flood's attack takes everyone unawares. Lookouts have been posted to monitor the river level, but with the approach of darkness their task is hampered. In the lower ground areas frantic efforts are continuing to clear the radiology unit. Everything portable has been carried upstairs and technicians are working to dismantle the MRI scanners and linear accelerators, the new Gamma Knife and multiple-leaf collimators. There is £25-million worth of equipment down here but it's not just a question of expense. These machines are vital; if they are lost or out of use for any reason, then patients can't be treated and some will die.

Barricades are being strengthened at critical installations. Workmen are shoring up doors, wrapping polythene around electrical junction boxes and sealing off boilers and generators. Sewage contamination will pose a major threat to health and fresh water must be stockpiled for washing and lavatories.

Stocks of drugs have to be moved from the pharmacy. Their safe storage presents difficulties. Electricians are endeavouring to isolate the upper floors in order to keep power running. The wiring has been designed with this in mind, with in-feeds at different levels, but though these are periodically tested, they are seldom used extensively and there are problems to be sorted out.

A team of students and nurses are ferrying patients across the main road into Archbishop's Park at Lambeth Palace, where RAF Puma helicopters are waiting to fly them out from the sports ground. With winds gusting to over sixty knots it is a desperate operation. A Puma can fit twelve patients: six stretcher cases and the same number seated. It takes a quarter of an hour to load the helicopter and lift off. So far they have managed three trips and flight control is warning that this may be the last. Conditions are just too dangerous.

A student doctor is helping two nurses manoeuvre a trolley between the lines of stationary vehicles when a policeman comes running down the road, blowing his whistle. All three hesitate for an instant, wondering what to do. Then the trainee glimpses streams of water snaking along the pavement and swings the trolley round, shouting to the others. Frantically they race the patient back to the safety of the hospital, bumping the trolley over the pavement and up the slope to the A & E entrance with water tearing at their feet. A mob of pedestrians and occupants of vehicles caught in the flood follow them through the doors.

Inside the hospital, alarm bells are shrilling. People sprint between buildings. In Lambeth Palace Road, the sandbag barrier across the ramp leading down to the vehicle entrance car park has been too hastily laid and collapses. Down below, wide glass double doors give access to the lower ground-floor level of Lambeth Wing. There has been insufficient time or resources to strengthen these properly.

Meanwhile, to the north of the site, the surge level continues to rise, climbing relentlessly up the stone wall bordering the river walk. The wall is in a weakened state and not designed to give protection against flooding. Before long water is spilling over the crest, running across the grass towards the main pedestrian entrance and pouring over the sides of the walkways into the car park below.

This area is now filling very fast with floodwater cascading down from overhead in many places, and the noise booms terrifyingly under the concrete roof of the parking bays. At half a metre deep the water pressure against the glass doors is of the order of twenty-five tonnes. The doors themselves are made of toughened glass and do not break but the panels are forced out of their supporting rims and levered inwards, allowing a mass of water to burst through into the rear regions.

At the same moment, the stone wall facing the river overhead gives way along most of its length. A tidal wave of water and rubble roars inland. At the eastern end of the site the initial impact falls on the Thames Terrace canteen at the corner of North Wing with a momentum that shakes the block. Great chunks of masonry smash down from the exterior wall, gutting the interior and carrying the contents of the canteen before it, through the convenience store and the bookshop next door and on into the main reception area.

There are approximately two dozen people here. Many have run in from outside and are trying to reach other parts of the hospital. Against an inrush of water alone, some of them might have stood a chance. As it is, the avalanche obliterates everything in its path. Victims' screams are drowned in the thunder of wreckage. Propelled by the swollen river behind, a torrent of mud and stones pulverises partition walls, crushing furniture to matchwood, ripping out electrical wiring and severing phone links.

In A & E, porters and nurses are battling against a horde of refugees from outside who are blocking their way as they try to wheel their patients to safety. At this point another section of the river wall to the north collapses, releasing a metre-high surge across a building site for the new 140-bed Children's Hospital and into the rear of the East Wing at their backs. To anyone watching, it is as if the wall itself sweeps forward across the cleared ground where the South Wing used to stand, a moving battering-ram of rubble and mud. It smashes down the doors of the East Wing and blasts on through, tearing down walls and doorways, battering, crushing, drowning everything in its path. Like a landslide of scree on the move, the enormous mass of material storms onwards through building after building, dragging wreckage with it, shouldering aside any obstruction, forced along by the unstoppable pressure of the swollen river to debouch catastrophically into the waiting area for A & E.

The Accident and Emergency entrance is approached up a ramp from Lambeth Palace Road. People still marooned in their vehicles outside hear a roaring sound and look up to see the front of the hospital bulge suddenly. The doors and windows darken, then explode outwards, vomiting tongues of mud and debris with such violence that cars in the roadway are swamped and buried where they stand.

How many die will never afterwards be known. Some bodies are swept out into the road, others are mangled unrecognisably or ground to pieces in the avalanche of rubble. The fortunate ones are killed instantly, crushed by masonry or boulders or impaled on splintered timbers or steel reinforcing bars picked up in the flood. Countless more drown or are suffocated by rivers of liquid mud. All night long rescue parties struggle through the wreckage, dragging out corpses. Even then the killing is not over. Parts of the building are so badly damaged that they collapse inwards, dropping whole floors into the morass underneath, entombing rescuers and dead alike.

Up in Riddell House, the Chief Executive is frantically trying to raise the radiography unit when the power dies. To the rear of the block the murderous torrent of rubble has overturned a 32-kW freestanding generator, crushing one man to death and drowning another. Nearby, an air-conditioning unit weighing two tonnes is rolled against a fire escape, pinning a student nurse in waist-deep water for eight hours.

Down in the basement areas, radiographers and IT specialists in the nuclear medicine centre, alerted by the alarm bells, are scrambling for the stairs when the flood bursts in on them and the lights go out. Screams pierce the darkness, mingled with the crash of glass and boom of toppling furniture as they retreat along the corridors, wedging doors shut to hold back the water swirling round their legs. A woman in a white coat slips and goes under. Her limbs churn the surface but she is caught up in some cables and can't fight her head free. Her hand torch glows for a moment beneath the water and dies.

The combination of flooding and catastrophic physical damage ruptures services to every part of the hospital. The upper floors are plunged into chaos as lights fail and life-support systems beep their alarms. Frantic nursing staff struggle with trip switches and relays. Some generators and battery back-ups kick in of their own accord, others require manual re-sets. A proportion, for one reason or another, are dead. Everywhere, circuits have to be switched over, computers re-booted, non-critical functions suspended. A theatre with an urgent operation in progress continues by torchlight.

On the fourth floor an over-hasty electrician connects a temporary lead to by-pass a blown fuse. With power fluctuating wildly, a circuit goes into overload. The cable heats up to flash-point and smoke percolates into a blacked-out ward, triggering panic. Melanie Sykes seizes a fire-extinguisher when the sprinklers open up, drenching the corridor. She hears her name screamed from the ward, where distraught nurses are trying to hand-pump ventilator patients, and runs back to help.

As she crouches over the wheezing pump, shivering with cold, her clothes sodden, with sounds of terrible destruction coming from below, all she can think is that this is only the beginning.

49

It is almost three hours since parliamentary business ended but the emptying of the Houses of Parliament is proceeding slowly. At the Speaker's invitation, Members and staff are helping move furnishings from the ground floor to upper levels. Teams of backbenchers stagger through the corridors, lugging paintings from ministers' offices or rolls of carpet. Computers, filing-cabinets and desks are trundled into lifts. The seats have been removed from the Chapel of St Mary and the firearms from the rifle range.

Leech, Head of Security, applauds the enthusiasm but wishes more of them would go home. At a rough estimate there are a thousand people still in the building. Many MPs talk openly of sitting out the flood in the bars and sleeping on sofas. The prospect of going back to a small flat in Clapham or Pimlico with no power or heating holds small attraction. Leech has sent fifty of his officers back to general duties. He could release more if only he could get the Palace cleared, but his first duty is for Parliament's security. The Speaker promises to do what he can, but is adamant that he will be remaining. Leech wonders if people have any idea of how very unpleasant conditions are likely to be.

At 3.15 pm the Assistant Commissioner orders him to send half his remaining force of police officers to help the traffic-division men attempting to clear Westminster and Lambeth bridges. Leech asks how vehicles are expected to move off the bridges with the roads at either end blocked? Traffic in Parliament Square has been at a standstill for the past hour with many cars abandoned by their drivers.

Then comes news of the Barrier failure. Leech hastens over the road for another urgent meeting with the Speaker and Black Rod. He pleads with both men to get their members away while there is still time left. Black Rod says most of the Peer's side is now clear. Leech's chief inspector at the Palace adds that some staff who left earlier have returned after finding it impossible to reach home.

Shortly after 4 pm Leech's radio warns him that the river level at Tower Bridge is 'rising very rapidly'. Overtopping is expected to begin within the next fifteen minutes. Together with the Government Chief Whip he begins an urgent search of the ground floor, chasing people upstairs.

Ann Dodbury is a Member for a West Country constituency and, at thirty, one of the youngest in the House. She has been looking forward to a game of bridge to pass the time but with TV images coming in of flooding in Docklands, the bravado is starting to fade. At the urging of colleagues she elects to go home. First, though, she wants to draw some money from an ATM. There is a rumour that the banks are going to close. With others about to leave she takes the river-front terrace staircase down to the ground-floor level.

Leech is checking the ministers' rooms beneath the House of Commons chamber when his radio bleeps again with urgency. Officers stationed on the Embankment report the river spilling over by Westminster Pier. Leech orders fire alarms to be sounded throughout the building. He runs back, making for the Lower Waiting Room stairs, his heart thumping. This is it, he tells himself. According to the Director of Works, the parapet along the terrace is half a metre higher than the walls elsewhere. Sufficient perhaps to give people a few vital extra minutes to get away.

The terrace is over two hundred metres long, with thirty windows and four doorways opening onto it. The doors have been reinforced so far as possible in the limited time available, but Leech doubts if they or the windows can hold out for long. The lights flicker and then steady again. Across the capital, electricity company technicians are furiously juggling supplies as sub-stations go down. Leech checks the torch in his pocket. The thought of being down here with water spilling in and no light is frightening.

He meets a trio of MPs walking towards him. The one in front says they are making for the cloakroom. They don't seem to have noticed the alarms pealing. Without ceremony he herds them back the way they have come. They have just reached the stairs to the Lower Waiting Room when a security guard runs back from the direction of the terrace, his face glistening with fear. The river is streaming over the terrace wall.

Leech steadies him. 'Did you leave anyone else back there?' Yes, the man nods. A whole bunch of MPs went past him in the direction of Star Chamber Court. 'Go to the top of the stairs,' Leech orders, 'and don't let anyone else down.' He runs back along the passage. In normal times these corridors are a favourite haunt of Members engaged in plotting with one another. Now the place is deserted. Through the pealing of the alarm bells he can hear the wind howling outside.

The terrace is reached by a glass door. As he approaches, Leech's heart stops. The lamps on the river wall are still burning, illuminating a ghastly scene. The terrace with its pavement and awnings has gone, vanished, swallowed up by the flood. In its place is an evil expanse of tossing water. Out of the heaving darkness beyond, white-capped waves shoulder up, to break against the crest of the wall, flinging over bursts of spray that crash against the glass. Already the water is lapping almost to the top of the door arch. Leech can see thin streams squirting through at the hinges and hear the splintering sounds of waves hammering on the windowpanes in the rooms either side – rooms that will be flooding rapidly, the water mounting against the internal doors, the pressure straining at the locks. And those doors open outwards into the passage.

Forty metres along and Ann Dodbury has reached the head of the queue at the ATMs. In front of her at the terminal is a florid-faced ex-minister. 'Wish they'd turn those bloody bells off,' he grunts, punching in his pin number.

'Come on now, George,' says a man waiting.

'Leave some for other people.' George blinks at him. They are from opposite parties. 'Bugger off,' he mutters. He taps in £300 and waits for his cash to appear. There is a crash from up the passage. 'What was that?' Ann looks round startled. George is grumbling. The machine has run out; it can only let him have £250. It is his last coherent thought.

At that moment the doors of the terrace canteens implode. Seconds later the hinges of the armoured glass panel of the passage door give way under the pressure behind. The water bursts through the three openings as though the spillways of a dam have been released. It hits the group by the cash machines with a force that knocks them off their feet, like bowling pins in an alley. Ann Dodbury has a fleeting memory of being blasted by a water cannon at a student demonstration in France years ago. Except what is different this time is not the force of the water but the temperature. It is like being stabbed with knives all over her skin. It is so cold that she feels her chest squeeze tight with the shock. Her entire body goes into spasm so she can't breathe and she thinks she is going to die right there.

Of fifteen people around the ATMs when the flood breaks through into the building, only four manage to keep their footing, clinging onto handholds where they can find them, clutching at doorways. Somehow they force their way back against the current to the stairs. The others are all swept down the corridor under the building.

Ann Dodbury is able to notice the lights in the corridor still shining through the foaming water that engulfs her. She is aware that the sensation of cold has diminished. She feels herself bounce off the wall, and instinctively twists her upper torso to face the direction in which she is being pushed, at the same time kicking down with both feet to bring her head above the surface. Her mouth snatches at the air and her chest expands to fill the lungs but water smothers her again. It is filthy and foul tasting and she sinks back choking.

She is now in absolute darkness. Somewhere in the corridor water has penetrated a light switch, allowing the current to arc between two contacts, overloading a circuit-breaker and causing it to pop from its socket. Ann's ears are filled with roaring noise and now she is being tumbled about until she doesn't know which way up she is. She is completely disoriented. More important, she is running out of air.

The most sensible thing for Ann to do right now is not to fight the current, to let herself be carried along until she gets another chance to breathe. Unfortunately every other instinct is urging her to struggle. So she is depleting her air supply fast. Now the brain is detecting an excess of carbon dioxide in her blood. It is telling her that unless she takes in more air, she will pass out. Her struggles are slowing down, a sign that her vital systems are growing sluggish. In a desperate effort to stave off unconsciousness, her brain is diverting what oxygenated blood there is to itself, shutting down the supply to the limbs.

Ann has been under water for a full minute now. Few people can last for much longer than this. Divers can train themselves to hyperventilate, saturating the blood supply with oxygen, to enable them to hold out for as long as four minutes in extreme cases, but this is rare. The majority of drowning victims lapse into unconsciousness after ninety seconds under water.

All the while she is fighting desperately for breath, a part of Ann's brain is following events with a sense of detachment. Is this what it is like to die? The fact seems curiously unimportant. It is a sign that the conscious brain is losing control. Random thoughts flash up, hallucinatory images resulting from the build-up of carbon dioxide in the blood. This is why drowning is sometimes said to be a pleasant way to die. The pain in her chest eases. A few more seconds and oxygen starvation will shut down the central nervous system, the autonomic will kick in and Ann will involuntarily open her mouth to suck water into her lungs.

At this point the coldness of the water is working in Ann's favour. She has stopped breathing. Her heart is beating irregularly and her pulse slows. Ann's metabolism is winding down, she is actually dying, but in this state her oxygen needs are reduced to 50 per cent of normal.

After the initial rush, the water in the passage is not quite up to the ceiling. Leech takes his torch and wades in up to his neck. He meets two men and helps them to the stairs, then goes back again for another two. On the third trip his feet encounter a body near the doorway at the far end and with difficulty he succeeds in hauling the person to the surface. It is a woman, her head lolling lifelessly, mouth filled with foam. Leech gets her back to the stairs where other officers are helping to pull people out. Two of them carry the woman up to the lobby and lay her out on the floor.

Opening the mouth has triggered a defence mechanism in Ann's failing nervous system. The instant water hits her larynx, it touches off a violent contraction of the muscles controlling the vocal cords, which closes the trachea and prevents her lungs from filling. This is why drowning victims can be resuscitated, because they have so little water in their airways. Talk of pumping out the lungs is nonsense. It is only the contents of the mouth and larynx that need to be emptied. Turning the person onto their stomach does that. The lungs are then worked to restart the heart. But this needs to be done quickly.

Luckily for Ann Dodbury the officers have been trained in first aid and the technique of cardio-pulmonary resuscitation. After only a minute or two she comes round to find herself lying face down on the floor of the Members' Lobby, feeling very sick and with no recollection of how she got here.

The mood in the Palace is sombre. At least six Members are dead, with others unaccounted for. While survivors are taken to the Speaker's apartment to recover, Leech goes on a tour of inspection. The flood is flowing fast into Parliament Square; New Palace Yard and Old Palace Yard are both under water. All the ground-floor level is submerged, power, light and heat are out and the phones no longer working. People huddle together over candles in the bars, trying to remain cheerful. The Palace is an eerie place in the gloom. The darkened Chambers echo with strange noises, the wind battering at the shuttered windows, the thud of waves surging against the river wall and the gurgle and slop of water in the drowned rooms below.

50

In Belvedere Road, behind County Hall, Fireman Wilson Palmer is helping people caught in the flood up to Waterloo Station. He is using a wooden pallet he's found to push as an improvised raft when a woman tells him she's seen two kids hanging onto the rigging of the London Eye, down by the river. There is no one else to send, so Wilson sets out alone.

The water is up to his chest as he turns the corner into Jubilee Gardens. Waves are crashing through here. It is like being in the open sea. The walls are all gone, only the tops of the lamps projecting from the water, some of them still functioning, astonishingly. And there is the great wheel, ahead and to his right, hanging out over the river, with two small figures clinging to the rim at the base.

How they got there Wilson can't imagine. More to the point right now, how is he to reach them? The river pier used for boarding has either been submerged or swept away by the flood. Only a few sticks of wreckage remain. The lowest of the glass viewing capsules is hanging a foot or so above the water and the children are wedged in among the steel frame wheel rim above it.

Water is running two metres deep along the Embankment path. All he can do is strike out, clinging onto his pallet to keep him afloat and praying that his boots and other equipment don't drag him under. The current is still sweeping inwards across sunken walls and he has to fight against it. Halfway across his foot catches on something underwater, most likely part of the railing along the pier, and he has a horrible thought that now he is actually in the river. Then a piece of white steel tubing appears before him. He grabs for it and hauls himself up beside the kids. A boy and girl, sick with fear and frozen nearly to death. He guesses they may be ten or eleven years old, skinny little things, dark eyes, dark hair plastered against their heads. He hopes they speak English or at least understand it.

Fortunately they do. Spray from the waves is drenching the wheel rim continually. It is very apparent that if they stay where they are all three of them will be carried away and drown before long. The nearest capsule is too low down to be safe; they will have to try one higher up. The Eye is constructed like a bicycle wheel made from tubular steel sections, with the observation capsules hanging off the outside rim. Clamped to the inside of the rim is a metal escape ladder. All they have to do is climb along it.

The storm and the crashing waves make talking impossible. By shouts and hand signs Wilson explains to the children that he will take them up one at a time. He tells the boy to hang on till he comes back and pushes the girl up the ladder ahead of him.

In fact, the climb is relatively easy. The wheel is

swaying in the wind but to begin with they are not climbing so much as crawling on all fours. Not till they have passed the next capsule along does the ascent sharpen. 'Keep going,' Wilson calls to the girl. The higher up they can get, the safer they will be and the better their chances of being seen and rescued. They pass another capsule and then a third. Now the ladder is starting to slope steeply. They are high above the river and the swaying motion is more pronounced. The girl looks back anxiously.

'This will do,' he tells her. The capsule they have stopped beside is hanging more nearly horizontal to the ladder. It is a simple matter to step across to the escape hatch in the roof. A twist of the handle and it opens. Wilson has been prepared to have to force it with his hand axe but that's unnecessary. He lowers the girl inside and returns for her brother.

In another ten minutes they are all three safe inside the capsule. Wilson closes the hatch and they slump down on the floor, huddled together for warmth. Outside the glass, the swollen river surges on between darkened banks, while to the east an ominous glare hangs over Docklands. Lulled by the rocking motion of the wheel, the children doze.

Upstream, the Oval cricket ground is a rapidly filling lake and water has entered the basement of Tate Britain, flooding the restaurant. On Vauxhall Bridge Road the water is running level with car roofs. Patients at the private Gordon Hospital have been evacuated by a fleet of chartered ambulances.

In Pimlico, to the west, firemen have been called to Tatchbrook estate off the Grosvenor Road. Forty elderly residents are penned in a care home; social services can't get through. The average age of the patients is seventy-six. Around half are bedridden and must be moved on stretchers.

The crew end up bringing the residents out themselves. It's a two-storey building and the lifts in the home can't be used for fear the power will go off. The wheelchairs go first, then the bed cases, carried down the stairs one at a time and put into high-wheel trucks borrowed from a TA depot.

By the time they are through, overtopping has begun. The drivers report water up to the trucks' wheel arches; if they don't leave now they'll be stuck here for the night. The crew chief is bringing out the last of the nurses on his back when the lights fail all across the sector.

A stone's throw from Buckingham Palace, a short canal once ran from a basin near the Royal Mews out to the Thames by Chelsea Bridge, half a mile away. When land was required for a new railway station, the basin was drained and the canal became a cutting for the tracks, which crossed the river by a new bridge two hundred metres west of the old canal entrance. Today, Victoria Station is the capital's busiest terminus, the mainline gateway to the south of England.

Down in Pimlico, the railway sidings are visible through the railings fronting the embankment beside the bridge. All trains have been run out south across the river to high ground and the flood pours through unobstructed into the cutting. A little further on, hard up against Chelsea Bridge, is the entrance basin to the old canal. At one time refuse was brought here to be loaded onto barges and taken down river. Now the wharf is used for storage of building materials. The river swarms through here, flooding over the lock gates into a thirty-metre stretch of the canal that is still in use, until its spread is checked by a brick wall.

On the other side of this wall, in the cutting, a three-storey modern building belonging to the Transport Police overlooks the tracks. There are only three officers on duty here, all the others are helping with the evacuation of the Underground system. As the flood swells, the wall gives way, collapsing with a rumble that shakes the ground.

In the operations room, the three officers have no warning. A tidal wave sweeps into the cutting, pouring through the ground floor, knocking out power and lights. Pursued by the flood, the men fight their way upstairs, stunned by the fury of the maelstrom that has appeared out of nowhere. A tree cracks behind them and a thunderous crash rocks the building, shattering windows and ceiling panels, and sending men and furniture tumbling. Dimly they are aware of something huge grinding past outside on the flood, but what it is they have no way of telling. All they can do is hang on and pray.

Beyond the sidings, the cutting runs under Ebury Bridge into the heart of Belgravia, channelled by sheer walls of brick, backed by tall buildings. The effect upon the water is similar to the narrowing of the estuary. The enormous weight of the flood pouring in from the river squeezes the torrent higher, at the same time as it ratchets up the speed. It is no more than four hundred metres from Victoria Station.

★

Flooding from Westminster has already reached Victoria Place, inundating the bus terminus on the station forecourt, causing a rush of people onto the concourse. A subterranean rumble comes from the steps leading down to the Underground and suddenly a foaming geyser belches from the entrance. Water is filling the system from all points, creating a ram effect in the tunnels. A woman hurrying past catches the full force of the spout and is knocked flying. As she flounders in the torrent there is a hideous gurgling from below and the backwash sucks down the steps again, dragging the screaming victim with it. Two men run down after her but the water comes surging back up, swallowing all three. One is pulled out alive, the woman and the other man are lost.

The lights are still burning inside the station. People queuing at the phone booths on platform 7 see a mountainous dark shape rear up against the far end of the arched roof. Squeezed now to a height of more than four metres and travelling at a velocity matching that of an oncoming train, the surge approaches with a hideous inevitability. For a few seconds it seems to hang, poised over the station, then the roaring cataract bursts in upon the platforms with the impact of a tidal wave. Riding the crest, caught up and swept along from the canal basin is a floating pontoon, twelve metres long and weighing as much as a container truck.

Fronting the platforms at upper-floor level is a raised gallery of shops and restaurants where many people have taken refuge. The avalanche explodes over them as the pontoon smashes clean through on the centre line like a monstrous battering-ram, catapulting a hundred victims to their deaths in the surging water below. Momentum hardly slackened, the missile lunges on into the concourse, its huge bulk snapping cast-iron pillars supporting the curved roof as if they are made of barley sugar. Glazed panels shatter as the roof sags, crashing among the unprotected crowd on the concourse, razor-edged shards as big as a door that can cut a man in half.

The entrance arch to the forecourt is jammed with a panicking mob clambering over one another in a desperate attempt to escape. The pontoon snuffs out a score more lives, ramming its blunt bow into the arch with a jarring crash that shakes the station like an earthquake.

Bottled up in the concourse, with only narrow passages to escape through, the floodwater surges to lethal heights. Shops and sales booths become tombs for customers caught inside. A teenager trying to reach the stairs up to the shopping centre sees a man pinned against a wall by a train of baggage trolleys while the water rises above his head, and thinks she is living through a nightmare. Her friend, watching blue flames spark from overhead wires, is convinced they are about to be electrocuted.

Many people are too frightened for their own survival to take in the full horror of what is happening. A central-heating engineer from Tooting notices that the water around him has a curious red tinge and realises it is his own blood leaking away. His left arm has been sliced open from shoulder to elbow, yet he feels no pain, only surprise.

As the lights fail, throwing a pall of darkness over the devastation, the cries of injured and terrified survivors echo like a litany through the ruined station.

51

On the north bank, the line of flooding now stretches west of Victoria through Chelsea into Fulham and Hammersmith. Between the King's Road and the Embankment, council vans are patrolling past some of the most expensive property in the capital. '*Urgent – Flood Warning – Evacuate Basements*', the loudspeakers blare. '*Residents of Flood Street, Flood Walk, Chelsea Manor, Oakley Street, Cheyne Gardens, Cheyne Row . . .*'

Outside a house on the corner of Cheyne Walk, a team of builders is packing up for the day. They have heard the announcements but aren't bothered. After the council vans came round there was a flurry of activity in the street. People moving gear up from basements, wheeling bicycles into hallways, driving cars north. Comical really. None of the builders believes there will be a serious flood. Maybe a couple of inches perhaps but no more.

Now water is tumbling over the Embankment wall in a frothing wave, spilling between the cars in the road. The builders stare mesmerised as it surges nearer. The road is awash as well as the area of grass in front of the houses. Their mates are running for the van; buckets and kit disappear on the flood, banging and clattering as they are swirled against iron railings.

Along the borough boundary of Chelsea, close to a metre of water is shooting over the Embankment, uprooting paving stones with its suction, spreading out rapidly into streets and squares. At Royal Hospital, a group of Chelsea Pensioners in their scarlet coats are caught in the current, swept off their feet and half drowned before they can be rescued. Fingers of muddy river creep across to the King's Road and shoppers drop their purchases and flee in panic. Water laps greedily against glossily painted front doors and chequerboard tiled porches. At pavement level it is knee deep and frightening. Below ground level, in designer basement kitchens, it is life threatening.

Further west, the football pitch at Stamford Bridge is swamped and the Exhibition Centre at Earls Court has to be evacuated. At the Victoria and Albert Museum storage annex in Olympia, security staff have gone off duty, leaving valuable collections of art, textiles and furniture on open shelves in a repository as large as Harrods. In Brompton Cemetery, tombs and mausoleums stand like islands in a lake. And across the river at Battersea Dogs Home, volunteers and staff are evacuating six hundred strays up to Clapham Common on foot.

Holly Smith and her husband, Jay, a software graphics designer, moved into a houseboat on the river four and a half years ago. They have views of Battersea Bridge and in summer the sun on the water fills the cabins with shimmering light. Swans come up to the kitchen window to be fed. When Darin, their son, was born, Jay made a cot for him that swings from the ceiling like a hammock on rough nights.

They discussed the situation at breakfast before Jay cycled to the office. It was obvious conditions were going to be rough. Gales from the east on a high tide, but the family has ridden out winter storms in the past and it has never bothered Holly before. She has slackened off the moorings and lashed everything down, the way Jay has taught her, locked all the cupboards and damped down the wood-burner. We'll wait here till you get home, she told him on the phone at midday. If it's still bad, then you can check us into a hotel for the night. Now she is wondering if that was a mistake.

All their neighbours have departed for the land. It is dark and the storm is frightening. The boat is pitching so violently that books and toys fly off the shelves. Holly has taken the pictures down from the walls and stacked them on the sea-grass floor. Darin is looking nervous. Holly is sure he would feel happier on shore. What is really spooking her, though, is the talk on the radio about fires downstream. She has tried Jay's mobile repeatedly but can't get through. She puts Darin into his life vest that they always use in choppy weather and packs a few things in a bag.

When she goes to the door though, she realises she has left it too late.

Down in Hammersmith, Harriet Binney lugs a Gro-bag across the kitchen. She planned on having her own tomatoes last summer but never got round to buying the plants. Luckily, she thinks ruefully. Water is streaming into her garden and under the conservatory doors. The kitchen floor is awash and she is frantically trying to block the step into the living room before the flood wrecks everything in there. Harriet has rolled up her trousers and removed her socks and shoes and her feet are numb with cold. The bag is unwieldy and when she finally gets it into place, it is too short. She is wedging the gaps with scrumpled carrier bags when a piercing wail comes from above. In the next instant Miranda is pounding down the stairs, shouting that the loo is overflowing.

'Jiggle the handle, it sticks,' Harriet responds automatically.

'Not the cistern, Mummy. The loo. There's shit coming up!'

Harriet grabs a mop and bucket and follows her daughter. Both stop abruptly at the bathroom door. The lavatory looks like a witch's cauldron. Filthy brown sludge is rising and bubbling in the pan, oozing over the seat, dripping down onto the white tiled floor.

'Do something, Mummy. You've got to do something!' Miranda cries, her sleeve pressed up against her nose, but Harriet can't think what. Gingerly, she leans forward to flip the lid. It holds for a moment, then the muck inside forces its way up, splattering over even faster than before.

Tears of frustration course down Miranda's cheeks. 'It's not going to get out,' she declares desperately. 'It's not getting into my bedroom.' And ripping down the shower curtain, she starts to construct a barrier from the waterproof sheeting and rolled up towels.

Harriet remembers she has a pile of dirty towels in the machine and dashes down to fetch them. On her way she passes the front door. They boarded it earlier with bin bags and the crates of wine Henry gave her for her fortieth. To her horror, water is trickling in. Rivulets that swell and spread as she looks. And now the floorboards all around her are starting to seep. With frightening speed, pools and puddles are appearing. Panicking, Harriet rushes through to the kitchen, sloshes across to the washing machine and presses the release catch.

She has no time to get out of the way. The machine vomits a deluge of foul water over her. She grabs the door and tries to get it shut again but the force of the water is too great. It keeps on coming, a filthy gushing stream. Harriet's jersey is soaked now as well as her trousers, the fabric clinging icily to her skin. Shivering, she retreats into the living room.

Water is swirling in here too. It is level with the skirting already, brown and cold and dirty. Carrier bags and other junk bob mockingly on the surface. All the moveable items in the room are stacked high, but sofa and armchairs stand marooned in the growing lake. The carpet will be wrecked. The piano too, Harrier fears. It was her grandmother's and she feels guilty, as if she has failed to care for it properly.

Outside the window, the street is a river. Front gardens have disappeared and parked cars look like toys in a child's bath. Dustbin lids and other debris toss about. Harriet watches a woman struggling to get through on a scooter. The water is too deep and she abandons the machine against a wall and comes splashing over on foot. Only when she is almost at the gate does Harriet recognise who it is. She is so accustomed to seeing Sophie de Salis looking immaculate.

And then, with a sickening jerk of memory, Harriet realises why Sophie is here.

'Goddamit, what planet are you on, Harriet?' Sophie's voice is sharp with anxiety. 'There's a flood warning and you let the kids run off to the shops!' She is sitting on the edge of the bay window she has just climbed through, an expression of utter incredulity on her face. The water inside the house has reached the wall sockets, knocking out the table lamps in the living room. The ceiling lights in the hall and kitchen remain on. Harriet looks distraught.

'They said they'd come straight back. They were only going up to the corner shop. It was before the water . . .' Harriet falters.

'Well, they're not there because I passed the shop and it's boarded up.'

Harriet's fingers are twisting in and out of one another. 'I'm sorry, I'm so sorry. I didn't know it was going to be as bad as this.'

Sophie bites back a reference to news bulletins. What right has she to blame Harriet? Harriet who is always there when Sophie is late from work, which is often. Who is as loving and generous to Chrissie as she is to her own daughters. She places a hand on Harriet's shoulder and squeezes. 'Forget it, honey. It's not your fault. But we're not helping any standing here.'

Miranda, who has been listening to the exchange from the stairs, pokes her head round the door. 'I bet I know where they've gone,' she says. 'They took the video rental card.'

Down on the Bakerloo track the situation of the passengers is now desperate. Battery power for the emergency systems is failing and the tunnel lights are so dim that the column is groping its way by the beams of hand torches. To add to their terrors the first signs of flooding have appeared. Their feet splash through puddles, which grow longer and deeper until there is a continuous pool spreading right across the tunnel. Dean Stacey's trainers are already soaking and he scarcely notices now when he sinks in to his ankle, but for others, the women particularly, it makes the final part of the march almost unendurable.

Up on the surface, a station controller from Paddington has at last reached the scene, summoned by urgent messages from the NCC. The controller opens up the emergency store and breaks out first-aid packs, torches and stretchers. He uses his radio to contact Central Command Complex at Hendon to drive home the scale of the disaster looming. Ambulances are available at University College Hospital in Bloomsbury, but police vehicles and fire appliances in the vicinity are fully committed. A reserve troop from Watford is heading for an assembly point being established at Regent's Park. It is ordered to divert to the scene and a motorcycle unit sent to escort them through the traffic.

The controller leaves one man at the entrance to act as guide, while he descends to the Bakerloo platform with the firemen to start the rescue operation.

*

Paul Suter almost weeps when he sees the lights approaching. Not to be the only one responsible for these people any longer is like a huge weight being lifted off him. The relief party have torches and stretchers and their arrival galvanises the marchers. Word passes along the column and passengers step out with renewed hope. The stretcher parties work their way back along the tunnel to bring out the casualties.

'What news on the flood?' Paul asks anxiously as soon as he arrives at the station. 'How long do we have before the water breaks through?' The controller can't tell him. Things are bad along the river, and the NCC has been evacuated. As he was leaving to come here, he thinks he heard someone say water had reached Oxford Street.

Dean can't understand why the rescue is taking so long. The column of marchers seems to have come to a dead halt at the mouth of the tunnel. Up ahead there are lamps bobbing about on the platform and voices shouting. Hampered by increasing amounts of water flowing across the platform and restricted space to work, firemen struggle to help people out. The darkness and bad air in the tunnel are making matters worse. An urgent appeal goes out for paramedics and doctors. And from the senior fire officer comes a demand for power to the tunnel lighting and emergency evacuation points and to work lifts and ventilation fans. 'And for Christ's sake hurry! We've a thousand people down here.'

From the platform, passengers face a further ordeal. Police and station officials are doing their best to move people up to the surface but there are no working lifts or escalators and many of the rescued are too exhausted to face the stairs without a rest. One exit passage is closed off by a locked grill and no one has a key. As a result the narrow platform is becoming crowded, further slowing the rescue effort.

Paul is helping a group of elderly Italians along the passage to the escalators when the noise of the approaching water is first detected. Out on the platform it sounds like the rumble of a distant train. Except that trains aren't running any longer. As the volume increases, people stop and stare. Suddenly a gush of liquid emerges from the mouth of the tunnel. Shrieks break out and there is a rush for the platform as the water foams waist-deep along the track. For several minutes pandemonium reigns. Passengers jostle one another to escape the water. Frantic parents hold out their children, pleading for rescue.

It is the fire chief who saves the situation. 'Stop!' he bellows in a voice of brass that rings through the station and shocks everyone into stillness. 'Get a hold of yourselves,' he tells them sharply. The water is flowing on down the tunnel. It's not getting any deeper. There's no immediate danger so long as they act sensibly and don't panic.

His words have their effect. Order is restored. People are still anxious but their desperation subsides. Even those in water up to their chests wait patiently for their turn to be helped out. A fireman uses his axe to force the locked exit gate and get more people off the platform. Then Suter returns from his trip to the surface. He pushes his way to the platform edge, aghast at what he sees.

'Hurry! Get everybody out!' he shouts to the nearest fire officers. 'It's starting to back up.'

A look of horror comes into their faces as they grasp what is happening. The dark river sluicing along the track is no longer running freely. It has slowed and begun inching its way up the station wall. Water flooding down the far tunnel has reached the train blocking the track half a mile away and is backing up behind it. Very soon it will be spilling over onto the platform.

A desperate race renews to get everyone up the escalators to the second level. The remaining passengers on the tracks can sense the water rising about them and are panicking again. Firemen jump down onto the track and begin heaving people up bodily for Paul and others to herd towards the escalators.

A woman in front of Dean Stacey is hauled onto the platform by paramedics. Dean scrambles up after her. The blonde tries to follow but slips back onto the track and Dean reaches down a hand to her. Behind, a gasping stretcher team emerges from the western tunnel, bearing the heart-attack victim shoulder high. His wife follows, supported by two firemen. The flood is frothing around them and the woman's face is a mask of terror.

Water is running across the platform. It is more than ankle-deep and the ambulance men are struggling to hold the stretcher steady as they hand the sick man up. One of them loses his balance and goes down. The stretcher lurches sideways, pitching the man into the flood. His wife shrieks. The firemen drop her and plunge over, feeling for the body. But the current is now a torrent; it is all they can do to prevent themselves being carried away. They've only their helmet lamps and the water is black with filth from the tunnels. It's impossible to see a thing.

Paul helps drag the woman out, while the men dive below the surface, trying to find her husband. In another minute the water is up to their chins. Their mates shout to them to leave it and save themselves. There is no chance the victim can have survived. He must have been swept into the tunnel.

The station is a terrifying place to be in suddenly. Paul is wading up to his waist, he has lost his torch and the only light comes from the firemen's helmet lamps. The entrances to the passages are shrinking fast as people crowd through. Water is pouring in at a tremendous rate.

Inside the passage it is worse. There is total confusion, shrieks and cries echoing against the roof. People have lost all sense of direction and blunder about, some trying to head back towards the platform in their terror. Firemen and guards shout directions, torch beams flash and disappear. Children cling round their parents' necks, wailing in fear. An elderly woman floats face down, forgotten and ignored. Another victim no one has strength to spare for.

At last Paul emerges into the escalator hall. Water is flooding in fast from the Jubilee tunnels but there is more head height here and transport police are using torches to light the way. There are only two escalators though and the climb is steep. Frantic people fight to reach the steps, yelling at those ahead to climb faster. Paul pushes the woman in front of him, forcing her upwards. This is the lowest level of the station so there will be another climb after this one.

They are about halfway up when there is a renewed outbreak of screams. A stream of water comes rushing down the steps. More flooding must have penetrated along the Circle Line at the next level. The woman stumbles sideways with a cry. As she falls she clutches at Paul, dragging him down with her. More bodies tumble down on top of them. Dozens of people are falling backwards, knocking down those below. A foot kicks Paul in the head. The weight of bodies is crushing the air from his lungs. He can feel water gushing around him and lashes out in panic.

He manages to get a grip on the centre handrail and ruthlessly drags himself clear. Someone cannons into him with a violence that is stunning. Bodies are pitching down the stairs like bowling pins. Paul falls across the central divide and slides down onto a No Smoking sign. He clings to it desperately. Another man comes sliding down onto him. Paul grabs his coat to stop himself being swept away and the two hang on.

The flood coming down from above is increasing. 'We've got to make it to the top,' Paul shouts. The man with him nods back. He is strongly built. On the stairs, those who have managed to stay upright are starting to claw their way against the torrent. Paul and his companion climb back onto the escalator and follow. After a few steps they find a woman with an injured leg and drag her between them.

As they near the top, firemen come down to help them. Up in the ticket hall the water is hardly knee deep. Other officers run past with ropes and portable lamps. Looking back down the escalator, he sees people fighting and climbing over one another in an attempt to save themselves. A mass of bodies writhing in inky water. A snapshot from hell. Their cries echo up the shaft.

Paul is too exhausted to stand. He has done all he can. A paramedic helps him to a casualty clearing post set up in the main station concourse. Amazed passers-by gawk at the flashing lights of the ambulances and the desperate figures being brought up from the flooded tunnels below. As Paul slumps thankfully to the ground he hears his name being called. Someone grabs his arm. It is Hew Thomas from the NCC, just arrived on the scene. 'Paul, thank God you've made it,' he says. 'You've been a hero.'

52

'OUR POSITION HERE *is now desperate . . .'* Lauren Khan dictates. '*I am sitting crouched on the floor of one of the sub-river tunnels beneath the Barrier. Beside me, leaning against the pipes with his eyes closed, is the Tide Defence Manager. He is cradling an arm that has been crudely splinted and bandaged. Other survivors from the piers huddle on the gratings. The serious cases are back in the first-aid post by the stairs. We are too tired even to mourn for Angus Walsh . . .*

'*Our foam supply is exhausted. Helicopters are on their way and we have been ordered to Piers 4 and 5 ready for evacuation . . . the fires on the north bank in the Royal Docks have made the first three piers too dangerous to use . . .*

'*Still no sign of the helicopters . . . and now a fresh danger. A few minutes ago one of the car ferries from Woolwich drifted up against the Barrier with a petrol tanker still aboard. The vessel is burning fiercely, her stern pinned against pier 6, sixty metres from where we are gathered . . .*

'*We are going down into the tunnels. The risk is too great . . . if the tanker explodes we could all be burned alive . . . a team of volunteers from among the firemen will attempt to board the ship over the stern from Pier 6. They hope to open the fire hydrants on the main deck and drench the tanks with foam . . .*

'*We pick our way down the stairs to the level of the tunnels. Everyone is sombre. We have watched the fire teams on Pier 6 assembling for the attempt in their protective suits. One team will cross onto the ship while others spray water on them to beat back the flames . . .*

'*We wait below like civilians in an air-raid bunker. An engineer stands at the bottom of the stairs in radio contact. The first men are aboard the ship. They are searching for the valves . . .*' a long pause '*. . . suddenly a thudding noise that sets every nerve on edge. We feel the thick concrete quiver under our feet . . . then a harsh scraping of heavy steel along the roof overhead, the hull of the wreck settling against the pier. The engineer drops the radio and we hear him running up the stairs. We crowd at the bottom staring after him. When he flings open the door there is a blinding pulse of light, and a gust of air, searing hot like an oven opening . . .*

'*The survivors are stumbling down the steps . . . screams, groans . . . we help as best we can. One is terribly burned . . . crying out for painkillers. Six firemen are missing, caught in the blast, dead. The pier took the full force of the fire . . .*

Later '*. . . the four central piers are all on fire. Impossible for helicopters to reach us. The steel doors are red-hot; we have placed wet rags to keep back the smoke. Our water will hold out for a while but there are thirty of us down here and no one knows how long the air in the tunnels will last . . .*'

Out on the river, the two Lambeth fireboats are operating close to their limits. With only one monitor apiece, they are not designed to fight conflagrations on this scale and their low freeboard makes them hard to handle in rough conditions.

It takes courage to stay close enough to the flames for the monitors to have effect. Visibility is down to a few metres only. The fifty-knot wind is filling the air with a blizzard of flaming droplets. More than once the Lambeth boats have to train their water cannons on one another to douse flames that have taken hold on the deckhouses.

Now *FireDart* is steering into trouble. The wind is driving the flames towards her and the GPS system shows a pontoon fifty metres ahead to starboard. The skipper can't see it yet but he is not going to risk a collision.

What the GPS can't tell him is that there is a sunken barge tied up to the pontoon. The surge has swamped it and now it is lying waterlogged just under the surface. The current has swung it outwards so that the stern is leaning some forty metres into the stream.

Two tongues of burning oil are pushing out from the shore. A blue flash explodes on the water as a vapour cloud ignites and flames sprint across the gap. The skipper puts the helm over and the water jets throb as the boat wheels to get clear. A jarring crash shakes the vessel. The bow rears up, then slews at an angle, canting the boat over to port.

The skipper slams the engines into reverse. There is an ugly clattering sound from below and the hull shakes violently but stays fast. They're aground. As if seizing the opportunity to pounce, flames roar up astern of the stricken vessel.

The monitor crew pumps desperately, but the

heel of the deck prevents them directing their jet effectively. The skipper is on the radio, calling for help on the emergency frequency. To their relief it is only a minute before their sister vessel emerges from the smoke. She manoeuvres alongside and the men scramble aboard.

There are no casualties from the incident, but the boat is a write-off. In the hiatus of its sinking and the rescue of the crew, a 150-metre-wide patch of flaming hydrocarbons detaches from the main fire front and drifts out into mid-river.

The ferocious wind is making air operations extremely hazardous. As Raikes's helicopter flies him into Hyde Park, he spots the twisted wreck of a Puma and two trees down. The volume of machines and equipment being gathered here is impressive. Helicopters, boats, amphibious vehicles, if only half of this had been available earlier they might have had some effect.

The helicopter settles on the temporary pad by the Barracks and engineers appear with a refuelling hose. Raikes and the pilot stay aboard. After a short wait the passenger door is slid back and Venetia Maitland scrambles in, wearing a flying suit with her silk scarf tucked in. As the Gazelle lifts off again she reaches out to take his hand momentarily.

Raikes has ordered the pilot to fly down river. The radio chatters, warning other aircraft of their presence. Columns of heated air bounce the helicopter as they cross the City and approach Docklands. Intermittently through the smoke they glimpse hot patches of fire glowing below.

'Where are we now?' Venetia asks.

Over the Royal Docks, he tells her, unfolding the map. He taps the pilot on the shoulder and points his finger downwards. The man nods and the Gazelle's nose dips in response. Suddenly the cabin fills with lurid orange light. Venetia gasps. They have come down through the smoke and, spread out below, stretching to every point of the compass, is an inferno of liquid fire. The intense heat beats up through the glass windows. All three occupants stare in silence till the smoke closes over again, mercifully blotting out the apocalyptic vision.

Raikes begins speaking. His message is bleak. He has brought Venetia up here to witness for herself the scale of the threat facing them.

'The aircraft lights you can see are helicopters lifting out people trapped on the Isle of Dogs. The burning oil is carried along on the flood and the water is too deep for fire appliances to get through to fight the blaze.' It may look bad from here, he continues, but it is nothing to what will follow. So far the spread of the fires into populated areas has been contained by high ground or by natural features like the River Lee and the line of the Outfall Sewer.

Now the slicks have broken through at Canary Wharf, spilling over into the Lower Pool at Limehouse. 'Rotherhithe is burning and fireboats can't get through to help. Wapping will suffer the same fate within the next few minutes.'

Venetia stares at the map. For the first time there is a look very like fear in her face. The fire is at the gates of London. If they fail to halt it, the city will be lost.

'We must make a stand, but where?'

He points at the map. 'Assuming LFB can deploy equipment in time, our best line of defence will be here at Tower Bridge. If we can't hold that, our only course is to fall back from bridge to bridge, praying for the winds to drop.'

Venetia turns her face to his. Her jaw is resolute again. 'If we can't stop the fires, then we must get people out. Now, all of them, while there's still time.'

She bends over the map. 'Contact Triple-C and tell them to start evacuating everyone back behind the ten-metre contour line.'

They both stare at one another. There must be two million people at least down there, Raikes thinks. For most of them it will mean abandoning their homes and wading out into the freezing night through water up to their waists for as much as two miles. Maybe further. There will be old people, invalids and children.

Venetia can read his thoughts. 'It's better than burning to death,' she says grimly. 'Get them moving.'

Some evacuations have already begun. Over in Rotherhithe, on the bend in the river between the Isle of Dogs and Wapping, the authorities are urgently trying to move the remaining population out of the path of the fires. Burning oil, escaping past Canary Wharf, has crossed the river, setting fire to hotels and warehouses on the waterfront. Rotherhithe is the next thing to an island, bordered by river on three sides and slashed across by docks and canals.

Fire-engines can't get through to tackle the blaze.

Mechanical diggers and four-wheel drives are commandeered wherever they can be found but, with water flowing a metre and a half deep in streets along the river, their use is limited. Appeals are broadcast on radio for residents to make for the railway embankments. Many are reluctant to abandon their homes until the flames are almost upon them. Some leave it too late. A fireman from the Deptford station sees one elderly couple, hair and clothes ablaze, jump from a fourth floor window.

The fireman has been ten years with the brigade but nothing has prepared him for the scenes he witnesses tonight. The shivering families wading through drowned streets, terrified children clinging to their shoulders. The woman of sixty who carries her crippled mother a mile to a railway station only to find she has died of cold. The hysterical parents searching for a son swept away on the flood, never to be seen again. A family of four run down by a truck carrying refugees and the mother killed.

For one soldier, a nineteen-year-old guardsman from Wellington Barracks, it is a night seemingly without end. The cries of fire victims will haunt him for years to come. 'Blocks of flats crackling like torches as they burn . . . the people inside screaming to us for help . . . Mother of God, the screams!' Other soldiers from the same unit break down the door of a house the flames have missed to discover a family of six inside, all dead, suffocated by smoke and heat.

Even those who do flee are all too often escaping into danger. In the howling darkness, without streetlights and with smoke gusting, a wrong turning can mean death. Groups of refugees stumble into canals or stretches of open water blocking escape routes. The bodies of twenty-two will later be pulled from Greenland Dock alone. Others mistakenly head deeper into the infernos or are swept out into the river.

Near Globe Wharf, a lofty tower crane sways in the bloodshot smoke, then topples like a falling giant. At the Surrey Quays shopping centre, a survivor notices bales of paper from the *Telegraph* printing works being rolled along the roadway like giant hoops, while around the corner looters are stripping a bicycle store. Some survivors are brought out by a tractor belonging to Surrey Docks Farm, a local tourist attraction. An eight-year-old boy hides his face in his father's coat, convinced they are all going to die. For his little sister, clutching a soft toy, the sparks and flames in the sky are the most beautiful she has ever seen, better than the Fifth of November. And, when finally they reach a reception centre, a woman gives her a drink of hot Bovril, her favourite drink.

Avril Thompson is a volunteer on duty at a sports hall in Dulwich. Her previous experience has been limited to assisting with evacuees from bomb scares. Now she is being worked off her feet, helping to provide food and shelter for a never-ending stream of homeless. Armed with pads of forms, Avril works her way along lines of soaked and smoke-stained people, documenting families, trying to list the missing. Many survivors have lost everything they possess and are too dazed to speak. Others are traumatised by horrors so dreadful that she can hardly bear to listen. They seem to her not so much Londoners as aliens from some different and terrible world, one that she can only dimly imagine.

Between the Tower of London and the Isle of Dogs, the former marshland of Wapping on the north bank protrudes into the Thames in a shallow bend a mile long, bounded to the east by Shadwell Basin and to the west by St Katharine's Dock. The main road, The Highway, cuts across the base of the bend, following the line of the ten-metre contour. Once an area with an unsavoury reputation for crime and poverty, Wapping has become fashionable. The old warehouses by Execution Dock, where Captain Kid was hanged for piracy, have been converted into executive flats and inland there are new housing developments.

South of The Highway, flooding has penetrated inland as far as the huge News International printing works, Wapping's largest employer. With virtually the entire district under a metre or more of water, burning oil slicks moving up-river from Canary Wharf have set Shadwell Basin ablaze and are spreading westwards.

Assistant-Divisional Officer Mike Rosen has been sent from Lambeth to assume command of fire-fighting in this sector. A university graduate noted for his forthright views, Rosen scans the area map at Joint Emergency Services Control on Cable Street and sums up the situation in a single word, 'Deathtrap.'

In the narrow streets with names like Cinnamon, Penang and Rum Close, where high Victorian warehouses crowd the pavements, residents who sought refuge on the upper floors are now in peril of their lives. With fire encircling them on three sides from the river, their only safety lies in reaching high ground. Except, as Rosen points out bitterly, that escape northwards is blocked by the half-mile-long Western Dock Canal, crossed by two roads, one already overrun by fires, and a single footbridge.

Wapping's four fire units are already in action, fighting the flames in Limehouse to the east. Fire-engines are known in the Brigade as 'pumps', and the normal attendance for a fire is two pumps. Any larger fire requiring more pumps either for manpower or equipment is classed as a 'make-up'. The standard sequence for make-ups runs in twos – 4, 6, 8, up to 12, then 15 and 20, or very rarely, 30 pumps.

Now as the flames close in on Wapping, Rosen dispatches an urgent assistance message. EAST AREA OPS FROM ADO ROSEN AT HIGHWAY WAPPING E1. MAKE PUMPS TWELVE.

Along Spirit Quay on the south side of the canal, the water is coursing round Chief Inspector Harry Lime's waders. Military and civilian trucks are working a shuttle service, picking people up and taking them down to the bridges. But the fires are burning nearer and more residents keep emerging. If only they had left sooner, Harry thinks.

Smoke and sparks fill the air; each time they pass a cross street or alley the heat hits them a physical blow. In a scene of mingled horror and beauty, plumes of coloured flame flare into the sky, painting buildings and water in a pulsing, dusky red light.

The noise is numbing; the fires burn with a deep roar punctuated with the crackle of timbers and the rumble and crash of falling masonry. A constant rain of sparks and burning fragments falls hissing into the water. Harry's respirator is no longer functioning; his head is giddy from the fumes and heat. It is acutely dangerous down here. Burning oil is filtering through the maze of streets to the south and east, threatening all the time to cut them off. The biggest risk, though, is from clouds of inflammable vapour given off by the blazing slicks that can drift hundreds of metres ahead of the flame front. Only minutes ago Harry witnessed one of these ignite without warning, turning an entire street into a boiling inferno.

The first tongues of fire are coming into view. The canal here is lined with modern three- and four-storey townhouses, brick built under slate roofs. A two-bed flat rents for £1,000 a month. Trees have been planted either side to make attractive walkways. Beyond them, iron railings project from the water, marking the line of the canal. There is a blaze of light and a thunderous concussion to his right and flames blossom among the houses on the far side. Harry's heart sinks. A vapour cloud has jumped the gap.

Knots of people come struggling through the smoke, their faces contorted with fear. There is a crash of glass and the windows of a house behind blow out, tongues of flame licking greedily at the roof. Everything they own has just gone up in smoke before their eyes. They paid a fortune to live here on the canal; now their lives are all in ruins.

He spots two small figures clinging to a tree by themselves. A girl of around twelve and a younger boy, waist-deep in water. Harry wades over. 'I'm a police officer,' he yells above the noise. 'Is anybody with you?' They shake their heads, eyes round with fear. Harry grabs the girl's hand and lifts the boy, taking them in the direction of the bridge. They will have to hurry to make it before the flames close in.

At that moment a vehicle comes charging along the quay. It is a four-wheel-drive driven by a panic-stricken woman. Ignoring Harry's signal to stop for them, she accelerates past towards the bridge, tyres churning the water furiously. She is fifty metres off when the roof of a four-storey house ahead falls in with a cloud of sparks. A side wall sags and the front façade topples drunkenly outwards. The nose of the vehicle slews violently round as the driver wrenches the wheel over to avoid the flaming rubble. The front bumper crushes the nearest railings. The cab lurches but it can't stop. The front tips down and before their horrified gaze, the vehicle plunges under the water, vanishing instantly.

Harry is powerless. The canal is all that remains of the old dock system. It is six metres deep. Vehicle and passengers must have gone down like stones. There is no one else near and he can't abandon the children to attempt a rescue. He is fumbling for his radio when choking smoke engulfs the quay and sheets of flame roar up all around them. The children let out shrill cries of fear. Shielding them with his arms, Harry hustles them to the railings. 'Can you swim?' he shouts.

At Highway fire station, Mike Rosen has just dispatched his most urgent assistance call yet. ALL STATIONS ALL AREAS ALL CONTROLS.

FROM ADO ROSEN AT HIGHWAY WAPPING E1. MAKE PUMPS THIRTY.

Looking out at the crimson smoke plumes towering to the east and south, Rosen wonders how much help there is left to send. The Brigade has only 175 pumps for the whole of Greater London.

On Pennington Street at the News International headquarters, the tide has peaked out at the southern edge of the main building but storm-force winds drive thirty-metre flames through the plant. Four newspapers print five million copies every day of the week here and burning paper stocks turn buildings into 1000-degree furnaces. A fireman sees water from the crew's hoses evaporate in clouds of hissing steam while steel supporting beams glow white-hot and brickwork disappears into ash. Toxic fumes from burning plastics gust through offices as computer housings and copiers flash up. So intense is the heat that the transparent roof over the two-storey newsrooms melts, deluging firemen with a rain of liquid glass.

Three hundred metres up, on The Highway, firemen trying to save the local swimming pool shout at residents to get clear. Flames have reached the chlorine store and clouds of yellowish gas are seeping from the basement. Near the same spot, a middle-aged woman opens her front door and leaps back for her life. Fifty metres away on the corner, a dairy tanker truck has caught light and boiling butter is running knee-deep down the street. She and her family escape out the back, clutching the children's pet rabbit, and make for the railway line.

*

The canal is deep but not so freezing as Harry Lime expects. Perhaps it is the heat of the flames round about or the adrenaline coursing though his blood that is responsible. He and the children have shed boots and coats and the children are clutching onto his belt, one either side, forcing him to swim with a kind of dog paddle. It is taking all his strength to keep his head above water. Each time he looks up to breathe, the railings opposite seem as far away as ever. He is terrified the current is carrying them sideways into the flames.

Then, through his splashes, he glimpses a figure on the far bank. 'Over here!' Harry shouts, trying to wave a hand. His head sinks under momentarily but when he looks up again, the man is throwing a rope. A coil falls beside him and Harry grabs for it desperately. He checks right and left. The children are still there, their pale faces gasping with effort. 'Hang on!' he tells them as the pull comes. Moments later they are at the railings and clawing their way out.

Up on the Highway, help is getting through. ADO Rosen has thirty-three tenders fighting shoulder to shoulder along a mile-long front, backed up by four hundred combat troops and a host of volunteer firefighters to tackle spot fires breaking out in the small shops and curry houses to the rear. The government is funnelling reinforcements into this vital sector as fast as they become available but the roads northwards are choked with fleeing refugees, hampering operations. At one point eighty extra men are helicoptered in to replace crews so exhausted they are dropping where they stand.

It is terrifying up close to the fires. The oil-rich smoke is so thick firemen are working by touch while the heat cracks the glass of protective goggles. Walls of flame roar out of the blackness to leap the main road and are beaten back. Already one appliance has been trapped and burned to a blackened shell. Eight men are missing. Rosen estimates that between St Katharine's and Limehouse Basin three hundred acres of waterfront are ablaze. All he can hope to do is contain the fires and stop them spreading northwards. If winds fan the flames into densely populated Whitechapel, the conflagration will become unstoppable.

53

Brent. North London. Bill Thurgood is a former aeronautical engineer, married with grown-up children. Retired two years, his principal recreation is sailing his dinghy on the local reservoir. He is at home watching the television, thankful none of his family is caught up in the floods, when two policemen bang at his front door.

'You are secretary of the Brent Sailing Association?'

'Yes. Why, is there a problem?' Bill is momentarily alarmed. Instinctively he looks past the officers. The estate is built right under the reservoir dam, which looms over the houses like a cliff. It's an earth-core dam with enough water behind it to take out all Neasden and Wembley if it collapsed.

The policeman speaks fast. He is telling Bill he needs to round up as many of his members as possible at short notice. 'You've got ninety minutes to have all your boats out of the water.'

'You've got to be joking! All the boats out of the water? At this time of night? It's not possible. Where's your authority? The reservoir is nothing to do with police; it comes under British Waterways.'

'Sir, we have emergency powers.' It is speedily apparent to Bill that the officers are in deadly earnest. If he refuses to co-operate he faces arrest. All police have been told is that it's to do with fighting the fires on the river. Bill can guess the rest. There must be a plan to bring in water-bombing aircraft, filling their tanks from the reservoir. Though how they are going to do that in the dark, he can't think.

He shouts to his wife to start ringing round the other members while he pulls on boots and warm clothing. Outside he can smell the smoke on the air. There are few people about. He drives up the steep lane to the club gates, the police following.

The clubhouses of the different groups that use the reservoir are clustered at the western end with many boats tied up to the dam wall. The rest are mainly moored inside two small jetties. The dam is a quarter of a mile wide, faced and topped with concrete. A path runs along the crest to a small pump-house in the middle. On the other side of the path the grassed rear of the dam slopes down towards the gardens of the first row of houses of the estate.

The reservoir extends back for a mile along a shallow valley in the ridge of high ground overlooking North London. The left bank is scrub; on the opposite side are lights where the North Circular road runs up to join the M1 going north. Westminster is around seven miles away as the crow flies.

A furious gust rattles the masts of the boats. There is a strong chop out on the water, with waves of half a metre. 'There's not a lot we can do till the owners get here,' Bill tells the officers. 'All the moorings are padlocked.'

One of the officers flourishes a pair of heavy bolt cutters. 'Not for long.'

An hour later Bill is frozen and wet to the skin and more tired than he can remember. A dozen other members have turned out and between them they have managed to bring all the boats moored on the open water in behind the jetties. Bill has convinced the authorities that those up against the dam are safest left where they are.

There is a lot of activity. The military have taken over from the police. Tankers for fuel and foam clog the car park. Airforce ground crews are busily setting up lights along the dam and installing radar and communications. Bill's clubhouse has been turned into a control post and two motorboats belonging to members have been pressed into service as rescue tenders. They are out on the water now, scouring for debris that might damage the planes.

According to the airmen, the planes expected are Canadair amphibians flown by French pilots; they can pick up a load of six thousand litres in only twelve seconds. 'They zoom in from fifty feet, lower a scoop as they skim the surface and fly on out without stopping. They drop their load and then come back for more.'

Bill does the calculations in his head and figures that a single drop will deliver as much water as a land-based fire appliance can pump in two minutes. The difference is that the water bomber can hit targets beyond the reach of conventional machines.

He looks up at the sky. Even from here, the smoke plumes and clouds of sparks are clearly visible, towering up from the conflagrations along the Thames. Officers' radios crackle on the freezing air. They sound anxious. If the planes don't get here soon it will be too late. London will be burned out.

'*In the interests of public safety . . . residents of Westminster, Pimlico, Chelsea, and Hammersmith and Fulham . . . are directed to leave your homes immediately and walk northwards to Kensington High Street and Shepherd's Bush, where you will be directed to a reception centre for the night. Put on warm clothing and bring any medication you need; otherwise take only what you can carry easily. If you have pets you may bring them with you. Anyone elderly or housebound should make themselves known to neighbours . . .*'

At Battersea Bridge, there is still no sign of Jay Smith. The hinged walkway that leads to the pontoon mooring for the houseboat and six other residential craft of the river hamlet has torn from its fastening and has been carried away. Waves, big waves like ocean rollers, are sweeping in from a river that has swollen to terrifying proportions. They surge against the side of the houseboat, hurling bursts of freezing spray into the rigid inflatable chained up under the prow.

Vainly, Holly scans the other craft for signs of life, but she and Darin are the only ones left. The big pontoon is pitching dangerously now and two of the smaller houseboats are taking a fearful pounding. Even if she could launch the inflatable, and somehow get Darin into it, they would never make it ashore in these conditions in the dark. And if Jay does return, how will he reach them? They are trapped.

Back inside, Darin looks at her fearfully. Holly gathers him up in her arms on the settee and shivers. All they can do is hold on and pray.

In the waterlogged streets of Hammersmith, Miranda Binney is scared. She regrets, now, having mentioned the video rental card and she wishes Sophie would slow down. They are trudging down to King Street together, Sophie leading, Miranda trailing behind. Harriet has stayed at home in case the girls turn up. The water is over the top of Miranda's boots and her legs are solid blocks of ice. With no way of telling what is under the surface, both women stumble constantly over kerbs and submerged objects. Miranda is terrified of falling down a lidless manhole. So far, she has managed to keep her upper clothes dry. She can't bear the thought of getting them soaked too.

A savage wind blasts at their backs and all the buildings are eerily dark. Only an occasional street lamp shows; in between there are great pools of blackness where people grope their way by torch, mostly heading in the opposite direction. They push past, elbowing their way selfishly, heads bent against the wind. The pub near the bus stop is blacked out and deserted but a single light flickers in the mini-market. Miranda can see the owner and his wife inside, moving stock to upper shelves. The woman's sari is hitched up between her legs.

They round a corner into a startling glare of lights. Miranda blinks, shielding her eyes. There are heavy vehicles ahead, massive military machines that look menacing and out of place in a city setting. She can make out figures moving, a barbed-wire barricade being unrolled across their path. Sophie shouts at the men to let her past. 'I've got to find my daughter!'

It is no use. The barrier is vicious and immovable. Burly, unsmiling men in waders and helmets shoulder them roughly away. 'Turn back. King Street is out of bounds and dangerous. Anyone attempting to pass will be forcibly detained.' The message is bleak and utterly convincing.

Back at home, Harriet Binney is distraught. It is nearly an hour since Sophie and Miranda left and there is nothing for her to do except listen to the radio and worry.

It is becoming bitterly cold. She has changed out of her wet clothes but is shivering nevertheless. All the lights have failed and a single candle burns on the bedside table. Harriet wonders if the gas is still working. She could boil a kettle and make a hot-water bottle. But she can't face going downstairs and getting wet again. Every few minutes she peers out of the window but all she can see is blackness. Over and over again, she reproaches herself. She shouldn't have let the girls go, she should have been firmer about them coming straight home.

A sudden loud rapping on the door shakes the house. For a moment Harriet is motionless as joy and relief overwhelm her. It has to be the girls. 'I'm coming, I'm coming,' she races down the stairs, rolling up her jeans to cross the hallway. 'The door is sandbagged, you'll have to use . . .'

The words die in her throat. Something is wrong.

Then the hammering again, right in front of her now, and a deep male voice breaking through her disappointment. 'Evacuation order . . . risk of fire . . . all occupants to leave the area at once.'

Harriet can't take it in. Flood . . . fire, what does the man mean? Surely they cancel each other out? She struggles to pull the door open, gives up and goes into the living room. Through the window she sees a torch beam jinking and a man in waders splashing back towards the gate. Moments later there is the same urgent knocking on her neighbours' door.

Out in the street a megaphone is repeating the command. '*Leave your houses now. Take only what you can carry easily. Head north, away from the flood zone. This is a government order for your own safety, issued under the Emergency Powers Act. Leave . . .*'

What Harriet does in those last chaotic minutes has no structure or sense. A photo of the girls, coat and gloves, a favourite book slipped into a pocket, almost forgetting credit cards and money in the rush. Scribbling a note to her daughters, pointless in its futility. Leaving food out for the cat. Then climbing like a thief out of her own window into the freezing water. Joining the anonymous crowd of refugees.

Wapping is lost; the fires have spread through into the basin of St Katharine's Dock on the north bank, hard by the Tower of London. On ten acres of water, 150 yachts and other craft are blazing at their moorings. Among them is a refuelling barge with a hundred tonnes of diesel in its tanks. Many other vessels also have fuel aboard and are burning furiously. Developments here include a 500-room hotel and the London World Trade Centre, housing the Commodity Exchange and the International Petroleum Exchange, where a billion dollars worth of oil and natural gas is traded daily.

There is high ground close by here and residents and workers have safely evacuated. Fire crews are making a stand behind Commodity Quay. Conditions are appalling. Radios snarl with staccato appeals for assistance. Exhausted firefighters dragging hoses, connecting up bulk tenders, helping comrades injured or overcome by smoke. Casualty rates in all emergency services are heavy. Everyone knows that at best this is a holding operation to gain time for sufficient forces to reach Tower Bridge. Many appliances are running short of foam concentrate and replenishment is difficult. Flooded drains have cut neighbouring roads. Army engineers are improvising with pumps mounted on military trucks but water alone is useless against oil fires.

In the intense heat, bizarre objects succumb to the flames. A bronze sculpture by the Tower Hotel, 'Girl with a Dolphin', 'melts like ice' according to one observer. Many boats are built of aluminium alloys that burn at 650 degrees, often with explosive violence and releasing clouds of toxic vapour. There are shortages of air breathing sets, recharged bottles and resuscitators.

Triple-C has ordered supplies of foam to be given top priority. There are stocks available all across the country, but getting them to where they are needed means using helicopters and these are desperately required for evacuations. The RAF is stripping men and machines off its airbases and flying them into London. All this takes time and the appalling weather only makes the situation worse.

Tower Bridge is choked with refugees streaming across as the flames on the south bank draw relentlessly nearer. Burning slicks have penetrated up an inlet to reach the Jamaica Road, three hundred metres inland, leaving this whole sector with no other escape. A fireman looking upwards in the cavernous alley of Shad Thames, criss-crossed at different levels overhead by latticed iron bridges, observes refugees by the hundred 'crawling to safety through the smoke like so-many rats'.

A vast relief operation is under way on this side of the river, where a million and a half people are being moved from their homes. Ruthless policing has cleared the M25 eastbound of all but emergency traffic and established access routes inward to the flood zone. Four-wheel-drive trucks and construction vehicles fan out in search of evacuees, ferrying them back to designated rendezvous points. From there, buses, military and civilian lorries, even empty container trucks, transport survivors out to schools and reception centres in the suburbs.

Meanwhile, up to quarter of a million people are believed to be walking out unaided on the elevated railway tracks.

54

The glow of the flames in the sky is visible from the M25. Dawn Fraser is one of the crew of Tender 4 from Basingstoke South station of the Hampshire Fire Service. Hers is one of the appliances ordered to the capital by Venetia Maitland at the start of the emergency. To begin with, when they were first put on stand-by, it was to be a flooding job. Then came word they were to stand in for crews from the suburbs sent to fight the fires in Docklands. Finally, when they reached the outskirts of London, they were directed to Tower Bridge and told to go into action.

Dawn is twenty-five and she has been a firefighter for three years. The crew are excited but apprehensive too. Theirs is part of a convoy of a dozen vehicles escorted through the streets by police outriders, sirens screaming. The immediate vicinity of the bridge is choked with vehicles and equipment. Dawn counts more than forty appliances, pumps, Bronto Skymasters, bulk foam units, command vehicles, hose layers.

Frantic activity is going on to make ready the bridge. Electricians are setting up searchlights on the walkway that runs between the twin towers of the central drawbridge. To supplement hydrants on the piers, engineers from the water company have laid 200mm-steel mains from Tower Hill the full length of the bridge, four runs either side, with branches off for hose connectors every twenty metres. To shield firefighters against the heat of the flames, pipes fitted with nozzles for a spray curtain are being run along the outer edges of bridge and piers. Other spray lines are being strung overhead so that at the turn of a valve the entire span can be drenched in a curtain of mist.

A separate main carrying foam concentrate is being laid to resupply the pumps as they run short. Extra breathing sets and air bottles have been placed in dumps on the piers. Spares of every kind are loaded aboard the appliances waiting to set off: dry clothing, gloves, boots, radios, first-aid kits. Life vests are issued. A lot of use they'll be, Dawn thinks, with the river covered in burning oil.

The fires are so close now that the crews being held on Tower Hill can hear the roar and crackle of flames. News cameras film the firefighters as they suit up, adjusting the harnesses, settling the heavy air bottles on their shoulders. A senior officer briefs them. This is going to be tough, he says. This is an oil fire, so wear BA sets at all times. Watch out for dehydration; drink plenty whenever you get the chance. There are medical-aid points at the control posts in each of the towers and at the bridge's north end. Just remember, he adds, if we don't stop these flames, we could lose London.

As their vehicle rumbles down onto the bridge approach, Dawn's crew get their first real glimpse of what they are going to be facing. The bridge looms ahead of them, a tunnel of fire. On the far bank, a mighty warehouse is a smoking inferno and the width of the river in between rages with sheets of flame that boil and leap on the water like a glimpse into the mouth of hell. Dawn can't believe a fire can be this massive. It is not just this sector either; the whole river is burning for miles.

Two vehicles up, Rod Crocker, a veteran of nineteen years in the Hampshire force, reckons some of the flames are reaching higher than the bridge towers. Rod is reminded of a description his grandfather, himself a fireman, gave of the London Blitz: 'the whole bloody world was on fire.'

Without checking, the pumps drive onto the bridge, under the gatehouse and through the arch of the north tower. Marshals direct them to both sides of the road. When Dawn's engine pulls up, she jumps down to find herself on the central span between the two towers. The crack in the roadway where the two leaves – the bascule halves – meet is a few metres away to the north of her.

'Hose connections, on the double!' Officers urge their crews into action. Dawn grabs the end of a preconnected 7-metre length of 150mm hydrant hose and drags it across to the nearest mains branch. Other crewmen are connecting lengths of hose to the discharge valves at the rear of the pump. Dawn screws the hydrant hose onto the branch. 'Ready!' she shouts to the officer at the pump panel. She gets the sign, spins the valve open and feels the jolt as water enters the hose.

Over by the balustrade, members of the crew are clamping two jet fog monitors to the railings.

Alongside them, other crews are doing the same. By Dawn's estimate there must be forty appliances at least on the bridge, a third of them on the upstream side, ready to douse any flames escaping underneath the roadway.

Rod Crocker is one of those manning a monitor by the water's edge. His partner signals ready, but the flames are not yet in range. Overhead the night sky is a hideous orange, so bright the lights aren't needed, except when clouds of smoke smother them in. The heat beating at them is fearful but just then the spray curtain comes on, dousing the bridge in a cooling mist.

The fires draw closer. Balls of soot spin past on the wind. Rod can hear sparks hissing into steam against the spray. His partner taps his shoulder. He has had the signal. Rod opens up the monitor and a jet of foam arcs outward onto the burning oil, pumping at two thousand litres a minute.

The bridge defence has its own Tactical Commander, who has set up his control post on the upper floor of the north tower. 'We appear to be having success,' he reports to Local Control on Tower Hill. A TV commentator, watching from the walls of the Tower of London, observes swathes of blackness being carved into the oncoming flames. '*London saved at the eleventh hour!*' he proclaims to an audience of millions.

To Dawn Fraser and Rod Crocker and their colleagues, the outcome appears less certain. As fast as they dowse a line of flames in front of them, another advances to take its place. The defences are pumping three thousand litres of foam a second onto the oil, but ferocious winds are blowing much of it away. Rod fears that they may only be extinguishing the flames temporarily. Crucially, the foam is failing to form a seal on the oil slicks. Where this happens, air can get in underneath allowing re-ignition to occur. Local Commander thinks the same. He urgently recommends that a second line of defence be established on London Bridge to the rear.

Up at Brent reservoir, everything is ready but still there is no sign of the planes. Bill is impressed with the way the military have improvised an operational base in so short a time. The flight path is marked out with green lamps along the water's edge and red markers strung along the dam itself. Word from the flight controllers in the clubhouse is that the lead aircraft are thirty minutes' flying time from the capital.

Meanwhile on Cannon Street Bridge, rescue efforts to bring out survivors from the Dome ferry are urgently continuing. Searchlights have started to pick up signs of oil on the water, moving up-river from Tower Bridge. Even if the firefighters there succeed in halting the flames, there is acute danger of reignition. An RNLI lifeboat from Teddington, manned by volunteers, is assisting and fire pumps have been brought onto the bridge to spray a protective barrier of foam around the wreck.

Passengers capable of walking are being evacuated via a makeshift ramp erected along the side of the bridge. The forward part of the upper deck has been crushed to less than half its height.

Firemen crawl on hands and knees to cut away seating so that paramedics and doctors can reach victims. A mobile crane has been driven onto the track and is swaying stretchers up to waiting ambulances. So far twenty-two bodies have been recovered.

The crushing of the upper deck has collapsed the stairwell exit from the forward section of the lower deck where the Exeter school party is located. Rescuers have to smash windows in order to let them out one at a time. It is an agonisingly slow process. Although none of the children has been seriously injured, other passengers nearby have and their distress adds to the general anxiety. Peering from a porthole, Claire Panton can see white flakes swirling in the glare of the searchlights. For a moment she imagines it must be snow, then she realises that, no, it is ash.

Dawn Fraser has relieved one of the monitor operators for her tender. It is exhilarating being up at the front line, playing the nozzle at the flames, seeing the fire wall wither beneath the deluge of white foam. To right and left of her, other crews are keeping up the pressure. Together they form an impenetrable barrier through which the flames cannot break. Word is that water bombers are on their way to join the battle. Fire tugs are working up from the east. It is only a matter of time, she is sure, before they have the conflagration under control.

And now disaster strikes. From time to time, patches of burning oil have been escaping under the bridge. It is the task of the crews on the piers to watch for these and extinguish them as they occur.

This is not always easy, especially when thick smoke obscures the bridge. The twin arms of the central lifting span are operated from machinery rooms under the towers. These are vulnerable and Tactical Commander has stationed teams there, ready to deal with any emergency.

Fire breaks out in the northern machinery room. Flames on the water have set light to grease on the bridge hinges and spread from there to the winding gear inside. A lot of smoke has been drawn into the machinery room already and the danger is not immediately apparent to the team on watch. As soon as they realise what is happening, they run a hose in to quench the flames. By this time, however, vapour given off by the fuel has collected in the chamber, forming an explosive concentration. The flashover kills all four members of the crew outright, blowing out the fire doors and sending a tongue of flame leaping up the stairwell to the floor above.

On the first floor, Tactical Commander and his staff seize extinguishers and try to fight their way out, but the fire is too fierce and they are overcome. Out on the bridge, amid the noise and smoke, several minutes pass before a badly burned paramedic from the first-aid post staggers out to raise the alarm. The captain of the nearest appliance himself leads the counter-attack. They are successfully quenching the blaze on the ground floor when their hose pressure fails on them.

Precise details of what has happened remain unclear. The 1,200-tonne bascule arms of the central drawbridge are electrically operated. When the emergency began they were locked in the lowered position. Somehow the lock on the northern arm has been overridden and the lifting sequence initiated. Rod Crocker is returning to his tender for a fresh air bottle when he feels the roadway heave underfoot. The bridge is rising. The roar of the flames drowns out the sound of the machinery but there is a widening split in the road and the mains pipes are bending up into a V-shape. One after another they tear apart, spewing torrents of water and foam across the road.

Rod braces his feet instinctively to stay upright. The tender beside him tilts and starts to move. He leaps for the railings, shouting a warning to a crew further along by the tower, who are staring in open-mouthed amazement. The eleven-tonne appliance lurches, then topples over onto its side with a crash that shakes the bridge.

The wall of foam along the crossing shuts off abruptly. All appliances have their own tanks, but at the rate they are pumping these are drained in fifteen seconds. The firefighters on the southern sector try vainly to connect up to hydrants in the tower and gatehouse, but heat has cracked the main under the bridge and there is no pressure to be had there either.

With so much smoke and confusion, Local Commander up on the hill can't tell what is happening. But he sees the foam jets die back and tries urgently to reach his Tactical opposite number. When this fails, he orders teams from relief appliances waiting on the hill to give assistance.

Out on the bridge there is frantic activity. Mercifully, after jacking up a distance of some two metres, the north drawbridge has stopped rising. The gap is too wide to jump; it will have to be scaled with ladders. Firemen and engineers are working to uncouple the damaged ends of the water mains and fit stop valves. With pressure restored to the northern half of the bridge, they can then run hoses into the tower and deal with the fires there.

Meanwhile, the wind is driving the wall of flames down upon the bridge. With the spray shield no longer in operation, the heat is now intense. Dawn Fraser can feel it through her protective gear. Smoke and fumes are so thick that visibility is near zero. In stifling blackness, colleagues work by touch to spread ladders across the gap between the two drawbridges. Behind them other crews are coupling flexible hoses onto the now useless mains pipes. A fireman scrambles up a ladder with a rope attached to a hose. As he prepares to fling a loop across, there is a roar and flames erupt through the gap like a Bunsen burner.

In an instant, it seems, the tyres of a pump near the edge catch alight. Dawn grabs an extinguisher; others follow suit. The flames are smothered momentarily, then return with a rush. 'Get back!' someone shouts and they scatter as the fuel tank detonates in a wave of heat. Dawn stumbles and falls. There is fire all around her. The road surface is burning, boiling tar running beneath the vehicles. Flames have spread under the bridge and out to the far side, enclosing them in a furnace.

Frantic shouts come over the radio. More vehicles are on fire near the south bank. It is only a matter of time before the entire span becomes an inferno. By the northern tower the overturned pump vehicle is also burning, blocking rescue attempts.

Local Commander makes his decision. With two hundred firefighters trapped and burning oil engulfing the bridge he has no choice. There is no way that a foam barrier can be re-established now. The crews on the southern half of the bridge must abandon their appliances and retreat up the tower and over the catwalks to the safety of the north bank. For Dawn Fraser, the climb up three hundred steps with a heavy air bottle on her back, followed by the scramble across the glazed catwalk, where paint on the rails is bubbling into fist-sized blisters in the heat, is an ordeal made harder by the knowledge that they have failed.

The fires have broken through the last barrier into central London. And now the evacuations upstream begin in earnest.

55

The suddenness of the disaster at Tower Bridge leaves the authorities no chance to organise defences upstream. It is less than half a mile from the Tower to London Bridge. With the tide flowing in at four knots, by the time news of the collapse reaches Triple-C, the leading oil fires are already drifting down upon HMS *Belfast* at her mooring on the south bank.

The old cruiser lies empty and abandoned. Her steel plating glows red hot in the flames while the White Ensign still flies defiantly amid the smoke. Along the shoreline, block after block of warehouses and office developments smoulders and catches light as the fires take hold.

Modern buildings are constructed to high standards of fire resistance, but retardant coatings and fire doors can only delay the flames, not hold them back forever. Installers drill holes in concrete floors to run phone conduits. Cheap printers mean more paper is stored. Bundles of cables act like twigs in a grate; the more there are, the better they burn.

And how they burn! Ten- and twelve-storey buildings, grouped tightly together and connected by alleys so narrow that the fires leap from block to block faster than a speeding car. Open-plan offices where the contents flash over, exploding into flame, generating heat that blows plate-glass windows bodily into the streets and shatters stone cladding to fragments. Superheated gases that boil through buildings, moving so fast that thermal detectors and fusible link shutters are burned out before they have a chance to trigger.

Most buildings have been evacuated in a hurry. Normal security patrols have been discontinued. Fire doors have been left open, water supplies to sprinkler systems shut off. As burning oil spreads through ground-floor halls, open stairs and lift-shafts act like giant chimneys, turning whole blocks into infernos.

Within an hour of the onset of the flames, the intensity of the blaze has reached such a pitch that fires are sucking air into the core zone at hurricane speeds and steel trusses buckle in the heat. Hot gasses from the burning streets can actually be seen as a shimmering blue cone pulsing hundreds of feet into the air.

The crew of HMS *Belfast* have long since fled. There is no one left aboard. At around 4 pm, when the flames are at their height, her moorings part, steel cables softened by the ferocious heat. The ship is drawn out into mid-channel, her stern swinging round into the wind. A moment later the racing current seizes the old warship in its grip once more and drags her back towards the south bank. She is headed straight for Hay's Galleria, the focal point of the area known as London Bridge City. Here, a clutch of old tea warehouses have been linked with a vaulted glass roof on iron columns and turned into upmarket shops, restaurants, offices and private apartments.

With awesome momentum, the 10,000-tonne behemoth demolishes the embankment wall and drives unstoppably over the riverside walkway, straight into the heart of the arcade. Walls crumble under the impact of the armoured prow. Iron columns shatter, glass shards rain down. The current still has the cruiser by the stern. It swings her like a giant crowbar, pulverising one side of the development as if it were made of mud. Façades slide and walls crumble. Offices and apartments cascade down upon the forward turrets in an avalanche of destruction.

Around the wreckage, flames roar up greedily.

'Where do we make our next stand?'

At Triple-C in Knightsbridge the smell of panic is palpable. Ministers and civil servants can see the situation sliding out of control. Short of a miracle, the fires will rip the heart out of the capital. Only Venetia Maitland's icy calm holds them together.

The experts' answers are grim. To have a realistic chance of halting the flames, sufficient forces must be concentrated. That takes time. Even then, with the south bank burning, any defences will be outflanked.

Unless aircraft can be brought in to action in numbers within the next thirty minutes, we shall lose Westminster to the flames, is the Chief Fire Officer's bleak forecast.

*

At Cannon Street bridge, the position is critical. Flames have swallowed Swan's Pier on the north bank, barely a hundred metres away. Despite the efforts of hose teams spraying water to keep the ferry cool, conditions on the lower deck are dreadful. The trapped passengers can see the approaching fires and are half-crazed with terror. A power saw has been sent for. When it comes, firemen succeed in cutting an opening into the lower deck. The schoolteachers bundle the children through with frantic haste. Claire Panton is one of the last to leave.

Inside the ruined upper deck, a doctor struggles to free a victim trapped by the leg. A fireman crawls in on his stomach beside him. They can hold off the flames for no more than ten minutes, maximum.

The man's leg is crushed beneath a heavy spar. Fire crew have brought in jacks but they might as well be trying to lift the whole bridge. The doctor is BASICS qualified, meaning he is specially trained to work on accidents like these. 'All right,' he says to the men alongside. 'Get ready to pull him free.'

He checks the victim's pulse. The man is unconscious and in shock. He daren't sedate him any more. Speed is what counts now. 'I want the hoist standing by to sway him up the moment we bring him out. Warn the paramedics to expect an amputation.' And he reaches for his saw.

The crane lowers a pallet down onto the ferry's rear deck. Minutes tick by. Steam hisses from the river where the hose jets beat at the flames. Smoke and sparks are enveloping the bridge and the heat is ferocious. A young fireman from the Barbican wonders what the hold-up is. How long does it take to cut off a leg? There is a shout from below. Four men emerge carrying a stretcher, the doctor following. The stretcher is placed on the pallet and the doctor kneels beside it.

There is a sudden cry of warning. The steam clouds part and out of the smoke emerges the prow of a ship, burning fiercely. It is a wooden schooner from a slipway on the far bank and it is only twenty metres away. The men below have seen it too. They leap onto the pallet, clinging onto the chains. The crane operator lets in his clutch, winding in as fast as he can. The group with the stretcher clutch at one another for support as they swing up and over the side of the bridge. The drifting derelict is very close now. The men on the bridge leap back as it crunches into the ferry's stern. Flames shoot up and a shower of burning debris falls around the waiting ambulance. Hoses sweep it clear. The stretcher is loaded aboard. Doors slam, a siren whoops. Voices are shouting urgently. It is time to be gone.

Along both banks of the Thames now, tall buildings blaze like candles. In Cousin Lane by Cannon Street, the London Futures Exchange, with a trillion pound a week turnover, is a burnt-out shell. The scorching air is charged with fiery droplets of oil and burning fragments, a deadly blizzard driven before the flame front, spreading ruin on every side. Between Southwark Bridge and Blackfriars, St Paul's Cathedral stands on the site of an earlier church razed in the Great Fire of 1666. The Dean leads a team of firefighters out onto the stone gallery surrounding the great dome, the second largest in Christendom after St Peter's, Rome.

Blazing debris has lodged on the lead flashing of the roof, threatening to burn through into ancient wooden beams, collapse the brick cone between the inner and outer domes, and bring the 850-tonne stone lantern crashing down into the nave. Risking their lives, the firemen clamber up onto the stone coping around the dome's shell, a hundred metres above the street, to dowse the flames with hand extinguishers.

Through a gap in the smoke Tate Modern on the south bank is briefly visible, silhouetted against the flames behind. Smoke and fire spouts from the mighty central chimney of the former power station, flaring like a giant Roman candle. A helicopter darts in to lift survivors off the roof.

A fire truck slews round the corner into Trafalgar Square and pulls to a halt outside the National Gallery. A solitary fire officer dismounts from the cab, slams the door and pounds up the steps. The big doors are locked shut. First with his fist and then with the blunt side of his axe, he hammers urgently. After a long wait, the door opens a fraction. 'I've got to see the director,' the officer says in a voice that doesn't admit questioning.

Dame Susan Crawford is in her office talking to her Head of Security. The power is still off and they are checking rosters by the light of a battery lamp when a restorer bursts in. 'Did you hear? Tate Modern has gone! Burning from end to end. The entire collection lost.'

At that moment the fireman blunders in on them. Dame Susan has a fleeting impression of sweat and grime and fatigue. 'Evacuation order, Ma'am. The fires are close to Charing Cross and we can't guarantee to hold them. The military are sending a truck for the pictures.'

'Surely the sprinkler system . . .?' Dame Susan begins, but the fireman cuts her short with a look. The fire he is speaking of will not be dowsed by sprinklers.

It takes only a moment for the Director to recover control. She exacts an estimate of the time they have left and dismisses the officer with an assurance of co-operation. When he has gone, she buzzes her secretary. 'Page all Curators. I want them in the Committee Room at once. Tag the message "utmost urgent".'

Inside five minutes, the group is assembled. Eight men and women of differing ages, background and academic allegiance – collectively, the guardians of two thousand of the most important paintings in the world. Dame Susan comes directly to the point. According to her calculations, they will be able to crate and remove to safety a maximum of eighty pictures. The others will have to take their chances with normal fire precautions. 'We may succeed in moving others without protection, simply packing them into lorries and cars, but we can't count on it.' Her gaze sweeps the room. 'The choice of what to take has to be made swiftly.'

Shock hangs in the air as the eight struggle to make sense of what they have heard. The fate of the pictures to be left behind is too horrifying to think about. They must concentrate on what to save.

A young man in a spotted bow tie is first to speak.

'Number one has to be Van Dyck's *Charles I* on horseback,' he declares. 'It's the most popular painting in the Gallery.'

A frissance of resentment stirs the table. The Curator of Renaissance Art rocks back in his chair. 'If decisions are to be based on postcard sales in the gift shop,' he sneers. His own collection includes works by Bellini and Raphael, as well as Leonardo da Vinci's cartoon of the *Virgin and Child*, bought for the Gallery by public subscription.

'I think we should concentrate on our own national treasures,' a quiet-spoken woman suggests. 'John Constable's *View on the Stour* and *The Hay Wain*. And Gainsborough's portrait of *Mr and Mrs Andrews*. The gun under Mr Andrews's arm and the detail of the Suffolk landscape are so quintessentially English . . .'

'Is this a provincial gallery or an international institution?' the only American in the group drawls, crushingly.

The awkward silence is broken by the Curator of Seventeenth-Century Dutch, demanding an extra quota for the Rembrandts. 'We have two entire rooms devoted to his work. He has to be the greatest artist of all time.'

It is an explosive remark. 'You have no basis for claiming that,' three people cut in at once, all starting to list other contenders for the title.

Dame Susan has been silent, the impassive onlooker at a ritual display. Now she rises. 'To use an all too apt analogy, we are fiddling while Rome burns. On a strictly numerical basis, each of you is permitted ten works. Select those you consider the most important, most representative or most valuable from your collections. They must be packed and ready for transport within thirty minutes. Alarm systems are being deactivated as we speak.'

Chairs draw back from the table. 'A final word,' the Director's eyes fix on one man. 'We possess two Vermeers in the Gallery; there are only thirty-six worldwide. It is my personal belief that the loss of both would be an incomparable tragedy.'

In the galleries, emergency lighting casts a weak illumination on jumbles of packing material and hurrying figures. Piles of wrappings and crates are dumped down the centres of rooms. Technicians struggle to unscrew the security devices that fix the frames to the walls. The larger frames are heavy in themselves and, with the added weight of laminated glass, there are constant calls for help lifting.

Wardens lug in long rolls of polythene that will be draped over those paintings remaining to protect them from water and foam sprayed by firemen. Curators and Assistants hurry by, heads bent in consultation. 'We have the Corot, we don't need another landscape . . .', 'Holbein comes before Bosch . . .', 'Our *Pope Julius* is the original, the Ufizzi would never forgive us . . .'

Wherever possible a picture's custom-made travelling box is used, but more often bubble wrap and an open crate has to make do. The packers, trained to take upwards of two hours for a single job, are on hands and knees on the wooden floor, measuring and cutting like madmen, battoning and padding, sniping at passers-by to keep their distance. Tempers all round are frayed.

Now heavy booted squaddies join the scene. 'Transport's waiting,' one yells, hefting a smaller crate. There are cries of protest. 'Take care, the pictures are fragile!' The soldier is unabashed. He has seen the blaze at Blackfriars. They'll be lucky to get half this lot away, he reckons.

The government is throwing everything it can into the battle to halt the conflagration. A Sea King helicopter from the Royal Navy base at Culdrose in Cornwall has reached the capital at last with a sling-loaded Bambi Bucket. The Bambi is a bright red rugged fabric container that holds ten thousand litres of water. The helicopter dunks it into the nearest available water to fill and flies the load over the flames, where a clever motorised dump valve allows a solid column of water to be dropped precisely on target. Depending on availability of water, a crew can average ten drops an hour.

The Sea King's crew has been given a map reference to a point near the head of the flames and they need it because visibility is zero; smoke has turned the sky blacker than night and they are flying on instruments. According to the screen they are over Southwark, approximately half a mile from the river. The stench is vile; all the crew are wearing oxygen masks. As they descend, the heat blasts them like an oven.

They fly north till the line of the river comes up on the radar screen, then bank west to follow it upstream at five hundred feet. There are tall buildings up ahead so it is safer to stay over the water. The infra-red sensor under the helicopter's chin picks up vast patches of incandescence thrown off by the burning fuel.

'Looks like clear water below,' the navigator calls at last. 'The London Eye is coming up five hundred metres to port.'

The helicopter shudders in a pocket of superheated air as the pilot eases down on the collective and they descend through the smoke while the wipers smear sticky globules across the windshield. At three hundred feet the blackness is still total. The winchman slides open the hatch a moment to peer out, then slams it shut again. 'Shit, even Kuwait wasn't this bad,' the crewman mutters into his face mask.

The radio is busy with chatter, passing messages between flight control and the tugs down on the water. At two hundred feet they catch their first glimpse of water and gasp. The pilot levels out above the river and holds the hover at a hundred and fifty feet, while the winchman clips on his safety harness and leans out through the hatch, shouting directions. Out of the smoke the glare of the fires is bright enough to read a paper by.

'Twenty descending, ten, eight, five, three, two, one,' he calls the altitude in three-foot units. The line hanging from the cargo hook is ninety feet long and the bucket is another ten, making a hundred feet in all.

'Height is good.' The base of the bucket is touching the surface of the water. 'Down three, two, one, and steady.' The rim of the bucket disappears beneath the surface. 'And up three, and steady.' Leaning out into the slipstream, the winchman sees the bucket rise dripping from the river, brimming over with water. He checks to make sure the thing hasn't snagged on anything, then gives the all clear. 'Hoist is good. Easy up and away.'

The pilot brings the helicopter up smoothly in a banking climb towards the north. Fully loaded, the bucket weighs over four tonnes and in any violent manoeuvre it can acquire a momentum sufficient to snap the strop. The navigator operates the switch to inject thirty-five litres of Class A foam concentrate into the bucket from an on-board tank. The concentrate increases the effectiveness of the load by as much as fifteen times, turning a single bucket into the equivalent of 150,000 litres of water. Because foam expands on release it is ideal for use in urban areas. The drop loses forward speed quickly, increasing accuracy, and is lighter in weight to leave buildings undamaged.

'Good,' the pilot says. 'Now ask control to give us a target.'

RAF Northholt, London. High winds have closed Heathrow and Gatwick. Civilian air traffic is being diverted to airports on the west coast and Scotland. Military transport flights are being directed to a government aerodrome normally reserved for VIP and Royal flights. The C-130 Hercules with the black Luftwaffe crosses rolls to a stop on an apron already crowded with other machines. Even before the propellers have ceased spinning, vehicles are pulling alongside. The hatch opens and an RAF lieutenant pulls himself aboard.

'Welcome to the party,' he greets the crew. 'Afraid you had a rough flight.'

*

'Your call sign is *Bismark*. It guarantees absolute priority. No other aircraft will be permitted to use this runway.'

'Fuel, water, retardant?' The senior pilot is a major, older than the Englishman, with a neat moustache. His flight suit reads Jost Metzler.

'Everything on tap, sir. You halt here each time you land and our chaps will connect the hoses. They will service you and you alone. Food and hot drinks will be put aboard. Anything you want, anything, just say.'

The Germans smile. 'Cold drinks,' the navigator says. 'Fire-fighting is hot work.' The lieutenant flushes, but the major waves the matter away. Time is critical. He is studying the maps the RAF has supplied. He wants to know the location of the fires and the whereabouts of tall buildings along the flight path.

The Luftwaffe plane is equipped with the Modular Airborne Fire-Fighting System, a transportable pallet that slides into the Hercules's huge belly, containing water tanks, pumping gear and twin dump pipes to discharge the foam mixture through the rear loading ramp. Fitted with the system, an aircraft can drop 14,000 kilograms of retardant on target in six seconds. This is twice the Canadair's load, even if it lacks the other's rapid refill capability.

While the airmen and their English navigator check the map, RAF mechanics refuel the aircraft and connect up a trailer of pre-mixed retardant. An air compressor spins into life, pumping the mixture into the aircraft's capacious tanks. The Luftwaffe systems operator watches his dials and calls enough. Hoses are disconnected, hatches slam shut. The major asks for clearance and receives an instant affirmative.

Fifteen minutes from touchdown, the black cross is rolling up the runway again.

56

Up at Brent Reservoir, Bill Thurgood has fallen asleep in spite of the cold. There is so much activity going on that the sound of aircraft overhead doesn't wake him immediately. It is not until the search-lights click on that he comes alert with a start. Everyone is staring up the lake to the north. He is just in time to catch the plane's lights lining up.

The lights dip downward and a streak of silver splits the surface in an instant, like a rip in a sheet of black paper. The noise of the engines grows louder as the plane ploughs towards them. Bill can make it out now, growing larger by the second: a boat-shaped nose and twin engines set above the wings, high tail almost hidden by a plume of spray. It is barely two hundred metres away when suddenly the spray cuts off and the plane lifts, skimming over the dam, engines blaring under full power. Bill swivels, straining to track the tail lamps as they vanish into the murk.

A second aircraft comes sliding in from the same direction as before. As it lifts off over the dam again, Bill catches a glimpse of the tricoleur roundels and a lump comes into his throat. He is filled with a sudden affection for these men who have flown through the storm to London's rescue.

Between Blackfriars and Waterloo, three ships are on fire and have come adrift, driving like Viking funeral pyres before the storm. One is blown across the river and ends up ramming the façade of the London Television Centre. All Southwark north of the railway lines is ablaze. On the grand terrace of Somerset House, one of the capital's architectural masterpieces, Assistant Curator, Gordon Pringle, watches the flames licking around the brutalist concrete terraces of the South Bank Arts Centre opposite and tells himself grimly, better them than us.

Pringle has spent the early part of the afternoon transferring gold and silver artefacts of the Gilbert Collection from the boathouse under the terrace to rooms in the main building. Now everything has to be moved again, and this time not only the Gilbert treasures. The principal rooms of Somerset House have been transformed into an outstation of St Petersburg's fabulous Hermitage Museum. Into the boots of their cars, Pringle and his colleagues frantically throw priceless wonders: Catherine the Great's silver thread wig, gemstones engraved with the Empress's portrait, and, in an ironic coincidence not lost on the curators, classical sculptures from Pompeii. All to be driven out like household baggage before the fires reach them.

Attempts to form a defence line on Waterloo Bridge have failed. By the time appliances reach the bridge in sufficient numbers, patches of burning oil have spread through into King's Reach and are threatening Charing Cross. The rail bridge here is a sole means of escape for people fleeing along the embanked tracks to the safety of the north bank. With flames surrounding Waterloo Station, this route is threatened and the Luftwaffe Hercules, call sign *Bismark*, is tasked to the area.

'There,' the English liaison officer points down through the smoke at the expanse of curved glass roof.

The plane banks low over the river, swinging in to cross the land from the east. As they skim over Stamford Street an entire block erupts in a cauldron of fire, spouting geysers of orange and yellow flame beneath them. A wave of superheated vapour blasts in through the open ramp and the Englishman gasps for breath as paintwork bubbles and blisters. The plane staggers, as though struck by an invisible hammer. Beside him, the bombardier's gloved fingers stab at the pumping console and with a violent rumbling noise the five huge tanks behind them void a drenching cloud of water and retardant mixture through the twin discharge pipes on to the inferno below. Freed of its load, the Hercules bounds upwards and a gale of cooler air sweeps through the fuselage.

The Englishman blinks, wiping sweat away. 'Does that happen often?'

The last of the discharge dribbles from the pipes. The bombardier shuts off the valves. With a whine of hydraulics the cargo ramp starts to rise up. He grins nonchalantly back, his grey eyes creased with amusement. 'All the time,' he says.

The Englishman takes a final glance before the

end of the ramp reaches the roof. The station is hidden beneath plumes of steam. The crew have judged the run perfectly, dropping the load right on target.

But the respite earned is brief. Coverage is not complete and already the wind is tearing at the foam. It is essential that repeated loads be delivered before the fire has time to recover. A round trip to Northolt and back takes half an hour. A second Luftwaffe aircraft is on the apron there now. It will take five minutes more to finish reloading its tanks and another ten for it to reach the drop zone.

But one of the Canadairs is available. Air Traffic Control radios the French crew. The liaison officer aboard scrawls a cross on the map; the pilot nods and adjusts the course for the new target. Check the radar, he tells everyone, and keep a sharp look out.

To the east of Waterloo, meanwhile, on the Peabody Estate, several families are in a desperate plight, marooned on the roof of a burning tenement. Flames have reached the topmost floor; the heat and smoke are unendurable. They have only minutes left to live.

The message is passed to emergency control. A helicopter is retasked and responds, swooping down through the smoke. But there is only room aboard for half the group and fighting breaks out. Screaming refugees hammer on the cabin doors. As it lifts away, a petrol tank in a nearby garage explodes, sending out a pulse of heat. Four men clinging to the landing gear drop away and, freed of the weight, the helicopter lurches upwards, momentarily out of control in the turbulence, straight into the path of the oncoming water bomber.

The French pilot has no chance. He has been told the route is clear. No one aboard sees the helicopter until the last second. By then it's too late. The port wing of the Canadair slices into the helicopter's fuselage and the two planes wrap around one another in a catastrophic fireball.

The crash slams the wreckage of both aircraft into the ground at a hundred knots, obliterating twenty houses in a street east of The Cut. The nose section and engines of the Canadair careers along the roadway, burying itself in the rear of a theatre on the main road and exploding the building in a cloud of pulverised rubble. A handful of pedestrians, who have taken refuge from the flood on the upper floor of a stranded double-decker bus outside, are caught in the explosion and wiped out.

A quarter of a mile away at St Thomas's, rescue work in the shattered ruins of Accident and Emergency is continuing. Everyone who can be spared is helping. With water two metres deep in places, some casualties have to be brought out on makeshift rafts. Surgical teams are operating in wartime conditions. The atmosphere of shock is total. Almost everyone on the medical staff knows someone who is missing or injured or dead.

One young nurse has fallen when an upper floor gave way. She lies unconscious and bleeding from the head for two hours before firemen dig her from the rubble and she is brought by stretcher to the North Wing. Melanie Sykes suspects fractures of the leg and pelvis and rushes her through to theatre.

'Looks like she landed on her right hip,' she tells them.

At least the need to cope takes Melanie's mind off the fire threat. The flames encroaching along the south bank are now in plain view from the upper floors and many patients are horribly frightened. News that the government has ordered an airlift for all those who can be moved gives only partial reassurance.

The sky overhead is an angry red that flickers with an ominous pulse. The world seems hideous and terrifying. Perspectives are distorted, heights foreshortened. Once familiar buildings seem shrunken and far away. The worst moments are when gusts of smoke descend, blotting out all vision in a nightmare darkness.

A Green Giant helicopter with USAF markings appears swinging in low over the river – 21 SOS now operating over the capital for the first time. The aircraft takes up a hover over North Wing and lowers its ramp. The winchman peers out, directing the pilot as the helicopter descends foot by foot till the lip of the ramp touches the safety rail surrounding the flat roof. 'Down one more.' Under the weight of the descending ramp the rail crumples slowly till the lip is resting solidly against the roof. 'Okay, hold it there,' he shouts into his microphone.

From a stairwell at the other end of the roof, teams of nurses and porters emerge. Ducking their heads against the hammering downdraught of the rotor, they manhandle a line of trolley-borne patients up to the ramp. A crewman leaps out from the cockpit to help.

The process of loading is slow. Patients have to be lifted off the trolleys on stretchers, carried up the ramp one at a time and strapped down inside. It is exhausting work and depends on the helicopter holding its position in spite of being battered by gale-force winds. When twenty-two patients have been brought aboard, the aircraft lifts off and another takes its place.

At Triple-C the main map of the estuary has been replaced by a large-scale one covering the central area of the city. Burning slicks have passed under the railway bridge at Charing Cross, the Chief Fire Officer reports. Flames have set light to the bridge and the fires have spread up the tracks into the station. Embankment House, the big development over the station, is burning. Fire crews are establishing a new defence line hinging on Trafalgar Square.

'My men think they can hold the north side of Whitehall, but without heavy support from the water bombers we shall lose the ministries along the river, including the Norman Shaw buildings and Portcullis House.'

Portcullis House is the new office building for MPs, erected at a cost of hundreds of millions. It stands above Westminster station, directly across the road from Big Ben. The fires are threatening the very heart of government, Downing Street, the Foreign Office, the Treasury, Westminster and the Abbey. Venetia Maitland's gaze strays across the map over to the south bank. Smaller buildings, mean homes clustered together, hospitals and . . . people.

What is the position at St Thomas's? she wants to know.

'Helicopters have so far brought out approximately two hundred patients,' an RAF officer responds. 'Our information is that as many as four hundred patients and six hundred medical staff remain in the complex.' Loading the patients is what takes time, he says. 'Once they are out of the way we can stuff a hundred doctors and nurses at a time into a Chinook for a short flight.'

The question is, will the flames hold off long enough to complete the rescue operation?

'If we deploy all the water bombers on the south bank,' the Chief tells her, 'we shall lose the Houses of Parliament and possibly Westminster Abbey as well.'

The colour ebbs from Venetia's face at these words. Everyone in the room is looking ashen. Westminster is the nation's centrepiece, symbol of Britain's identity around the world.

Raikes interrupts. We are missing the point here, he says. 'We have to stop the oil from spreading. As it moves up-river the area of the blaze gets larger all the time. There are more fires to fight and our resources are depleted. We are using up stocks of foam faster than we can resupply the fire crews. Every pump engine we have is committed to action.'

What is needed, he says, is a barricade across the river that will skim off the oil and halt it. 'Once we stop the oil moving, we can leave it to burn out on the water, while we target the planes against the fires in the city.'

'Where could we make a barricade?' Venetia asks him.

'Our best choice, in fact our only one, is Westminster Bridge. The headroom there is three metres lower than Tower Bridge or Waterloo. We could drop metal boats, pontoons or empty steel drums, on the water to create a blockage. Some oil will still get round the flanks, but the great bulk will have been stopped.'

The Fire Chief agrees. 'At the moment my crews are being run ragged with fresh fires breaking out every other minute. They don't know where to turn next. If we can contain the blaze, then we can deal with it.'

'Then let's do it,' Venetia orders.

Mary Lucas has been trying to interrupt for some time. Now she pushes forward and manages to catch Venetia's eye. 'Well, what is it?'

Mary's heart is in her mouth. In all her training one thing has been hammered into her, the need for objectivity. To tell the truth and not simply what people want to hear. But how to be sure? How to know whether to believe the data she has been handed? Has the judgement of her colleagues been clouded by a desire to make things right?

No, she tells herself. She can trust the Central Forecasting team to give her the facts straight and unvarnished by hope or speculation.

'Well, what is it this time?' Venetia repeats, impatiently. Her jaw is set, bracing herself for more bad news.

'Rain,' Mary says. New pressure readings have come in from the North Sea. The anti-cyclone centred over Germany is moving away eastwards and filling. If the pattern holds, winds can be expected to drop, with a chance of precipitation later.

'Four to six hours,' she adds.

The looks of hope around the table subside into dismay. Four hours might as well be forever.

Venetia's back straightens. 'Four hours,' she says firmly. 'We can hang on somehow till then.' It's hope, she is saying. For the first time, hope.

'Will it be enough to halt the fires?' someone asks doubtfully.

The Chief Fire Officer nods his head. 'It could be,' he says. 'If these damn winds would drop we'd have a chance at least. The gales are driving the flames on so fast we're outrun at every turn. New outbreaks spring up and my men can't reach them in time to stop the flames spreading.

'It's the same with the slicks. Rain will cool the oil. Light rain will lie on the surface, shutting out the air. Smaller patches will snuff out. There will be less risk from sparks. Rain is good.'

'How can we be sure rain is coming?' another minister says suspiciously. 'The Met Office has been wrong all along.' There are murmurs of agreement.

Mary Lucas flushes. Venetia steps in, 'Of course we can be sure. This is England and winter; rain is the one thing we can count on. We have to hold on till it reaches us.'

Trafalgar Square. Dame Susan Crawford stands on the steps of the National Gallery and tries to keep the fear out of her mind. She has come out here to gauge for herself the closeness of the fires. The sight has left her so numbed with horror she can scarcely think.

It is the crimson sky to the east that terrifies her. The lurid, pulsating radiance that has Nelson wavering on his column and weird shapes flickering in and out of view against the buildings. The fantastic light that Turner captured 170 years ago, when he painted the Houses of Parliament burning. A baleful glare as if the fire has a life of its own, a monstrous force that consumes everything it touches.

The noise is hellish, an all-consuming, deep-throated bellow, punctuated by sudden detonations and the wail of sirens. Her eyes are streaming with the smoke and the stench is sickening, a mix of burning plastic, leaking gas and escaped sewage, that makes her stomach heave. There is a row of fire-engines pulled up across St Martin's Place and the church of St Martin-in-the-Fields, famous as the inspiration of the American Colonial style and a refuge for the homeless, is crackling merrily like a children's bonfire. The firemen's pumps are sucking water from hoses attached to the fountains in the square.

A mob of fleeing refugees scuttles past on the road below, bundled possessions slung over their shoulders – Londoners driven from their homes like a scene from some third-world disaster. Two more fire-engines come swinging down Whitcomb Street, swerving wildly to avoid a huddle of abandoned cars.

With a shudder she pulls herself together. There is still work to do. A short time in which to get a handful more paintings away before she and her staff are driven out by the flames.

Please God, someone knows what they are doing, she prays. Please God, we can stop this in time.

*

Across the river, up in the capsule on the London Eye, the sound of aero engines jerks Wilson Palmer abruptly alert. Where before there was only darkness, now an ominous red glare suffuses the sky, illuminating a hellish scene of blazing buildings and belching smoke palls. Far below, patches of burning oil are visible drifting around the base of the Eye; the eastern end of County Hall is ablaze. Across the river, the white fortress of the Ministry of Defence is burning furiously, huge flames shooting up from the roof, making an eerie and magnificent sight.

And there is something else. A tremor runs through the capsule. Looking down, Wilson realises they are much higher than before. The capsule is moving round. Debris on the water, a drifting barge, must have struck against the wheel, breaking the lock mechanism and causing it to turn.

His view is blotted out momentarily. A thick veil of smoke descends on the capsule like a black shroud. The children have woken and are staring round, alarmed. Wilson tries his radio but it is hopeless. Water has ruined the circuits.

They are trapped up here and surrounded by fire.

57

Giant American aircraft have begun arriving at Heathrow bringing amphibious vehicles from military bases in Germany. A column of these, manned by Marines in combat gear, rumbles through central London. They will be used to ship men and equipment into Westminster and bring out survivors.

In the meantime, heavy earthmovers and construction machines are crawling through the water to dump concrete building blocks at the approaches to Westminster Bridge. Raikes hopes by this means to prevent the defences from being outflanked, on this side at least. On the north side of Whitehall, the great ministry buildings are being fortified with concrete block and sandbag barricades. Army engineers are installing pumps and generators for the firemen and bringing up supplies of foam.

Helicopters are busy transporting in empty freight containers to be lowered into the water against the bridge. Other containers are being filled with sand and water and placed in streets leading up from the Embankment to form an impenetrable defence against flames. The plan is to stack them two high on the terrace of the Houses of Parliament as a precaution should the fires break through.

But time is desperately short. The winds have dropped a little but not enough to matter. Already advance patches of burning oil are drifting up against the bridge piers. With the barricade only two thirds complete, fire crews are being rushed to the scene and ferried with trailer pumps onto the bridge by amphibious trucks. Among them are American teams from air bases in East Anglia.

While the Luftwaffe unit sweeps the south bank, the French Canadair pilots, as if furious to avenge their fallen comrades, scream down the river at suicidal heights to splash retardant on the advancing flames.

Helicopters vitally needed to fight the fires at the bridge are having to be diverted to lift out patients from St Thomas's, where the evacuation is not yet complete.

On the eighth floor of North Wing, Melanie Sykes struggles to keep patients calm. 'We'll all be leaving together,' she repeats. 'The helicopters are on the roof and our turn will come soon.'

Smoke is eddying through the corridors. Chunks of burning oil have started fires on the ground floor. Firemen, brought in by the same aircraft evacuating patients, clatter down the stairs with their equipment. Noises of the battle are clearly audible on the wards.

A senior surgeon comes round to perform a triage rating. Those patients with the best chances of survival are to be flown out first. Hopeless cases may have to be left behind. The High Dependency cases can't be moved. They will die anyway when their machines are turned off. As for the others, 'We must do what we can for them.' Melanie is to prepare a stock of morphine and syringes. He promises to back her up in whatever action she deems necessary for patients' best interests.

The battle of Westminster Bridge is entering its critical phase. The span is marked by lines of fire and arcing hose jets. Foam drenches the flames and bursts back in sheets of spurting steam. Torches and searchlights flicker in the smoke like ghostly eyes.

If only they can get more material to complete the barricade in time, Raikes tells himself. The best things are the big shipping containers. Lowered into position against the piers by helicopters, they need to be lashed down by cables and anchors to form a fireproof wall against the flames. Each one measures six metres; another dozen should suffice.

Some oil is getting through still, streaming along the south bank. St Thomas's is burning. Fire crews and water bombers are fighting a desperate rearguard action to hold back the flames long enough for the evacuation to be completed. Patches of burning fuel have spread down past Lambeth into Vauxhall, setting light to the Oval cricket stadium. But the main mass of oil is being checked. If only they can hold on until the rain comes, they might beat it.

As he watches, a Puma steadies over the southern span and starts to lower the metal box dangling from its strop. They have the system organised now. Fire teams cover the engineers as they drag up steel cables. Shackles are attached and at a signal the winchman aboard the helicopter lets go the hoist. The container drops with a mighty splash into the river, jerking short against the lashings. The fire teams crawl forward to smother it in foam, gaining precious yards.

The river side of Whitehall, from Trafalgar Square to Westminster, is a mass of flames. The MOD roof has fallen in, releasing showers of multi-coloured sparks. Fires lick around Portcullis House by Westminster Station. Liquid glass from the windows streams down the marble façade like giant tears. Across Westminster Square, in the Abbey, the Archdeacon listens to the steady drip of molten lead from the ancient roof. The square itself is a war zone of sunken vehicles and burnt-out or shattered equipment. Tracked military ambulances lurk in side roads for their quotas of casualties. People are dropping like flies from heat and fumes. Some alleys are choked with bodies.

Frantic efforts by water bombers and helicopters with buckets are still holding off the flames from the main part of St Thomas's. All patients capable of being moved have been evacuated. Only a handful of doctors and nurses remain tending to the High Dependency cases. Melanie Sykes is among those refusing to leave.

Inside the Palace of Westminster, another desperate operation is under way to save the regalia and other precious artefacts from the two Chambers. The Serjeant at Arms himself carries out the 16-pound silver-gilt Mace from the Commons. Also at risk are the archives housed in the Victoria Tower, six miles of steel shelving on twelve floors containing master copies of every Act of Parliament since 1497 and many other historical documents, including the original Bill of Rights and the trial record of Mary, Queen of Scots.

Shouts ring through the lofty central lobby of the Commons. A fresh sense of urgency penetrates the building. Torch in hand, Superintendent David Leech runs along the East Corridor into the Lower Waiting Hall. A marble bust of Oliver Cromwell and an Epstein on loan from Tate Britain are both missing from their plinths. Leech suspects that a fair amount of items being rescued will never be seen again. He takes the stairs up to the first floor. Overlooking the river here are the committee rooms of both Houses. It is pitch dark. Hoses snake across the corridor and helmeted figures blunder in search of hydrants and mains connections.

Leech gropes his way into the nearest room. The shutters have been opened. Two firemen are peering anxiously out. In contrast to the gloom in the corridor, the whole room is filled with lurid red light. One of the men shouts at him to get back. But Leech has had one glimpse and that is enough. Out on the river, a raft of burning oil, at least a hundred metres across, is moving down upon the terrace.

There is a roar of engines overhead. The men by the window duck back inside as a huge shadow swoops past. There is a thud and a woomph sound, followed by an insane hissing, as from ten thousand steam jets suddenly opened. The firemen look out and curse vividly.

Leech peers over their shoulders. Seven thousand litres of retardant have overshot their target by fifty metres. The bridge approach is frosted with white foam. The flames swarm closer, the stench of oil eddying sickeningly through the window. The firemen have turned on their hose, but against that inferno they might as well be pissing into the wind. Leech fancies he can hear the crash of the terrace windows shattering in the heat.

'Get out!' the men scream at him again. 'Get out, while you've the chance!'

Leech pulls himself away. Hoses alone won't hold the flames for long. The men are right. He must get people out now, before it's too late.

With helicopters in desperately short supply, individual rescue is frequently a matter of luck. On the Millennium Wheel, Wilson has been endeavouring to signal for help from the capsule with his hand torch. But it is a colleague who has reported him missing, who galvanises the authorities into mounting a search.

Military air is being co-ordinated out of RAF Strike Command High Wycombe. As the Sea King from Manston approaches the river, instructions come through to divert. A man and two kids are trapped on the London Eye. Reed, the co-pilot, calls out the fresh heading and switches channels to speak to local emergency control.

Pilot Lieutenant Ralph Nichol has the river on radar. He drops down below the cloud base almost on top of the Eye. The base of the giant wheel is surrounded by patches of burning oil and the big building nearby pulses with a flickering glow from the fires inside.

Nichol circles overhead, keeping an eye on the glass capsules round the rim of the wheel. They reflect the firelight and make a good reference point. Smoke, thick and dark, charged with flames, eddies through the central spokes. Reed plays the searchlight downward. Nichol can see it glinting off a spider's web of cables. Suddenly there is a cry from the winchman behind; he has spotted a figure on one of the capsules.

Reed has him as well. He centres the spotlight and Nichol picks the man out, clinging to the framework of the wheel's rim, shielding his eyes as he stares up into the beam. In the capsule beneath, two smaller figures are visible. The children.

By the open hatch the winchman, Seb Heywood, is clipping on his harness over his neoprene suit, ready to drop. Seb is twenty-three and, as of last week, father to a baby girl. He is not a specialist rescue-swimmer but he is a member of the Royal Marines Special Forces, so his training is multi-skill. Nichol tells Seb to back off a minute. He wants to take a good look first before they go in. There must be a couple of hundred damn wires down there, he is thinking.

Reed has emergency control on VHF. They tell him the Eye is 135 metres in diameter with a central hub like a bicycle, supported by A-frame pylons sixty metres high. Also that the wheel may or may not be in motion.

This is worse than the rigging of any ship. Nichol needs to set Seb down on a hundred-metre line with a wind still gusting to fifty knots. There is no way it can be done from this height without risking getting him tangled in the wires. They have to get in closer.

Reed adds to his troubles. 'See that big gas-holder about two klicks west? Fire is pushing close to it. Control say the thing could blow any time.'

This low over the fires there is a lot of turbulence. Nichol is having a hard job to hold the aircraft steady. Pockets of heated air bubbling off the flames bounce the Sea King like a toy. Reed struggles to hold the small group on the wheel in the searchlight.

'Look at those cables on the landward side,' Nichol tells Seb over the intercom. 'See how the ends are belayed down to the ground to keep the legs tensioned? The fire must be heating the wire up red-hot by now. If they give way, it'll drop the big wheel smack in the river.'

'What are they doing?' the girl wails. 'Why is it taking so long?'

The fury of the storm is increasing and with it the shaking of the capsule. Heavy tremors run through the structure like the strings twanging on a giant double bass. The cables howl in the wind and Wilson can feel the wheel shudder in the gusts. And that shouldn't happen. The Eye weighs two thousand tonnes. It is built to withstand a hurricane. Something must be causing it to fail.

The children cling to the edge of the hatch, trying to see what's going on. Smoke, rising off the water, sets them coughing. Even at this height the heat from the river is ferocious. The helicopter is hovering directly overhead now, the searchlight holding them in its beam like dazzled insects.

All at once they can see a man's feet in the air immediately above them. 'Stand still,' Wilson shouts. 'Wait for him to come to you.'

The man is so close now they can hear him chattering on his radio. The wash of the rotors crushes them against the roof of the capsule. He drops down and his feet meet the glass nose section with a bump. He is three metres from them but the angle of the nose and the buffeting of the wind make it hard to climb. He drops to a crouch to stop himself sliding downwards. Wilson flings a hank of rope for him to catch.

'The little one first.'

The girl wriggles up from the hatch. Seb grabs her and slips a sling over her shoulders. He tightens it under her arms. 'Okay, up,' he calls into the radio. Thirty seconds later she is in the helicopter and Seb is dropping back down again. This time he lands right by the hatch. Wilson lifts her brother out, Seb puts the sling around him and he too is safely away.

Wilson readies himself. From down below comes the crash of a capsule bursting in the heat. Another tremor runs through the wheel, stronger than before. Seb comes dropping down again. Wilson stands up on the capsule, ducks his head under the sling and looks upwards at the helicopter's belly.

The searchlight cuts out. A giant hand jerks him off his feet and then an instant later slams him down again with bone-crunching force. A mile and a half west, flames have just detonated the gas-holders by the Oval cricket ground. A million cubic metres of gas flashes off in the space of seconds. In Vauxhall and Kennington the ground heaves and buildings buckle and slide at the terrific concussion. A block of council flats takes the full force of the explosion and is pulverised. Many residents of low-lying properties have taken refuge here on the upper floors and the carnage is frightful. The blinding glare of the ignition lights up the capital as bright as the sun and the southwestern sky is suffused with the glow of a tremendous fire. For a mile around the site, windows are blown out and roofs stripped of slates.

The fireball boiling into the sky is the only warning Lieutenant Nichol gets before the aircraft is hammered sideways by the shock-wave a split-second later. Nichol has never flown in combat but it is like what he imagines a missile hit would be. The nearest he can get to it is the time he was in a light plane that was struck by lightning over West Africa. The Sea King staggers in the air as if it has run into a cliff, jerks upwards, then drops again like a stone. Loose gear bursts from lockers. An insanely loud clattering noise erupts from the cabin behind; simultaneously, alarm bells shrill as the flight deck fills with smoke.

The hoist wire jerks tight instantly beyond its breaking strain but the fail-safe mechanism clicks in, trips the cable-cutter and the wire runs right out into the murk below. Seb and Wilson fall on the rim of the capsule. They are winded and the only thing holding them is the still taut wire. When it goes slack they slide off into thin air.

The shock-wave of the explosion has swung the Sea King across the smoke plumes belching off the river. On the flight deck Lieutenant Nichol is suddenly flying blind. With the main hatch open great draughts of filthy fumes are sucked inside. In the space of seconds, vision for the entire crew is shut down. The smoke is so thick it seems, in Nichol's own words, 'like grease in gas form'. When it fills the flight deck he can't see a thing. He can't make out the windshield wipers. In fact he can't see the windshield at all.

He flips down his night vision goggles that are fixed to his helmet. He has been flying without them because the patches of fire on the river cause the NVGs to back off and go blind. Even with them on now, Nichol still can't see a thing. The flight deck is completely opaque and even NVGs require some fraction of light to operate. Either that or oil from the fumes is condensing out on the lenses.

Back in the cabin the children are crying and the radar operator who doubles up as winch controller is hanging onto the combing of the hatch trying to see what has become of Seb and the last survivor. Something looms out of the smoke alongside and to his shock there is one of the Eye's glass capsules right by the tail rotor. 'Up! Up! Up!' he shouts urgently.

Nichol hears the signal for a Low-level Abort. Instinctively he pulls maximum power on the collective. In less than three seconds the Sea King jumps two hundred feet straight up. The rate-of-ascent goes off the clock. Literally. The engines are screaming, alarms and buzzers filling the flight deck. All the lights have gone out. Yanking full power has over-torqued the gearbox, causing the generators to go off-line.

Nichol has got no radio, instruments, automatic flight control or infra-red. The crew-alert panel is dead and the flight deck is shaking so hard the dials are a blur anyway. From somewhere behind comes a noise like rocks being spun inside a steel drum. The Sea King powerplant comprises twin Rolls-Royce Gnome turboshaft engines mounted side by side above the cabin. That noise means either a broken turbine blade or worse a catastrophic gearbox failure.

The engines are down to 50 per cent power and the aircraft is wallowing around the sky like a drunken sow. Nichol shouts to his co-pilot to kill Number Two. Reed reaches out with his gloved right hand and fumbles for the nearer of the two T-switches. Pulling cuts off the power to the engine and a twist anti-clockwise fires an extinguisher into the engine compartment. Reed pulls and twists hard. The appalling din in his left ear dies to a rattle. The fire bell peals for a few seconds longer, then falls silent. The aircraft breaks out of the smoke and a modicum of visibility returns. Nichol is using the switches on the collective to regulate the remaining engine. Reed flips the flight-deck power supply to back-up mode and re-starts the generators. Lights come on and some, but not all, instruments resume function.

Down below, Wilson and Seb are miraculously still alive. The cable holding them has snagged between the capsule and its mounting, snatching them up short with a jerk that almost snaps their spines and leaves them dangling two hundred metres up over the flaming river. Seb is hanging upside down and the hoist wire is wrapped around Wilson's right leg causing agonising pain. Seb manages to reach up and grasp the hoist, taking some of the weight off and pulling him upright, but he can't disentangle him. The helicopter is no longer visible but he can hear it in the smoke still somewhere close.

Overhead Nichol banks round. The radar operator whose name is McCabe, at thirty-four the oldest man aboard, has hooked another cable onto the winch and makes ready to drop. Reed unclips the intercom wires from his helmet and leaves the flight deck to see him down as Nichol steadies into the hover. The Eye is now leaning drunkenly. One set of cables has burned through completely and the two men on the broken hoist are swaying through a 30-degree arc. At the last moment before he jumps, McCabe grabs a pair of wire-cutters from the tool kit and cradles them on the descent.

McCabe drops right alongside the pair. He reaches out to grab Seb's arm but their arcs are out of synch and they swing apart like acrobats. Nichol is desperately trying to hold the hover and stay close to the wheel but it's on the verge of collapse. One leg has broken free from its concrete mooring and the other is twisting and buckling under the strain.

McCabe swings back and this time manages to get a hold on Seb's harness. He pulls in close and drops the sling over his head and tightens it in the same movement. He wraps his legs round Wilson, grips him tight with one arm and snips the hoist wire with a single cut with his free hand. Together the three men swing back out over the water. Wilson is fainting with pain. McCabe can't be sure if he's hooked on safely so he is keeping as firm a grip on him as he can, but Wilson is a heavy weight. Seb can't help because he's facing the wrong way.

Up in the hatch, Reed has his finger on the winch button and the moment he sees the signal he starts reeling in. McCabe thinks he can feel Wilson slipping. The strength in his fingers is giving out. The swinging of the rescue line is making it worse. All he can do is grit his teeth and pray. Just as he's thinking he is going to have to let go he sees the hatch coming up. Reed leans out to grab a hold of Wilson's collar. There is a ripping sound and a handful of fabric pulls away. Wilson slips from McCabe's grasp but McCabe still has a leg hold and manages to check him for an instant. Just in time, Seb twists round and grasps Wilson by the belt. Between the three of them, they successfully haul him back.

Reed swings the hoist in and suddenly they are all safely aboard.

As the helicopter flies slowly away on its remaining engine, Seb snatches a final glimpse of the wheel through the hatch. Fire has weakened the last cable. The remaining leg shears and two thousand tonnes of steel crashes forwards into the river. Through the smoke palls Seb has a momentary vision of snapping cables and glass capsules descending amid a ruin of flame before a veil of darkness falls.

On the bridge, someone screams a warning. Raikes jerks round to see a black wall twice his own height sweeping towards him. Two thousand tonnes of steel toppling into the river, partly from a height of over a hundred metres, has the impact of an earthquake jolt. Raikes has a single second in which to grab hold on a crawler tractor behind him before a tidal wave of oil-burdened water swamps the bridge.

Blind and breathless, all he can do is hang on for his life, while the water tears past him. He can feel the icy chill of the water and oil smearing him with its greasy weight, turning his fingers slippery till he feels he must lose his grip and be swept away. Then, suddenly, the ferocious current slackens. The water drops away and he can breathe again. It is only a respite though. Seconds later, like the aftershock of an earthquake, another great wave comes crashing into the bridge. It must have rebounded off the buildings along the riverside. Once again water sweeps over Raikes's head. Not so deep this time though.

He is covered all over in a coating of slime. There is oil in his eyes, in his hair, in his mouth. Oil burning in his throat. As he vomits up gouts of filthy muck, he can hear others coughing and retching around him. How many have been washed away, Raikes can't tell. Fifty? A hundred? There is no time to think about their fate. Some of the oil is still alight. The roadway beside him dances with flickering flames.

'Hoses here!' he shouts. 'Fire parties!'

Jets of foam lance out to quench the burning fuel. People are pulling themselves together, getting back into action. An amphibious vehicle, a Buffalo, comes lumbering across from the north bank with reinforcements. A water bomber roars in to dump its load beside the bridge. Another follows. The flames fall back.

But the fires have one last trick to play. The wreckage of the Millennium Wheel is preventing most of the oil from passing under Westminster Bridge, but enough has made it through to deal one final deadly blow. As the weary defenders glance behind them, they see the Houses of Parliament burning 'like the Day of Judgement' in the words of one observer.

The fire crews on the upper floors are falling back. Leech can hear their whistles as they pound down the stairs. Flames are eating their way inwards from the terrace. Stone tracery crumbles, carved pinnacles break away in the heat. The roar of the flames is submerged in a continuous roll of ruin and destruction. Stone splits, timbers crack, roofs cave in and walls collapse. Centuries of British history dissolve in a cataclysm of fire and flood.

Stumbling down the stairs from Poets' Hall, Leech finds himself back in the Central Lobby. The magnificent arched windows are smashed and broken. Smoke eddies through. Flames flicker in the direction of the Commons Chamber. As Leech hesitates, the huge chandelier overhead emits a warning clink. Leech glances up and flings himself through the west door and down the steps into St Stephen's Hall. Behind him, the high roof of the great Central Tower comes crashing through the lobby's vaulted stone ceiling, collapsing the floor, where he has been standing a moment ago, into the cellar beneath.

Yet amid all the destruction, one symbol remains. The Clock Tower, Big Ben, still stands, soot blackened and charred but so far unharmed.

Fire swarms through the Speaker's apartments next door, sparks flare upon its spire, but still its hands continue to mark the time. And all the world waits.

Up the river comes a humming shape. An aircraft bearing the black cross insignia. Crewed by men whose grandfathers in a different century might have flown similar missions but bent on destruction. It swoops in and unleashes its cargo of fire-smothering foam. Clouds of steam explode upwards from the drop. A second German aircraft screams down to empty its load, so low it almost scrapes the clock tower as it pulls out of the dive. The flames are snuffed out. Fire crews race to hose down the smouldering ruins. But Big Ben is saved.

Across the river in St Thomas's, Melanie Sykes has lost count of time. The roar of the flames and the thunder of the aircraft bombing the fires have numbed her senses. By the light of her torch she stumbles from bed to bed, checking air pumps and drips. Battery power is getting low and there aren't enough medics and nurses left to work the equipment by hand. At least for most of the patients the end will be brief when it comes.

She has seen the London Eye fall and the Houses of Parliament burning but she is too drained to feel anything. For the moment the flames have been checked at the bridge but for how long? Then, all at once, as she stares from a shattered window, she notices a change. Something different in the air. Drifts of steam are rising from flaming buildings and the burning slicks on the river. Not the explosive bursts of the water bomber drops but a gentler, more persistent sound. She puts out her arm and feels the patter of drops upon her palm. Rain. Rain, and the tears stream down her face in response. A steady downpour falling from the blackened sky. Rain from heaven. They are not going to die after all. Rain.

Hammersmith. Flooding has spread across the Uxbridge Road into White City. Directed by police in waders, Sophie de Salis and Miranda Binney slosh northward along Bloemfontein Road towards Westway. It is dark, but some streetlights are still working and the glow from the fires to the southeast drenches everything a hideous red. They move in a daze, too exhausted and cold to speak any longer. The Uxbridge Road and all the neighbouring streets are jammed with people wading in the same direction. A quarter of a million residents turned out of their homes by the threat of fire. Some wheel pushchairs and barrows laden with possessions thrown together in haste; others hump suitcases or backpacks. The majority, like Sophie and Miranda, have left everything. The elderly, the handicapped and the injured are carried on makeshift stretchers. A few fortunate ones get lifts on trucks. The whole vast torrent of human misery is making for Wormwood Scrubs where a huge reception centre has been opened up on the common.

At Westway they reach the limit of the flood at last. Police have closed off the dual carriageway to all non-essential traffic. As the refugees splash onto dry ground columns of buses arrive to take those unable to walk further. 'I've lost my daughter!' Sophie pleads again and again.

At last an officer hears her. 'Go to the reception

centre. Everything's being organised there. They're taking all the names. Children are top priority and they may be able to locate her for you.'

Dragging Miranda by the hand, Sophie heads toward the common, desperately searching faces in the gloom. 'Please God,' she implores silently, 'let me find her safe.' The prayer of every mother since time began.

Drops of water are filtering down out of the sky. People are shouting to one another with relief. Rain! Rain to put out the flames! Sophie turns her face upward and, forgetting her worries for a second, allows the cooling shower to wash her skin. She hears a cry and turns to see Miranda, arm outstretched, pointing. Sophie's eyes are blurred by the rain. She wipes the water away and scans the ranks of strangers. And then she spots them. Harriet Binney and Jo, pushing frantically through the crowd. Chrissie is close behind.

Tears course down the two women's cheeks as they hug their lost daughters. Out of so many, their pleas at least have been answered.

Rain. Within sight of Big Ben, Roland Raikes, soaked and oil covered, clambers up into the back of an American amphibious vehicle. A marine passes him a blanket. Venetia Maitland settles it around his shoulders. Rain hammers on the roof and they smile wearily at one another. Rain. The forecasters' promised miracle, England's ancient and most reliable ally of all. Rain. Rain.

The rain falls steadily, cooling the heated oil, expunging flames. But it cannot put out all the fires.

For the remains of this night and into tomorrow the emergency crews will battle on to contain the infernos raging across the city. Countless numbers will fall victim to the flames and yet more will be driven from their homes before the blazes are brought under control. Even in those areas spared from burning, the night will be long and wretched with water lapping the second storeys in boroughs near the river. Hundreds of thousands will spend many nights to come in tents and reception centres. Others fill hospitals and the makeshift casualty clearing stations which have opened up across the country. But they are the lucky ones. Already people are speaking of one hundred thousand dead.

24 December

It is twenty minutes before midnight on Christmas Eve. The curfew is in force; it is an offence to be on the streets in the flood zone after dark without authorisation. The pavement is treacherous underfoot as Roland Raikes stumbles along Whitehall. Layers of mud and slime coat the neighbourhood of the river and are knee-deep in places. He uses his torch sparingly. The batteries are failing and black marketeers have cornered the supply. There are no street lamps, no lights in the windows. Much of the city is without power.

Outside the Treasury, sentries huddle around a brazier, swathed in greatcoats. Near medieval conditions visited on the centre of government. Raikes turns down his collar so that they can recognise his face and utters a greeting. His breath smokes in the sharp air. On this side of the thoroughfare the buildings were spared the ravages of fire, but on the river side it is a different story. Only blackened shells remain. He crosses over and picks his way through the rubble and wreckage to Westminster Bridge. Heavy pipes snake from the entrance to the Underground station, pulsating to the distant clank of pumps below. Army engineers are labouring round the clock to clear the flooded tunnels. As fast as they pump, more water drains in from above.

By the Embankment the devastation is random. Breaches in the wall hastily patched with sandbags and concrete blocks, the roadway choked with uprooted trees and paving slabs torn from the sidewalk by the water's suction. Downstream, a pale beam swings across the surface of the river. One of the searchlights mounted on the bridges to pick out bodies coming down on the current. The stench is everywhere, of oil, of stagnant water, of mud and rottenness, of death. At the rampart, Raikes pauses to look over to the charred remnants of the south bank. Homes, offices, public buildings razed to the ground. And beyond, it's a desolate land. Light, heat, water, sanitation, all lost. Before the food distributions got properly under way there were pitched battles here between looters and police. The talk is of a million homeless but the real figure is anyone's guess.

Raikes turns back towards Parliament Square. It is eerily forbidding. They have had machinery clearing here, and water-filled pits and spoil heaps loom like the aftermath of a battle. Over the mess broods the burnt-out skeleton of the Houses of Parliament, stark and silent, backlit by a moon glinting through shreds in the cloud. As he draws near to the Abbey, Raikes mingles with groups of people hurrying in the same direction. It is a result of Venetia Maitland's insistence that the mass is being held. There were voices of dissent: warnings of transport problems and crime in the darkened streets. But her instincts are proving right. The building is packed to capacity, its ancient stones and timbers mellow by candlelight.

Raikes slips into a pew across the aisle from Venetia. She turns her head to look at him momentarily. It is good to see her smile. The tentative wheeze of the organ, still damp from flooding, breaks the stillness. And then, piercingly beautiful, the notes of the opening solo:

'*Oh come all ye faithful,*
Joyful and triumphant . . .'

A message of hope in a world gone dark.

Acknowledgements

A great many people and organisations have assisted in the research for this book. Among those deserving special mention are:

Association of British Insurers – Chris Mounsey, Malcolm Tarling
Barking Power – Peter English
BASICS – Dr Ken Hines
Brent, London Borough of – EPO Keith Gosling
British Telecom, Central Operations Unit – Colin Penny
British Transport Police – PC Mike Powell
Cabinet Office – Commander David Morris
Coastguard Agency – Claire Chapelle
Corporation of London – EPO Stewart Thomas
Dartford Crossing Control – Chris Dixon
Ministry of Defence – Major-General Andrew Pringle, Lt.-Cmdr. Damian Beljeanne, Lt.-Col. Geoff Cook, Jack Fiscal, Ian French
DEFRA – Dr Jim Park, Chris Whitehead
Devonport, Queen's Harbourmaster – Petty Officer Allen
Drinking Water Inspectorate – Chris Davis, Robin Millar

East Anglia Ambulance Service – Steve Green
Environment Agency – Richard Logan, James Moore, Archie Robertson, Dr Geoff Mance, Roy Davey, Dave Fullwood, Peter Borrows, Tim Lewis, Jed Kennedy, Linda Jameson, Martin Whiting
Essex Catchment Office – Tom Miller
Essex County Council – June Thompson
Essex Police – Chief Inspector Dave King
Esso, Purfleet – Bernard Bradshaw, Mark Wentworth
ExCeL – Kate McReedy
Furtherwick Park School, Canvey – John Hunter
Government Office for London – Scott McPherson
Greenwich, London Borough of – Lynette Russell
Guy's and St Thomas's Hospital Trust – Mark Atkinson, Claire Barber, Bronwyn Vick
Hammersmith and Fulham, London Borough of – Colin Denyer, Adrian Price
Department of Health – Dr Duncan McPherson, John Orsulik
Home Office Emergency Planning Division – Kevin Wallace, Dr S. Athwal
Howard Smith Towage – Tom Drennan
Institution of Civil Engineers
King's Lynn Borough Council – EPO Ron McCarthy
Lambeth, London Borough of – Paul Randall
Lewisham, London Borough of – Tony Harper
London Ambulance Service – Andy White, David Taylor
London City Airport – Natalie Grono, George Beck
London Electricity – Paul Phillips, Jane Francis
London Fire Authority – Brian Riordan, Barbara Hyde
London Regional Transport – Dennis Tunnicliffe
London Underground Ltd – Derek Smith, Mike

Gellatly, Paul Ebbet, John Greenaway
Meteorological Office, Storm Tide Forecasting Service – Dave Smith
Metropolitan Police – Inspector Mike Free, Chief Inspector Tom Pine
Middlesex University, Flood Hazard Research Centre – Prof. D. Parker, Colin Green
Mobil, Coryton – Pat Robson
National Gas Canvey – Norton Jensen
National Grid – John Washburn, Diane Owen, Robert Corey
National Marine Aquarium – Juan Romero
New Millennium Experience Co. – Fiona Cline, Doreen Andrews, Anthony Day
Newham, London Borough of – EPO John Page, Roy Walker
OFWAT – Dilys Plant
Ordnance Survey – Dave Dell, Dave Lovell
Houses of Parliament – Director of Works, Henry Webber
Port of London Authority – Barry Wade, Captain McQueen
Powergen PLC – Mike Pollak
Privy Council Office – Stephen Pearl
Proudman Oceanographic Laboratory – Dave Smith, Lisa Carlin
Queen's Harbourmaster, Devonport – Petty Officer Allen
Shell UK – Sarah James, John Brown
South Thames Regional Health Authority – Christopher Gundry
Southend Borough Council – James Mackie
Southwark, London Borough of – EPO Martin Clements, Mary Woods

Tate & Lyle PLC – Charles King
Thames Barrier – Andy Batchelor, David Wilkes, Georgina Roberts, Karen Roberts
Thames Water – Greg Holland, Richard McLaughlin, Alan Lenander, Dave Middlemiss, John Lawrence
Thurrock Council – EPO Kevin Smith, Alan Dawkes
Tower Hamlets, London Borough of – EPO Brian Wood
Transco – Bill Smith, Julie Smith, Louise Martin, Mike Walpole
Van Ommeren Terminal – Peter Smith
Waltham Forest, London Borough of – EPO John Law
Wandsworth, London Borough of – EPO Nigel Powlson, Peter Newman
Westminster City Council – EPO Brian Blake
Canary Wharf Ltd – Suzanne Wild
Wick, Harbourmaster – Norman MacLeod

Mrs Billie Burnett and John Burnett, M.P.
Dr Amanda Ferris
Dr Keith Greene
David Hooper of Pinsent Curtis Biddle
John Horner
Christine Mackay
Kate Pringle
Andrew St Joseph
John Trent
Steve Whalen

In addition, I would like to thank, for their help, criticism and encouragement: my agent, Desmond Elliott, and his assistant, Justin Gowers; Oliver Johnson and Ana Cox at Century; copy editor Monica Schmoller, and Diana Greene and the Focus Group.